FLIGHT FROM SUBJUGATION

BY ELLEN M JAMES

Copyright © Ellen M James 2019

All rights reserved

No part of this publication may be reproduced or transmitted in any form or by any means without the prior written consent of the author.

All characters and events in this publication are purely fictitious and any resemblance to real persons, living or not, is purely coincidental.

Other books written by Ellen M James

TEEN/YOUNG ADULT
The Other House

CHILDREN 8-11 YEARS
Molly and the Grumpy Angel

The Grumpy Angel Strikes Again

The Magic Bubbles

The Magic Clock

The Magic of Pan

The Magic Calling Crystal

CHAPTER ONE

April lowered her head against the wind, tucked her chin in and trudged on. This was ridiculous, she thought; this daily charade of walking up and down the hill, or mountain as Miss Abigail insisted on calling it, simply to prove to the outside world that the girls were well cared for. They never headed anywhere in particular anyway and no one actually ever saw them. They just reached the summit and gasped in feigned delight at the view on all sides and then turned round and headed back down again. April gritted her teeth and curled back her top lip, trying not to snarl or wince. The back of her heel was blistering. The boots were so stiff.

It was the same every morning. Immediately after breakfast the girls put on their jackets and boots, dependent on the weather of course, and formed an orderly queue. Miss Abigail would then march to the front carrying a riding crop in her hand, reminding them and anyone else they might miraculously happen to meet on the dreaded walk that it was purely for safety. A group of girls together and one always had to be careful! But the girls knew different. The crop was to ensure that they behaved on their walk and didn't step out of line. It was to make certain that none of them ran off and that they kept up. In the past there had been girls who had tried to run away but they had always been caught and punished. No one ever escaped from Avondale House. April turned her head and spat out a particularly lumpy mouthful of porridge that had been glued to the back of her teeth for the last half hour. That was another thing. They always had porridge for breakfast, taking turns joining Cook in the kitchen and helping her with it. Today it had been Bertha's turn and it was disagreeable and lumpy just like her. Bertha was well known for her lack of culinary skills. But, unfortunately, the porridge had to be eaten. Every bowl had to be returned empty or another bowl would be filled and dumped in front of each girl and that would be cold as well as disgusting.

To the outside world Avondale House was the perfect developmental home for difficult girls. But the girls weren't difficult, except perhaps Bertha, and April wasn't in the least surprised that she had been returned from her first work placement. Despite being an exceptionally hard worker she was the least likely of any of the girls to be kept on in such a position. Bertha hadn't minded coming back though. She had been forced to work much harder in her placement than she ever had for Miss Abigail at Avondale House. She had also been rejected by the head of the household as unacceptable breeding material although Bertha wasn't aware of this. Anyway, she had rebelled so much and contrived to work with such an air of hostility that she was back at Avondale House within three months and now had extra chores - but she seemed happy. She even managed a slight smile for Miss Abigail every now and then. The management, in other words Miss Abigail and Cook, at Avondale House let her know that they were glad to have her back and considered her one of their success stories as, since her return she had been pliant and uncomplaining.

The girls were at the House for different reasons. Some had been in and out of care for years and Avondale House eventually became their only stability. Some had been dropped off at a boot camp and left there. Their parents simply handed in false paperwork and disappeared, never to be seen again. Some of the younger girls were on a special 'at risk register' and were eventually taken away from their homes for their own safety. Their time would come later. Then there were those, like April, who had simply become one too many. April had many siblings and there was barely enough food or clothing to go round so she was sent away, primarily to work at the House, in return for a little money being sent home so that her younger brothers would fare better with their education. It didn't matter that April had a good head on her; she had become superfluous to requirements. She was a girl and under the regime of the new Government boys were of greater significance in the household as they would inevitably become the main earners and providers upon reaching adulthood. It was imperative that this ruling was not challenged and over what seemed to be a very short period of time it became the general consensus of opinion that girls were of little value or worth. In April's grandmother's day there had been equality between the sexes but no longer. Gradually and almost imperceptibly that had changed. There had been too many girls born into forward thinking households and then suddenly they had grown up and were working and had important careers and there were no babies and no husbands and no families until one day, as if by magic, a new Government stepped in. No one voted the new Government in. It appeared from nowhere, was comprised of twelve men, and their rule was absolute. Seemingly innocuous, the men smiled and simpered and waved as they enforced their new regime, making light of the possibility of consequences; men with balding heads and paunches, men who looked very much like the average man on the street or the friendly neighbour next door. Wolves in sheep's clothing! The primary goal was that girls should no longer have careers, although this was not at first apparent. Reproduction became compulsory or there would be no future generations and so girls really must stay at home. The future as a whole was at stake and with the new Government change was inevitable. So young girls began to take on the previously discarded roles of domesticity in which they washed and cooked and gardened and ironed and scrubbed and laboured until they were worn down, ill and exhausted, and looked old before they needed to.

A lot of the girls chose this option, little knowing or even thinking about what would happen to them. As soon as the new Government voted themselves in there were banners and posters everywhere stating that under their wondrous new regime girls would be looked after and that they would be treated like Princesses. They wouldn't need to work. They were worth so much more and their brave, heroic husbands would go out and earn excellent wages in order to take care of them. Life would be perfect. Pictures and photographs of handsome men were everywhere, on every wall, in every doorway and stapled to every tree and fence, and each eligible female would be in a position to pick and choose whom they wanted as a husband. And the girls fell for it; they fell for the entire cooked-up propaganda, in their hordes. But their perfect lives were so far from the truth. The young wives were treated like Princesses for precisely one year and then things changed. Ultimately they became baby-making machines and they had to keep going until each girl had pushed out at least three boys. If a wife died in childbirth then another girl was immediately chosen as the new wife and so the process continued. The girls existed as nothing more than objects to be used for the purpose of reproduction and their lives resembled those of cooped up battery hens, except that they produced children and not eggs.

April knew it hadn't always been like this. She remembered meeting her grandmother once, a tall, fine lady who wore a knitted suit and pearls, and who had looked at her in dismay and with a degree of sadness in her eyes. Her grandmother had been passing through, or so she said. She lived a long way away, at the foot of a range of mountains and the authorities either didn't know about her or weren't interested in her because she was old. She had somehow managed to slip through the net. She had acquired the relevant paperwork needed for travelling and, being so well presented, looked to all and sundry as if she was a visiting dignitary. She was well past the age of child-bearing so after a cursory nod or two and a glance at her papers she was waved on and ignored. There were very few people who lived at the foot of the mountains but she was one of them. There had always been rumours that the simmering volcano in the middle of the range was ready to erupt and that the lava was just waiting to spew its way up and over, destroying everything in its path exactly as it had done once before and so no one willingly chose to live there, except for a few elderly couples or so it was whispered. When the new Government voted itself in however it suddenly seemed the ideal place to live. April's grandmother had watched as her daughter became more and more brainwashed and finally realising that there was nothing she could do to help her she had simply packed a bag one day and left, taking all her valuables and hiding them on her person, for what use would they be to her daughter now that she was going to be treated like a Princess with many gifts supposedly to be bestowed upon her? On that day when she had returned, paying her one and only visit out of guilt, interest and love, she had looked at April and known her future and had whispered under her breath: "There will always be a home with me if you need one." April had smiled politely and said nothing. It was clear to her that she would always be her mother's favourite and she had no idea what her grandmother was talking about.

But then came the awful morning when her mother took her to the local GP surgery and left her. April underwent a thorough medical health check and when it was finished she was told to wait in the next room. There were four other girls there. Bertha was one of them. None of them seemed to know what was going on or if they did they weren't telling. They sat and stared at the floor, feeling very confused and expecting their mothers to arrive at any moment. But their mothers never came. Instead in flounced Miss Abigail wearing a smart, red suit and black, patent leather boots and carrying a riding crop.

"Line up now, line up."

Most of the girls ignored her. Was she talking to them? Was her daughter amongst them?

"Get up girls. You're all coming with me. You are about to start a new life and you will behave as you are meant to right from the beginning."

The girls slowly stood up, looking round at each other in some bewilderment. What was happening? Who was this awful, bossy woman with her tightly-fitting suit and riding crop? Miss Abigail prodded one of them roughly with the end of the crop.

"Not you dear. You're not fit. You need to spend some time in the sanatorium."

Sanatorium? What was the woman talking about? There was no sanatorium. The last sanatorium any of them were aware of had operated out of the run down hospital with the broken windows at the end of the road and that had been closed for years.

"I'm waiting for my mother," said April, attempting to clarify what was going on.

"You no longer have a mother," retorted Miss Abigail sharply. "None of you do. You are to come with me and earn a living. Here are your papers. Read them and know that from now on you belong to me. Your parents have given up all responsibility for you."

There was only Bertha who didn't have any papers. She obviously knew Miss Abigail as she had stood up straightaway when she entered the room. Her eyes were lowered and a cynical smirk played about her lips as if Miss Abigail's arrival was part of a huge joke but the joke wasn't on her, it was on everyone else.

"I don't believe this," muttered April irritably. "Why would my mother give me away?"

"You are fit and healthy and ready to earn money. Your siblings need to be fed."

"This is ridiculous. She would have told me. I'm not going anywhere with you."

"Stand in line behind Bertha now," ordered Miss Abigail and her crop flicked out and caught April smartly around the shoulders. April winced but didn't move. The crop flicked out again, not once but three times in quick succession and April yelped in surprise and pain. Bertha grabbed her and pulled her in line behind her.

"Better do as she says if you don't want more," she hissed.

April couldn't believe what was happening. Why was this sniggering, square-shaped lump of a girl telling her what to do? It wasn't possible that her mother had given her away, especially not without mentioning anything or saying goodbye. She knew that things had been difficult at home of late but that didn't necessitate her leaving. She had always helped her mother out around the house with the cooking and cleaning. Her mother needed her. She was useful at home so why would her mother want to get rid of her? She couldn't believe it was just for money. Perhaps her father had had something to do with it? Her mother had been upset a lot of late and it always coincided with her father drawing her aside for a private word or two after he had come in from one of his meetings. Her father didn't love her; he didn't love any of them. He was not that kind of man. April didn't even think he loved her mother. He had been called to meetings a lot lately. They were meetings for men; no women were allowed, so it was impossible to know what went on in them? It was always such a big secret and he generally returned home even more surly and bad-tempered than ever.

April stood still. The girls were in line now except for the skinny, pale one who had been poked with the crop.

"I am Miss Abigail and I expect to be addressed as such. Now follow me for we are behind schedule and I do not like to be late."

Miss Abigail headed for a door at the back of the room and opened it. It led out into an alleyway that April had never noticed before with a white van parked at the end. A burly man was standing on guard next to the van and the girls followed Miss Abigail over to it before being roughly manhandled in. The burly man shoved the door shut behind them and padlocked it, giving it a good bang with the side of his fist so that the driver knew it was time to go. Miss Abigail climbed up in front, sitting demurely next to the driver but with a good distance between them. April recognised the burly man as the father of one of her friends. What was going on? Was this some kind of conspiracy? Girls went missing all the time but in school she was told that they had gone to live in the homes of prospective, handsome husbands until they were old enough to be married and that it was a joyous day for each and every one of them. Soon their turn would come and then it would be a time of great happiness for the new Princesses; something quite wonderful to look forward to!

  There was a small, dirty, barred window at the back of the van and April peered through it. Everything on the outside looked perfectly normal. Indeed it was a perfectly normal day out there and people were walking to and fro about their daily business. The bakery was open as was the post office and also the chemist. She even heard the jingle jangle of the corner shop bell as they drove by and suddenly caught a glimpse of her mother coming out. She gripped the bars of the window in shock and shook at them violently.
  "Mum!" she yelled. "Mum!"
  "She's never coming for you again," said Bertha, sniggering. "She can't hear or see you. You ain't going nowhere except in this van so if you know what's good for you you'll shut up and take notice."
  April glared at Bertha knowing that what she said was true and that her mother couldn't hear her. This was obviously some hideous and terrible mistake though and her mother would return to the surgery and find her favourite daughter gone. What would she do? How would she be able to find her? Would she look for her? She watched as her mother disappeared from sight and then sat down with her head in her

hands. She felt so angry. Her knuckles were white with tension where she had gripped at the bars and she so wanted to thump this disgusting, lumpy girl who seemed to know exactly what was going on and was enjoying every moment of the shock and misery around her.

"You're all gonna work as you've never worked before," continued Bertha. "You think you worked hard for your families but that was nothing. They'll get their money's worth out of you at the House that's for sure, and when you're of age there's another surprise coming and it's certainly not about being a Princess, I can tell you. There's special rooms for you then and you'll have another job to do." Bertha grinned and her face contorted into a sickly leer. "I don't know what's worse, the hard labour or the coming of age."

April finally looked up. "Are you in one of the special rooms then? You have to be of age!"

Bertha grunted. "No, I got out of it. Not good-looking enough. Not suitable for placement either. Prefer it at the house anyway and so will you when you know what the special rooms are for."

Bertha turned her head away in defiance and stared sullenly at the side of the van with tightly pursed lips and that was all April could get out of her for the rest of the journey. She had obviously hit a nerve.

There were about forty girls residing at Avondale House in all. The majority of them had been there since they were fourteen, with a few younger girls interspersed amongst them, and when April arrived a group of them was preparing to celebrate the great 'coming of age' – all on the same day! None of them looked very happy about it though. There was to be a lavishly extravagant party and the girls would wear Princess dresses and have their hair done along with their makeup. A great fuss would be made of them and Miss Abigail would flit about congratulating them on the next stage of their journey through life. The girls would be treated to pedicures and manicures and full body massages and facials – all carried out by the younger residents who had no real idea what was happening and didn't understand why the coming of age girls weren't happy. When they were dressed and ready and they saw their reflections in the mirrors they were delighted – briefly – for they truly looked like Princesses! After the celebration party there was dancing and a lot of champagne, too much champagne! Then the coming of age girls were led out of Avondale House and driven down the road to Avondale Manor never to be seen again. Numerous rumours flew around as many expensive cars with dark, tinted windows drove by that evening and it was difficult to make out who was in them. They parked at Avondale Manor, as that was the next property further along the road, and the girls at the House could only assume that the new Princesses were going to meet their future husbands and get married. Little could be further from the truth and it was Pat, Bertha's supposed partner in delinquency, who provided most of the horrifying and incredible gossip. Pat had been there. She had been to Avondale Manor after celebrating her coming of age but once there she had been rejected; just like Bertha, but in her case it was because of the numerous scars that covered her frail, underdeveloped frame and so she was promptly sent back to the House. For Pat it was a lucky escape.

Sister Charlotte ran Avondale Manor but as a nun there was nothing holy about her. She lived by her own unusual interpretation of the bible and this included twice weekly bouts of self-flagellation whereby she concluded that if she could bear it then so could the coming of age girls. She took great delight in using her cat o' nine tails on the tender flesh of those in her care, taking care not to lash so fiercely that she would break the skin. Truth to tell, she didn't care for men. She possessed a distinct proclivity for young girls and generally succumbed to a state of ecstasy shortly after her disobedient charges had stripped off and knelt down with their arms neatly crossed over their hearts waiting for their punishment to begin. She took great pleasure in walking around them with her cat o' nine tails, flicking sharply and unexpectedly at vulnerable, exposed flesh, shivering in delight as she did so. When the girls eventually began to cry she would stop what she was doing, kneel down with them and beg their forgiveness, at the same time reminding them it was for their own good. Salivating, she would stroke them better and then lean forward to kiss away the pain that she had inflicted. She never, ever struck so hard that the freshly erupting, red weals wouldn't fade. That would be more than her life was worth at Avondale Manor and she certainly didn't want to lose her position there. She remained in a state of intoxicated bliss whilst she punished her girls so she knew it was the right thing to do. Some of the girls determined not to cry as they deplored the idea of Sister Charlotte touching them but then the punishment would go on and on and on until there were red marks over every inch of their fragile bodies and eventually they couldn't help but cry out or break down and Sister Charlotte would work herself into an even greater frenzy than usual with her stroking and fondling and kissing. She knew it was her duty to make them feel better after all that whipping. Eventually after much discussion amongst the girls it was decided that the best way to foil Sister Charlotte was to cry as soon as possible and then the punishment and subsequent kissing would be over within the space of about five minutes and they could get away from her and on with their chores.

There were not many chores at Avondale Manor. Work there was a doddle compared to the House. There was the daily cleaning and upkeep of the Manor but spread between so many girls these barely took more than a couple of hours. The main duty of the day was in beauty preparations for the afternoon and evening visits. These visits were from discerning men who arrived at the Manor and chose girls with whom they would like to spend time before ultimately planting their seeds in the innocent, often unyielding wombs and in return for such pleasure they discreetly handed over large sums of money to Sister Charlotte. This money contributed to the upkeep of Avondale Manor and to Sister Charlotte's grand holiday each year. Eventually, with so many visits, bellies began to grow and then the girls would be gently led away to rest in a large, luxurious dormitory and to be treated like Queens for the remainder of their confinement. There was a special room in the bowels of the Manor where the girls would be taken to give birth. This room was totally soundproof and the agony of childbirth was never heard by the remaining mothers to be. Sometimes a young girl died in childbirth. Sometimes there were complications which led to a choice having to be made between a mother and a male child in which case the mother would be sliced open, often without anaesthetic, and the child would be saved. There were plenty more mothers who were available on the premises and a male child would fetch a high price indeed. When a mother was not seen again Sister Charlotte spread joyful rumours amongst the girls that she and her newborn had left the Manor in order to be married and to live happily ever after.

Pat's stay at Avondale Manor was short-lived but not so short that she failed to notice what was going on. Her body was covered in scars, the legacy of an abusive parent, but her face was beautiful. Sister Charlotte took a particular interest in her and longed for her to misbehave. Shortly after her arrival at the Manor Pat threw a tantrum because she had come of age and was being treated differently from the other girls. Pat didn't understand what was going on. Sister Charlotte brought her in for punishment. She knew about the scars but had not seen them. However, as soon as she saw the wounds on the slim, delicate body she flung down her cat o' nine tails, fell to her knees and begged Pat's forgiveness for wishing to inflict pain. Later that day she took her to the dormitory where the pregnant girls were resting and showed her how to change the bedding and a few days after that she felt she was strong enough to witness the birth of a dead foetus and the subsequent bleeding to death of its mother. Both had to be wrapped in white sheets and taken to the huge oven which supplied the heating and hot water for the entire Manor and which needed constant fodder. Pat was shocked to the very core by what she saw and utterly thankful then that she had been rejected by each and every suitor. She said nothing but determined to remain close to Sister Charlotte and in her good books until it was deemed necessary to return her to Avondale House. This was the only way in which she thought she could save herself. For the short period of time that Pat was under Sister Charlotte's wing there were very few punishments meted out. Pat was often taken to Sister Charlotte's quarters to share a meal and to have her scars kissed better and although Pat disliked such preferential treatment she considered it the lesser of two evils and a step nearer to safety. The other girls were relieved beyond belief at Sister Charlotte's temporary lack of interest in discipline and Pat became the star of the Manor throughout her duration there.

Pat and April arrived at Avondale House almost at the same time, Pat being returned from the Manor, much to Sister Charlotte's dismay, and April from the back of the van. Sister Charlotte had sent Pat back to the House knowing that she could no longer keep her at the Manor in safety as there was a certain gentleman who had noticed her beautiful face as she went about her household duties and now he continually asked after her on every visit. He was told about the awful scars that covered her body but this didn't deter him. She was the girl for him and he became obsessed with her, seeking her out and idly watching and lusting after her as she worked. Sister Charlotte became more and more concerned and then possibly did the only unselfish thing that she had ever done in her adult life and sent her packing. Pat was grateful but didn't relish the thought of the hard labour back at Avondale House. She saw April kicking out and struggling as she was manhandled from the van and recognised her as the sort of girl who could be a worthy ally. Late at night when the work duties for Miss Abigail had been completed and the girls were in bed she sought her out and told her everything she knew. April recoiled both in horror and disbelief at Pat's stories but felt she was out of danger for a while, at least. She was still traumatised by the fact that her mother could have disposed of her so easily and knew instinctively what the arguments with her father had been about. She wondered what cock and bull story her father had relayed to her mother and if her mother really knew what was going to happen to her eldest daughter. Now, as she listened to Pat and absorbed all she was telling her, she realised she had landed in the middle of a living nightmare. She watched hopelessly as the girls got ready for their coming of age celebrations knowing that she had to remain silent. There was nothing she could do to help them. For those brief moments when they looked so beautiful they were filled with happiness; she couldn't take that away from them. The girls had their suspicions as to what lay ahead at Avondale Manor but chose not to believe the rumours that such things could and would really happen. They were far too eye-catching and gorgeous for such horrific futures and they determined to enjoy their last moments at Avondale House. They were the girls who would be chosen as happy ever after brides. April wondered if there were places all over the country like Avondale House and if being sent somewhere similar to Avondale Manor was what happened to every teenage girl when she came of age.

So it was on this particular, fateful morning and halfway up the hill, which seemed as if it was big enough to be a mountain when they were climbing it, and exactly how Miss Abigail always referred to it, that April decided to escape. It had to be today; she could wait no longer as she had been at Avondale House for months now and there were only a few weeks left until her own coming of age and of course, from an impulsive point of view, there was no time like the present and what was she waiting for?

The girls always walked up the hill in pairs but there was one part of the track which narrowed so much that for a short period of time they were forced to walk single file and it was here that April recognised the possibility of escape. Pat was walking next to April and saw from her expression and by the way her eyes flickered nervously from side to side and then quickly to Miss Abigail and back that something was going to happen. She could hear April's breathing becoming harder and faster as if she was preparing herself mentally for something.

It was a damp, misty morning and conditions were perfect for invisibility. The clouds hung heavily, suspended in a grey torpor and the sun's rays, having made several attempts to peep through, were ready to give up and admit defeat. April looked up at the sky and decided it was now or never. She hadn't really thought out a plan of escape but the more she considered what was going to happen to her in the very near future the more she realised that it was her only option. They were approaching the curve on the hill where the track narrowed and it was at this point that Miss Abigail gave three short, sharp blasts on a silver whistle that hung around her neck on a matching silver chain. This was the signal instructing the girls to walk in single file and that it would be advisable to do so immediately. April looked down at the patches of prickly furze and thickly spread bushes below her and suddenly ducked and launched herself at them. She gritted her teeth as she landed awkwardly and uncomfortably on her hands and knees and proceeded to crawl as fast as she could away from the group and then to roll. She closed her eyes and put her hands protectively around her head as her body gathered speed, turning over and over, bouncing slightly as she went. Pat saw what she had done and an involuntary squeal escaped her. Instantly she knew she had to do the same. She could not be left behind to stay at Avondale House without April. It was inevitable that she would be returned to Avondale Manor at some point. April was the only girl who spoke to her apart from Bertha. She had to go with her. She bent down and flung herself into the bushes also. They were full of thorns and prickles but the pain was nothing compared to the long ago pain inflicted by her cruel father in one of his drunken rages. She could bear it. An image arose of Sister Charlotte tenderly kissing her scars and suddenly she felt euphoric. That was the only love that she had ever experienced. Sister Charlotte was the only person who had ever stood up for her in her entire life. Sister Charlotte would be proud of her for making a bid for freedom for wasn't that why she had been sent back to Avondale House in the first place? She closed her eyes and rolled, just as April was doing and hoped that they would land in the same place.

"What's going on?" called out Miss Abigail. "What's all that noise? Stand still everyone and let me through."
Miss Abigail began to push her way through the group of girls who now stood shivering and motionless on the curve of the hill. It was slow progress as she didn't want to slip on the damp earth and hurt herself or tumble down into the depths below. She weaved in and out cautiously amongst the girls grabbing hold of arms and shoulders to support her as she did so.
"It's me, Miss Abigail. I've hurt me ankle," called out Bertha.
Bertha had seen April and Pat plunge headlong into the bushes and was filled with what could only be described as a curious rush of adrenalin or was it an impending sense of doom? She was unable to distinguish between the two. On one hand she wanted April and Pat to escape as no one had ever managed it before but at the same time her spiteful self wanted them to be caught because the punishment would be glorious. Somehow her better half won and she threw herself to the ground, grabbing at her ankle as she did so, moaning and writhing in false agony. She didn't know if anyone else had seen April and Pat disappear into the murky depths of the hillside as it was very dull and gloomy around them and the girls generally walked with their heads down attentive only to their own thoughts but April and Pat deserved at least half a chance and she was going to make sure they got it. Perhaps if Miss Abigail was distracted by her ankle she wouldn't even notice that the two girls were gone until everyone was back at the House. She

sniggered briefly and then pulled a face of excruciating misery as she noted Miss Abigail crouching down beside her.

"Can you walk?" asked Miss Abigail. "How bad is it?"

"I don't know, Miss. Perhaps if a couple of the girls were to help me up I could try."

"You girls," said Miss Abigail, pointing to the two girls in front of and behind her. "Grab Bertha under the armpits and help her. And be careful! We don't want anyone disappearing down the side of the hill, do we?"

Bertha tried not to snigger again as she felt arms grip her beneath her shoulders and attempt to heave her onto her feet. She exerted as much force as possible in the opposite direction and snorted with pleasure as she was raised no more than a few inches from the ground before sinking heavily down once more. She was certainly not going to make things easy for her helpers. The greater the distraction the better as far as April and Pat were concerned. Eventually though Bertha was standing and it was decided that, as she could barely hobble without support, they should turn around and head back down the hill, returning to Avondale House in order to have the ankle examined and then to get on with the daily chores. It was such a misty day that they wouldn't have been able to see the beautiful view from the top of the hill anyway and if the mist rolled down any further there was a definite chance that the track in front of them would disappear from sight and they might end up getting lost. Miss Abigail didn't fancy being reported as missing on the hillside with a bunch of frightened girls.

Things went exactly as Bertha hoped and Miss Abigail completely forgot to take a head count. She was so involved in making safe progress back to the House that by the time they arrived a couple of hours had passed and April and Pat had a good head start on their journey to freedom. Bertha felt smugly satisfied. She had a couple of fresh bruises on her ankle where she had knocked into the corner of a bedpost earlier that morning and so she was given an icepack and told to rest. It was much later before anyone realised that April and Pat had not returned to Avondale House and were missing.

CHAPTER TWO

April rolled and rolled until finally she landed with a bump against a solid mound of earth hidden amongst the bracken and foliage. Shortly afterwards Pat crashed into her, arms and legs akimbo, letting out a pain-filled gasp as she did so! Both girls were wet through and battered and bruised from their rough descent. Their clothes clung to their bodies like desperate limpets, unwilling to escape. Their boots were soggy and covered in mud. April sat up, pushing a lock of hair away from her face in disgust, and stared at Pat.

"What are you doing here?" she demanded. "Where are you going?"

"With you," replied Pat meekly. "I saw what you did and I just knew I couldn't face going back to Avondale Manor, ever. And I will be taken there again at some point, you know."

April said nothing. She knew that what Pat said was true. She shrugged her shoulders.

"We'd better get going then before they notice we're missing. We need to cover as much ground as we can in as short a time as possible."

Pat nodded. Both girls stood up and shook off the excess dirt and foliage.

"We look a right state," said April, trying not to smile. "No one will recognise us like this."

Pat grinned cheekily in response, relieved that April was going to let her accompany her.

April continued: "I think we should head off to the left. There's a huge hill there and hopefully we can find somewhere to take shelter. It seems brighter down there too. The mist can't have got that far yet."

The girls began to walk, treading carefully through the undergrowth and prickly furze that sprouted abundantly around them. They could see no more than a few feet ahead of them at any one moment but they surmised this to be a good thing because it would make it harder for anyone to find them – if perhaps they were looking. They stopped at every sound they heard and waited, waited until the scrabbling or rustling came to an end or grew quieter and moved away. Was it a rabbit, a deer, a fox? They had no idea; they couldn't see. The mist around them was too thick. They walked and walked and walked until April knew by the grumbling noises coming from her stomach that it had to be lunch time. She had no idea where they were or what they were going to eat. She hadn't thought that far ahead. Although food at Avondale House was limited at least it was there and at regular intervals too. Pat said nothing. She didn't want to moan or complain in case April changed her mind and decided to leave her behind, continuing her journey alone. She didn't relish the thought of trudging through the mist without company.

As the girls continued walking the mist slowly began to lift and the sporadically persistent sun managed to push a few weak rays through so that it looked as if any foliage around them was covered in random shafts of sparkling dew. April and Pat felt their spirits begin to rise. At least they could almost see where they were going now. They had been climbing a new hill for some time and it was far less green than the last one. They seemed to be approaching an area of barren rock with tufts of grass and ferns sprouting here and there in the sheltered crevices of the craggy boulders. They could hear the sound of water trickling somewhere nearby and April suggested they keep an eye out for it. Within moments of saying this Pat almost stepped into a small stream.

"It's here!" she cried. "Look!"

She bent down and thrust her hands into the icy cold water, rubbing them together briskly to clean them before cupping them so that she could drink. She dipped her hands in again and then rubbed them back and forth across her face, smiling. April watched her and laughed before she too bent down and did the same thing. The stream meandered its way in and out of the rocks trickling over a shallow layer of pebbles as it did so. It was only a few inches deep but surprisingly fresh and clean.

"It's freezing," called out Pat joyfully.

"But delicious," added April. "We need to find something to eat now."

"There are berries," said Pat. "I saw a few on the way up but I didn't want to stop and eat any in case I lost you."

"Let's have a look around," said April. "And don't worry. We're not likely to lose one another. No one is going to spot us either. Our grey tunics and jackets blend in perfectly with the rock face. It's just your wispy, blonde hair that stands out, even though it's full of leaves. It looks like a bird's nest. Take a look at yourself in the water."

Pat laughed and bent over even further, gazing at her reflection with interest.

"Hmmm, I think I could pass for a wood nymph. Quite romantic actually; I could go for this look."

She ran her fingers through her hair and shook her head. Bits of twig and moss flew out.

"Most attractive, I'm sure," she added. "There are some berries over there. I can see them. Look!"

Pat pointed in the direction of a large boulder a little further ahead and stood up. April followed her until they came to a spot in which a few stubby trees sheltered an abundance of almost over-ripe berries. The stream had pooled a little here allowing for the tree roots to take hold and subsequently promoting growth.

"There's an elderberry bush too. We can get drunk. Yum!"

The girls gorged themselves on the berries, their fingers and mouths staining black in their eagerness to fill their empty bellies. They washed in the stream and suddenly realised that the sun could clearly be seen above them now and that it was a lot warmer. The chill had gone from the air and the heat from the rays had almost dried out their hair and clothing. Their boots still felt uncomfortable though.

"I can see steam rising from your tunic," said April.

"Yours too," giggled Pat in response.

It was the first time that they had experienced any freedom since their arrival at Avondale House. Even if they were caught now it would be worth it, thought April. It would be worth it for the discovery of the stream and the berries and the sun and the camaraderie that she and Pat were sharing.

"I don't feel full," said Pat. "I feel a bit sick actually."

"That's nerves and all that rolling," answered April. "We would have to eat pounds of berries to feel satisfied. We'd better get going again. Miss Abigail must have discovered that we've gone by now. We've been away from the group for a good few hours. I don't want to get caught."

"Do you have a plan?" asked Pat. "Do you have any idea where we're heading?"

"We're going to walk to my grandmother's. I only met her once but she said there would be a home for me with her whenever I needed one. I didn't know what she was talking about at the time but now I reckon I do. She must have known about all the things that were going to happen. She must have known about the nightmare I was going to end up in."

"But what about me?" queried Pat. "Do you think she'll want me? I don't want to go back to my dad. He hated me. He was always drunk and I was his favourite punch bag. He used his belt a lot too and I don't ever want that to happen again. At least Sister Charlotte only had a piffling cat o' nine tails and she never touched me with it anyway. She was creepy in lots of ways but she looked out for me."

April looked at her. Pat had obviously been through a lot more than she had. She was such a little thing too and looked much younger than she was.

"We're sisters from now on," she said impulsively. "Nothing will separate us."

She was taken aback by Pat's response as a sudden, revealing smile lit up her face and transformed her.

They trudged on, the sun rising higher and higher in the sky and a frisky breeze arriving and snaking its way here and there and all around them. A few boulders further and they would be out in the open and in plain view for everyone to see. They would have to take a rest and find shelter and set off again at dusk. There was no way otherwise that they could avoid being seen except perhaps by taking a long detour and that would mean travelling back for some way before being able to move forward again and this in itself would present a much greater risk of discovery. April could sense that Pat was getting tired and didn't want to wear her out. She had spotted a few cave-like holes in the rocks around them as they had been walking and thought that exploring them might be a sensible option. Even if the caves only went back a couple of feet they would at least be protected from the elements and out of sight.

"Sit down a moment, Pat," she said. "I'm just going to look at those shadowy areas over there in case there's somewhere we can rest for a bit and hide."

"Don't leave me, will you?" returned Pat anxiously, not knowing whether she should follow April or simply do as she had been told. April stared at her wistful expression and was reminded of a needy puppy with separation issues that her mother had once brought home. Her father had soon got rid of it calling it an extra expense and a lot of extra work, although of course he hadn't been involved in any of it!

"Don't be daft," she said, laughing. "We're sisters, remember."

Pat smiled and sat down. April was right; it was too hot to keep going. Her feet were sore anyway and she didn't seem to have much strength these days. She hoped she wasn't going to start coughing. She had been doing a lot of that lately. But perhaps she wouldn't, not out here in the fresh air. Perhaps she only coughed in the damp dormitory which most of the girls shared at Avondale House. She didn't want to go back there. No one seemed to like her and she couldn't think why. She had always worked hard at her chores and never got anyone into trouble. Still she was branded as difficult. What a joke! Perhaps it was because she grew tired before anyone else did and Miss Abigail thought she was lazy. She had believed the girls were fascinated with her stories of everything that really went on at Avondale Manor but perhaps she was wrong about that too? Maybe they thought she was attention seeking or maybe they were shocked and horrified and thought she was telling lies? She could possibly have been spoiling their dreams of future happiness as they didn't want to think that life wasn't going to be perfect immediately they came of age. After all, who wanted to hear that they were going to become baby mothers and remain in confinement for months on end? Who wanted to hear about the corrupt Sister Charlotte who delighted in looking at the bodies of young girls and loved to punish them so that she could exist in a semi-permanent state of blissful ecstasy? Of course she never really hurt anyone but she was weird all the same. Pat missed her in a peculiar sort of way. She had felt safe and protected whilst she was under her wing and it had never been like that at Avondale House. But everything felt much better now she was with April. April was strong and decisive and knew exactly what she was doing. She was a leader and now she had chosen Pat as her sister. Pat had never had a sister or brother before. Her mother had died in childbirth and her father had brought her up. There had certainly been no love lost there. He had always seemed to blame her for the death of her mother and more often than not he took his rages out on her and punished her for it. Pat had never known him not to drink but she had heard that he had been a different man once, before her mother died. Maybe now that she was out of the way he would be able to pull himself together. After all, there was no one to remind him of his wife now! Pat shrugged. Funny old world! She had been taken out of the frying pan simply to be thrown into the fire. No, that wasn't absolutely correct. She had been taken out of one frying pan and plonked into another. She hadn't quite been burnt in the fire yet and she seriously had no intention of ever being so!

 April returned. She hadn't been gone long at all.
 "We can shelter down there," she said. "I've found a small cave behind some ferns. You can't see it from the outside so we should be okay. Come on, let's go. You look as if you're about to fall asleep."
 Pat nodded and got up. She followed April off the track to a large boulder and from there to a smaller one behind it. She watched as April pushed aside some ferns, bent down and disappeared. Pat raised her eyebrows in surprise and pushed aside the ferns too. Behind them was a shady recess which went back about three feet. The rocky roof came down to within a couple of feet above their heads and the whole space was just big enough for two, small people to be able to snuggle up together and fall asleep. The earth below their feet was covered in a carpet of dried moss and felt soft and spongy. Pat sat down again immediately. This was more like it. The perfect hiding place! No one would find them here except maybe a wild animal or two but then she and April were together and so everything would be alright and it was still daylight. There was nothing to worry about.

 April sat down too. "We must rest," she said. "It's dry and warm in here and we'll be safe for the time being. Let's lie down and try to sleep for a couple of hours. As soon as the sun starts to set we'll get moving again. We'll blend in more with the scenery when there's less daylight."
 Pat didn't need any persuading. Within moments she had sunk to the ground with her head resting on the moss and had curled up into a tiny ball. April tucked her body in tightly

beside her to keep warm and closed her eyes. Seconds later both girls were asleep and oblivious to anything that might be going on around them.

CHAPTER THREE

They awoke with a start. What was that awful sound? It was so loud it seemed as if it was coming from somewhere in the cave with them, although that was impossible of course. Pat let out a terrified shriek and April quickly clamped her hand over her mouth so that she couldn't make any more noise. There was no way of knowing who or what was wandering around out there or how close they were to the cave entrance. They didn't know how long they had slept either, although the cave was quite dark now making both girls strangely disorientated. For a moment Pat couldn't even remember where they were or what they were doing there. Then it all came back to her and she shuddered with fear.

"Stay here and I'll take a look outside," April whispered, though why she was whispering she had no idea as the noise was so deafening that very little would be heard over it. It sounded as if a huge engine was running and there was a strange, whirring noise too. Perhaps the hunt was on and Miss Abigail was close by heading a torch lit search team? That wouldn't surprise her. Miss Abigail would feel completely out of control and in a state of rising hypertension with the loss of two girls. April grinned to herself at such a thought.

She crawled slowly to the cave entrance glancing back at Pat who was hugging her knees in fright wondering what was going to happen next. April cautiously pushed aside the ferns and then immediately let them fall, overcome by the glare of strong, powerful beams of light. She shook her head, blinked rapidly, waited a few seconds and then tried a second time, squinting and turning her head slightly to the left so that she didn't have to stare directly into the full intensity of the beams in front of her. Even so she felt dazzled by them. What on earth were they? She waited and waited until the glare no longer seemed to be quite so piercing and she could make out the dark shape behind the light and hazard a guess as to what it was.

It appeared to be an enormous, grey machine. It looked like a battleship, a flying battleship, similar to pictures in books she had once read or flicked through, and the whirring noise emanated from three sets of large, heavy duty propellers turning round on top of it. These were gradually slowing down and coming to stillness and the lights, which looked as though someone had fixed car headlamps at intervals around the machine, were growing dimmer and dimmer as the sound of the engine died away. The machine had landed on a rocky plateau close to the cave and the sight of it was awesome, yet also terrifying! April popped her head back into the cave and now she couldn't see anything at all. She knew Pat was there though.

"It's some kind of flying machine!" she hissed. "It must be a warship. It's amazing! Come and have a look! Hurry up; we can't stay in here any longer. We've got to get going again. Let's find out what it is. Maybe we can hitch a ride. The further we are away from Avondale House the better. I don't think it's anything to do with Miss Abigail. She wouldn't have that kind of authority."

April raised her eyebrows as she made this remark making light of the matter and knowing that Pat would be feeling far too afraid to move. She waited whilst Pat summoned up enough courage to crawl over to her where she remained close to her side as April lifted the curtain of ferns again. Whatever the machine was it was definitely too big for Miss Abigail to have drummed up or organised at such short notice.

There appeared to be no one around and both girls stared in wonder and confusion. Then, suddenly, a door in the side of the machine grated its way open and a thin, twitchy-looking man jumped out. Pat crouched down even further peering out from behind April's shoulder. The man fished around in one of his pockets and April watched as he took out a small tin, withdrew from it what appeared to be a pinch of tobacco and rolled it in a slip of paper, sealing it by licking it from end to end before finally popping it between his lips, cupping his hands around it and lighting it. She gasped! Cigarettes weren't allowed and that included roll-ups. They had been banned since The Twelve had come into government as they were deemed detrimental to public health and of no beneficial use whatsoever. Taxes could be levied in other ways. This man must have got his supply of tobacco on the black market. April hadn't seen any cigarettes in a long time but she had seen pictures of tobacco and she knew the history of it. The man was enjoying a roll-up and it had a very strange smell indeed. The smoke wafting over made her feel a little woozy. She had never inhaled anything like it before. She remembered the last time she had seen cigarettes. It was on the day when the townspeople were ordered to take their supplies down to The Square and dispose of them on a large bonfire. Every ounce of tobacco and every cigar and cigarette disappeared that day, or at least she thought they had. At precisely seven in the evening the bonfire had been lit and the unwelcome deed had taken place and anyone caught with any form of tobacco after that knew they would be heavily punished. The men had stood around watching and a deep, reverent silence had ensued as the flames took hold and flickered and fluttered their way up into the sky, crackling and popping, exuding the most intoxicating of smells and exhibiting the most psychedelic array of colours. The men breathed in deeply, surreptitiously glancing at one another, saying nothing and savouring the last aroma of tobacco they might ever have the pleasure of experiencing. April's father never touched another cigarette. At least she never saw him with a cigarette but there were times when he returned home from work with the lingering remains of a certain smell emanating from his clothing, but who was to say that he'd been smoking and that he hadn't just been in the company of someone who bravely, or perhaps stupidly, defied the new regime. Needless to say, the tales of chastisement that came from those unfortunate enough to be caught were enough to make those who persisted in smoking very careful indeed.

The man from the machine stared around expectantly almost as if he was waiting for someone. The more he drew on his roll-up the less he twitched. He closed his eyes each time he sucked in and then slowly exhaled with satisfied sighs of pleasure. He moved away from the machine and began to walk about, stretching his legs. He reached up with his arms, twisting his torso from side to side and then gave a great yawn. Perhaps he had been travelling for hours, flying through the sky and fantasising, dreaming of a new life? April knew this was what happened on long journeys. If you didn't fall asleep you would drift off into another world with your own thoughts and hopefully they would be happy ones. It had been a long journey from the alleyway at the back of the surgery to Avondale House and after feeling angry with Bertha for a while she had nodded off into a dream world and done exactly this.

The man began to walk around the machine, nonchalantly tapping here and there, checking that there was nothing loose and that all looked well.

"Now!" hissed April. "Now! We've got to get on board while he's distracted and can't see us. Come on Pat, get out from behind me and get in through that door."

Pat looked at her in surprise and then did as she was told. She ran quickly and lightly on her toes to the door which was at least two feet off the ground and gave a fawn-like leap into the air. Within seconds she was in. Now it was April's turn but the man was coming back. He would be here at any moment, in front of the machine again. April dithered, uncertain as to whether she ought to make a move or not and by the time she had decided to follow Pat the man had returned, stubbed out his roll-up and hoisted himself up and in. April was horrified. She hoped that Pat was squirrelled away somewhere out of sight. It would be a nightmare if either of them were caught. She didn't know what she would do if that happened. But she couldn't leave Pat on her own. They couldn't be separated. She had to think what to do next!

Moments later the man was back in the doorway again and this time his arms were full of cardboard shoeboxes, or at least they looked like shoeboxes. He didn't jump but balanced precariously in the doorway, using his elbow to push a button at his side so that a set of steps unfolded neatly in front of him, and then he walked carefully down, his feet splayed outwards on the narrow treads. The shoeboxes were piled so high in his arms that he couldn't see where he was going at all. He placed the shoeboxes neatly together on the rocky earth below and then went back into the machine to collect another armful. He began to pile the boxes up. Each one was marked with a red cross. He noticed one with a blue cross on it and tutted irritably. Lucky he had spotted it! It was obviously not meant to be there. He picked it up and carried it carefully back into the warship and then came out again, sighing heavily before sitting down on the steps to wait. Or at least that was what he appeared to be doing. April was incredibly curious. She wanted to know what was inside the boxes. What was the man waiting for? And why had he landed his strange machine or warship or whatever it was on a desolate expanse of barren, rocky earth in the middle of nowhere? As she watched, wondering what he was going to do next, she began to hear movements. They came from behind her on the rocky incline she and Pat had traversed earlier. Soon she could make out the dim shapes of people approaching. No, not people – women! Women were stealthily making their way across to where the man was seated. They were coming out of the shadows, emerging as if from nowhere and there were about twenty of them altogether. They walked with their heads lowered, covered in heavy, woollen scarves and disguising their bodies in long, dark, shapeless garments, so that they remained as inconspicuous as possible. The man didn't move until he was sure everyone had arrived and then he slowly stood up and stretched again. As if this were some kind of secret signal the women quickly moved to the boxes and began to open them. April heard gasps and chuckles of happiness and delight. Some of them even bent down and kissed whatever was in the box they had just opened. Two of the women were carrying a large, hand woven basket covered with a cloth and they placed it carefully on the rocky earth in front of the man before each picking up a box of their own. One of them stared directly at the fern curtain behind which April was hiding and then looked away. April gulped. She was sure the woman knew she was there. It was a scary feeling and a flicker of uncertainty ran through her. The man removed the cloth cover and reached deeply into the basket. He then lifted a handful of leaves to his face, closing his eyes and inhaling steadily. April caught a whiff of the strange tobacco again and had to pinch her nostrils tightly so that she didn't sneeze. She turned her attention back to the women. As soon as they were satisfied with whatever was in their boxes they picked them up and carried them away, clutching them possessively and disappearing into the gloomy rocks and crevices from which they had so covertly surfaced. Everything was quiet now. It was as if the women had never been there. It was as if they had never even existed. April shook her head in confusion. The whole episode had taken place in a matter of moments and felt most surreal. There were no boxes left. One woman had taken two and April watched her give a great beam of delight before she too vanished amongst the rocks and undergrowth. The man stood up.

"Pleasure doing business with you," he muttered obligingly to the empty air. There was no one around to hear him except for April and possibly Pat. The women had gone. They had left nothing behind them except for the large basket of aromatic leaves.

Amazing, thought April! If I had closed my eyes for five minutes I would have missed the entire scenario. She watched as the man opened his tin and began to fill it with a handful of crushed leaves from the basket. Tobacco, that's what it was. The women had given him tobacco. It was no ordinary tobacco either. That was quite obvious from the silly grin that spread across his face as he carried the basket up the steps and onto the warship. He disappeared inside leaving the door open behind him. April waited a few seconds before she darted over. She had no choice. She couldn't leave Pat alone on the warship. Who knew what might happen to her? She crept up the steps as quietly as she could and peered cautiously inside. Pat was nowhere to be seen and neither was the man. She climbed in ducking down as she did so as if that made her less visible. She could hear the sound of tuneless singing coming from somewhere ahead of her and she decided to explore in the opposite direction.

"Pat," she whispered, "where are you?" But there was no answer.

"Pat!" she whispered again, a little more loudly this time.

"Over here," she thought she heard a very small voice reply.

April crouched down and began to crawl forward on her hands and knees. The interior of the warship was dim and dusty but beautifully warm. There was another door in front of her and April reached up to turn the handle. She found Pat sitting on the floor behind it, shivering with fright, her face stained with rivulets of tears.

"I thought you weren't coming," she whimpered. "I thought you were going to leave me here with all these dead things."

April shut the door carefully behind her.

"What dead things?" she asked.

"In the shoe boxes," replied Pat.

"Let's not worry about that now," said April. "We need a good place to hide so that the man can't find us. I'm sure the warship or whatever it is will be taking off soon and, as I said before, the further we are away from Miss Abigail and Avondale House the better."

"I found somewhere," said Pat. "There's an old wooden kennel with a blanket in it at the back of the boxes. The man must have had a dog on board at some point. The kennel smells a bit musty but there's only a small entrance to it and we'd never be seen unless someone knew to look for us."

April nodded and followed Pat behind piles and piles of closely stacked boxes. She would have to find out what was in them. She was very puzzled certainly, but not yet. It was more important that they made sure there was no one else on the warship except for the twitchy man and they needed to wait until the warship took off and he was occupied before they could do any snooping.

The wooden kennel was old and well past any sell by date it might have once had but it had obviously been loved in its time and was a suitable hiding place for the two of them. Pat crawled in first and April followed her. April leant back and closed her eyes once she was inside and Pat sat next to her, resting her head against her shoulder. They waited. Presently they heard the sound of footsteps and then the slamming of a door. The man was humming under his breath. Soon after they heard what could only be the sound of the engine starting up and finally the whirring of propellers. The warship was taking off. April and Pat had never been up in the sky before and the experience encouraged strange lumps to form in the back of their throats. They had to swallow over and over in order to try and remove them and to unblock their ears. Pat kept her fingers in her ears, screwing her eyes shut tightly until things grew quieter. Fortunately the sound that came from the engine and propellers, after the initial roar into life, was much less aggressive inside the warship than it had been from the outside.

"Thank goodness that's over," said April. "You can take your fingers out now. I'm going to have a look around and make sure there's no one else on board apart from that man. Do you want to stay here or are you going to come with me?"

"I'm coming with you. I don't want to be on my own. Are you going to have a look inside the boxes?"

"Not yet. We have to make sure there's no one else around first. Come on, let's go."

She crawled out of the kennel and stood up, stretching. Pat followed her. The belly of the warship was empty. There were only dead things in boxes around them according to Pat. They could still hear the man humming. April headed off in the direction of the humming.

"I'm pretty sure we're the only extra bodies here. Let's stay in the kennel," said Pat, grabbing hold of April's arm. April shook her off.

"No, we must check properly. I'm not being taken back to Avondale House and I'm certainly not going to the Manor. Wait here if you don't feel brave enough to come with me. I'm going to take a sneaky peep up front where the engine is. I think there's a window I can look through."

April left Pat standing stiffly with her shoulders hunched and her fists balled at her sides and continued walking. She was close to the cockpit now. She crept to the side of the door, ducked down and took a deep breath. Then she slowly stood up and leant forward, shading her eyes with her hand as she tried to peer through the small, grubby window in front of her. There was no one in the cockpit except for the twitchy man, only she couldn't describe him as twitchy any longer because after a few drags on his roll-up his behaviour had changed and he seemed to be calm and composed. He appeared perfectly at ease and very pleased with himself and April decided he must be totally unaware of any other presence on his warship. He was in a world of his own, a world pleasantly enhanced by the tobacco fumes he was constantly inhaling. She wondered how long they would be up in the air for and where they were going. She could only just detect dark clouds rolling by through the glass at the front of the warship and knew they were moving further and further away from the rocky plain. She sighed in relief. They would soon be beyond the reach of Miss Abigail and Avondale House. No one would ever think of looking for two girls on a warship. She almost felt happy and that was twice in one day now. She hadn't experienced that emotion in such a long time. Happiness and contentment had become practically alien to her. She had smiled and nodded a lot in agreement at Avondale House but the smile had never reached her eyes and she had never been happy and neither had any of the other girls as far as she was aware – with the exception possibly of Bertha who often appeared smug and self-satisfied, for reasons known only to herself. However, April felt she was in no position to judge her for hadn't she been the one to create a diversion so that she and Pat could make good their escape? Or had there been a hidden agenda behind her unusually supportive behaviour? Was she even now waiting for them to be captured and for their shamefaced return purely to take pleasure in the punishment that would most certainly follow? But this was something that didn't even bear thinking of and so April shrugged and dismissed such thoughts. She needed to focus on what she and Pat were going to do next. She withdrew her head from the window and crept back to her.

"It's all clear," she said. "You were right. There's no one else on board except Mr. Twitchy. Let's find out what's in those boxes."

Pat nodded in agreement, still clenching her fists at her sides but starting to look more relaxed. "Can we go back to the kennel though? We don't want him leaving the cockpit and discovering us, do we?"

"A pilot can't leave his controls. There's no one to take over," said April reassuringly.

"He might be able to," continued Pat. "What if he can switch the controls to auto and this machine can fly itself? What if he needs to have a pee or something or wants to stretch his legs?"

April raised her eyebrows. "You could be right," she said, "but I haven't seen a toilet anywhere, have you? There was a bucket next to him at the front. Perhaps he uses that?"

"Eugh! That's disgusting," said Pat. "There must be a loo on board or at least somewhere to dispose of any mucky stuff. Anyway I'd feel a lot happier if we were near the kennel. There are plenty of boxes there."

"Okay," said April.

They made their way back to the kennel as quietly as they could, just in case the man decided to leave the cockpit for any reason, and then April carefully lifted down one of the boxes. There was a thin pipe of tubing attached to the side of it and April was careful not to dislodge it. She placed it on the floor and both girls knelt beside it. April looked at Pat and they nodded at each other before she slowly raised the lid and looked inside. She gasped in shock and immediately replaced it.

"Well," said Pat. "I'm right, aren't I? There's a dead thing inside, isn't there?"

April said nothing. She was trying to compose herself. She removed the lid once more, this time with shaking hands.

"Look!" she whispered. "It's a baby!"

"What!" gasped Pat. "Let me see! That's impossible! Who would put a dead baby inside a shoebox?"

"The baby's not dead. It's alive," said April. "I can see its chest going up and down. It's asleep and it's breathing."

Both girls peered into the box and April cautiously extended a hand towards the baby's chest.

"It's warm," she said. "And I can feel a heartbeat."

The cardboard box was packed with insulating material, silver in colour and quite thick. The baby was lying naked in the middle of it. The inside of the lid was insulated too so that the baby was kept warm and its body temperature remained stable. There were tiny holes in the lid to let in air but now that the lid had been completely removed the body was beginning to cool down. The baby stirred and let out a small cry. The girls could see that it was a tiny boy. There was a thin tube going up through his nose and the other end of it left the box through a small puncture at the side.

"He's waking up!" hissed Pat, with a note of panic in her voice. "We don't want him waking up and crying, do we?"

April shook her head and instantly closed the lid on the box. Immediately there was silence. She opened another box, quickly glancing inside before replacing the lid, and then another and another.

"They're all boys," she said. "Every single box has a boy in it! Oh no, wait a minute. There's one with a red cross here. The man must have missed it. If what I'm thinking is correct this one will contain a girl."

April lifted the lid on the marked box and sighed. A couple of tears rolled down her cheeks.

"Why are you crying?" asked Pat.

"Because I'm right," said April sadly. "All the boxes that the man took outside had red crosses on them and women came and took them away. Don't you see; the women took all the girls away. There are only boys on this warship now. These babies all have mothers somewhere and the mothers can't have just given them away. Why would they and why would they put them on a warship? They've all just been born. Would you give your newborn baby away? There's something very wrong about this. I don't like it."

Pat shook her head. "What's going on then?" she asked.

"I don't know," replied April. "But this entire warship must be filled with baby boys except for one little girl. Or maybe there are more baby girls on board, hidden amongst the piles of boxes and the man missed them. Goodness knows where he's taking all these babies. And they're so small too. They're too small. They must have been born ahead of their time and there are so many of them and that's a reminder of something else that is particularly horrid."

She glanced at Pat and knew she couldn't tell her that she thought all these babies had been prematurely induced. She had heard of such things from her mother who had told her that this was done when it was thought that there would be a problem with the birth but as she stared at the boxes she had a feeling that whatever had happened to these babies had not been done with the health of any of the mothers in mind. It was another good reason to be as far away from Avondale House and Avondale Manor as possible.

"We can't worry about that now though," she continued. "At least the babies are alive. I'm sure we'll discover more of what's going on when the warship lands. I think we should find out where those tubes go to and what's in them. It looks as if the babies are being fed through them. Perhaps we might find enough food at the end of the tubing for us to be able to eat something. My stomach's rumbling like crazy. Isn't yours? We're going to have to eat soon."

April began to inspect the sides of the boxes examining the thin, plastic tubes that came out through the small, puncture holes in each of them. Finally she came across what she had been looking for; a thicker tube that ran along the ground. Most of the tubes seemed to be attached one box to another but this particular tube ran along the ground with lots of pieces of thin tubing attached to it, away from the boxes, against the side of the wall and from there to a large, white machine that looked like a freezer. There was what appeared to be a timing device on the front of the machine and a red light but no handle with which to open it. As April watched the light turned from red to green and a creamy, white liquid began to trickle into the tube.

"It must be milk!" she whispered in wonder. "Amazing! It's all piped through from here. This is how the babies are fed. Look, Pat. The milk comes out of this machine and down this tube and into all the boxes. The babies are kept asleep somehow. Maybe the milk is drugged. And then they're fed through that pipe going up their noses. We need to think of a way to get some milk for ourselves. There's obviously plenty in the machine and so we won't be depriving the babies, will we?

Squeeze round to the back if you can and see if there's any way we can open it and get some out. I'll check the sides."

April was too big to fit between the machine and the wall but it looked as if Pat might be just the right size. Pat glared at April in horror but did as had been suggested, squeezing her thin frame into the gap, having to turn her head to the side in order to do so.

"It's disgusting back here," she hissed. "It's full of dust and dirt. I can't see anything. There's nothing, no button to press, no handle, nothing. I'm coming out."

"Keep looking," said April. "There has to be something. Where does the tube go? It has to go into the machine from somewhere. Look along the floor."

Pat lowered her eyes and tried to look down, finally catching sight of a small switch in the bottom right hand corner.

"I'll have to come out and stretch my arm in on the other side," she said. "I can't stay here much longer because I'm about to sneeze with all the dust and it's going to be so loud that the babies will probably wake up and the man will hear me too!"

"Have you found something then?" asked April. There was silence. Pat was in the process of squeezing her way out from behind the machine again. She held her breath as she did so. She pinched her nose for a moment or two in order to prevent the anticipated sneeze before eventually brushing at her clothes with grubby hands.

"Eugh!" she said. "There were cobwebs everywhere. I nearly scraped my nose just then. I'll get you back for making me go in there, you see if I don't." And she grinned at April. "There's a switch at the bottom on the other side. If I stretch my arm in I might be able to flick it down. I don't know what it does but we can find out, can't we?"

April nodded and watched as Pat crouched down on the other side of the machine. Pat reached into the gap between the freezer and the wall and then began to grope around. Suddenly there was the sound of a click and the humming noise that had been coming from the machine stopped. A door at the front, which previously had been hidden from view, began to swing open.

"You've done it!" called April, catching hold of the door. "Come and have a look!"

Pat pulled her arm out and rubbed at it.

"I get all the worst jobs," she grumbled. "This milk had better be worth it. And what if it is drugged? We'll fall asleep then too, won't we?"

"If we're hidden in the kennel it won't matter. And I could do with a good rest. I woke up a long time before you did in that cave. You were out like a light and I was just drifting in and out of sleep making sure that you were okay. When I finally did manage to fall into a deep sleep we were woken up by Mr. Twitchy and his warship."

Pat sniffed. "You need to talk quietly. You're getting too loud," she complained.

April ignored her and pulled the door open wide. "There are huge packets of stuff in here, look. The packet at the bottom is the one with the tube coming out of it. That must be the one that feeds the babies. Help me lift one of them out and we'll try and open it. I'm starving. Those berries only filled my stomach for five minutes."

She reached up and began to tug at one of the packets. It was heavy and she needed all her strength to pull it forward along the shelf. Pat reached up to help her. Finally they were able to grab hold of it and lower it gently to the ground.

"It's freezing," said Pat, blowing on her fingers. "That man can't possibly be giving freezing milk to the babies. Their little bodies wouldn't be able to take it. They'd be awake and screaming in no time, wouldn't they?"

April frowned and leant across the floor to the main tube, before pinching it gently.

"This tube is warm," she said. "There must be something that heats the milk up as it leaves the machine and passes along the tubes. I think the machine has to be some kind of sophisticated freezer, don't you? I don't know what else it can be."

"Open the packet then," said Pat. "Come on, I want to get back to the kennel. We don't want the milk to start turning cold for those babies either, do we? Who knows what we've done by flicking the switch and opening the freezer?"

April grasped the plastic lid on top of the packet and turned it. It opened quite easily.

"There are some extra bits of tubing in the freezer. They must be spares for other babies. Pass me one please," she said to Pat.

Pat obliged and April popped one end of it into the milk and began to suck through the other end like a straw.

"What does it taste like?" asked Pat.

"Yummy," answered April in between sips. "It's quite sweet. Your turn now."

And she passed the tube to Pat, grinning as she did so. She shut the freezer door whilst Pat was drinking and stared at her.

"There's definitely a little extra something in it," she said. "Can you taste it?"

Pat nodded and continued sipping.

"Not too much," said April. "We need to get back to the kennel. Can you flick the switch at the back again?"

Pat stopped drinking and puffed out her cheeks, blowing through them in exasperation. She reached into the gap once more and felt around until she found the switch.

"Done," she said. "Let's drag this milk back to the kennel with us. We don't know how long we're going to have to stay there. I'll keep hold of the tubing."

"Okay," said April, screwing the lid back on again. "At least we know where we can get something to fill our bellies with now, don't we? Let's see if we can lift the packet between us first before we resort to dragging it along the floor. It won't be too heavy as we've both had a good drink from it."

The girls found that the weight of the milk packet was manageable and slowly they carried it back to the kennel. They were just about able to get it through the small opening, Pat pulling at one end and April pushing at the other.

"Let's hope the man doesn't notice that there's a huge packet of milk missing," said April. "That would be a disaster."

"He might not even look inside the freezer," said Pat. "After all, why would he? The babies are fine so he doesn't need to."

April nodded. The man would have to change the milk packet when it became empty at some point but it wasn't worth mentioning to Pat. It would be just another worry for her. She realised she was feeling a little light headed. Obviously the extra ingredient in the milk was beginning to take effect. She lay down on the stale-smelling dog blanket and closed her eyes, smiling dreamily at Pat as she did so. Pat looked at her new friend and felt a surge of warmth rush through her. April was a much nicer friend to have than Sister Charlotte. She curled up next to her and soon the pair of them had drifted into a dreamless oblivion.

CHAPTER FOUR

Miss Abigail was furious. Having thoroughly inspected Bertha's ankle at Avondale House she decided that the girl was making a terrible fuss about nothing and withdrew to her room in a great huff. Miss Abigail hated to be made a fool of. She would have to think of a suitable punishment for Bertha but unfortunately she couldn't really prove that the girl hadn't hurt her ankle, could she? It was a dilemma. The journey up and down the hill had taken the whole morning instead of the usual one hour and she was now very behind with her duties. Due to the fact that she had been obliged to keep a close eye on Bertha the other girls had played up and had behaved in a childish and silly manner, giggling and sniggering throughout the rest of the walk. It was most frustrating. Before she knew it she would be supervising lunch and she hadn't even partaken of the simple pleasure of her morning cup of tea.

At last she was in her room though and could relax. She had taken her boots off at the main door downstairs and instructed one of the younger girls to clean them and now she could change out of her walking outfit into something more befitting the Director of such a prestigious, developmental home. Should she wear her blue suit or the red one? The red would imply that she was feeling motivated and in extreme and efficient working mode so the girls had better beware but the blue would fool everyone into thinking that she was calm and collected and totally composed. She decided on the blue. She didn't want the girls to think they had won and that they had managed to ruffle her feathers in any way. But first she must shower. Bertha had slithered and slid about an awful lot on the way down the hill and on one occasion she had actually slipped over, clutching at Miss Abigail as she did so and taking her with her. The girls had tried to stifle their titters, thrusting their fists into their mouths as they turned their heads away, but Miss Abigail had heard them and hadn't appreciated the funny side of it at all. She had hurriedly scrambled to her feet, gritting her teeth in displeasure, desperate to make light of the fact that she was covered in mud and had then proceeded to encourage them to continue walking as quickly as possible, almost as if nothing had happened.

Miss Abigail felt much better after her shower. There was something particularly exhilarating about a hard, hot shower. It picked one up, she thought. She loved it when her hair felt squeaky clean and the skin on her body had been rubbed down and exfoliated with a rough towel. Life's problems took on a gentler perspective after a good scrub. She sat in the chair in front of her dressing table and examined her face. No lines yet. Well, she would take her time with her beauty routine. The girls would be having lunch soon and she could leave the rest of the preparations to Cook. Cook had noted her late arrival and irritable manner and had nodded understandingly at her. She would give her recovery time, as she called it. Miss Abigail would eat in her room – a tasty salmon salad would go down a treat, she thought. She would summon two of the girls to do her hair and maybe her nails too as a couple of them were chipped from scrabbling about in the mud. She shuddered. It didn't bear thinking about! She needed to feel lovely again.

Miss Abigail rang the bell above her head and soon after one of the girls arrived, bobbing a respectful curtsey to her as she entered the room. Miss Abigail passed on her instructions and within five minutes she was able to lean back in her chair, closing her eyes in deep satisfaction whilst a face pack was applied and her hair was blow dried. She sank so deeply into a reverie that she almost forgot about the Bertha incident. It was something she didn't want to deal with anyway. It would be more than convenient to pretend nothing had happened and to move on but she knew she would never be allowed to do that. She had an image to uphold but just for once she wished that she could let her guard down and show the girls how much she really cared and that she didn't like what they had to do and neither did she want any of them to leave Avondale House and go to Avondale Manor. After all, it was a situation that she had managed to escape – fortunately!

At Miss Abigail's medical examination it was discovered that she would never be able to conceive naturally. At the time this meant very little to the young Abigail but the news came as a complete shock to her mother. The repercussions of such a revelation didn't bear thinking about. Luckily Abigail's father had some influence in the community and so she had been sent to an educational, developmental home where she learnt to tutor and to be useful. Abigail had kept her head down, worked hard and had subsequently risen through the ranks becoming well respected by her seniors until finally she was awarded a supervisory position. But such deferential treatment came at a price! Miss Abigail, as she became known, had no friends. No one liked her or wanted to spend time with her. Abigail knew as soon as she arrived at the developmental home that she would have to make herself indispensable or she would quickly be disposed of. How she would be disposed of she had no idea but it would certainly occur. She had watched it happen to other girls. Once they became worn out and ill with all the hard work they endured they simply disappeared. She didn't want to disappear, never to be seen again. So she had made herself indispensable, but not to the girls, only to the staff. And this was what cemented her unpopularity amongst her peers. She exerted herself and made sure that she was capable of doing every single job that needed to be done. She offered to help out as soon as a batch of new girls arrived and made it clear that she would be perfectly happy to take on the responsibility of showing them the ropes. Little by little the staff relied upon her to take charge. Her consistent, hard work couldn't help but be noticed and after a few years it was inevitable that she should be offered a managerial position especially as the older women always moved on. Still, Abigail had to be ever watchful and vigilant as there were often petty jealousies, spiteful remarks and veiled threats made in such an establishment. She knew that no one would dare confront her though as once, having been the object of intimidation, she had retaliated by holding a penknife to the bully's throat whilst pulling back her hair and threatening her. Word had spread like wildfire! After this she was left well alone. One did not mess with Abigail. She was tough and she was dangerous!

And this was the way Abigail liked it. When it eventually became clear that she was too old to remain where she was she was sent to a newly opened developmental home called Avondale House to take her place as second in charge. This was a position that suited Abigail as it meant that she didn't have to take ultimate responsibility for the girls. She could always pass things on to be dealt with at a higher level. Unfortunately, quite soon after Abigail's arrival, her superior became ill and one day she was hurriedly bundled out of the House and driven away in the back of a van never to return. Abigail was told that she had been taken to hospital for an operation but with a sinking feeling she knew this to be a far cry from the truth. Time was up for her superior and she was being disposed of. Now Abigail was in charge and had to be addressed as Miss Abigail, waking every morning with a sick feeling in her stomach, knowing that she would have to spend the next twelve hours being hideously officious and making sure that the day ran smoothly without any hiccoughs. She steeled herself, standing tall with a straight back and things generally went well. She appeared ruthless and disciplined and ran a tight ship. This morning however things had not sailed according to plan. Miss Abigail let out a deep sigh. Today there had been a hiccough and she had yet to deal with it.

She turned her attention to happier thoughts. She was finding it more and more difficult to be overbearing and unforgiving in her dealings with the girls for Miss Abigail, the demanding and unyielding Miss Abigail, had fallen in love. It was something that had taken her completely by surprise and not something she had ever planned on. She rarely came across any suitable men in her working environment and she certainly didn't have a social life so love had never been part of the agenda. Of course there was that pig of a man, the sleazy, slimy superintendent, who arrived periodically to check on her work and assess the girls. He had made random passes at her, which she chose to ignore, as if it was his right to have any woman he wanted. Once he had unexpectedly come up to her room and thrown her down upon the bed ready to force himself on her. As he leered at her, unzipping his dirty trousers with his grubby, fat hands, Miss Abigail had enough presence of mind to reach behind her and tug at the bell pull. The situation cooled rapidly when two of her girls walked in. After that Miss Abigail made sure that the bell by the main door was connected to every room in Avondale House so that she could be alerted as soon as the superintendent arrived on the premises and so she might never find herself in such a compromising position again. She shuddered every time she thought of him and she certainly didn't want any of her innocent girls to be caught unawares. The two girls who had saved Miss Abigail from a fate worse than death that day were rewarded with ice cream at tea time and word quickly spread amongst the envious onlookers that they would receive the same attention if they were able to protect Miss Abigail from the sleazy pants superintendent. None of Miss Abigail's girls liked him for they were astute enough to notice the gleam of lust in his eyes and the bulge in his trousers on Inspection Day shortly before some of them were due to come of age.

And just as the girls had saved Miss Abigail from the superintendent's lechery so she made it her duty to protect them. On Inspection Day she flitted here and there, not letting the sorry excuse for a man out of her sight and never allowing any of her girls to be alone with him. He resented this as he couldn't misbehave in any way and had to toe the line. It was more than his job was worth to interfere with any of Miss Abigail's girls in public. With grim satisfaction Miss Abigail knew she had won a small battle. A few more of those and they might even win the war, she thought. She couldn't prevent her girls from taking the next step of their journey after their time at Avondale House but she could at least help them to enjoy their coming of age celebrations without being poked and prodded in their private parts by that licentious and disgusting pig of a man. The girls could leave Avondale House having known some happiness no matter what lay ahead of them.

Miss Abigail had fallen in love with one of the Town Drivers. She hadn't noticed him at first for he dealt efficiently with his deliveries and then was gone. He rarely ever got out of his van. But one day he climbed out, approached and addressed her. He mentioned his daughter. She was going to be arriving with the next batch of girls and he was interested in knowing exactly what happened to the girls at Avondale House, what their lives were like and how long they were required to stay there. Not that he would want to change anything of course because that wouldn't be allowed but he was intrigued. Miss Abigail had contemplated his words suspiciously and said very little. It was wise not to trust any man. But when he next arrived to deliver medical supplies he approached her again and this time he told her his daughter's name. Miss Abigail looked at him with a degree of curiosity but once again she said very little. There was something about his eyes that attracted her however. She didn't quite know what it was but she thought it might possibly be compassion. She thought that perhaps he could be a man of sensitivity and empathy. Then she corrected herself. What a ridiculous idea, she thought, how totally ridiculous! He was just a man and they were all the same. But he had caught her attention and now she began to think about him. She couldn't help herself. He came into her thoughts at the most inconvenient and random of moments for here was a man who seemed to care about his daughter and she had never met such a man before or even been aware that there were any in existence. Her own father, a quiet, work driven man, had barely seemed to notice her. He had never been unkind to her or abused her in any way. In fact he had often patted her on the head and smiled if she came to his attention, but he never had time to speak to her. She started to have fantasies about the Town Driver late at night when she was in bed, imagining him kissing her and telling her how beautiful she was, reaching the climactic heights of orgasm as she did so. By the time his daughter finally arrived at Avondale House she had convinced herself that she was in love with him. She didn't consider the possibility that she might be incredibly lonely, or even plain desperate, not having received any affection or spoken to anyone on an intimate level since she was a child, or even that she was drawn to him because he had seemingly sought her out and was now paying her attention, albeit in the most innocent of ways. These thoughts never crossed her mind. She had vague memories of her hard working, absent-minded father, or she thought she had, and in due course she transferred these memories and a hormonal desire for love to the Town Driver.

The Town Driver, however, didn't have a clue! He was simply concerned for the welfare of his daughter. He had heard all sorts of stories about Avondale House and he determined to find out the truth for himself. He knew that there were much worse developmental homes but he just couldn't bring himself to agree to the idea that his daughter was going to be groomed ultimately to become part of a reproduction line. The very thought of his daughter as a sexual commodity was abhorrent to him. He knew it was supposed to be a great privilege and honour under the rule of The Governing Twelve but he was an older father and, if the truth be told, he liked things as they had been and not particularly as they were now. He remembered when girls met their boyfriends and husbands through a natural process, how they left school and went to university and then went on to have interviews, leading to good jobs with excellent wages, finally making decisions as to what they should do next with their lives. Should they have a family? Should they wait for a while or should they start one straightaway? Who was going to be the main breadwinner after the baby arrived and were there any family members around to help them out and would they be prepared to do this? Now everything was much more straightforward. Girls didn't have any of these things to consider because equality no longer existed for them. Girls left their homes as soon as they hit puberty in order to go to the surgery for the obligatory medical examination and then were never seen again. The young fathers were happy with this arrangement for there was little concern for the welfare of daughters, having been brought up as nothing more than a prospect of financial gain. Each father was given a lump sum of money for surrendering a daughter and this paid towards the greater education of sons. Under the new regime each wife had to continue to give birth until three boys were produced. Only then could she stop and by then the young husbands were bored with their flabby wives and looking elsewhere anyway. There was very little respect for the latest generation of girls and women under the Rule of The Twelve. The male population was all powerful and females were subservient and totally compliant.

The Town Driver had just dropped his daughter off at Avondale House and was miserable because of it. He had managed to procure permission to drop her there as he was a trustworthy delivery driver but it was still painful. He had stepped out of the van to hug her goodbye with tears in his eyes and Miss Abigail had never seen anything like it. For some reason this simple, loving gesture tugged at her heartstrings as nothing else ever had and she wished that she was the one in the Town Driver's arms on the receiving end of such a heartfelt embrace. She stood discreetly behind the main door watching as the Town Driver said his goodbyes. There were no sons in his family so far, just daughters, and so his wife had to keep reproducing. He had received an official letter from the Town Council stating that he would have to take a new wife soon if his current wife was unable to bear him a son. At the moment he was the proud father of four daughters. And he loved every one of them. He didn't know what it was like to have a son and he loved his daughters and his wife devotedly. He had chosen his wife many years before and had remained faithful to her ever since. He had no desire to look elsewhere but he knew that in the next year it was imperative that he and his wife produce a son if they were to stay together. There were ways around this, as he was informed in the official letter, but at the moment he didn't want to explore any options that existed beyond the walls of his own bedroom. He kept the members of the Town Council at bay with news of the latest pregnancy but his wife was three months gone already and there was very little time left. If his wife had one more daughter she would be designated to the scrapheap, either to work on the lowest of levels or to be used in experimentation in a clinic for women whose genetic makeup or misfortune meant that they had not borne any males. And he would have to start again. And now he had just lost one of his daughters and he was feeling devastated. It was all too much for a loving husband and father.

    He stood twisting his cap in his hands and watched as his daughter walked up to the main door. She had no suitcase with her, nothing, just the clothes she was wearing. The Town Driver knew she wouldn't have those for very long either as any girl that he had ever seen at Avondale House wore a brown, linen smock and thick tights with either walking boots or pumps. He sighed heavily. His daughter looked so fragile and vulnerable. He watched as Miss Abigail welcomed his daughter into Avondale House, briefly resting a hand on her shoulder as she did so, something she had never done before and which took her by surprise. Was she doing it because she was aware that the Town Driver was watching or did she genuinely feel compassion for his situation? Miss Abigail was confused by the conflict of emotions churning away inside her. The Town Driver turned to climb back into his van, his shoulders drooping heavily, when suddenly he heard the rapid click clack of heels behind him. It was Miss Abigail. She had run down from the main door and was panting, out of breath.

"Don't worry," she cried. "I'll make sure she's okay."

The Town Driver stared at her. Although he had previously spoken to her of his daughter he hadn't really taken much notice of her. He regarded her curiously. In front of him stood a young, brittle-looking female who was obviously feeling quite awkward. She seemed as upset as he was.

"That's very kind of you," said the Town Driver. "My name is Bill."

As he stared he felt a rush of optimism and courage. "Would it be acceptable for me to knock at the door next time I arrive with a delivery and make enquiries?"

Miss Abigail found herself immediately flustered.

"Yes, yes, of course," she said, blushing and lowering her gaze. "Come to the kitchen entrance after your deliveries and we'll sort you out with a drink and a sandwich. I can talk to you about your daughter then."

Even as she said this Miss Abigail knew she was heading for trouble. Tradesmen were not permitted to step inside the premises, not under any circumstances, and to invite one in for something to eat, well, such a suggestion could easily end in disaster. She knew Cook wouldn't say anything. She saw so few people outside Avondale House that she would probably enjoy the company. Miss Abigail would think of a plausible excuse for Bill's visits later. She couldn't say he wanted to ask about his daughter, or could she? Was there really any harm in a father being concerned for the welfare of his daughter? She sighed. Bill, that was a nice, simple, down to earth name, she thought. As long as he was never there at the same time as the slimy superintendent she thought it was possible that everything might be alright.

"Thank you," said Bill. "I make my rounds here once a week on a Wednesday."

"Lovely," replied Miss Abigail. "I'll make sure I'm available then."

As if she didn't know when he arrived with his deliveries at Avondale House? She had been standing at the window watching out for him for days, ever since he had first mentioned his daughter. She had spent hours dreaming and fantasising about him and now she had actually spoken to him. Her face broke into a broad smile of delight and Bill looked at her in surprise. He had been visiting Avondale House for some time and had heard many stories regarding its occupants, particularly Miss Abigail, and none of them fitted in with her current behaviour. Still, gossip was gossip and not much of it was ever true and if she could help him keep an eye on his daughter then he was prepared to give her the benefit of the doubt and ignore any idle chitchat that reached his ears. He stretched out his hand. Miss Abigail slowly extended hers and they shook on their words.

Bill drove off shortly after that and made his way to the local pub. There were hardly any of these left now as under The Twelve they were considered to be time consuming and wasteful. But this pub was in the basement of a friend's house and the men who came to drink there all did so under the pretence of belonging to a company which supposedly had dealings with import and export. The sign hung above the door – 'Davis and Sons'. It couldn't possibly have read 'Davis and Daughters' even though daughters were all that Tom Davis had because then he would have found himself in deep trouble.

Each man who came in to drink at the pub in the basement of 'Davis and Sons' suffered the same problem! None of them had any sons but they had beautiful daughters. The men were each of a certain age, close to retirement in the old world, and they didn't want their wives to have to keep reproducing. They were tired of rearing offspring purely for the sake of it. They loved their daughters and were good fathers but they didn't want any more babies in their lives. It was such a lot of hard work and inevitable heartache. Now was the time when they ought to be thinking about retirement and spending more time with their wives, and not just in the bedroom with the heavy burden of 'boys' dominating their lives. One only had to leave the house to see that there were babies everywhere. Young mothers congregated on every street corner and in every shop and park. There were too many of them and it was becoming ridiculous. The pavements were choked up with young girls pushing double and triple prams and buggies around, trying to make the most of the fresh air and their short-lived moments of freedom, especially when the sun was out and their husbands were away from home. The older men who visited the basement of 'Davis and Sons' wanted to enjoy their latter years and to make the most of whatever time they had left. They also needed to remind themselves that they were not the only ones living in daughter blessed circumstances. They met twice a week in the basement in order to reminisce and then to discuss the current situation in which they had inadvertently found themselves and what they could do about it, if anything. Today was one of those twice weekly days and Bill couldn't wait for a double whisky. His wife knew he would go to the basement pub after he had dropped his daughter off and that she would see him later after he had attempted to drown his sorrows in drink. She would be the one to watch him walk quietly through the front door filled with sadness and despair. Then she would comfort the man she was growing old with and who chose to stay with her out of love, resisting for as long as he could the moving on to a younger model as so many men were obliged to do now. He would be devastated by the loss of their daughter and they would support each other in their grief and bereavement, for that was basically what it boiled down to. Their daughter was, to all and sundry, dead to them and they might never see her again. Little did Bill's wife know that her husband had sown a seed of connection with Miss Abigail and that he would return home feeling more positive about life than he had done in a long time. He had news to communicate to his friends too and perhaps he would be able to help them in future situations with their daughters. A small flame flickered in his heart ready to grow and for the first time since The Twelve had taken over in government he allowed himself the privilege of feeling mildly hopeful.

CHAPTER FIVE

Miss Abigail stretched out her hands so that the girls could apply nail polish. A pearly pink would go down well today, she thought. Pink always implied innocence and youth and Miss Abigail had remarkably pretty hands. She had managed to avoid plunging them in hot water too much and always kept them well creamed. Now that her hair had been gently teased into soft, cascading waves by the girls and her face felt smooth and clean the cares of the morning were rapidly evaporating. What did it matter if Bertha hadn't really sprained her ankle? What difference did it make if the girls were behind in their chores? Who would check up on her? No one! She was in charge and if the bedding wasn't changed today it could always be done tomorrow.

Miss Abigail was feeling much better and the thought of seeing Bill in an hour's time was simply the icing on the cake and brought with it a thrill of happiness. It was Wednesday and Wednesday was delivery day. Today all the cleaning products and tissues and toiletries would arrive along with the groceries. It was Miss Abigail's favourite delivery day. She had decided to let the girls select their own shampoos and deodorants, within reason of course, as there wasn't actually a great variety to choose from. They worked hard; they even grew their own vegetable produce which they cooked and ate. They boiled up their own soap and flavoured it with mint and lavender from the herb garden, and sometimes they even used rose petals, and they made their brown tunics out of that rough, coarse linen with which they were supplied. They even hand embroidered the edges of the blankets, sheets and pillowslips which were on their beds. Miss Abigail's girls worked very hard indeed and perhaps it was time for a small reward.

She had only entertained such kindly notions since she had fallen in love with Bill and the girls were surprised and excited. Suddenly Miss Abigail was popular and the girls liked her and it was a feeling that she enjoyed. The girls had recently started smiling at her as they bobbed their curtseys and once or twice Miss Abigail had had to force herself to purse her lips and frown in order not to smile back. There was a brief moment wherein she thought that perhaps Bertha shouldn't be allowed to choose shampoo and deodorant and then Miss Abigail dismissed such thinking. They were late; she could prove nothing and it didn't really matter.

She asked the girls to leave her hair as it was today and not to pin it up as they usually did. She flicked it back from her shoulders and was aware of its gloss and shine. Surely Bill would notice. He had been no more than respectful and polite on each visit so far but perhaps if he saw her long, lovely hair floating down her back, framing her pale, eager face he might start to think of her in a different way. Miss Abigail had been able to pass on favourable reports of his daughter every week and today she had decided that she was going to let him see her. She would have to be discreet of course and he would have to hide somewhere out of sight as he wasn't allowed to have any contact with his daughter. She thought that he could peep out from behind the scullery door as the girls were choosing their toiletries and then he might see how well they were taken care of. She knew this would give him pleasure and she hoped that perhaps he might warm towards her. Any small gesture of affection would be most gratefully received. She glanced down at her nails, smiling happily.

"Thank you, girls," she said. "They look lovely. You may have an extra dessert at lunch but before you eat would you bring up the salmon salad I ordered from the kitchen? I would be most obliged. I have decided to allow April to supervise lunch today so I'd like you to let her know and then mind you do as she says."

Both girls smiled at her.

"Yes, Miss Abigail," they chorused before bobbing out of the room.

The girls looked at each other with feigned horror as they ran downstairs. Miss Abigail didn't know that neither April nor Pat had returned from their daily walk and that they weren't anywhere in the House. Oh dear, it was going to be such a moment when she found out! They hoped that she wouldn't find out too soon as then they would certainly be deprived of their recently awarded privileges. They would have to spread the word that everyone had to be on their best behaviour during lunchtime or they would never get to choose a shampoo and deodorant. The longer it was before Miss Abigail found out that anything was amiss the better.

Soon Miss Abigail was eating her favourite fish with a well dressed salad. She hadn't had salmon for at least a week. She had made a deal with the fishmonger in the nearest town early on during her placement at Avondale House. Her girls would repair and alter any items of clothing he sent in and after a certain amount of work had been done Avondale House would be rewarded with the delivery of a large slab of choice salmon. Of course the salmon was only for Miss Abigail but she always shared it with Cook as she wanted its arrival on the premises to be kept as quiet as possible. All the girls knew about it but no one said anything. The girl who returned Miss Abigail's tray to the kitchen after she had finished eating would stop at the turn of the staircase, make sure no one was around and then pick and lick the plate clean before going merrily on her way. What a treat! Miss Abigail never ate the silvery black and grey fish skin and it was gulped down with relish before the licking and long before the tray reached the kitchen. No one was ever any the wiser!

  Miss Abigail put down her knife and fork and wiped her mouth. An oily residue lingered. She would need to clean her teeth again and reapply her lipstick. She went into the bathroom and washed her hands. Oh what a glorious day it was going to be! Bill would be arriving in ten minutes and she was going to be in the kitchen to greet him. She would take her own plate down today. She felt sure there must be a little salmon left over and she would ask Cook to prepare Bill a sandwich with the remains. She knew that Cook wouldn't mind and she could imagine Bill's delight! He didn't look as if he was used to having many treats. Well, she would spoil him and take great pleasure in doing so. She was well aware that Cook would have secreted a portion of salmon away for herself by now. Miss Abigail and Cook understood each other very well. Cook resided at Avondale House along with Miss Abigail and had no home of her own. She had arrived shortly after Miss Abigail and was determined to keep her position there. She had her eye on Bill too but Miss Abigail wasn't worried in the least. Cook was not the most eye-catching of women and even her good, solid cooking was not enough to attract a man like Bill.

  When Miss Abigail finally finished in the bathroom she looked at her watch and gasped. Bill would have arrived by now. She grabbed a pale blue cashmere cardigan and flung it around her shoulders, casting a final admiring glance in the mirror at her appearance. She skipped eagerly down the stairs grabbing her plate and fork on the way. She didn't want any of the girls finding Bill in the kitchen. Once at the bottom she took a deep breath in order to regain her composure and fixed a bright smile on her face. She opened the kitchen door in sublime anticipation. She was safe. Bill was sitting at the large, deal table tucking into a salmon sandwich. Cook had read her thoughts and was even now presenting him with a mug of strong, black coffee.

"There you are, dear," she said, depositing it in front of him. She looked up then and noticed Miss Abigail.

"My goodness, I didn't recognise you with your hair like that. Would you like me to pin it up for you? Couldn't you get one of those lazy girls to do it today?"

Miss Abigail blushed and raised a hand to a wisp of hair that had somehow managed to stray across her cheek and stick there. She pushed it back and gave her glossy locks a small flick.

"Thank you so much Cook, but no! I've just washed it after slipping and sliding about in all that mud outside earlier on and it's still quite damp."

Her hair was nothing of the sort of course but Miss Abigail was simply desperate for Bill to notice her. Bill placed both hands around his mug, took a gulp of coffee and nodded at her.

"It's very nice, loose like that," he said.

Miss Abigail blushed and melted. She felt her eyes begin to prickle and lowered them quickly, staring unnecessarily at the salmon sandwich.

"I'm so glad you thought ahead Cook and used up the rest of the salmon on our guest. Great minds think alike and I don't know what I'd do without you!"

Cook gave a broad grin, revealing the gap in her front teeth where she had been punched by her drunken husband one night. Yes, she was happy and always treated with respect at Avondale House and she had no intention of jeopardising her position there.

"So Bill," continued Miss Abigail, "I thought you might like to see how your daughter is doing. Obviously she's not allowed to know you're here so we'll have to hide you but I think we can manage. How do you feel about that?"

Bill gulped at another mouthful of coffee, spilling some of it down his chin in shock and excitement. He couldn't quite believe what he was hearing. Girls were never allowed to see their parents after being dropped off or taken away. He rose to his feet, almost knocking the remains of his coffee over as he did so and wiping his mouth with the back of his hand. He picked up his cap and began to twist and wring at it nervously.

"I wouldn't like to get you into any trouble, Miss," he said, looking straight at her.

"It will be fine," replied Miss Abigail, sounding most confident. "And if you could call me Abigail I would appreciate it very much."

Bill smiled then, a grateful, I'm most obliged, sort of smile and I'm very surprised at the same time too.

"That would be wonderful," he said, and after a slightly puzzled shake of his head, "Abigail."

Cook stared hard at Miss Abigail. Had she taken leave of her senses? If anyone saw Bill in the kitchen or hiding anywhere there would be hell to pay. And Cook was being drawn into her scheme, making her culpable too. Miss Abigail was turning Cook into a non consenting partner in crime and Cook didn't know quite how she felt about that. She didn't even think Miss Abigail had given any thought to it. Yes, Cook was attracted to Bill but she wasn't sure she liked him enough to risk losing her job over him and she certainly didn't relish the prospect of being sent to some awful behavioural Home instead of remaining here at Avondale House where she felt secure and generally content. Right now everything was running smoothly and she knew her place and where she stood with Miss Abigail. She really didn't want the boat rocked in any way. Was Bill worth that? She stared even harder at Miss Abigail and as she did so, quite unexpectedly, everything fell into place with a number of rapid clicks. She saw what had happened from the softness in Miss Abigail's eyes and the loosening of her hair and the painting of her nails and the care she had taken in dressing and ultimately even the slightly vulnerable way in which she was standing. Of course! Miss Abigail thought she was in love with Bill! Cook sighed and a great wave of sadness and tenderness swept through her. Miss Abigail could never be with Bill. She was infertile; she was of no use to any man except for convenient sex and whilst she was at Avondale House she was fortunate enough to be able to avoid that. And as Cook processed everything she suddenly saw Miss Abigail as the daughter she had never had.

"I'll help you," she said.

Miss Abigail beamed with pleasure then and her face looked bright and beautiful. Cook had never seen her look so lovely. Her loneliness and the lack of love in her life tugged at Cook's heart and she determined to assist her in any way that she could.

"We could let the girls choose their shampoo and deodorant in here and Bill could hide behind the scullery door and if we leave it open a little he could peep through," suggested Miss Abigail breathlessly.

Cook nodded. "The girls should almost have finished lunch by now. I'll open the boxes and lay everything out on the table. Bill, it would be a good idea if you were to get out of sight behind the scullery door."

Bill did as he was told and Miss Abigail left Cook to deal with the boxes. It was quiet in the dining room, very quiet, much quieter than usual. The girls were obviously on their best behaviour. Miss Abigail would have to leave April in charge more often.

"Girls, girls," called out Miss Abigail, clapping her hands together. "If you have finished your food you may stand behind your chairs and then make your way in single file to the kitchen. Your behaviour has been exemplary and as a treat you may each choose a deodorant and shampoo. I am very proud of your hard work and your high standards. Well done, girls."

There was a scraping of chairs as the girls stood up. They grinned sheepishly at one another, not only because they would be getting a treat but also because they knew that Miss Abigail had yet to discover that Pat and April were missing. They did not relish that moment and were quiet as mice as they filed through from the dining room into the kitchen. The tension that filled the air was almost palpable.

CHAPTER SIX

When April and Pat next awoke the engine was still making the same droning sound of flight and both girls felt groggy.

"Whatever is in that milk is very strong," muttered Pat, rubbing her eyes. "I feel lousy."

"Yes, my head feels pretty thick," agreed April. "Can you imagine what it's like for those babies? They must be completely out of it. Let's take a peek at some of them and see how they're doing."

They crawled out of the kennel and lifted the lids on several of the boxes.

"They're still breathing," said Pat, "and their cheeks are rosy. I wonder if they're hot. They look as if they're going to wake up soon."

"This one's eyes are flickering. I'm going to put the lid down. I don't want to be the one who wakes it up so that it screams its head off and we get caught."

Pat nodded in agreement and quickly closed the rest of the boxes.

"There," she said. "What shall we do now? Shall we explore again? I wonder how long we slept for?"

"I don't think there's much more to find here," said April. "Let's go back to the cockpit and I'll see if I can glimpse any scenery through the window."

They moved quietly to the front of the warship and April stared through the window. She could see the back of the man's head and from there more and more hills and mountains.

"It looks just the same," she whispered. "The hills go on forever. There are no villages or anything. There's nothing to see. This is crazy. We could be in exactly the same place we started out from. Mr. Twitchy could have been going round and round in circles for all we know. He could have landed half a dozen times without us being aware of it. I don't like it. Even the journey in that van from the surgery didn't take this long and there have to be some houses and buildings around somewhere. I wonder where we are. I really don't like it."

"The babies are starting to make sounds," whimpered Pat. "Perhaps we should go and hide in the kennel. We'll be safe there."

"Yes," agreed April. "Come on."

By now the tone of the engine had changed and they could tell that they were going down. The warship was making its descent.

"I'm going to check on that girl baby first," said April. "I want to make sure she's alright."

Pat nodded at her. "I'll see you back at the kennel. Don't be long, will you?"

April patted her on the shoulder. "I'll only be a minute, don't worry."

She turned away from Pat and made her way to the back of the pile of boxes. The box containing the girl baby was easy to locate because of the red marking on top of it. April lifted the lid and stared inside. Something was wrong. The baby was a strange colour. She looked as if she was turning blue. April put her hand in and gently touched her cheek, withdrawing it quickly. The baby's cheek was cold. She placed her hand on the tiny chest and thought she could feel a faint heart beat. She checked the side of the box. The milk tube was empty. There was no milk coming in. The box felt cold too in spite of the insulating material inside it. April shook her head and grimaced. This was no good. The baby was going to die if she didn't receive help. She carefully began to pull at the thin tube going up through the baby's nostril. The baby didn't stir. Soon the tube was out and April had the baby girl in her arms.

"I'll save you if it's the last thing I do," she whispered, bending over to kiss her on the forehead. She held the baby close to her chest and then picked up the box. No good leaving an empty box behind for the man to find as he might wonder what had become of the baby. There were no empty boxes on the warship. Each one had a baby in it and so there was no point in arousing suspicion. She tiptoed quietly and quickly to the kennel, throwing the empty box ahead of her as she approached, and then crawling in after it.

"What do you think you're doing?" hissed Pat. "You just clonked me on the head with that box! Idiot!"

"I've got the baby girl," responded April. "She's freezing. I couldn't leave her there in the box without any food. She would be certain to die. And I couldn't leave the empty box behind for Mr. Twitchy to find, could I?"

"Why didn't you just leave her in the box and bring her over in it?" grumbled Pat. "That would have been the most logical solution."

She rubbed at the painful spot on her head and stared at the baby in April's arms. Within moments her face softened and she smiled. She couldn't help herself.

"She's beautiful," she whispered. "But how are we going to keep her quiet? She is a baby after all and babies don't understand when you tell them to stop crying."

April nodded. "Once I warm her up and get some food into her she'll be fine. That milk shouldn't be too cold now. It's been out of the freezer for ages. If you could just let me get at the milk packet and that piece of tubing I'll have a go at feeding her. I'm not going to push the tube up her nose. That's not normal. I'll try squirting a little milk into her mouth. I'm going to wrap her up in that dog blanket as well. I know it's not very clean and that it's covered in black hairs but it might do the trick. Poor thing! The man obviously thinks he's given all the baby girls away. When we land again we'll find a good home for her. Do you think that's a good idea?"

Pat didn't respond. She wasn't convinced. April was taking an enormous risk, she thought, and carrying a baby around with them was sure to attract attention. There was no way they could keep the baby quiet forever either. Nevertheless she moved aside so that April could get to the milk packet and tubing and watched as April swaddled the baby girl in the blanket. She certainly looked comfortable and cosy by the time April had finished with her.

"Can you hold her for a minute so that I can feed her?"

Pat took the baby whilst April dipped one end of the tube into the milk and then carefully inserted the other into the baby girl's mouth. She squeezed slowly at the tube so that the milk began to seep through. Drops trickled down the back of the baby's throat. There was no movement from the baby.

"Do you think she's already dead?" asked Pat timorously? "She's a strange colour, isn't she?"

"No, just half dead," responded April. "Does she feel any warmer yet, do you think?"

"Maybe," said Pat. "But I don't really know. I'm not used to babies."

"I've got younger brothers and sisters," said April. "When they were babies they sometimes became sick and I had to look after them. They were never cold though. They were usually hot and I had to pat them all over with a damp cloth to bring their temperatures down. I'm not really sure what to do with cold babies. I can't think of any way of warming her up other than what we're doing. Perhaps if I put her under my clothes with her head peeping out at the top she might respond to the warmth of my body? What do you think?"

Pat nodded eagerly and handed the baby over. April unbuttoned her tunic and settled the swaddled baby beneath it, cringing at the roughness of the dog blanket as it scratched against her bare skin. She picked up the tube again and continued to feed her.

"It's working," she whispered after a while. "Her eyelids are fluttering. Look! She must be dreaming. Perhaps she's dreaming of her mother?"

"Oh yes," agreed Pat. "That's wonderful! I dream of my mother sometimes even though I don't have her any more. She was always kind and gentle. She tried to protect me from my father when he was annoyed but it didn't really work as he would just use his fists on her first before coming for me with his belt. Then after she died he was so angry with me. I don't know why he hated me so much. I never had any brothers or sisters so you would think that he would love me, wouldn't you? After all, I was his only child. I was all he had left. Perhaps that was the problem; perhaps he wanted more children. Perhaps he just wanted lots of boys and then he would have been happy. Boys are important, aren't they?"

April looked at Pat and thought awhile before she replied.

"Of course they're important, yes, but so are girls. We're as important as each other. Why shouldn't we be? But something has gone wrong. My mother used to tell me stories of the amazing jobs girls had after they left university. That was when they were allowed to go. She told me how they earned good money and how they bought their own homes and that they were very independent. And there were lots of girls who weren't married either. They chose to be single so that they could travel and have top positions doing work they enjoyed, making the most of life and having great holidays around the world and they wanted babies later in life too. Imagine that! Imagine a world where girls made their own choices and were successful and happy. I can't imagine it, can you? When I think about the stories my mother told me it seems like an impossible dream. All I've ever known have been families dominated by males and I know now why lots of girls were hidden away, especially if there were no boys in the family. We've been treated like unpaid slaves and even if we had mothers who tried to protect us the fathers have always had to follow the rule of The Twelve so that they weren't arrested. There are lots of men out there ready to snitch on each other. I heard of some fathers who were caught after going against The Twelve and they were given a public beating before being sent to prison. And that was the last of them as they were never heard of or seen again."

Pat looked at April in wonder.

"One of my friend's fathers was whipped in the village square in front of everybody and then he was bundled into the back of a van and never seen again," she whispered. "He was quite an old man and he only had one daughter. When he finally sent her to the surgery for her medical she was well past her coming of age and that was his punishment for hiding her away."

"We're best away from it," said April, sighing. "And if we can make it to the mountains where my grandmother lives I know we'll be okay."

Pat leant across and kissed April on the cheek. Then she blushed with embarrassment.

"I'm so glad I escaped with you and that we've become friends," she said. "I never had a friend before."

April wrinkled her nose in pleasure and smiled at her. "We'll get through this, don't worry."

By now the noise from the engine had completely died away and the girls concluded that the warship had landed. Some of the babies were crying and they could hear rustling sounds as they wriggled around in their boxes.

"Don't move," said April. "And stay quiet. We need to find out what the man's doing. I'm sure we'll hear him soon enough."

"You certainly will!" a voice suddenly roared in front of them.

Pat let out a scream and grabbed at April who accidentally pushed the tubing down the baby's throat so that she started to cough and choke. Mr. Twitchy's face loomed large at the kennel entrance and Pat clung to April in shock. Both girls began to shuffle and slide towards the back of the kennel trying to appear as small and insignificant as possible.

April removed the tube from the baby's mouth and patted her on the back, comforting her. She was desperately trying to assess the situation and thinking about what they could do next. No matter what happened they had to stay calm. The man stared at all three girls and then let out a huge guffaw of laughter.

"Did you think I didn't know you were here?" he announced. "I heard snoring as I was doing one of my checks and couldn't help but find you. One of you snores very loudly."

April glared at him. She knew she had to be the noisy culprit.

"So what are you going to do?" she asked bravely. "What do you plan to do with us now that you've found us?"

"I have to turn you in to the authorities of course," replied the man. "There's a fat reward for anyone who turns young runaways in."

April and Pat stared at him in horror. The baby began to cry.

"We know about the girl babies," continued April boldly. "We know what you got in return for them too. I saw everything."

"Do you really think you're in a position to blackmail me?" continued the man. "Who do you think would believe you?"

"I've got one of the girl babies here," continued April.

"So you have," said the man. He laughed even more. "Of course I'm not going to turn you in. Don't be stupid! I would get into so much trouble for allowing a couple of stowaways to hide on my warship. I have two daughters of my own and I would hate it if they were in your predicament. Luckily no one knows about them so far. We don't all conform to the rule of The Twelve, you know. Not everyone agrees with their rulings."

"Really?" whispered Pat. "You're really not going to turn us in?"

Tears of relief began to roll down her cheeks and then she started to sob. April glared even harder at the man and held the baby closer. She wasn't sure whether to believe him or not.

"No, of course not. You haven't been reported missing yet but that's not to say you soon won't be and there is always a fat reward for girls your age. I simply presented you with the worst scenario. My van is parked close by. I have to deliver the boy babies to the next town. It's not a long drive. I could take you with me if you like."

"You don't know where we're going?" challenged April.

"Well," responded the man. "I'm assuming you don't want to do much more walking across this rough terrain, do you? No food, no drink, and always looking over your shoulder to make sure no one is around to see you. And now you've got a baby to care for, and a girl at that! You won't want to return in the warship to where you've just come from, and I will have to head back you know? It would be easy for the authorities to catch up with you then, wouldn't it?"

April scowled at the man. What he said made sense but she didn't like feeling that he was in control of their situation.

"I'll drop you off in the town and you can make your way to the Wine Sellers. A friend of mine, George, runs it and he'll be able to hide you for a couple of days."

"How will he know that he's supposed to hide us?" asked April. "And why should we believe you? You might be leading us into a terrible trap."

"I might be," replied the man. "But I have to drop off the boys and then go and collect some older babies for a different town. What do you have to lose? If you stay on the warship there is a greater risk of being captured as a group of men will load the next lot of babies on board and after my trip back you'll be exactly where you started. If you go to see George you'll be much further ahead on your journey."

"But you don't know where we're going?" interrupted Pat, wiping away her tears.

"I can guess," said the man. "Everyone who escapes from anywhere heads for the foot of the volcanic mountain.

That's the safest place to be and no one will look for you there. Am I right?"

April and Pat stared at him and said nothing. This man knew too much by far. April still didn't feel as if she trusted him.

"So what was the deal with those girl babies then?" she asked finally.

"I did the best I could," responded the man thoughtfully. "I'm supposed to dump them and go, leaving them for the wild dogs or wolves to devour. But I just can't do it. I have a group of contacts who put the word out when I'm in a position to make a drop. There are plenty of families hiding in caves and in densely wooded areas and when they hear the warship they come out to collect them. You saw them, didn't you? Away from the towns and the rule of The Twelve these families bring up their young as they used to hoping against hope that one day things will change, just as I do. In this way I can pretty much save all the girls on my warship. It's a small step in the bigger scheme of things but who knows what the future holds? There are many men out there making deliveries from warships but I'm not aware of anyone else who risks his livelihood in order to help any girls. Men do as they are told or it's the worse for them and their families."

"Well, you get paid with that strange-smelling tobacco, don't you? April told me. You don't do it for nothing, do you?" objected Pat. "You're not that goodhearted!"

"That's true," responded the man. "But I have two daughters to feed that no one knows about and I can trade some of the tobacco for fresh meat or milk or eggs or even leather to make clothing and shoes with. It's all swings and roundabouts!"

Pat turned with a puzzled frown to April. Swings and roundabouts! What had eggs and milk to do with swings and roundabouts? The only swings and roundabouts she knew about were growing old and rusty in parks that no one played in any more. She had once run away from her father and hidden in one but as night had fallen it had become too cold and she'd been forced to return home for a beating. She hadn't a clue what the man was talking about.

"I think we should go and see George at the Wine Sellers," she said. "That sounds like a good option. The further we are away from Avondale House and Manor the better."

April nodded and turned to address the man again. "How will George know that he's supposed to help us though?"

"I'll give you some tobacco to take as a gift and then all you have to say is that Tim sent you. I'm going to unload now and transfer the boxes to the van. Wait here until I let you know that it's safe to come out."

And with that Mr. Twitchy, or Tim as he had just announced, withdrew his head and left them.

CHAPTER SEVEN

"Can you carry the milk if I take the baby?" asked April.

"Of course I can," responded Pat. "Do you think we can trust that man, Tim, then?"

"We'll have to," said April. "We've got no choice. The baby's going to sleep again now. Look! We'll have to think of a name for her. She's so beautiful. I feel as if I love her already."

Pat looked down at the baby, snuggled cosily beneath April's tunic.

"I think I love her too," she said, extending her little finger in order to stroke her cheek. "And I've got the perfect name for her. We can call her Hope. I think she's come into our lives to give us some, don't you?"

"She couldn't have a better name," said April. "You're right. So can you grab Hope's milk and try and find some tissues from somewhere. I've just felt a leak of hot, wet stuff running down my stomach and there's a very strong smell coming from it."

"Eugh!" said Pat, wrinkling her nose in disgust. "Perhaps I don't quite love her yet?"

April laughed. Hope's milk had to come out at the other end at some point and she was used to cleaning babies. Unfortunately though, there was no spare clothing for either Hope or April to change into and they would have to remain damp and smelly for the time being.

Pat returned with a few, almost clean tissues and April removed the soggy blanket that she had swaddled Hope in and dried her as best she could. She hid the stinking, urine soaked blanket at the back of the kennel, chuckling as she did so. Tim could deal with it later. That would be a nice surprise for him.

"Go and have a look and see what he's up to, will you?" she said to Pat. Pat nodded and left the kennel once more. A minute later and she was back.

"He's finished. He says we can go out now and get into the back of the van."

April crawled out of the kennel clutching Hope closely to her chest.

"Don't forget the milk, will you? That's all the food we have. We won't get very far without it. And it will help to keep Hope quiet too."

Pat reached back into the kennel and grabbed the milk.

"There's only half a packet left," she said.

"We'll have to make sure we find the Wine Sellers as soon as possible then, won't we?" said April. "Maybe Tim will have some more on the van that we can take with us?"

Outside the warship it was getting dark and they could only just make out the shape of the van in the dusky half-light.

"I don't know where the time disappears to," said Pat. "I don't know what day it is or anything."

"Neither do I," replied April. "Who knows how long we slept after drinking that drugged milk? Look what it's done to Hope. But at least she's not cold any more. She's breathing peacefully and her little cheeks are quite pink."

Pat clambered into the back of the van and carefully took Hope from April so that she could climb in too. Tim came round to lock the doors.

"Get behind the boxes and stay low in case we're stopped on the road. Recently there have been spot checks everywhere. It's never been as bad as this before. I don't know what the road police are looking for. It can't be the two of you.

There must be something else going on because, quite frankly, you're not that important in the greater scheme of things."

April and Pat did as they were told. Tim sounded worried and they certainly didn't want to risk the possibility of getting caught. They crouched down out of sight and heaved a sigh of relief as the van's engine turned over and they set off.

"I hope this isn't going to be a long journey," said April. "I could do with stretching my legs. I feel as if all we've done is curl up and keep out of sight, not that it stopped Tim from finding us and I'm sure I was seen when those women came to collect the baby girls. One of them stared straight at the cave entrance where I was hiding. You were on the warship by that time and it was quite spooky. I think she was letting me know that she knew I was there, but it was definitely spooky. It sent a shiver up my spine."

"But why didn't she say anything or come up and speak to you?" asked Pat.

"I'm not sure," replied April. "Perhaps it was something to do with the fact that the women were rescuing the babies? Or perhaps she was just showing me that she was on my side? Maybe if I'd been a boy hiding behind that ferny curtain she would have raised the alarm? Who knows? Anyway, we're well away from all that now and hopefully we're a lot nearer my grandmother's house. I wish we had a map to tell us how far away we are or at least a compass so that we could tell whether we're heading in the right direction or not! That would be a bonus, wouldn't it?"

"I don't care how long it takes us," said Pat. "The most important thing is that we're away from Avondale House and I'm sure that after a while they'll give up searching for us."

"That's if they are searching for us," responded April. "Tim didn't think we were that important, remember."

Suddenly the van skidded across the road and screeched to a juddering halt. Pat lost her balance, falling forward and striking her head on a sharp, metal corner. She let out a high pitched squeal before clutching at it, moaning. The girls heard the sounds of raised voices issuing orders followed by a single, solitary gunshot. Acknowledging that there was no time to inspect Pat's injuries April held her down against the floor of the van and covered her mouth with her hand to encourage her to be quiet. Luckily Hope was sleeping so deeply that the firing of a cannonball wouldn't have awoken her.

"Shhhh!" hissed April. "Don't move and don't make any noise."

The back doors of the van were flung wide allowing a sliver of light to filter through and they could hear the dragging sounds of boxes as they were pulled from the van and then a lot of sniffing and snorting as they were opened.

"Nothing unusual here!" said a gruff voice. "Show us your papers!"

This last command was obviously directed at Tim who had said nothing as yet but April assumed he must be standing in a show of mute respect by the van doors. There was the rustle of paper being handled and then silence.

"So you're a baby transporter?" continued the gruff voice eventually, as if it wasn't obvious. "Everything appears to be legit but we need to unload the rest of the boxes so that we can be certain."

"You're more than welcome," said Tim calmly. "However, I'm already behind schedule and I would hate to have to report the reason for this extra delay. The work I do is of paramount importance and my orders come straight from the top. You would also be putting the lives of the babies at risk and that would be most unfortunate, wouldn't you agree?"

"It's more than our jobs are worth to let you through without a thorough check," responded the man with the gruff voice. He turned to speak in hushed tones to another man and then turned back to Tim.

"Unless you can compensate us in some way," he grunted, coughing and clearing his throat.

There was an intense period of silence after this request and April held her breath. She hoped Tim wouldn't give them up as being handed over to road police would be the worst outcome possible. Who knew where they would be taken or what would happen to them? She had heard of girls being abandoned by the side of the road after they had been abused and mutilated by such officials. Miss Abigail had told the girls at Avondale House many times of all the terrible things that could occur if any of them tried to escape and were picked up by the wrong people. There were a lot of evil men out there, not just good husbands. April felt her body stiffening as she considered the possibilities that lay ahead and she could feel Pat's body responding to her own and becoming rigid with tension beside her. The next few minutes seemed to take forever, until finally the girls heard the sounds of boxes being reloaded and retreating footsteps.

"What's happening?" whispered Pat.

"Hush!" replied April. "I don't know."

Within seconds the engine was turned over and they were on their way again.

"Do you think Tim's driving or someone else?" whispered Pat.

"It has to be Tim," replied April. "I don't think he'd give up his van or the babies without a fight. He would be in serious trouble if he did."

"That's a relief," said Pat. "My head really hurts. I didn't half give it a crack." She put her hand up to her forehead and gently patted her temple with two fingers. "It's bleeding. There's blood on my hand and I can feel it running down the side of my face and into my eye."

"Let me see," said April. "Yes, you've got a nasty cut there. It doesn't look deep though. We need to find something to cover it with."

She began to poke about at the back of the van opening tins and half empty packets to see what was in them. There was very little chance that they would be stopped again, she thought. That would simply be too much bad luck in one day. Hope was secured so completely beneath her tunic that April's hands were free to investigate and explore. Eventually she came across a battered and rusty first aid box. She pulled out a roll of bandage and a tube of antiseptic. She also managed to find a large piece of gauze and debated whether or not to attach this to Hope's bottom in an attempt to keep her clean but decided finally that Pat's injury was more important.

"Stay still while I sort your head out," said April. "I've no idea how long any of this has been here or how clean it is but it's the best I can do for now."

Pat winced as April applied the antiseptic. The cut stung madly but at least the bleeding had stopped. April then gently patted the gauze into place before unravelling the roll of bandage and wrapping it around Pat's head a few times.

"You may need stitches. We'll find out when we get to the Wine Sellers. George is bound to help us, isn't he?

"I hope so," agreed Pat. She felt nauseous and her head ached. She lay on her back and closed her eyes. The whole trip was starting to feel like a nightmare and there was a part of her that was having second thoughts and wishing she hadn't rolled down the hill after April. Life hadn't been so bad at Avondale House. She had been able to cope with the cleaning and cooking and washing and ironing and everything else. She had been fed and clothed and she had slept in her own bed. It was Avondale Manor that was the problem. And she certainly didn't want to go there again even if she was taken under Sister Charlotte's wing for a second time. Sister Charlotte had always been extra kind to her but who knew what she would eventually have wanted in return. Pat had watched as she became more and more intimate with the girls she punished and recoiled in horror every time she thought about it. She knew the other girls had been relieved and even pleased when Sister Charlotte had shown such a special interest in her as that meant she would leave them alone. Some of them had even passed on morsels of food in appreciation or had done some of her cleaning for her but none of it made up for the gut-wrenching sense of apprehension she experienced every time Sister Charlotte called her into her office.

As soon as the door closed behind her Pat was always asked to remove her clothes so that her body could be inspected for any new or recent marks. Sister Charlotte wanted to make sure that no one ever harmed her again, or so she said. Pat had been obliged to undress slowly and to fold her clothes neatly on a chair in the corner. She then had to stand very still in the middle of the room trying not to grimace whilst Sister Charlotte walked around her lightly touching her here and there asking if anyone had hurt her. And Pat always shook her head most adamantly. It got to the stage where it became a daily ritual and once, most shocking of all, whilst Pat was undressing, Sister Charlotte removed her habit and stood naked and trembling in front of her. Pat had no idea what was expected of her at this point and rather than stare in obvious horror and trepidation she had simply closed her eyes so that Sister Charlotte could carry out her inspection as per usual. She felt Sister Charlotte stroke her scars with the gentlest of fingertip caresses and for a moment there was an awareness that perhaps she had brushed her body against her own as softly and as delicately as the fluttering, powdered wings of a butterfly, but when Pat eventually opened her eyes Sister Charlotte was fully robed and seated at her desk scribbling vigorously on a notepad as if nothing had happened.

CHAPTER EIGHT

It was a glorious moment for Bill as he watched his daughter come into the kitchen with her new friends to select her deodorant and shampoo. He felt his cheeks blaze red with pleasure as he stood hidden and out of sight behind the door. He could sense his daughter's delight as she turned to smile at the girl next to her. All too soon it was over though and Cook was leading the girls out. Miss Abigail came to join him for the last few moments as he gazed after his daughter, moving to stand in front of him. He could hear her breath coming in small pants and smell the warm fragrance of her perfume as it lingered at the nape of her neck. She turned and glanced back to smile at him; a smile full of promise. In that instant he knew what she wanted. Of course he couldn't see his daughter without payment. Payment was always required in the world of today. He frowned knowing that he had to satisfy Abigail – as she wished to be called. It wasn't something he had considered. She was so very young and he had thought she had allowed him to see his daughter out of the goodness of her heart. A lump of disappointment settled in his stomach. What had humanity come to? Standing still and processing the awkward situation he was in he became aware of her pert bottom pushing against him and, without expecting it to happen, his body began to respond. Bill was shocked. This was something he hadn't considered. He felt her reach down with her hands, pressing back harder as she slowly rolled her tight skirt up along the sides of her thighs until it stopped at her waist. With a gasp of surprise he realised that she was wearing only a skimpy thong beneath it. He groaned and closed his eyes. The temptation was overwhelming. An image of his middle-aged, loyal wife taunted him briefly and he experienced a pang of guilt - but not for long. This was something else. This was taut, young flesh teasing him; taut, young flesh wanting him. He gritted his teeth and pursed his lips, aware that he was thinking with his groin and not with his head, a sensation he had almost forgotten existed. Feelings of strong desire began to course through his veins. He felt Abigail reach down with one hand and caress him. He groaned again, overcome with lust, and automatically reached for her breasts, squeezing them hard. He couldn't help himself. The temptation was too much. It was all there, being offered on a plate, right in front of him. Abigail let out a small, eager squeal and tugged frantically at the zip of his trousers. He inhaled deeply and bit into her neck moving his hands down towards her buttocks. He then slipped a hand underneath the skimpy cotton thong, pulling it aside as he did so. She parted her legs slightly. He crouched down a little, positioned himself comfortably and then pushed his way in. She was so tight. But of course she was; she was probably a virgin! His head and body were suffused with an almost aggressive hunger! He was going to a place where none had been before. He thrust again and again letting out all the pent up frustrations that constantly eroded the enjoyment of his daily life. He allowed himself to be consumed by her warm, velvety embrace. She made no sound and neither did he but he was aware of the whiteness of her knuckles as her hands pressed against the door. He plunged on and on until finally it was over and with a shuddering sigh he tucked his limp member away. He stood kissing her neck from behind and breathing heavily until his emotions were once more under control and the carnal sensations faded away to nothingness. He experienced a fleeting moment of shame but that was all. The whole thing had taken less than five minutes and as she turned to him he saw the brightness of her eyes and that she was radiant with joy.

"You love me, don't you?" she whispered.

"Yes, yes, of course," he stammered, not having the heart to hurt her.

"We'll do this again," she continued, rolling down her skirt, rearranging herself and opening the door, walking into the kitchen as if nothing had happened and looking the picture of perfect respectability. Bill hurriedly zipped up his trousers, guilt now beginning to sweep through him.

"Cook!" Miss Abigail called. "Cook!"

Cook returned to the kitchen. "The girls are putting away their toiletries," she said. "All is well."

"Good," responded Miss Abigail. "Could you see Bill out, please? He has been reassured by the sight of his daughter and needs to get back to work."

Bill nodded at Cook and lowered his eyes shamefacedly, still feeling flustered by what had just taken place. Miss Abigail left the kitchen and walked hastily upstairs to her room. Cook smiled at Bill and ushered him to the back door. Bill saw that he would have to squeeze past her oversized body in order to leave Avondale House. It was obvious that Cook had no intention of moving out of the way. She grinned at him, displaying a gaping, black hole where her front teeth had once resided, and he caught sight of a momentary flash of lust in her eyes and wondered what on earth he was getting himself into. Sex mad women, he thought. That's what came of never having any contact with men. He had to admit that he had enjoyed his few stolen minutes with Abigail but he resolved not to go down the same path with Cook. She was simply not in the same league. And what if he did and the two women found out about each other? It didn't bear thinking about. His path had unpredictably taken a new turning and there could be no going back. What he had done was completely out of character and his thoughts were drawn regretfully towards his wife. Sex with her had become routine and was performed as a means to an end. It hadn't always been like that. He had been attracted to her once but over the years as babies popped out her body had become soft and loose and flabby. He loved her anyway and so had never even thought of looking elsewhere until today. He couldn't quite believe what had just happened. He knew he ought not to do it again but the thought of Abigail's obvious desire, her readiness and welcoming depths made him start to perk up again. He tried to push away such thoughts knowing that there would inevitably be another time and that it would hopefully last a little longer and possibly be more intimate. Perhaps he would be able to push her head down upon him and obtain relief that way. He used to enjoy that so much when he was younger but his wife no longer wished to pleasure him. For her sex had become nothing more than a marital chore that took place every night as a means to an end and one that needed to be over and done with as quickly as possible. She was a good wife and never refused him but neither did she encourage him. She just rolled onto her side so that penetration was easy and waited until it was over. Then she fell asleep. Bill smiled as he drove away from Avondale House knowing that he would return within a week's time and then who knew what might happen.

    Miss Abigail was getting changed. She pressed a hand gently against her swollen vulva and sighed with pleasure. Bill loved her. He had just proved it and he had told her so as well. Life couldn't be more perfect. He found her desirable and even with such hard thrusts he hadn't hurt her. She wondered how that could be. She had been told so often by her mother and by Cook that the first time was painful and generally unpleasant. But it had been wonderful with Bill. She had ached for him to make love to her. She had had such fantasies about him and now they were starting to come true. It had been over too quickly but she would make sure there was a next time. Oh, things were simply getting better and better. She was in two minds as to whether or not she should confide in Cook though. Cook might disapprove or worse still, she might put someone else in the picture and then there would be such trouble. She reflected on why Bill's lovemaking hadn't hurt. There had to be a reason. She remembered all the medical examinations she had endured in order to work out the size and shape of her uterus and exactly where it was positioned within her body just in case there might be the possibility of childbirth at some point in the future. The doctor had told her mother she was a most unusual case and had seen her every day for two weeks, examining her, probing with his fingers and making copious notes. His fingers became more and more exploratory with each visit and she often felt his hot breath upon her private parts as he worked. She would lie on his table with her knees up and her legs open and once he slid a cushion under her bottom so that her legs flopped even more widely apart and he could clearly see what the problem was or so he said. It was on that day that part way through the examination he bent his head down, pulled back the head of her pubis and sucked at her, tickling her with his bristly moustache. She wondered why he had done this and what part it could possibly have played in his examinations. She found she enjoyed the sensations it aroused, pushing up against the doctor's probing tongue and mouth as he physically and eagerly analysed his latest findings. But sadly that was the last session and on her way out she saw a younger girl going in and wondered if he was going to repeat the same exploratory process with her. She never said anything to her mother about what the doctor had done as she was naïve enough to think that his examinations were completely normal and her mother wouldn't have brought her to the surgery so often if he had been doing anything untoward, would she? She dismissed the doctor from her thoughts and turned her attention back to Bill. What a wonderful afternoon she had just had.

    She sighed with happiness and smiled at herself in the mirror. She would have to make sure that there were more such wonderful afternoons. Now that she knew Bill loved her she would have to think of a way of getting him up to her room. It would be impossible to bring him through the main house as someone would be bound to notice but there was always the option of the rickety, fire escape outside. It led directly to her window and from there she would be able to let him in. He would have to enter her room at night though and it would have to be the greatest of secrets. The girls were usually asleep by ten and so an arrival at eleven would be perfect. She would go downstairs now and commend April for having taken charge of the girls so well. They had behaved so beautifully during lunch and after. They were a credit to her and to themselves. Miss Abigail felt confident and content. She would make sure her girls were always well looked after. She could do nothing about what happened to them after they left Avondale House but while they were in her care she would do her best for them. They deserved at least that much for their constant, obedient behaviour. She decided to put the Bertha incident behind her and not mention it. After all it was such a small thing and the memory of it shouldn't be allowed to spoil or disrupt the rest of her day in any way. She would go down and see how the girls were getting on with the clothing repairs.

At Avondale House the first two hours after lunch were spent doing needlework. The girls would sew on buttons, replace zips, patch jumpers and cardigans, stitch hems, anything that needed doing in the way of repairs in fact. As well as bringing groceries, medicines and products to Avondale House Bill also brought in bags of clothing. Each item had to be individually inspected and then placed in its relevant pile. Some of the clothes weren't fit to be worn and these were put aside to be recycled but some of them had surname labels sewn neatly at the neckline and these had to be washed and repaired if necessary before they could be ironed and finally wrapped carefully in brown paper ready to be returned to their rightful owners. Each girl was given a different job to do and so the result was generally that of a smoothly run operation that worked well.

Miss Abigail felt sparks of happiness flicker through her and for a moment she almost forgot herself as she skipped down some of the stairs. She paused on the last tread with her hand across her chest, attempting to still her fluttering heartbeat, and then opened the door leading into the workroom where she could hear merry chatter as the girls worked. She would have to calm them down. They were obviously in high spirits after having been given the privilege of choosing their own shampoo and deodorant. But it was supposed to be a time of tranquillity as they worked!

"Girls!" Miss Abigail called out. "Girls!"

An immediate hush descended and each girl withdrew to her allocated workplace within the room and continued with what they were supposed to be doing. Now the room was as it should be and Miss Abigail tried not to smile. She was in charge and discipline had always to be maintained. The quietness pleased her and showed her how much respect the girls had for her. Perhaps if they continued in such a way she would permit a scoop of ice cream with their supper. She knew Cook kept a variety of tubs hidden at the back of the freezer under the emergency ice cubes which she sporadically dipped into. Miss Abigail was in a very generous mood.

"April!" she called. "April, could you stand up, please?"

There was silence and the girls lowered their heads as they continued to work. Miss Abigail frowned slightly.

"April," she repeated. "April, I asked you to stand, please!"

Still there was silence! It was an uneasy silence, one that remained unbroken by the expected sound of a chair scraping back and the sight of April on her feet. Miss Abigail sensed a moment of bewilderment. What was April playing at? Where was she? Was this some kind of a joke? April was one of her best behaved girls; a little rebellious perhaps on one or two occasions but nothing that couldn't be quashed by a stern look from Miss Abigail. She closed her eyes for a moment in order to think. She really didn't want anything to spoil her lovely afternoon. She stood calmly as she considered her best option in this situation. Maybe April was still putting away her shampoo and deodorant or perhaps she had gone to the bathroom? It could quite easily be as simple as that although she was not actually allowed to leave the workroom without permission! Perhaps there had been an emergency? Miss Abigail was prepared to think only the best. She glanced round at all the girls and her eyes finally came to rest on Bertha who appeared to be smiling contemptuously.

"Bertha, do you know where April is?" she asked sharply.

Bertha instantly pulled back her chair and stood up. Miss Abigail noticed that she was still smirking but trying her best not to.

"Well, Bertha," Miss Abigail continued. "I asked you a question!"

Bertha raised her head defiantly. "She's not here," she retorted sullenly.

"She's not here, Miss Abigail, if you don't mind. Remember your manners, girl!"

Something was going on. Something was clearly going on and if she didn't deal with it quickly and professionally it was undoubtedly going to spoil the rest of the afternoon. Miss Abigail's lips thinned into a long, tight line and her nostrils began to flare. Two red spots appeared on her cheeks.

"Tell me Bertha, tell me the truth. Where is April?"

"She's gone, Miss Abigail. She's run away."

"Don't be ridiculous, Bertha. She's hiding in the building somewhere. She's playing some sort of childish game. She can't possibly have run away. I would have noticed earlier."

But even as she said this Miss Abigail knew it wasn't true. She had been too busy with Bill. He had taken up every moment of her thoughts after the girls had come back from their walk and she had also been so preoccupied with Bertha and her ankle that she had forgotten to take a head count. A wave of anger swept over her. She glared at Bertha.

"Exactly when did she run away?" she asked, knowing full well what the answer would be.

"On the walk this morning," muttered Bertha. "I didn't see anything, honest. I just noticed when we got back that April and Pat weren't with us."

Miss Abigail turned white. Pat was gone too! This was rapidly turning into a nightmare of an afternoon.

"Go to my office," she hissed. "And the rest of you are confined to your rooms until I say you can come out. Take your work with you and get on with it. You will be questioned individually. At least one of you knows something and you can rest assured that I will get it out of you! There can be no doubt about that!"

The girls stood up slowly, feeling subdued and not wanting to be noticed. They were wary of Miss Abigail's anger. It was so intense that it filled the room. She usually shouted and ranted and raved for five minutes and then it was over but this was a different kind of anger. This was an anger that sent chills down the spine, the kind of anger one didn't encourage. This was a quiet, venomous, threatening sort of rage such as the girls had never before experienced from Miss Abigail. What they had originally looked forward to as a potentially comic situation was rapidly turning into something else. They had thought Miss Abigail would flap about in shock and anxiety for a few moments giving little thought to them. They had pictured both Miss Abigail and Cook running about like headless chickens not knowing what to do and had giggled amongst themselves. They had never imagined this still, seething fury which was shortly to be inflicted upon each one of them in turn. The girls picked up their work, bobbed slightly in respect and concern, and hurried to their rooms.

Bertha was the first to be seen by Miss Abigail. After all she was the one who had created the distraction. It was perfectly clear to Miss Abigail that Bertha was the prime instigator in all of this but the insolent girl denied everything. Bertha was strong and rebellious enough to lie confidently and to look straight into Miss Abigail's eyes as she did so. Miss Abigail gritted her teeth and went through the process of seeing each girl one by one. Not one of them had seen either Pat or April slip away or so they said. And somehow, in spite of herself, Miss Abigail believed them. It must have happened very quickly. Miss Abigail would have to alert the authorities. The Town Council would have to be informed and would undoubtedly get involved. Perhaps a search party would be sent out? After all, the two girls couldn't have got very far, could they? They must still be on the mountainside somewhere. They would be cold and wet and hungry. It had been painfully damp on the walk earlier that day, the sort of damp that lingers, working its way into the bones and making one feel on the verge of shakes and shivers. Maybe the girls were on their way back to Avondale House even now? Perhaps they had changed their minds about running away? Miss Abigail felt a brief flash of sympathy for them. She might have run away if she had been in the same situation? Would she have enjoyed living at Avondale House knowing that she would soon be going to Avondale Manor to become a baby mother? Only of course the girls didn't know that, or did they? Were any of them aware that they left Avondale House after their coming of age celebrations in order to be used and abused? They were told that they were going to find perfect love and get married. But perhaps some of them did know the truth? After all both Pat and Bertha had spent time there. And then Miss Abigail considered her own situation. She was going to get into an enormous amount of trouble because two girls known to be in her care were no longer on the premises and their whereabouts was unknown. The authorities would be obliged to deal with her and her special and most coveted title could easily be taken away from her. What would happen to her then? What would she do if she didn't work at Avondale House? Where would she go? She held a respected position at the House. What would happen if it was taken away?

    Miss Abigail sat down and put her head in her hands. She had interviewed every single girl and had no idea what to do next. She was facing a troublesome dilemma which could potentially turn into a nightmare. The afternoon was completely spoilt as she had feared it would be. She exhaled heavily. Then a thought struck her! She could confide in Cook.

That was the obvious solution. She didn't really want to discuss the matter with her but it might help. Cook might have some sensible suggestions? Yes, that's what she would do. Cook was much older than she was and had undoubtedly dealt with many distressing and perplexing situations throughout her life. She would listen to what Cook had to say and follow her advice. She lifted her head and took a deep breath. Thank goodness for Cook, she thought!

CHAPTER NINE

"You must go now," said Tim, letting the girls out of the back of the van. He had pulled to a halt in a deserted car park. "I can't drive you any further into the town with me. The Wine Sellers is no more than two streets away but I can't drop you off at the door, I'm afraid. I'm running very late as it is and I don't want to lose any sales."

"Two streets won't make much difference," said April, not really understanding Tim's explanation or train of thought. "And what sales?"

Tim sighed. "The baby boys are for sale. They are all in perfect health and I take them to the Town Hall where they are bought by families who have no boys. It's a way out for the mothers who have only produced girls. They raise the boys as their own and in this way they are able to redeem themselves somewhat and comply with the rulings of The Twelve. Of course they have to get rid of their girls but that would happen anyway. It's a sorry state of affairs but that's the way it is and for the moment I can't imagine it ever being any different. Now please, you must go. There's no time to chat. I can't be seen with you. It's more than my job and, in fact, my life is worth. Just head down this road and into the next street and you'll see the sign above the door. Take the alleyway through to the back and give three short presses on the buzzer. George should answer you."

"We need some of those leaves," said Pat.

"Yes, of course you do," responded Tim. "Thanks for reminding me."

He handed a sealed paper bag to Pat and told her to hide it down the front of her tunic.

"Go quickly. There's a curfew and no one is allowed out on the streets unless they have the correct papers. You don't want to be seen in this neighbourhood at night time, that's for sure."

"Thank you," said April, a little stiffly. "Thanks for everything."

She could feel Hope beginning to stir and was starting to feel concerned. She was also processing what Tim had just told her about the baby boys. It was most disconcerting. Things were obviously much worse in the outside world than she had previously been aware of. She realised now that on some level Avondale House was something of a safety net and place of refuge for the girls who stayed there. They led a life of sheltered seclusion away from the disturbances of the neighbouring towns and villages. She shook her head, frowning, and was instantly dragged away from her worrying thoughts by Hope pummelling at her chest with her small fists. April winced and reached down to stroke the top of her head. She didn't want Hope waking up and making a racket. They needed to get to the Wine Sellers so that she could feed her.

"You're welcome," responded Tim. "I'd want someone to do as much for my girls if they were in trouble."

Suddenly Pat threw her arms around him and hugged him, then just as quickly she stepped back, startled by her impulsive behaviour. She felt tears prickling at the back of her eyes. Must be the head injury, she thought. She desperately wanted to lay her head down on a soft, comfortable pillow so that she could relieve the intense throbbing. She felt April staring at her and then smiled as April reached out and squeezed her hand.

"Tim's right, we've got to go. We've got to go now."

The girls watched as Tim climbed into the front of the van, gave a final wave and started the engine. Then they turned round and headed off in the opposite direction. They didn't look back to see him drive away but kept their eyes fixed on the gloomy road ahead. April was surprised at how vulnerable she felt and judging by Pat's farewell gesture she knew she must feel the same. In a short space of time they had built up a tentative bond with Tim especially as he had been their rescuer throughout a daunting situation. It was small wonder then that there should be an emotional response from both of them? They had been in the company of females for so long that they had forgotten much of what they initially knew about the behaviour of men except for the unsavoury particulars of what they took part in at Avondale Manor. But Tim was okay and so there must be more like him out there somewhere. There had to be more than one decent man in existence. Perhaps they would be able to trust George too if Tim said he would help them. April pursed her lips and shrugged her shoulders. There was no time to think about any of it now; they had no option but to get to the Wine Sellers as quickly as possible and away from the dark, threatening streets. She lowered her head protectively towards Hope and began to take longer and longer strides.

"Keep up, Pat. We don't want anyone to see us. Keep as far back from the light of the street lamps as possible."

A dog barked in the distance and Pat winced, both in pain and fear. She was afraid; very afraid of being caught. She didn't like built up areas. She much preferred the familiarity of wide, open spaces where she could see for miles around her. It was easy to be seen out in the open but it worked both ways and meant that she could see everything too. There was always a clear view of who or what was coming and there was generally a good chance of escape; but in built up areas with houses and shops and buildings all squashed together in higgledy piggledy rows and jutting out at different angles and levels it was difficult to tell who was hiding in a doorway or porch or who was lurking down a dark passageway gripping a knife and waiting to slit a throat or two for money, or even if there was someone crouching on top of a roof ready to jump down and strangle them. Pat's imagination was running wild. She shuddered and scurried after April keeping as close to her as she could. At least she wasn't on her own.

Shortly afterwards April stopped.
"This is it," she whispered. "Look, can you hear the sign swinging about up there? It doesn't half creak in the wind although there's not much of a breeze, is there? It needs a good oiling, that's for sure."

Pat followed April's gaze. She could just about make out the words on the sign above her head. She nodded at April.

"Follow me down the alleyway and stay next to me. We're safer if we're together."

April felt tense with worry. Pat grabbed hold of her arm and they tiptoed down the alleyway as quietly as they could. It opened out into a small, empty yard at the back of the Wine Sellers.

"Press the buzzer three times like Tim said," urged Pat shivering. She hugged her arms around her thin body and rubbed at them, shaking with cold and fright. April cautiously stretched out a finger and pressed. Then both girls retreated into the shadows to wait. It wasn't long before they heard bolts being drawn back and the door slowly began to slide open. A short, weaselly-looking man popped his head out.

"Yes, what is it? Where are you? What do you want? It's very late and I shouldn't be disturbed at such an hour as this. Hurry up and show yourself and state your business."

April gulped and a frisson of apprehension ran along her spine. She took a deep breath and stepped forward so that she could be seen.

"A girl! A girl! What are you doing here? Go away! I don't want any trouble! Go away! Go back to where you came from right now!"

Pat slipped out of the shadows to stand next to April and offer her support.

"We can't," she said. "We have something for you from Tim." She reached down into her tunic and took out the package.

"Not here, not here!" hissed the weaselly-looking man. "Who knows what you've got, although I've a fair idea, but we never know who's watching! What is that man playing at? Deliveries being made by girls! I've never heard anything like it. Come inside now and don't make a fuss. Hurry, hurry! You mustn't be seen."

He ushered the girls ahead of him, closing and locking the door quietly behind them. The lights were low and it was difficult to see clearly. As their eyes adjusted they realised that they were in a long corridor with doors leading off to the right and left. The weaselly-looking man was almost treading on their heels in his anxiety to hurry them to the end of it.

"Go through that door," he said, in a much more normal but slightly squeaky voice, no longer hissing though. "Yes, the one right in front of you. That's it. Turn the handle."

April did as she was told and suddenly they were in a small, snug kitchen consisting of a sink, a rickety table and four chairs and with the welcome warmth of an old stove being thrown out at them.

"Sit down, sit down whilst I inspect the goods."

The weaselly-looking man took the package and began to carefully open it. Then he thrust his long nose inside, sniffing in delight before spilling out a portion of the contents onto the table in front of him. He picked up a few of the leaves, crumbling them tenderly between his thumb and two forefingers as he did so. The aroma rising from them was pungent and clearly to his liking.

"You are George, aren't you?" interrupted April suddenly. "We have come to the right place, haven't we? Tim said you would help us."

The weaselly-looking man stared ponderously at her before responding: "Yes, I'm George. I can't believe Tim has sent you here. How does he think I'm supposed to help you?"

"We need food and shelter for a night or two before we head off again. My friend may also need a couple of stitches in her head."

"I'm not a doctor," said George. "You'll have to sort that out yourself or maybe I can get someone to help; I'm not sure. What have you got down the front of your tunic? Is it an animal; it's moving?"

"This is Hope," replied April, lifting her out carefully. "She was on Tim's warship. We've adopted her as our baby sister. She needs feeding and clean clothes too. She's been very good so far but at some point she's bound to start crying and you know how noisy babies can be, don't you?"

"What on earth made you decide to take a baby?" asked George, shaking his head in disbelief. "You're not responsible for her. After all, she's not either of yours, is she? You look far too young. She'll slow you down considerably and make your journey or wherever you're heading much more difficult than it has to be. I won't even be able to hide you away in one of my upper rooms just in case she decides to scream her head off and someone hears her. This is ridiculous! What was Tim thinking of when he got involved with the pair of you or rather, the three of you?"

April suddenly felt angry. Who was George to judge them? What did he know about their lives or what they had been through or where they were going? He was a stupid man and he didn't seem to be a very pleasant one either! Tim must have been wrong about him. It was obvious George hadn't any children or he wouldn't be speaking to them in such a manner. She drew herself up to her full height before answering.

"We couldn't leave her to die. That would have been inexcusable. It's not her fault she's been born into such a female-hating world, is it?"

There! It was out! She had said the very words she didn't even know she was capable of thinking. A female-hating world! They were living in a female-hating world! That was a sweeping statement, if ever there was one and a bitter one to swallow too! But even as the words tumbled out she acknowledged the truth of them. Girls and women had lost their place in society and there was no longer any respect or need for them except for reproduction. The Twelve had most assuredly seen to that and what was worse was that no one was attempting to do anything about it. Well, apart from Tim maybe, but he was an exception! He had saved a few baby girls and there were probably more like him somewhere, although he had said he didn't know any. There had to be! But everything had to be done in secret. That was part of what was so very appalling about the whole situation. She glared at George and her top lip curled slightly in disgust. He stared back at her pale, defiant face. Then suddenly he grinned and began to laugh.

"I'm not your enemy," he burst out. "If Tim has sent you then I'm your friend. I'm just tired, that's all, and that's why I sound grumpy. I'm tired of always having to look over my shoulder to check if anyone is watching. I'll help you in any way I can, I promise you. Sit down, please. You're making the room look crowded. The kettle's not long boiled so I suggest we have a cup of tea and try to relax and sort things out."

April eased herself down onto the seat of a rickety chair and gave an inward sigh of relief. "Pass me Hope's milk, would you?" she said to Pat, lowering her gaze and hiding her face so that George couldn't tell how overwhelmed and embarrassed she felt.

Pat handed over the half empty packet, trying to act as normally as possible. For a moment there things had been tense. She gave a sidelong glance at George. He was warming the tea pot by swirling hot water in it and humming to himself. He took three cracked mugs from a cupboard and placed them on the table with a small jug of milk.

"I hope neither of you take sugar," he said. "I ran out some time ago and have been unable to replace it. Thankfully with Tim's package I should now be able to do so. In fact, I should be able to buy decent food for at least three months. My work here at the Wine Sellers earns me enough tokens to allow the purchase of only the most basic of groceries. It's good to have a treat every now and then. I know men who would love some of that tobacco. I might even manage to get a little fresh meat in exchange for some of it. What do you think of that?"

His eyes sparkled as he looked at April and he rubbed his hands together gleefully. It was clear he had calmed down after his initial outburst and had no intentions of arguing with them. Neither did he want any trouble.

"That sounds great!" responded April. She still didn't fully trust him. He could so easily change his mind about helping them and decide to dispose of them or report them. But she wouldn't go down without a fight. If he planned to hurt them in any way she wouldn't make it easy for him.

George poured tea into the mugs and a little milk after. The tea was very weak as if the leaves had been used a few times already but the drink was hot and wet and after their bumpy ride in the van it was a welcome relief and settled their stomachs. April glanced at Pat. Her face was ashen and she looked on the verge of collapse. The blood had congealed on the side of her head and she must surely have a headache.

"We need somewhere to rest," April continued. "Somewhere warm if possible."

"I have the very place," said George. "It's sadly not on the upper level but it's a place of safety and it's warm too. I can give you a little bread right now but in the morning I'll be able to go out and get provisions. When you've finished you can follow me and I'll show you where you can get a good night's sleep."

It didn't take long for the girls to finish eating and drinking. They were so hungry that the semi-stale bread was swallowed in no more than a couple of mouthfuls and they managed to gulp down two whole mugs of tea in quick succession. Hope was fast asleep again and now there was only a quarter of a packet of milk left. What they would do when they couldn't keep her slumbering peacefully April had no idea?

It didn't bear thinking about. She would address that problem when they came to it. For now though they needed a good rest. The stress of hiding on the warship and then being stopped by soldiers during the van journey had taken its toll on both girls and April wasn't in a position to think only of herself. She had two others to care for. She tucked Hope back inside her tunic and stood up. George rinsed and wiped the mugs and put them away.

"Mustn't leave out any evidence, must we?" he said. "We don't know who'll be knocking on the door in the morning. You'd better hold onto Tim's package for the time being too. It will be safer with you for the night. I'll keep enough with me for one roll up before I go to bed and a little extra for provisions. Guess I'd better get some more milk for that baby too, eh?"

He scooped a handful of leaves from the package, nodding at Pat as he handed it back to her.

"Let's go," he said. "I'll show you where you can sleep."

The girls obediently followed George out into the corridor and then through a door leading down some slippery, stone steps into a cellar. This was where all the wine was kept and April hoped George wasn't about to say that this was where they were going to rest. It was dark and cold and the walls around them were slimy with mould. It smelled disgusting too, not of fine bottles of wine but of fungal spores and dampness. April shuddered and she could see Pat gazing about her unhappily. But George kept walking, right to the back of the cellar and behind the last shelves of well-stacked bottles to a barely noticeable door. There was no handle but somehow the door slid across at a touch from George and they found themselves in a box room. From there George rolled back a small rug and pressed his foot against a piece of wood embedded in the floor. Immediately a trap door clicked open. After climbing down a short stepladder they found they were in an even smaller room. George flicked on a light switch and finally, they could see properly.

The room was bare except for a mattress which took up most of it. There were no windows and the ceiling was low but the room was warm.

"We're almost directly beneath the stove," said George, as if in answer to April's next question. "The heat will come through until the morning and then I will turn the stove back on again. Sometimes it feels like a furnace in here especially during the summer months when I'm cooking. You won't have to worry about how much noise you make either. The stone walls are so thick that a bomb would have to explode for anyone to hear anything. I've already hidden a few people here and once I even had to hide Tim. He had officials and mercenaries hunting for him as they'd heard he was a tobacco dealer and they wanted his stash. It sells for a great price on the black market, you know, especially the kind of tobacco that Tim manages to acquire. No one dares touch him now though. He has friends in high places with all that baby transporting he does."

Pat flopped down onto the mattress and closed her eyes.

"I think I'll be asleep in five minutes," she said, yawning. "Thanks. I feel better already."

April felt the same. "Yes, thanks."

The rancid smell coming from Hope was hideously intensified by the warmth of the room and she wanted to sort her out as quickly as possible. The thought crossed her mind that she could just strip her off and let her sleep naked beside her.

"There are some items of clothing in the corner there," said George, almost as if he had read her thoughts again. "You may be able to make use of them. They were left behind by my last itinerant residents. I can't say how clean they'll be but I can say that they'll be better than what you're wearing."

April nodded. Weariness was taking over and she was desperate for George to leave the room so that she could see to Hope and then get to sleep. She stepped across Pat to reach the crumpled pile of clothes and began to rummage through them. There were trousers and tops and a couple of old jackets and there were handkerchief squares too; large pieces of cotton that had been left behind. April wondered what they had been used for. They looked clean. She picked one of them up. It was possibly big enough to cover Hope's bottom. She might be able to use it as a nappy. A slight smell of tobacco came from it and April thought it had perhaps been used to discreetly conceal twists of leaves. She sniffed again. She rather liked the smell. She removed Hope from her tunic and laid her on the mattress. Then she proceeded to clean her as gently and as best she could with one of the handkerchief squares. She folded a fresh handkerchief into a triangle, placed Hope on top of it and knotted it under and around the front of her tiny tummy. That was better. She hardly smelled at all now. George watched for a few moments and then discreetly and quietly climbed back up the ladder and left the room. He felt saddened and yet humbled at the sight of the girl child, for she was little more than that, looking after and caring for the unknown baby.

April removed her grubby tunic and covered Hope with it. She would be warmer than warm now and she was sleeping peacefully. She hadn't needed any extra feeding after all. She put on the cleanest-looking top she could find and lay down in between Hope and Pat. Exhaustion swept through her and as soon as her head touched the mattress her eyes closed and she fell into a deep slumber. After the events of the day it was what she needed.

CHAPTER TEN

It was April who opened her eyes first. She felt disorientated as there was no light in the room. She couldn't even think where she was at first or even how long she had slept for. She had been awoken from her dreams by Hope who had been uttering small cries of discomfort and wriggling around for some time. She had squirmed and fidgeted so much that she had managed to twist the tunic tightly around her tiny body and April could tell that her disgruntled sounds were on the verge of turning into high pitched squeals. There was only a little milk left and April knew she had to give Hope the last of it. She couldn't wait for George to arrive with fresh milk. Hope needed feeding now. That's what you did with babies. You didn't wait until you looked at the clock and saw that it was the right time to feed them. Babies couldn't tell the time. They just knew when they felt hungry or tired or uncomfortable and they would let you know by making a lot of noise. April crawled over to the wall and groped around for the light switch. Having found it she flicked it down, blinking as her eyes adjusted and then she rocked Hope softly from side to side with one hand whilst sorting out the milk and tubing with the other. She unravelled Hope from the tunic, popped the tube into her mouth and squeezed the last of the drugged milk through. Within moments Hope settled and dozed off again.

April turned to look at Pat. The gash on her head had developed a colourful bruise around it and was quite swollen.

Pat wouldn't be going anywhere for a couple of days, that was certain. She needed to rest. Oh well, the room was lovely and warm and perhaps George would be along soon and then she could ask him if she could go outside. And if he said no she thought she might still like to see the neighbourhood in daylight even if it was only by peeping through a grimy window. It had to at least be morning. Her befuddled, aching head told her that she must have been asleep for hours and her body hurt all over as if she had been mowed down by a truck or some other heavy vehicle. She sighed and raised a hand to her forehead. It was surprising how tired she felt and how groggy too. Fog brain - that was the name for what she had. A bit of fresh air would clear that up in no time. It had to be something to do with the stress of running away and the warship and the van and everything else they had somehow found themselves having to cope with. She thought back to her small, neatly made bed at Avondale House. Everyone would be up and about by now, she was sure of it. She could feel it in the pit of her stomach. It was rumbling hideously. She could hear it. It was making more than enough noise to wake Pat - only she didn't stir. April leant in towards her and put a hand gently below her nostrils. Yes, she was breathing. A waft of hot air flicked at her palm every couple of seconds. Thank goodness for that! It would be the final straw if Pat had died in the night and she was left on her own with a small baby to look after. She hadn't realised how much help Pat was or how much she needed her. She had never really considered whether or not she actually liked her either. There had never been time for relationships at Avondale House. But as she gazed down at her bruised and swollen face she knew she did. Poor Pat! She was such a fragile, skinny little thing and had already undergone such trauma in her short life. She would make it better for her though. As soon as they got to her grandmother's everything would be different. Pat would be the sister she had always wanted, along with Hope of course, and had never had. Pat could be the best friend she had often dreamt of and trusted. April smiled happily at her thoughts and lay down to rest her aching head. She drifted back to sleep.

Shortly afterwards George climbed down the stepladder. He noted that the light was on and the girls were asleep so he left a few provisions next to the bundle of clothes. He guessed April had fed Hope as the empty milk packet was lying crumpled in the corner. He also put down two mugs of steaming hot tea with the provisions although he knew the drinks would be cold by the time the girls woke up and found them. He thought he might enjoy cooking a late breakfast as he had managed to acquire bacon and eggs in exchange for some of the tobacco leaves and there was more than enough for everyone. All in all George felt content – a feeling he hadn't experienced in a long time. Each time he looked at the girls a rush of warmth surged through him. This came as a surprise as he had neither friends nor immediate family of his own and had never been looked upon as much of a catch by anyone. After several futile attempts at relationships he had given up and become grouchier and more sallow-looking and greasy as the years slipped by. He was aware that his appearance wasn't a particularly pleasing one and that he could do more to help himself, even with the most minimum of effort. He was perfectly capable of keeping himself clean and well groomed if he wanted to but he had never been much good at looking after himself and he hadn't earned enough to pay for the luxury of hot water for some time. But from today things were going to change. He decided not to pour a kettle of heated water into a bowl in order to slosh at his face and hands and the sweatier parts of his body as he usually did but to luxuriate in a full shower. Up until now he had rarely come into contact with anyone and so paying extra for electricity out of his meagre income had not been a priority. He didn't particularly object to his own bodily smell so why should anyone else? A great part of him had simply shrugged and given up on basic hygiene and self care a long time ago. But today was not the same as every other routinely drifting day. Today was going to continue in a flurry and a whirl as he had unexpected guests and they were females. Girls always liked to be clean and fresh. So George had sold some of the tobacco he had been given and topped up his electricity. He had been using the electricity very sparingly up until now but he had to admit that it would feel good to have a full body wash, especially now that he could. All in all he felt pleased with himself. The girls would be able to shower and wash their hair and put on a change of clothing and he would see to the wound on the skinny one's head and make sure it was on the mend. He knew he had a needle and thread somewhere if she needed stitches but he hoped it wouldn't come to that. Perhaps, once the wound was clean, he would find that it had healed quite nicely and simply be able to treat it with a fresh dressing. George picked up the empty milk packet and soiled handkerchief square and climbed back up the stepladder and out of the room.

By the time he returned he had showered and roughly shaved and eaten a huge hunk of bread with a little ham. He was wearing clean clothes and felt like a new man. He had certainly made an effort to make the most of his appearance. April was awake and rummaging through the provisions when he arrived and she stared at him, barely recognising him. Somehow his weaselly look had all but disappeared and he was smiling, a semi-toothless, disarming grin that made him seem almost friendly. It wasn't his fault he had a squint and a stoop. Having freshened up he appeared passably presentable.

"Thank you for the food and clothes," April said, forcing a bright smile upon her face. "That was really kind of you."

"Any friend of Tim's is a friend of mine," replied George.

He wasn't quite sure how to address April or how to have a conversation with her. It was such a long time since he had seen a girl, especially a teenage one. The streets around the Wine Sellers were full of older women covered up with hand knitted head scarves and long, woollen skirts and with very young children hovering closely at their heels. They kept their eyes lowered as if they didn't want to be seen. They shuffled along, pressing close to the walls, huddled into their bodies and well practised in the art of invisibility. The less they were noticed on the streets the better. Every young girl from about eight upwards seemed to have disappeared. It was said that they were kept at home until they were old enough to visit the local surgery and then they were taken away. But there were other stories about girls kept at home too, stories George didn't like to think about and would never dream of repeating to anyone. Who knew what would happen to him if he did? There was a certain sense of security and safety in his isolation and independence. In a way he could identify with the older women on the streets as he had no desire to be noticed or seen either.

"Is it daylight?" asked April.

"It certainly is," responded George. "You've slept the whole night and most of the day away."

"I'd like to take a walk outside," said April. "I feel as if I need some fresh air. I know we walked here from the van last night but it was too dark to see anything and we just concentrated on getting here."

"Well, you can't go out looking like that," said George. "There are no girls out there of your age and you don't want to draw attention to yourself. It's dangerous on the streets and you have to be careful. The more inconspicuous you are the better. I don't know if I dare risk being seen with you."

"I could go out alone," suggested April hopefully. "I really do need a breath of fresh air."

"I'll think about it," said George, "but first you must eat. I have bacon and eggs. How does that sound?" A snort of laughter erupted from him as he watched April's face light up.

"I've never had bacon and eggs before!" she gasped in surprise and delight. "I've heard about how delicious they are and I've seen Miss Abigail eating them but I've never tasted them. I took a plate up to Miss Abigail's room once and the smell was simply divine. I wanted to stick my finger in the yellow bit of the egg and lick it but I didn't dare."

George beamed at her. He had no idea who she was talking about but she obviously approved of his proposal of bacon and eggs. Pat was stirring by this time and had heard the end of the conversation.

"What did you take to Miss Abigail's room?" she asked, rubbing her eyes sleepily. "What yellow bit did you want to lick?"

"We're having bacon and eggs," replied April excitedly. "George has been out and bought some."

"Wow!" exclaimed Pat. "I once shared some bacon with Sister Charlotte and it was delicious!"

"Well," interrupted George, "this time you don't have to share. There's enough for everyone. Come up to the kitchen now and we can eat. I might even let you cook your own."

April looked down at Hope. She was still sleeping peacefully.

"We can leave Hope for a short while. I don't think she'll wake up just yet. And she can't hurt herself on the mattress, can she? There's nowhere for her to roll to. I'll put her in the middle and get rid of the tunic. It's lovely and warm in here so she doesn't really need it."

She removed the tunic, settling Hope comfortably and giving her a loving kiss on the forehead before following George and Pat upstairs. By the time she got to the kitchen Pat was already standing on a wooden stool using a spatula to turn over slices of savoury bacon that were spitting and spluttering in a well-oiled pan. George was making tea. April handed over the mugs that he had left downstairs. She had been surprised at how thirsty she was on first awakening and had gulped down both mugs of lukewarm tea in quick succession.

"I used to have a dog, you know," said George, whistling through his front teeth. "It was such a happy creature but I could never feed it enough. It just grew thinner and thinner before my very eyes until I could see every vertebra on its bony spine and play tunes on its ribs. I didn't know what to do with it. If I left it on the street it would have hung around the front door and everyone would have automatically known that it was mine. If I took it for a walk in the dead of night and left it far away it would probably have followed me home or someone would have caught it and killed it for next day's dinner. I couldn't bear to think of that. In the end Tim took it and it went everywhere on that warship with him. You smell like dog, do you know that, especially Hope? It's what reminded me of my dog."

"We found a kennel on the warship," said April, inhaling the appetising aroma of the semi cooked bacon. "Perhaps it was used by your dog. We hid in the kennel and slept there when we first climbed on board. I wrapped Hope in an old, hairy blanket for a while to keep her warm. Tim let us sleep even though he knew we were there. We didn't see a dog anywhere though."

"I'll have to ask Tim about it next time I see him," said George. "Drink your tea girls while I get on with the eggs."

He handed them fresh mugs of tea and removed the bacon from the pan, flicking it onto a side plate. It didn't take long to fry the eggs and soon everyone was sitting at the table tucking into the late breakfast of bacon and eggs and chunks of bread. There was a contented silence whilst they chewed and swallowed and then much satisfied grinning at one another once their bellies were full.

"I can quite honestly say that was the most delicious meal I've ever had in my life," said April, patting her stomach. Pat nodded vigorously in agreement and George let out a hearty belch and beamed at them both.

"I'd best clear away," he said. "I have a delivery arriving a bit later and I don't want any lingering smells. Everything has to appear as normal as possible."

"Can I go out though?" persisted April. "I won't stay out long. I really do need some fresh air. And I'd like to see what kind of area we're in."

George looked at her and then at Pat.

"Well, you can't go out dressed like that," he said finally. "Put on some of those clothes I left out for you. And do something with your hair. Tie it back out of the way so that no one can see it."

April stood up in excitement. She stared at Pat. Now that she had eaten she looked rather less pallid and her eyes were sparkling.

"Come on, Pat," she said. "You could do with some fresh air too especially after that crack on the head. We'll go out for a short while only and then you can rest again. Let's get ready."

George looked at them both and shrugged his shoulders. What was he letting himself in for now?

It didn't take long for April and Pat to find suitable clothing to wear. They ended up tugging on ill-fitting trousers and buttoning up large, crumpled shirts. There were no items of female clothing in the pile and, looking at each other, they began to laugh.

"You could easily be a boy," said April. "We just need to sort out your hair."

She pulled a shoelace from an old pair of boots and tied Pat's hair back with it.

"There, that's better. Now we need a hat for you."

There were a couple of flat caps in the pile and she plonked one on top of Pat's head.

"Very nice, dear," she said. "Now you truly look the part. A scruffy little urchin if ever I saw one!"

"Put yours on," said Pat. "Come on, I want to see what you look like."

April grinned and tucked her hair up before pulling her cap on.

"You still look like a girl," said Pat. "There's no getting away from it."

"I'll just have to huddle up and look down if anyone approaches, won't I?" answered April. "I'll stuff my hands in the jacket pockets and put on a grumpy face. Then everyone will definitely think I'm a boy."

Pat began to laugh. "Let's go and show George," she said. "Phew, it's hot in here."

April looked down at Hope who seemed to be smiling in her sleep as if she was enjoying the joke too. She bent over and stroked her cheek lovingly.

"Two sisters," she said. "I've got two sisters. Whoever would have thought it?"

She beamed happily at Pat and nudged her on her way up the stepladder.

Standing in front of George and staring down at the floor Pat and April could certainly be mistaken for boys. George raised his eyebrows in surprise.

"Those clothes are a very good disguise but there's just one thing we'll need to do before you leave and go on your way," he said, "and that's cut your hair. We won't think about that now though. It'll be dark soon and if you really want some fresh air we'd better get out there now. We're going for a short walk and that's it. I need to pick up the newsletter from the Town Hall. I have to keep up with all the latest government regulations. The more I know of what's going on out there the better equipped I am for survival. This town has been hit very hard by The Twelve."

He frowned as he pulled on an old overcoat and tucked a scarf around his throat.

"I don't want you standing too close to me when we're outside. You can follow me but at a distance. Try and take note of the streets we pass through and keep close to the walls and in the shadows. You don't want to draw attention to yourselves. Is that understood?"

Pat and April nodded, saying nothing. Pat had already decided that she would do the same as April and huddle into herself, keeping her hands in her pockets. Her head still ached and she hoped the fresh air would help. She hadn't said anything to April but every now and again she was overcome by moments of dizziness.

Outside a cool breeze gently curled round and lifted the creaking shop sign but apart from that there was silence.

"It's almost curfew," hissed George out of the side of his mouth. "Most people will be indoors by now."

April and Pat stared at him blankly. They waited until he had stepped well ahead of them and then began to follow him. Pat linked arms with April. She felt uncomfortable with so much quiet and stillness around them. The remains of a large, red, globular sun hovered uncertainly in the distance and Pat stared, fascinated, as it sank slowly downwards. George was walking quite fast and the girls had to hurry to keep him in sight. It wasn't long before Pat was out of breath.

"Can we stop a minute?" she whispered. "This is making my head throb."

April immediately stopped and turned towards her. A trickle of fresh blood was beginning to make its way down the side of her face from beneath her cap. Pat was looking pale again, pale and weary looking.

"We should go back," April said. "Perhaps this isn't such a good idea after all."

"What about George?" asked Pat.

"He'll be fine," said April. "We don't need to worry about him. Let's get you back and have a look at that cut of yours. We can get some fresh air another time. We've had enough for now. Come on."

She turned Pat around making sure that their arms were still firmly linked. Then she suddenly pulled her back into the shadows.

"Ouch!" winced Pat, lifting a hand to her head. "Why did you do that?"

"Ssshhh!" April hissed, gripping her arm tightly. "Look!"

April and Pat watched as two, long, gangly men in dark overcoats drew close and then loped by. Their focus was on George and, fortunately, they hadn't spotted the girls.

"Are they after George?" asked Pat.

"It would seem so," replied April. "I think you'd better sit down here in this doorway and I'll go after them and see if I can warn him. Sit as far back as you can and don't move until I return. I won't be long."

"Can't I come with you?"

"No, you're not well enough. You need to rest. Just wait here for me. I promise I'll be as quick as I can."

April looked up at the sign above the doorway so she would be able to recognise it on her return and then sprinted off after the two men. Pat slowly sank down into the corner and raised both hands to her head to try and stop the throbbing. She knew April was right.

It didn't take April long to catch up with the men. She darted across the road behind them and slipped into a narrow passageway from where she could observe them as they drew to a halt outside an imposing-looking building. George had just gone in through the main doorway. She watched as the men slithered about in the shadows, resembling a couple of slippery, predatory snakes preparing to strike at their prey. She had to do something. It was imperative that she warned George. She must be brave. She had no idea why they were following him but he needed to know. She took a deep breath and stepped out of the passageway. She tucked her head down and began to walk quickly towards the main door. She would be inside very soon and then she would be able to find George. She could feel her heart pounding and her breath was fighting to get out in short, sharp bursts. She walked faster, pulling her cap firmly over her ears, balling her hands into fists, clenching and unclenching them nervously at her sides. She didn't want to be grabbed suddenly by a pair of long arms or for anyone to notice she was a girl. And then almost without realising it she had arrived in front of the main door, was reaching out to push it open and stepping inside. She took in a great gulp of air. She was safe, for the moment.

April blinked. It was darker inside than it was outside. There was certainly no intention of wasting electricity here. A couple of dim lights sufficed to keep complete darkness at bay. She could make out groups of men milling about, dragging their feet as they shuffled along, each one of them acting as if his behaviour was totally unimportant and not the sort of thing that anyone would care to notice. Men were queuing to get to desks, queuing to have pieces of paper stamped and queuing to hand pieces of paper over. They were picking up leaflets, reading them and then putting them down again. They appeared to be stuffing rubbish into their pockets and they were all trying to be as unobtrusive as possible. April joined the end of the queue in front of her, lowering her head again as she did so and huddled amongst the men as they slowly crept forward. She glanced around every now and then to see if she could spot George. Finally she caught sight of him. He had picked up a sheet of paper and was holding it close to his face scouring every little detail. She tried not to grin. He couldn't possibly be that short sighted. She left the queue and shuffled cautiously towards him. She tugged at his overcoat. He made an irritable sound and then looked down.

"Two men have been following you," mouthed April. "They're hiding outside."

George stared but made no attempt to acknowledge what she had just said. April could tell from the look in his eyes that he understood though. With great deliberation he took the sheet of paper away from his face, folded it into four and put it into his pocket. He nodded briefly at someone he recognised and began to walk towards another door at the back of the room.

"Desperate," he whispered as someone raised a hand to stop him. The hand dropped and George walked on with April clutching at his sleeve. He pushed open the door and April followed him. They were now in a store room piled high with boxes on all sides except for a small space which contained a bucket and a corner sink. The bucket was full of acrid-smelling urine and the sink was grimy with hard water stains encrusted around the tap showing that it hadn't been used for some time. April wrinkled her nose in disgust. George made his way to the wire meshed window, inadvertently kicking the bucket over as he did so. Eugh! The smell of ammonia was even stronger now as the urine slopped out onto the floor and there was nowhere for it to drain to! He ignored the bucket, turned the stiff window handle and pushed; grunted and pushed until there was an opening big enough to squeeze through. He lifted April up so that she could climb out and jump down on the other side.

"Wait there!" he hissed as he thrust one leg through after her and then flattened his body against the rotting window ledge making a sort of rolling movement until he lost his balance and fell in a heap to the ground beside her. He stood up, wincing, and forced the window shut behind them.

"We'd better get out of here," he said. "Where's Pat?"

"I've left her in one of the doorways," said April.

"Show me where the men are," said George, "and be very discreet about it."

George placed a hand on April's shoulder and followed her down a filthy alleyway. From the familiar smell it was obvious what it was used for and the stench caught at the back of their throats and made their eyes water. They had clambered through a window at the rear of the building and the alleyway took them along the side of it directly to the front. As they approached the road April shrugged George's arm away and crouched down. She crawled on her hands and knees for the last few feet, grimacing and trying not to think about the filth her hands were sloshing about in, and then peered round the corner. She could see the men no more than twenty paces away in the shadows and could hear them whispering aggressively.

"Are you sure it was him?" hissed one of them. "We don't want to nab the wrong man or we'll be in serious trouble."

"Yes, it was him. I can tell by the way he walks. You shouldn't have taken your eyes off the door at the Wine Sellers. He sold a stash of stuff last night and we need to see if there's any more of it. We'll get such a reward when we hand it over and he'll get such a beating."

"Can't we keep it?"

"Don't be stupid. If we try to sell it someone is bound to report us and they'll be after us then, won't they? And we'll be the ones in line for punishment. We just have to wait here a bit longer, that's all. He has to come out soon. The place closes in half an hour. He can't stay in there all night."

April withdrew her head in dismay.

"They're on the other side of the road," she said. "I don't know how we're going to get out of here. They know about the tobacco and they recognised you earlier by the way you walk."

George frowned as he looked down at her and then he removed his overcoat.

"I want you to put this on and sit on my shoulders. You'll have to pull the collar right up around your ears. In the dark we'll look like a tall man. They won't be expecting that and we may get away with it."

April stared at him in horror and stood up. Without question she took the overcoat and put her arms through it. It was enormous. George crouched down so that she could climb onto his shoulders and wrap her legs about his neck. Then slowly he rose to his full height, buttoned up the front of the overcoat and folded his arms inside and across his chest, giving the impression that the pair of them together equalled one very long man. April tugged at the collar on the overcoat so that it touched the back of her cap and then fiddled around until she was sure that the hand clasping it was on the inside next to her chin and couldn't be seen. She left the other arm loose and swinging through the sleeve of the overcoat.

"Right, let's go," said George. "Don't move up there. And hit me with your arm when we're close to the doorway where Pat's waiting. Don't make a sound either. If any talking's to be done I'll do it."

"Okay," whispered April feebly. She didn't feel at all happy about being on George's shoulders. The overcoat was heavy and holding it in place by the collar was difficult. Her grip was tenuous at best and she could feel her hand and arm beginning to shake under the weight of it.

George started to walk. He assumed a rolling gait and April wasn't sure if he was doing this on purpose or if he had hurt himself as he fell through the open window. She gripped the sides of his head with her knees. She didn't want to lose her balance and give the game away. That would be the final straw of the evening. She stared down at the ground, trying to keep her face well hidden, as George crossed the road. She hoped the night would be kind to them and support them in their disguise. The two men stopped their banter and called out friendly greetings.

"Alright mate?"

"Yeah, alright?"

"Best get indoors," grumbled George. "Curfew, you know."

The two men muttered and mumbled in response and began to lope off down the road in the opposite direction to George and April. April turned her head slightly to the side so that she could watch them. She knew that as soon as they thought they could no longer be seen they would return and secrete themselves in the shadows once more.

A few minutes later they had reached Pat. She was curled up in a tiny ball in the corner of the doorway and looked asleep. She was breathing heavily. George undid the buttons of his overcoat, crouched down and allowed April to slide from his shoulders. She withdrew her arm quickly from the long sleeve and ran across to Pat.

"We're back," she whispered. "Come on, we've got to go."

Pat looked up through half closed eyes and didn't move. April gave her a slight shake and still she didn't move.

"There's something wrong," she said to George. "Something's not right."

George bent down to look at Pat. Her skin was pale and felt clammy to the touch. He put an arm under her shoulders and lifted her into a standing position. She slumped against him, barely moving, unable to remain upright on her own.

"I'll have to carry her," he said. "She may have a fever. She's such a fragile thing."

He picked her up gently and began to walk with her in his arms to the Wine Sellers. April hung on to the overcoat. It was the least she could do under the circumstances. This was a new worry. She didn't want to think about Pat being ill. She just wanted to be safe and sound at her grandmother's. But at least they would be in good hands with George. He seemed so different from the man they had met the evening before. First impressions were not always necessarily correct, she informed herself.

They arrived at the Wine Sellers within minutes and April cast a final glance behind her to see if the two, slippery men had realised what had happened and were hot in pursuit. But there was no sign of either of them. The dusk had turned to darkness and in response the street lights cast a golden gleam on the pavements below reminding George how late it was.

"Get inside," said George. "Be as quick as you can. It's curfew. Look, the lights are on. We're not allowed out on the streets any longer. Take the keys from my overcoat pocket and unlock the door."

April did as she was told.

"Pull the bolts behind you," said George as soon as they were in, and April did as she was told once again. She heaved a sigh of relief. This place was like a fortress. It was totally secure. No one would ever find them here unless they were invited in. She followed George to the windowless room below the stove and watched as he carefully placed Pat on the mattress. She was murmuring incomprehensible words and seemed to be slipping in and out of consciousness.

"We need to bring her fever down," said George. "I hope it's not that head injury. Go to the kitchen and get a bowl of warm water and a cloth. A sponge would be ideal but I'm afraid I don't have one."

April hurried off. Within two minutes she was back. George had stripped Pat to her underwear and April gasped in shock.

"I'm sorry but it has to be done," he said, noting her dismay. "Put the bowl down."

He dipped the cloth in the water and wrung it out. He then began patting it against Pat's chest, arms and legs. He tutted as he saw the scarring. Pat was no longer pale and clammy but flushed and obviously running a high temperature.

"Get another cloth and then you can do the same," said George.

April rushed off. Within moments she was back and copying him. There was a lump in her throat as she listened to Pat attempting to inhale in short, sharp rasps and then exhaling with a pitiful, whining noise. She felt tears begin to well up and to trickle down her cheeks. She tried not to sniff. That wouldn't help anybody and she didn't want George to see how upset she was.

"Who beat her?" asked George quietly.

"I think it happened when she lived at home," answered April. "She had her scars when I met her."

"No need, no need to do this to a child. No need to do such a thing to anyone," said George sadly, shaking his head. He dipped the cloth in the bowl and wrung it out once more. "I wasn't fortunate enough to have been blessed with a wife and children but if I had they would never have been treated like this. Times have changed so much and respect has become a word of the past. I have to appear unfriendly and hostile and behave in a crotchety manner so that no one will take advantage of me. I look after the best wine and champagne for the men running the Town Council and as long as they remain in control I will never be without work. You would be surprised what beauties are tucked away in my cellar."

April said nothing and continued to dab at Pat's body with her wet cloth. Pat seemed to be breathing a little more easily now. She still looked very flushed but appeared to be sinking into a deeper sleep.

"We're nearly finished," said George. "If we can get her through the night she'll be fine. It looks as if her fever is on the verge of breaking. It came on very quickly so let's hope it disappears just as fast. Don't cover her with anything. It's already more than warm enough in here. You'd best sort out that baby now. She's getting restless."

April moved away from Pat to tend to Hope. She'd forgotten about her whilst she'd been helping bring Pat's temperature down. Somehow Hope had managed to roll over to the corner of the mattress and onto her tummy and her legs and arms were kicking and flailing about in frustration. Who could tell how old she was? April had assumed she was a newborn because she was so small and delicate looking. But that wasn't possible. She must be at least six months old if she was able to roll about the way she did. She had been kept motionless and sleepy and under control with the drugged milk and now April could see that all hell was about to let loose. Hope's fists were clenched and her face was contorted and red. She was preparing to scream. There was no more drugged milk left. April climbed up the step ladder and made her way to the kitchen as quickly as she could. There was a container of milk standing in a jug of water next to the sink. She found a saucepan and quickly poured some of the milk into it and then heated it on the stove. How would Hope be able to drink it though? George wasn't likely to have any baby bottles hidden away anywhere. She picked up a clean mug. That would have to do. She didn't know if Hope would be able to drink from a mug. She had been used to milk being filtered through a piece of tubing and trickling down the back of her throat. April frowned. She would have to think of something.

In the tiny box room April crouched on her hands and knees on the mattress. Hope was already screaming and April was rapidly dipping her fingers into the milk and then putting them into her mouth to try and feed her. It wasn't working. So much for that plan! She couldn't get the milk in quickly enough. Hope was yelling and wriggling and tossing her head about so much that most of the milk from April's fingers was dripping onto the mattress beside her. April sat up and looked at Hope, frowning. There must be another way. Suddenly she spotted the piece of tubing and had an idea. She dipped the tubing into the mug and sucked up a mouthful of warm milk. Then, holding Hope's head still with her free hand she inserted the other end of the tube into her mouth just as she was about to let out a great roar. She began to gently blow the milk down the tube. Hope spluttered and coughed for a moment as the milk hit the back of her throat and then all of a sudden she was calm and stared up at April with a look of complete surprise on her face. April continued blowing the milk into her mouth giving her time to swallow without choking. She finished the mouthful and smiled at Hope. She lifted the mug and filled her mouth with milk and repeated the whole procedure again with the tube. Hope gurgled and gasped and then, quite unexpectedly, she began to suck at the tubing. April lifted her up in her arms and put her end of the tube directly into the mug of milk. Hope was now making little snuffling sounds of satisfaction as she continued to suck and to feed without help.

It wasn't long before the milk was finished and from the smell that wafted around shortly afterwards it was clear that Hope needed changing. She gurgled in delight as April cleaned her, replacing the soiled handkerchief square with a fresh one and then gave the most enormous of burps as she was rolled onto her tummy. April kissed her cheek and a wave of love coursed through her. She had no control over her feelings where Hope was concerned. Hope was simply that sort of baby, whether she was screaming or not. April sighed happily and turned her gaze back towards Pat.
"She'll be fine now," said George, smiling at her. "You've no need to worry. The fever's breaking already. She'll sleep right through the night without any bother, you see if she doesn't."
"Thank you," said April. "Thank you for everything."

George nodded. "You're more exhausted than you realise. Rest a while. I'm expecting visitors shortly. They're coming to deliver some wine so I'd better go and make sure there's no evidence of any of you in the kitchen. I'll check in on you later." He stood up and stretched. "You're good with that baby. It comes natural to you, doesn't it?"

Without waiting for a reply he turned round, climbed the step ladder and was gone. April stared after him and at the empty space left behind on the step ladder. She felt embarrassed but pleased by his compliment and she knew he was right about being exhausted. They shouldn't have gone out so soon after arriving at the Wine Sellers. They needed at least a couple of days rest before they would be fit to set off again. She didn't know what she had been thinking of, encouraging Pat to go outside so soon after their arrival. It was obvious she was unwell, especially with that cut on her head. She felt cross with herself for having behaved in such an irresponsible and selfish manner. At least Pat was sleeping comfortably now though and so was Hope. There was nothing left but to turn out the light, lie down and join them.

CHAPTER ELEVEN

It was noon the next day before any of them surfaced. George had cooked eggs and bacon again, this time adding a few mushrooms. April thought she remembered eating mushrooms when she was younger, much younger, before she lived at Avondale House. She had a vague recollection of going out to pick them, going out into the fields and woods with her mother and hunting for them. There had only been one or two varieties growing nearby and these had been perfectly safe to eat but Miss Abigail had always insisted they didn't touch mushrooms or toadstools on their walks as there were some that were hideously poisonous and would do terrible things to their minds and bodies if consumed or even touched in any way. April had raised her eyebrows as she listened but had said nothing.

"These are a special treat. They're delicious," said George. "The men who came to collect the wine brought them last night as a thank you. Would you like to try some?"

April nodded vigorously. The sight and smell of the mushrooms sweating in the pan made her think of a happy time, a time when she belonged to a family unit and had noisy little brothers running around and scrambling to take their places at a well-scrubbed table. She remembered her mother standing sticky and sweaty in front of a hot stove turning round to smile with wisps of hair escaping from beneath the brightly coloured headscarf wrapped around her head. April sat down in pleasant anticipation. Pat took a seat beside her. She still looked pale and fragile.

"Let me look at that cut," said April in concern. Pat pulled her hair back from her face and April gently lifted the dressing.

"It's healing up really well," said April. "It looks clean and I don't think you'll need any stitches."

"Thank goodness for that," responded Pat. "I've got a thumping headache and my neck is so stiff. The smell from those black things in the pan is making me feel sick. I don't know if I can eat anything actually."

She turned up her nose and sniffed in disgust. George shared out the food and then took a look at Pat's cut also.

"Your head is fine," he said, looking puzzled. "There's no sign of infection at all. In fact the cut is much less serious than I first thought it was. I can't think of any reason why you should have a headache except that you must still be tired."

"I feel completely exhausted," said Pat. "In fact I feel quite ill and I haven't even done anything to make me feel so ill. I've done exactly the same as April and she's okay."

She picked at a little of the food on her plate and then lethargically moved the rest around with her fork. George watched her. She was unusually unwell and he was worried. She pushed the plate away from her and as she did so George caught sight of a red marking on her wrist.

"May I have a look at your wrist?" he asked quietly. He reached forward and pulled back her sleeve. "This is what's causing you the trouble, not the cut on your head."

Pat stared at her wrist. She had a rash spreading out from a small, red, bite mark.

"I was bitten a short while ago on one of our walks with Miss Abigail. I didn't see anything or even feel anything but afterwards the bite bothered me and I wanted to scratch it. Then it seemed as if it was going away. This is the first time I've noticed a rash."

"Go and lie down again," said George. "I know what this is. I'll have to go out and get you some medication if I can."

"What is it?" asked Pat, still staring at her wrist.

"Don't worry about that now," replied George. "We'll get it sorted. Drink a glass of water and go and rest."

April said nothing. She knew what the rash around the bite mark meant. She looked down at the table and took a mouthful of bacon. Miss Abigail had warned them so many times and she was surprised that Pat had forgotten or maybe it was because she was poorly and she wasn't thinking straight. Pat stood up to leave the table and George passed her a large glass of water.

"Drink this. It will help clear your system of toxins."

Pat nodded and then obediently began to drink the water.

"Well done," he said, patting her gently on the shoulder. "Go and get some more sleep. That's when your body heals itself."

Pat gave him a thankful smile and left the kitchen.

"She needs antibiotics, strong ones," George said as soon as he felt Pat was out of hearing distance. "I don't know if I can get any. I have only one contact who deals in black market medication and I haven't seen him around in a while. If we don't get her the antibiotics soon there's a chance she could be really ill. Don't worry, it's not contagious but it is dangerous."

April felt scared and kept her eyes lowered as she finished the rest of her late breakfast.

"What about those men last night?" she said eventually, putting her fork down. "Do you think they know where you live?"

"I wouldn't be at all surprised," answered George. "They must have found out about the weed."

"Weed, what weed?" asked April.

"The leaves you gave me. It's called weed and worth a lot of money as it's something that's difficult to get hold of. People smoke it to feel relaxed and they also use it to help with pain. Those men either plan on using it themselves or they want to sell it for a good price or even collect a reward for handing me over to the authorities. Whatever they've decided I don't really want to be a part of it."

"I'll have a look outside and make sure there's no sign of them," said April. "They won't be interested in me. They'll think I'm just some street urchin out on an errand."

George stared at her. She was a brave kid. He didn't really want her going out again but neither did he wish to be caught carrying weed on his person. Her suggestion was sensible and he didn't see what else they could do. It was imperative that Pat had antibiotics and soon!

CHAPTER TWELVE

In the kitchen Cook was all ears and most sympathetic. She had heard about the disappearance of April and Pat and had been waiting to find out what Miss Abigail proposed to do about it. She didn't want anything to change at Avondale House. That would be a disaster. She had a good life at Avondale house and was perfectly happy with things the way they were. She liked working alongside Miss Abigail, who was a firm but fair Director, and she enjoyed the smooth running of Avondale House under her supervision. She had no desire to go anywhere else and start again. She was allowed the run of the kitchen and there were various perks to the job including the extra slabs of salmon and cartons of ice cream she was able to hide away. Cook and Miss Abigail had a wonderful understanding. They worked together extremely well. Cook would hate that to be spoilt by the thoughtless absconding of two silly girls.

"I have to call the authorities," said Miss Abigail, frowning. "I don't know what else to do. They will need to be informed at some point and I'd rather it was sooner than later. I have never had a girl run away from here before. This is a disaster. I must call the authorities and get it over with. Don't you agree?"

Cook stared at her and said nothing. She was mulling over an idea. She finished wiping the last pot and then spoke. "There was an unhappy occurrence in another House that I worked in. A young, foolish girl ran away and was found two weeks later in a ditch. She had frozen to death. It was tragic. She was brought back to the House for a moving funeral service and this served as a lesson to all those who had grand ideas about running away. It showed them that it was quite impossible to live away from their House and that there was no one out there in the big, wide world who would help them. They were only safe and cared for whilst they remained in their House. No one ever attempted running away again."

Miss Abigail frowned. "That is sad, yes, but how will it help us with Pat and April? We don't know where they are or even how they are. If the authorities start a search and find them we could still lose our jobs. There's no doubt about that. We would appear as incompetent fools and as if we had been too lenient with them or else how would they have managed to run away in the first place?"

"We don't have to find them," said Cook. "We can just tell the girls that they returned late at night and that by the early hours of the morning they were dead. Then we hold a funeral service for them and inform the authorities that two of our girls have passed away and because we've dealt with the situation and completed the relevant paperwork we will probably be able to stay here and nothing will change. The authorities certainly won't want to have to go to the trouble of setting up a search for two troublesome girls. It may even be possible to turn the situation around to our advantage."

"But what if April and Pat decide to come back? What will we do then if there has been a funeral service and they're supposed to be dead?"

Cook thought for a while: "We'll just say that the two girls who arrived half dead on our doorstep in the middle of the night were so badly bitten and ravaged by wild dogs that in the darkness it was difficult to make out who they were. We simply assumed they were April and Pat. We tended to their wounds as best we could and then wrapped them in blankets and let them sleep on the hearth next to the kitchen stove. We didn't want to upset our girls by letting them see their friends in such a state. When we went to check on them in the morning they were dead. We held the funeral and cremation as quickly as possible in case they were carrying any infectious diseases."

Miss Abigail nodded. She could envisage the possibilities of such an idea but it was rather farfetched to say the least. She had never heard of wild dogs roaming anywhere in the vicinity of Avondale House or of any attacks on humans but who was to say that there weren't any dogs on the hills and that attacks didn't happen? She and Cook would have to plan it carefully though and they would have to do it now. It was a matter of urgency. They didn't have much time. Declaring that the two girls had returned in the night meant that they wouldn't have to involve the authorities until everything was over. She couldn't think of anything else that they could do. She sighed. It seemed as if there was no alternative.

"We'll do it," said Miss Abigail. "We need to go out later on when the girls are in bed and get a couple of those old tea chests from the shed. We'll use them as coffins. They're big enough to hold two small girls, aren't they? We need to organise everything before we decide that the whole idea is ludicrous and I lose my nerve. Even the thought of what we're planning gives me the jitters."

"That's my girl!" said Cook, smiling. "There's no need to worry. The girls will believe whatever you tell them. We'll have an outdoor cremation ceremony in the morning and sing a few hymns and then it will be over and life can get back to normal. Go and rest now. You need to calm down. I'll get one of the girls to bring you some supper. I'll prepare something especially nutritious for you. You must be exhausted after all that cross-examination."

And she winked at Miss Abigail. Miss Abigail nodded gratefully. It was good to know that she had someone on whom she could depend.

"The girls have been confined to their rooms for long enough," she said decisively. "We'll have supper. It's not their fault that two of their friends have run away. Who wouldn't want to run away if they knew what was coming next. I certainly would. I can't blame Pat and April. I can't blame any of the girls for keeping it quiet either. But we will have supper in silence. I'll lie down for a while and then join everyone."

Impetuously she leant across and kissed Cook on the cheek.

"Thanks for everything," she said gruffly. Then she turned on her heel and strode quickly from the room, overcome by the gamut of emotions running through her. Cook watched as she left and then lifted a hand to the cheek that had just been kissed. She too was overcome. It was the first display of affection that she had been shown in years.

CHAPTER THIRTEEN

Supper was most certainly a subdued affair. There was an uneasy silence as Miss Abigail had not spoken after questioning the girls and so no one knew what was going on or what was going to happen next. The only noise in the room came from the sounds of forks and spoons clattering against plates. Cook had excelled herself in the kitchen and made huge pans of spaghetti with cheese and this was a real treat. To the girls it was confusing though as they couldn't work out whether they were being punished or rewarded. The questioning that had taken place earlier had been almost interrogation-like in its severity and had left each girl reeling in shock and horror. Even the defiant Bertha sat sullen and brooding at the table. The girls stared down at their plates as they ate, none of them even daring to peep at Miss Abigail. Eventually there was the sound of a chair scraping against the wooden flooring as it was pulled back and Miss Abigail stood up.

"Take your plates and cutlery to the kitchen when you have finished eating and wash and dry them. I would like you to queue in an orderly fashion whilst you wait your turn. Do not speak to one another and do not disturb Cook in her work. Then you will go straight to your rooms and it will be lights out in half an hour. There will be absolutely no noise as there has been enough disruption for one day. Do I make myself clear?"

"Yes, Miss Abigail."

The chorus of timid voices momentarily assailed her senses and Miss Abigail took a deep breath. She was still perturbed by the thought of what she and Cook were planning to do. She pushed her chair in, gripping the back of it, her knuckles displaying white and strained, and closed her eyes briefly.

"I'll take your plate, Miss Abigail," said Bertha quietly.

Miss Abigail opened her eyes, glancing at her in some surprise, and then nodded without saying anything. She turned on her heel, marching rapidly out of the dining hall, tears prickling at the back of her eyelids. The whole situation felt just too emotional for words. Even Bertha's behaviour was out of character. Miss Abigail desperately wanted to burst into tears and to tell the girls that she didn't want any of them to run away. She wanted them to stay, to stay with her at Avondale House for ever. She enjoyed being with them. She enjoyed their company. They were such a lovely group. She took great pleasure in the days they spent together and the way that everything seemed to flow along so nicely. She enjoyed looking after them and making sure they were safe and protected. She took great pride in her job and didn't want anything to change. She didn't like having to be so strict but that was just the way it was. Of course she couldn't say any of this and she hadn't even been fully aware of how she felt until now. It was only when challenging situations arose that it became obvious exactly how much was at stake. And now Bill was in her life too and she didn't want to lose him either. She so definitely didn't want to lose him!

Miss Abigail sat in the lounge in front of the roaring fire. One of the girls had made it up for her without having to be asked, just before supper, and that made Miss Abigail want to cry even more. She sat tense and upright in the high backed chair so that anyone entering the room wouldn't be able to see how upset she was and so that she would have a moment to pull herself together before answering any questions. Not that any of the girls would come in of course. She had made her wishes perfectly clear. Miss Abigail could feel a headache coming. She hoped it wouldn't turn into a migraine. She had endured enough stress for one day.

There was a gentle knock at the door and then Miss Abigail heard the turn of the handle. A moment later Cook was standing next to her with a mug of steaming, hot chocolate in her hands.

"I thought you could do with some of this after today's events," she said, handing it over to her. "It hasn't been one of our easiest days."

Miss Abigail grasped hold of the mug wordlessly. There was a huge lump in her throat and as she blinked she noted that her lashes felt wet. She didn't trust herself to speak. She tried to smile her thanks to Cook.

"Don't you worry now, dearie," said Cook. "Everything's going to be alright. Those girls have gone up to bed already and in an hour or so we'll go and get the tea chests. We'll have to find something to fill them with so that they have some weight to them and we'll have to make sure they're going to burn easily. We could use some of those old rags that we're supposed to recycle. No one will know."

Cook was forcing herself to be cheerful. She had never seen Miss Abigail in distress before and she wasn't sure how to cope with it. She was used to being on the receiving end of instructions, not the person who made suggestions but in the circumstances it seemed only right and fitting that she should offer her advice, in a restrained and deferential sort of manner of course. Miss Abigail nodded and lifted the mug of hot chocolate to her lips. Cook tentatively patted her on the shoulder and left the room.

Less than an hour later Miss Abigail and Cook made their way together to the shed wearing thick coats and gloves. Miss Abigail had only a dull headache, alleviated by the mug of hot chocolate she thought, and was feeling more optimistic. The night was bitterly cold and so their story of April and Pat returning and then dying began to seem all the more plausible.

They dragged two tea chests across to the remains of a bonfire which had been simmering during the course of the week and then began to rummage through the pile of rags. They collected everything that looked as if it would burn quickly and easily. The smell didn't matter because that would make the funeral pyre all the more realistic. Cook even found the carcass of an unidentifiable cat which she gingerly picked up by the tail, holding it as far away from her body and face as possible, and then walking disdainfully with it to one of the tea chests before flinging it in with a grimace and a snort.

"Let's hope we don't find too many of those lying about," she said, turning her nose up in disgust.

Miss Abigail grinned. Now that there was a definite plan and it was being put into action she felt much more confident about the way the situation would evolve. She hoped April and Pat were far away and travelling towards a better life. She knew that with Cook at her side everything was likely to take place exactly as was envisaged and between the pair of them they would be able to answer any awkward questions that the girls might ask and therefore put their minds at rest. It was much better this way. Miss Abigail planned a short meeting after breakfast and then instead of their daily walk it was decided that the girls would gather around the bonfire as it was being lit. Miss Abigail would say a few prayers pertaining to the sad demise of April and Pat and then Cook would lead them in the singing of appropriate hymns. Afterwards the girls would be given an hour or so for extra tea and biscuits as consolation and to get over the shock of everything while Miss Abigail telephoned the authorities and gave her account of what had happened. It was really quite simple. As long as she and Cook stuck to the same story there shouldn't be any problems. She didn't know what she had been worrying about or why in the first place. Everything was under control.

Upstairs in Avondale House there was a twitch at the curtains. Bertha was having trouble sleeping. The lights were out and everyone was supposed to be asleep but Bertha could hear unfamiliar noises. She pushed back the bed covers and walked across to the window. She drew the curtain aside a little, just enough for her to be able to see outside but not enough for anyone else to see in. She wondered if April and Pat had decided to come back and were even now struggling to open the main door. Maybe that was what the odd noises were. If so she would go downstairs and let them in. If they had returned there would be very little trouble and after a while Miss Abigail's hostility would die down and things would get back to normal and it would be as if nothing had ever happened. It would also prove Miss Abigail's point that no one ever escaped or left Avondale House. Bertha squinted and wrinkled her nose. It was too dark to see much. There was a sneaking sliver of a moon and the sky was bright with the glittering stars that so often choose to reveal themselves on cold, frosty nights. Nothing was happening by the main door but at the bottom of the garden there appeared to be the flickering of torch lights. Bertha stared and as she stared she could just make out the shapes of two figures moving around. They didn't look like April and Pat though. They looked far too big. They looked like adults. In fact one of them distinctly resembled Cook and if so the other one had to be Miss Abigail. What on earth were they doing at the bottom of the garden in the middle of the night? Something was amiss but it was far too dark to make out what it was. Bertha decided to go downstairs. She would slip out through the kitchen door and find out what was happening. The kitchen door was sometimes left unlocked. Bertha knew this as she often went down to raid the fridge at the most unearthly of hours and invariably tried the handle. She had frequently thought about running away, especially when the handle turned and she was able to stand in the doorway staring out at the back garden and potential freedom. Upon greater reflection though, she invariably changed her mind. It wasn't likely that she would ever have to go back to Avondale Manor and her position at Avondale House could be a lot worse. She had always wanted to learn to cook properly and she was optimistic that should she approach Cook on this matter Cook might teach her. Cook was getting on a bit and at some point would need an assistant, even if it was only for lifting the sacks of potatoes or cleaning and paring the vegetables. The girls took turns helping in the kitchen but Bertha was the strongest and always the most willing when it came to the heavy work. So Bertha chose to ignore the unlocked door and took a little extra something from the fridge to ease her hunger pangs and loss of potential freedom before returning to bed.

Tonight however would be different. Tonight she would go out through the kitchen door and see if she could find out what Cook and Miss Abigail were up to. She wouldn't be able to take a torch with her as she didn't want to be caught but it would be wonderful to be able to give the girls a little extra gossip in the morning. Bertha was aware of her unpopularity but snippets of gossip meant that the girls would feel compelled to talk to her and would huddle around her and she liked to feel important, even if only for a short while. She put on her dressing gown and lightly tiptoed down the stairs. She hesitated at the kitchen door, listening to see if she could hear anything. When she had satisfied herself that all was quiet she slipped on an old pair of Cook's well-worn shoes and stepped outside. It would be difficult to see anything in the dark and Bertha didn't fancy being caught in a beam of torchlight. She would have to be very careful indeed.

"I think we're finished now."

Bertha jumped. That was definitely Cook's voice. It sounded quite close too. Where had she suddenly appeared from? She had been at the bottom of the garden a couple of minutes ago.

"Yes, I quite agree. Everything is ready for the morning."

Now Bertha could hear Miss Abigail's voice. She ducked down behind the laurel bush at the side of the kitchen door just in time. The beam of a torch flashed in front of her and Bertha briefly caught a glimpse of Miss Abigail.

"Let's hope we don't have to do anything like that again and that it will soon be over and done with."

Cook was speaking once more. There was no answer from Miss Abigail and very soon the pair of them had disappeared inside the house. Bertha waited until she was sure that she was alone in the garden and that she felt calm and composed before she stood up. Her heart had been pounding so loudly that she couldn't believe it hadn't been heard. She had crouched with her hands across her chest expecting at any moment to be dragged out from behind the laurel bush and questioned ferociously, maybe even slapped a few times for good measure too, although why she thought that she wasn't sure as no one had ever been slapped at Avondale House - but there was always a first time. She could just make out the shapes of the two tea chests on the bonfire and resolved to investigate. The remains of the weekly bonfire were still glowing as Bertha approached and she rubbed her hands together to warm them, holding them a few inches away from the smouldering embers. Now she was here she might as well see what was inside the tea chests and find out what all the fuss was about. There was no lid on either chest and Bertha peered down, squinting, being careful where she placed her feet. The smell was dreadful, of urine and rotten food and mould. It looked as if the tea chests had been filled with dirty clothing and there was some kind of dead animal in one of them too. Bertha shuddered in disgust. What on earth were Cook and Miss Abigail up to? How ridiculous coming out in the middle of the night just to burn a few old rags and rubbish. What was going on? Bertha shivered. It was time to get back to bed. There was nothing more to be seen. She hurried up the garden path and in through the kitchen door, which fortunately was still unlocked, carefully removing the borrowed shoes as she did so. Everything was silent inside the house and Bertha stole upstairs to her bed feeling like a thief in the night. She would sleep now and wait and see what happened in the morning. Then she would let the girls know what she had seen and heard. She gave a snort of delight at the prospect of the glorious gossip ahead of her and then clasped her hands over her mouth to stop her giggles as she finally crept, shivering, under the bedcovers.

CHAPTER FOURTEEN

The next morning Miss Abigail and Cook entered the dining hall dressed in black. Cook had removed her grubby apron and pinned up her hair and looked quite respectable for a change. She stood quietly next to Miss Abigail in a gesture of support and solidarity. The girls had finished their porridge, which today had been sweetened with a little honey, and stared at them in some surprise. So many strange things were happening at the moment and Cook and Miss Abigail never did things together. An uneasy silence befell the dining hall.

"I'd like you to take your bowls and spoons to the kitchen and put on your coats and boots," said Miss Abigail. "However, we will forgo our walk today. Something terrible occurred during the night and I need to talk to you. You will line up at the kitchen door and then we will walk in pairs to the bonfire at the bottom of the garden."

The girls glanced at each other questioningly. What bonfire? Why was there a bonfire so early in the morning? They desperately wanted to know but no one dared speak. Whatever it was that Miss Abigail had to say it sounded serious.

"Go now please," continued Miss Abigail. The girls pushed back their chairs, picked up their bowls and spoons, and made their way to the kitchen. Soon they were queuing at the kitchen door waiting for Miss Abigail and Cook. Miss Abigail took her place at the front of the queue and Cook moved to the rear. They certainly didn't want any more girls to disappear. It was imperative they keep an eye on them. The group filed out into the garden and followed Miss Abigail to the bonfire where she instructed them to stand in a circle around it.

The air was crisp and cold with a wan sun desperate to make an appearance, no matter how fleeting. It sailed randomly in and out of the gloomy clouds attempting to welcome the girls with its brief, cheerless arrival and then forcing them to huddle together again upon its departure. There was a heavy, sombre dullness about the morning and the girls wished that Miss Abigail would hurry up and get on with whatever she had to say. There had been enough disruption at the House during the past twenty four hours and they just wanted to get on with the day and for things to return to normal. But of course nothing could ever be normal again because Pat and April were gone and this had shaken the very foundations of Avondale House and everything it stood for.

Miss Abigail coughed and the girls looked at her expectantly.
"This is a sad day for all of us," she began. "I never thought anything like this would happen during my time at Avondale House but it has and we must deal with it in the best way possible." She paused for dramatic effect before continuing. "April and Pat returned last night. They were cold and wet and hungry. In fact they were ill but Cook and I weren't aware of this at the time."
She glanced at Cook who nodded dismally. Miss Abigail let out a heartfelt sigh.
"We gave them food and dry clothing and as it was very late we left them to rest on rugs in front of the fire. It seemed to be the best solution at the time as we didn't want any of you to be disturbed so late in the evening. Little did we know what we would find this morning?"
Miss Abigail attempted to stifle a false sob but it came out as more of a nervous snicker than anything else. A few of the girls pulled faces at each other and then quickly lowered their eyes before Miss Abigail or Cook noticed.

"We came down early this morning only to find that they had both ...."

It was clear that Miss Abigail was struggling to find the words to convey her experience regarding what had happened. "They were cold and stiff and sadly no longer with us."

No one made a sound. The girls stared at Miss Abigail in shock and confusion. Was she saying what they thought she was saying? Had Pat and April gone somewhere else or were they dead? It wasn't possible, not in such a short time. They hadn't been away from Avondale House for even a day. Miss Abigail and Cook were obviously playing some sort of sick joke on them. People didn't die just like that. Suddenly Bertha spoke up and asked the question most of the girls were thinking.

"If they were no longer with us where were they?"

Cook gave her a sharp dig in the ribs. "Don't be facetious!" she responded irritably.

The girls began to shuffle their feet and glance round at each other nervously. Then, with a vague rumble of discontent, the whispers and murmurs began and the atmosphere started to feel mildly threatening. Miss Abigail felt a shiver of consternation run up her spine. This wasn't going quite as well as expected.

"There were wounds too. Both girls had been bitten," she continued hurriedly. "We dressed their wounds. However, in the dark we had no idea whether the wounds were infected or even how deep they were."

She stopped speaking and looked at the girls, her eyes growing wide and startled. She had no idea what to say next. The whole thing was such a colossal lie and in the stark light of day it sounded like one too. She turned to Cook and Cook could see that she was on the verge of panic.

"And so we've prepared a cremation ceremony for them," she burst in, rescuing Miss Abigail. "We knew that you would wish to say your goodbyes so we thought a simple service and some hymns would do nicely."

Cook watched from the corner of her eye as Miss Abigail visibly began to relax. She knew she had interrupted at a crucial moment and hoped she had said the right things and that they would be able to carry on with their plans whether they were credible or not.

"We thought you might like to light the bonfire, Bertha," continued Cook.

"Yes, Cook," responded Bertha meekly. Bertha was bewildered although she didn't show it. She knew exactly what was in the tea chests and had no idea why Miss Abigail and Cook had concocted such a story and why they were pretending that Pat and April were about to be cremated. What a stupid game this was! What was really going on? She took the matches however and complied with Cook's wishes.

The bonfire flared up quickly as the deep crimson embers from the previous evening were still warm and the crumpled pieces of paper that had been strategically placed around the tea chests flickered into flames almost instantly. An amber and gold blaze of light was soon licking its way hungrily into the air. Miss Abigail led the girls in prayer and then Cook began to sing. Cook had a beautiful voice, deep and full, and the sudden shock and anger at what the girls had just been told turned slowly and gently to sadness. One by one everyone joined in with the singing, familiar with the words and simple tunes. They weren't sure what to believe but as they watched the bright, colourful flames dancing and weaving snake-like patterns in and around the tea chests the ceremony took on a surreal and dreamlike quality. The girls reached out to each other and held hands. At least they were alive. They were safe at Avondale House and nothing could happen to them whilst they remained there.

All too soon the flames died down however and the girls found themselves walking back through the kitchen door and into the House. They were told that tea and biscuits were available to help them deal with the trauma regarding the demise of their friends and this encouraged them to discuss what had happened and to commiserate over their tragic and confusing loss. There seemed to be an awful lot of tea and biscuits on offer lately. Bertha waited until Miss Abigail and Cook had gone and everyone was conversing in low voices and sipping sweet tea before she dropped her bombshell.

"April and Pat weren't in those tea chests," she burst out suddenly. Immediately all eyes were on her.

"What do you mean?" asked one of the girls suspiciously.

"Yes, what are you talking about?" demanded another crossly.

"The tea chests were full of dirty rags and there was a dead animal in one of them," Bertha replied, rather imperiously. This was an opportunity for her to feel important and she was going to make the most of it. Also, she felt a sense of outrage at the absurdity of what they had just been subjected to.

"You're lying!" interrupted another girl. "Why on earth would Miss Abigail and Cook perform a ceremony for Pat and April if they weren't dead?"

"That's what I want to find out," continued Bertha, tapping the side of her nose and giving an all-knowing wink. "And I'm not lying!"

"And how do you know what was in the tea chests anyway?" asked the first girl.

"I heard noises outside last night and came down to investigate. You may have been fast asleep but I certainly wasn't. I was hungry and couldn't sleep. I sneaked out into the garden and looked inside the tea chests. There was certainly no sign of either Pat or April in them or in the House. And why would Miss Abigail and Cook dress their wounds in the dark? They've made up a crazy story and I'm going to find out what's going on."

Bertha felt affronted. She knew the truth of the matter and was disappointed that the girls didn't believe her. She could almost feel the waves of hostility and disgust emanating from them. Well, she would show them. She put down her cup with a clatter and stormed upstairs to the dormitory. She reeked of smoke and needed a wash. Dopey girls, always believing everything Miss Abigail said! They hadn't believed Pat when she told them of the horrors that went on at Avondale Manor either. Those dumb creatures had been brainwashed into thinking that the coming of age celebrations were all about becoming Princesses and getting married to wonderful, handsome Princes just like some sort of fairytale. But Bertha knew Pat was telling the truth because she had spent time at Avondale Manor too. The only other girl who believed Pat had been April and now the two of them were gone. At that moment Bertha half wished she had rolled down the side of the mountain too. She had told the girls the truth about the tea chests and the bonfire and they were conceited enough not to believe her! Stupid, stupid girls! She would find out why such a story had been concocted and give them one last chance and then that would be it. And if they didn't believe her, well, she would never speak to any of them again. They just weren't worth it. She would make sure she worked in the kitchen so she wouldn't have to spend any time with them and with what she knew she was certain she could persuade Miss Abigail to give her a bedroom to herself instead of having to share a dormitory with so many dull, brain-dead idiots! Bertha knew there were half a dozen empty rooms on the top floor and she would be more than happy to make use of one of them. She felt so cross. She stripped off and put on a fresh uniform, scrubbing furiously at her face and hands before doing so. The smell of smoke still lingered in her hair but it would have to do. She had wet it and it was now plastered down her back and stuck to her forehead and cheeks in slick, dark strands. She would read a book for a while. She knew where Miss Abigail kept the key to the library cupboard. Not many of the books were suitable for young girls as they were part of Miss Abigail's private collection and they were mostly full of slush and sex but she would find something to while away the time until she was called down to help prepare lunch. She would be surprised if anyone missed her anyway!

Downstairs the girls couldn't stop talking. They didn't know what to believe! Some of them had a sneaking suspicion that Bertha was telling the truth but if that was the case then why would Miss Abigail and Cook make up such a story? What was the point? Why pretend that Pat and April were dead? Why have a bonfire and a ceremony? It was certainly very strange. But on the other hand how had April and Pat died so suddenly? They hadn't even been gone for twenty four hours. There were tales of wild dogs and sometimes wolves roaming on the hillside but there had never been any actual sightings. No one had ever seen a paw print or a ravaged animal to prove that any such creatures really existed. It would be lovely to believe, as Bertha seemed to think, that their friends were still out there and on their way to freedom. It would give them some sort of hope although most of the girls couldn't understand why April and Pat had run away in the first place. Life wasn't so bad at Avondale House. They were fed and well cared for. Miss Abigail was strict but not unduly so. Cook sometimes slipped them surprise treats with their food when there had been an extra large delivery. Of course they were obliged to work hard but the rewards that were to come once they were old enough to go to the Manor would surely be worth it. Bertha was always making up wild stories in order to be noticed. She and Pat had concocted and relayed some hideous tales about Avondale Manor which the girls knew couldn't possibly be true. After all, it was obvious that they were in the process of being trained to be perfect wives and Princesses. How could they possibly instruct the hired help if they didn't know how to perform the menial tasks themselves? And so after a good half hour's heated debate and discussion the general opinion was that Bertha's story was no more than an attention-seeking fabrication and they preferred to believe Miss Abigail and Cook's version of events.

"Thank you for your support, Cook," said Miss Abigail, leaning heavily against the kitchen door. "For a moment there I thought we were in trouble and I could feel myself starting to panic."

"You're welcome," responded Cook. She grinned at Miss Abigail, exposing the gaps in her front teeth. "We make a good team, don't we?"

"We certainly do," responded Miss Abigail. "I don't know what I'd do without you."

The two women felt very satisfied. The bond between them had deepened and they knew that they could trust each other completely.

"I think a decent cup of coffee is in order, don't you?" said Miss Abigail. "I'll go and make that phone call to the authorities. I'll be back in five minutes. Once I've done that such a weight will be off my mind."

"Good idea," said Cook. She had a stash of delicious Columbian coffee hidden away which she had been waiting to make use of and which would be perfect for such an occasion as this.

Bertha grumpily made her way downstairs to the library. The rest of the girls were still chatting in the lounge and Miss Abigail and Cook were safely ensconced in the kitchen. She took the key from the tiny drawer hidden beneath Miss Abigail's desk and unlocked the cupboard with Miss Abigail's personal books in it. If there was one thing that Bertha loved it was reading. She kept it a secret though as it didn't suit the tough, sullen image she took such delight in portraying and it would be a disaster if any of the other girls found out. Books took her out of herself and almost managed to lift her from the daily drudgery of her life to another dimension, almost but not quite. And there were so few books at Avondale House. Somehow, since The Twelve had come into government practically every book had miraculously vanished. It was getting to the stage where people were forgetting that they'd ever been able to read, almost as if books had never existed and as if people had never had thoughts, ideas, facts or stories in their heads which they needed to put down on paper.

The disappearance of the books hadn't happened all at once but had taken place over a period of months as things began to change. One by one, libraries closed and shops removed magazines, books and periodicals from their shelves. Then a new job title was created – Book Investigators! As part of their job description the Book Investigators were required to search people's homes and make an inventory of every book before it was taken away. People hurriedly began to burn and dispose of their books as they didn't want to be on the list of those who flouted or disagreed with the rules and regulations of The Twelve. It was extraordinary! It was almost as if anything to do with any sort of unauthorised education or enjoyment had to go. But no, that wasn't quite true because Bertha had once seen a book fall out of an old man's pocket and he had bent down and retrieved it as quickly as possible making sure that no one had seen him. He hadn't noticed Bertha staring at him from the back window of the white van on the day she was being driven to Avondale House with April. And Bertha had seen a few, very old magazines scattered about in the surgery waiting room for people to browse through. They were pretty boring though as they were mostly about cars and horse racing and allotments and greyhounds; all the things that men were interested in or supposed to be interested in, and which no longer took place or existed – and generally innocuous.

No one knew that Miss Abigail kept books as the cupboard in which they were hidden was obviously filled with important paperwork. How Miss Abigail had managed to get hold of any books when they were clearly not allowed was also something of a mystery. In fact why Miss Abigail's office was called a library was a total enigma. Perhaps it had been a library many years ago and the name had simply remained as a reminder of a bygone era. The lumpen, surly Bertha was always on the lookout and had caught a glimpse of the books at the back of the cupboard one day when she delivered the post to Miss Abigail and from then on she watched Miss Abigail like a hawk. She studiously turned her back as Miss Abigail fiddled about beneath her desk but not before she saw her secreting her current book under a pile of paperwork as she entered the room. She obviously had plenty of time on her hands if she could sit in the library reading or perhaps the books were so exciting that she couldn't put them down. On one occasion Miss Abigail had become very red and flustered at Bertha's arrival almost as if she was afraid of being found out.

Bertha stared in wonder and delight at the rows of books beckoning her. She lifted a hand and gently ran a finger down the spine of one of them. No dust. She smiled. The other girls thought she was slow and she played along with it but she definitely was not. Bertha was highly intelligent and it was only her heavy, lumpish body and ungainly manner of movement that gave the impression of indolence and stupidity. She had long ago perfected the art of putting on a vacant expression in the company of adults so that she was automatically ignored by anyone in authority and such being the case she often overheard things that were not meant for her ears. Adults saw her but looked through her, almost as if she didn't exist. The other girls scorned her and rejected her company. This worked well for Bertha on some levels but not all for it meant she had no friends and no one to confide in. And Bertha desperately wanted a friend. She thought she might have gained the respect of at least one of the girls by helping April and Pat to escape but none of them even acknowledged her part in it. Not one of them had made the connection between April and Pat rolling down the hill and Bertha hurting her ankle. Bertha shrugged and turned her attention back to the books. There was a classic right in front of her, bound in crimson cloth and with the title embossed in gold. It was Black Beauty. She was surprised to find it in Miss Abigail's collection. Bertha took it down from the shelf and opened it. There was an inscription on the front page: 'Happy Birthday darling Abigail, love Nana xxx.' That was even more of a surprise. Bertha had never considered the fact that Miss Abigail had once been a child or indeed, had even ever been part of a family. She closed the book and cleverly secreted it down the front of her tunic just above the belt. Now she could lock the cupboard, replace the key and go upstairs and no one would be any the wiser. Excellent plan! She hoped Miss Abigail wouldn't notice that the book was missing. Bertha smiled smugly, feeling very pleased with herself. But no, someone was coming. She had to hide. Where could she go? She ducked down behind the sofa on her hands and knees and hoped that she couldn't be seen. It could only be Miss Abigail coming into the library. No one else would need to. She heard Miss Abigail go over to her desk and rustle amongst some papers. Then she picked up the phone. Bertha strained to listen. It sounded as if she was talking about April and Pat. Yes, she was. She was telling someone what had happened to them. Now she was being put on hold and Bertha tried not to breathe too heavily. She didn't want Miss Abigail to hear her. That would be a disaster and Bertha could only imagine the trouble she would be in if she was caught! Mind you, she was in possession of some damning evidence against Cook and Miss Abigail; she knew things no one else did. She might be able to make use of her knowledge later on.

    She listened as Miss Abigail told her story all over again. It seemed as if her explanation was deemed satisfactory because Miss Abigail agreed to some form filling and put down the phone. There was silence for another few minutes interrupted only by the sound of a pen scratching across paper and then Miss Abigail scraped her chair back, clicked her heels together triumphantly and left the room. Bertha waited until she was sure she had gone and slowly stood up. She crossed over to Miss Abigail's desk and put the key away. Then she picked up the piece of paper that Miss Abigail had been writing on. It was a form to be filled in for the report of deceased or missing girls and Pat and April's names were on it. Bertha stared. She felt shocked. Was this all the girl's lives amounted to, a few words scribbled on a piece of paper? It felt very final. She knew what Miss Abigail and Cook were up to now though. They were getting themselves out of trouble. It was as simple as that. No one was even going to look for Pat and April. As far as the authorities were concerned the lives of the two girls were done and dusted and no longer of any consequence. The relevant paperwork had been completed and no further action needed to be taken. But what would happen if the girls really did come back? What would happen then? Would they have to be killed in order to comply with Miss Abigail's ridiculous fabrication? Would the story need to be true? It didn't bear thinking about. Bertha hoped that April and Pat never came back. She also hoped that at some point they would decide to get in touch with her and let her know they were safe. They owed her that much at least. She sniffed. She didn't want to feel resentful simply because she was the only one who knew the truth and no one believed her. At some point she might be able to use this to her advantage. She would remember that. She was the one holding the upper hand and this gave her a feeling of empowerment. She could walk with her head high as she went about her daily duties at Avondale House whether she had friends or not. Bertha gave a low whistle before leaving the library and walked quietly back up the stairs hugging the precious book to her chest.

CHAPTER FIFTEEN

It took a further seven days for Pat to make a full recovery. George had managed to acquire five days worth of antibiotics and he and April began to see an improvement in Pat's health halfway through taking them. There was no rush to be on their way though as George kept reminding them. He enjoyed their company. The girls didn't need to leave; they could stay as long as they liked.

It was while Pat was getting better that Hope's appetite noticeably increased. She drank and drank and drank. The drugged milk that had previously kept her either asleep or passive had obviously not been enough for her and now, whenever she was awake, she was constantly hungry. This took April by surprise but luckily George was able to provide an endless supply of milk and during this short period of time Hope's cheeks began to fill out. Her eyes would light up and she would smile and gurgle every time she saw April knowing that food was on its way and April couldn't help but adore her.

Pat was beginning to put on a little weight too and looked much healthier, in fact much healthier than she had for a long time. There was even the hint of a rosy glow to her cheeks. April handed Hope over to her. She didn't want Pat feeling left out. They were a family unit now, a family of three. And she sensed that the time was coming when they would have to say their goodbyes and be on the move again. They couldn't stay with George for ever no matter how much they wanted to and, truth to tell, they were very happy in his company and in the warmth and security of the windowless room. The thought of continuing their journey and leaving the Wine Sellers was not a happy one. George allowed them the free run of the place during the day but as soon as it began to grow dark outside they were confined to the room beneath the stove. That was when there was the strong possibility of a furtive knock at the door followed by a couple of overbearing members of authority shouldering their way in and demanding bottles of the very best house wine. These uninvited guests knew better than to demand champagne or any of the vintage bottles from the last rack in the cellar as they had to be accounted for but George generally put by a few bottles of house wine that he knew wouldn't be missed for just such unwelcome visits. George always complied with the demands of these guests as he knew they could easily find a reason, any reason, to put him under house arrest and then he would be driven away in one of the state vans to be incarcerated and finally punished whether he was guilty of crime or not.

While the girls remained at the Wine Sellers George realised that for the first time in years he could describe himself as content. He thoroughly enjoyed looking after them and loved the fact that they were recuperating there. He was dreading the day when they would have to leave. April had said nothing as yet but he only had to look at Pat to see that she was blossoming and much stronger now. No one was saying anything. The subject was definitely being avoided. In fact it was almost as if it was a game and they were playing happy families and no one wanted to spoil it. The girls couldn't stay at the Wine Sellers forever though. Inevitably and at some point one of them would slip up and they would be discovered. It would only take the unexpected arrival of unwanted visitors during the daytime and a particularly shrill cry from Hope and the girls would be searched for and found and Hope was indeed becoming more vociferous with the passing of each and every day. George knew the subject of departure would have to be broached in the very near future but he just didn't want to be the one to do it. He was knowingly procrastinating. He was going to wait. He would let the girls decide. In the meantime he took it upon himself to make sure they were well prepared for their forthcoming departure. He cut their hair and used a henna preparation to dye their shorn locks a very dark brown. He searched amongst the old clothes he had accumulated over the years and made sure that April and Pat continued to dress and look like boys. He managed to procure a pair of well worn boots for Pat. They had seen much better days but were comfortable to wear as Pat's boots had split completely from top to bottom. They would be perfect for the long walk ahead of the girls, outside the town and across the barren, treacherous terrain which led to the foot of the mountains and the tunnels. He also found a rucksack, one which was roomy enough to pop Hope into and a particularly large donkey jacket for April so that both the rucksack and Hope could be hidden underneath it if ever the need arose. He tried to cater for every eventuality yet mentioned nothing.

It was on the very evening that he managed to obtain the donkey jacket that their most feared and discussed scenario occurred. George had called April and Pat up to the kitchen for their hot milk and bread just before they were about to turn in for the night when suddenly there was a loud knocking at the door.

"Go quickly, go!" George hissed. He had no visitors booked in to collect wine and it was very late. This was not the usual knocking either; this was a confident and almost threatening sound, a sign that something might be devastatingly amiss. The girls hurried away taking their bread and milk with them. George walked slowly to the front door tutting as the knocking grew louder and louder.

"I'm coming, I'm coming," he growled under his breath. "Give me a minute."

He drew back the heavy bolts and turned the key. Almost as soon as he did so, two long, loping men shoved their way past him, pushing him aside as they did so. There was a familiarity about them that George couldn't quite place and he cringed at the smell of alcohol and cheap tobacco emanating from them.

"We've got you now," one of them snarled.

"We certainly have," continued the other. "So where is it?"

George drew himself up to his full height, stepped forward and stared at the men in surprise. They certainly didn't appear to be the usual types who called at his door for a couple of bottles of wine. And they certainly weren't figures of authority. They weren't in uniform. Who were they and what could they want?

"We're going to report you anyway so you might as well hand it over. You escaped from us once but you won't get away a second time."

George thrust his chest out, clenching his fists, attempting to appear as if he was completely in control of the situation.

"What on earth are you talking about?" he asked.

"You know exactly what we're talking about," answered the first man as he moved closer to George. His stance had suddenly become threatening. The second man slunk up next to him and he too adopted an aggressive posture. It was clear that singly they would pose very little danger but together they felt strong and were comfortable united in the cowardice of pack mentality. They were much taller and broader than George and almost surrounded him. He tried hard not to feel flustered. A fierce, deep growl erupted from the back of his throat and he raised his fists in response to the situation, noticing as he did so that one of the men involuntarily took a step back. He seized the opportunity to stride assertively past them and flung the main door wide.

"Get out!" he growled. "I work for the authorities and will have no truck with the likes of you. I don't know who you are but I suggest you get out now before I do my duty and inform them."

He watched as the men displayed a moment's hesitation, glancing at each other in confusion. George's reaction had been unexpected.

"Get out now!" he repeated even more loudly, taking advantage of their uncertainty.

But the men stood firm again and were not to be put off. They had talked about the acquisition of George's tobacco for days, vocally encouraging and egging each other on, mulling over the possibilities of every situation in which they might find themselves, until finally deciding that the only option available to them was to knock at the door and force their way in, obtaining the aromatic leaves through intimidating behaviour and maybe even threats of blackmail. They had watched men come and go from the Wine Sellers on an almost daily basis and knew that George opened the door to everyone who knocked. They were determined to claim or steal their prize depending on how amenable or difficult George chose to be and were not going to leave without it. The taller of the two men lurched towards George thrusting a hand beneath the folds of his overcoat as he did so. George caught sight of a flash of silver. Immediately he kicked out taking the man by surprise and knocking him off balance and into his partner. He pushed his way past both of them and rushed into the kitchen, slamming and locking the door behind him. The main door was still open so the men could leave and retreat into the darkness if they so chose but George was now trapped inside, leaving them to decide what they were going to do next. And who knew what that would be? They might leave or they might break down the door and attack him. If they opted to explore the Wine Sellers and went down to the cellar the girls wouldn't be able to remain hidden for long. Hope was shortly due to have her last feed of the day and if April wasn't prepared she would start to scream. George would be in much greater trouble if the men discovered the girls than if he gave them some of his stash. As he stood with his back against the kitchen door it suddenly dawned upon him that that was what they wanted. There was nothing else it could be. How they had found out about it was a mystery although he was aware that there were always wagging tongues and citizens desperate for money or extra food. The men might report him to the authorities after they had taken his stash but they would inevitably keep some for themselves. George had no idea what to do. He stared vacantly at the grubby kitchen walls, his eyes coming to focus on a grey-green patch of mildew growing in the corner. The girls were his priority. His life had been so much more bearable since their arrival. He needed to think. And he needed to think about them!

Eventually a plan began to unfold. One of the windows outside led directly into the room next to the cellar. He would make his way to it and warn the girls. The girls would have to leave tonight. The untimely arrival of the two men made this imperative. There was no alternative. Somehow he would have to help the girls through the window and see them on their way. He didn't want to put them at risk; they had been through more than enough already. He would have to hurry though. The two men must not find the girls before he had a chance to help them. He clambered deftly up onto the kitchen sink and commenced battle with the kitchen window. It hadn't been opened for so long that it was well and truly jammed shut. He could turn the handle but that made absolutely no difference whatsoever. In fact after a minute or two of pulling and tugging the dratted thing came away in his hand. No use at all! He could smash the window but that might draw attention to what he was doing and he didn't want that. There was a crowbar somewhere. But where? Where had he left it and when was the last time he had used it? Under the sink, yes that was it. He jumped down and began to rummage around beneath the sink flinging bottles of cleaning fluid and old bits of cloth and carbolic soap aside as he did so. He finally found the crowbar he was looking for and stood up, gripping it firmly between both hands. Perhaps he should dispose of the two men before rescuing the girls? The image of himself lunging at the men with his newfound weapon was a decidedly welcome one but the girls were a priority so he climbed back up to the windowsill and instead began to use the crowbar as a lever wrenching it back and forth until the base of the window frame gave way and with a final jerk the window was open. George leapt down into the paved yard below and made his way to a large, metal waste bin. Behind it was the window he was looking for. He wheeled the bin aside and crouched down. The window was filthy, just below ground level and no more than a foot wide. You would never notice it unless you knew it was there. It hadn't been cleaned for years and was so thick with grime that certainly nothing could be seen through it. George leant across and began to tap at it, over and over again. He had no idea whether the girls would be able to hear him as the window wasn't part of the tiny room they were currently sleeping in but belonged to the room above. He began to tap a little louder.

"April!" he hissed. "April, are you there?"

There was no reply. He stopped and listened for a moment. He could hear nothing. This was senseless. He could spend hours tapping and calling, to no avail. Impulsively he tapped at the window with the crowbar and quite unexpectedly the glass began to shatter. There's a surprise, thought George. He hadn't considered that! The window pane was still in place but it was slowly and surely turning into a myriad of criss cross cracks and splinters. He tugged at the sleeve of his jumper until it covered the whole of his arm and hand and then pressed gently with his elbow against the pane. Immediately the glass fell inwards and onto the floor below with a blistering crash. George hardly dared breathe. He listened intently and realised that the two men were now arguing vociferously. With any luck they wouldn't have heard the glass breaking.

"April," he hissed again.

This time April heard him.

"What's going on?" she called up from her hiding place. "Why have you smashed the window?"

"There's no time for explanations," said George. "You've got to leave now. Get Pat and Hope and grab the rucksack. It should contain everything you need. You have to go. There's no time to lose."

There was silence and then a few minutes later he heard the sound of footsteps on the stepladder and saw the trap door being pushed open. April climbed out first having swaddled Hope in an old shawl which she had tied securely around her chest and waist. She had her arms through the donkey jacket George had found for her. Immediately behind came Pat carrying the rucksack on her back and struggling under the weight of it.

"Where are you?" whispered April. "There's glass everywhere. What's going on?"

"Look to your right," answered George. "You need to climb through the window."

He leant forward and brushed away the remaining shards of glass with the sleeve of his jumper. "Now!" he insisted. "Right now!"

April moved across to the window and beckoned Pat over. Pat looked worried.

"Pass the rucksack to George and go through after it."

Pat nodded, not daring to say anything. George extended his arm and grabbed hold of the rucksack. Then Pat crouched down and began to slither through, wincing as she felt her hands and the back of her neck being pierced by minute slivers of glass. There wasn't enough room for April and Hope to get through together so April untied the shawl and passed Hope carefully into George's outstretched arms. Now it was her turn. She could hear voices in the cellar. There wasn't much time. She didn't want whoever was in the cellar finding her or discovering the tiny room they had been hiding in. She tiptoed to the door and slowly slipped the heavy bar across. No one would be able to get through now, she thought.

"Good thinking," she heard George whisper loudly. "Hurry up. Come on."

April lay flat on her stomach and slid through. The glass was everywhere. That would be something else to think about. She and Pat would have to inspect each other and pick out the tiny fragments at some point. But she wouldn't worry about that for the moment. She stood up and secured Hope to the front of her body once more.

"Who was at the door?" she asked. "Why is it so important that we leave?"

"Do you remember the two men who followed me, when you had to sit on my shoulders in disguise?"

April nodded.

"It's them. They must have been watching the main door ever since. They know about the tobacco stash. They don't appear to know about you but it won't be very long before they do if you stay in that room."

"So what are you going to do?" she asked.

"I don't know yet," answered George, shaking his head. "I'll think of something. But there's no time for discussion. You've got to go. You've got to go now."

"Where?"

"Go to the end of the road and turn right and just keep walking. You'll eventually find yourselves out of town and heading across open land. Watch out for wolves though. Keep your eyes open and make sure you stay together."

April stared at George in horror. Wolves!

"Can't we get rid of the men and stay with you?" she asked.

"Yes, please," interrupted Pat. "Can't we just stay with you?"

"Not possible," answered George, a look of sadness on his face. "We knew this day was coming. You can't live in that tiny room for ever. Take the crowbar. That will afford you some protection at least."

He passed the crowbar to April who gripped it tightly, looking around her in anguish as if expecting to see the dreaded wolves coming out of the shadows even as they stood there. George bent down and impulsively kissed the top of her head and then reached out a finger to tenderly stroke Hope's cheek. Pat threw down the rucksack and hurled herself at him, sobbing.

"We've had such a lovely time with you even though I've been ill. I don't want to leave you. I'd be happy to stay in that room forever. We've been like a family, a real family and I've never had that before."

George could feel tears welling up as he hugged Pat and he gave a huge sniff, blinking rapidly and then coughing in embarrassment in an attempt to hide his emotions.

"You must go. I've got to go back and deal with those men. I'll have to try and do some sort of deal with them, give them some of the stash, you know."

He disentangled himself from Pat's arms and sighed heavily.

"It's been so good having you to stay with me. I feel so different from the person you first met. Go quickly, go before I change my mind and beg you to not to leave. You've got to find April's grandmother so that you can lead normal lives. Hurry now."

"We'll find a way to contact you," said April, tears running down her cheeks. "We'll really try. As soon as we get to my grandmother's we'll contact you and then you can join us."

"That would be wonderful," said George. "I'd like that. I've had enough of this place anyway. I feel as if my time's running out here and I need to move on. It's taken the three of you coming into my life to make me realise how awful it's been and for how long and what a lie it all is. I can't go back to the way things were before you arrived. I've got to try and move forward in some way. But first I've got to deal with those men. So go. Go, go, go before I change my mind and drag you back in with me. And don't worry about contacting me. I'll find you. You can be certain of that; I will find you."

And with such passionate, heartfelt words George hunched his shoulders, clenched his fists in anticipation, turned round and strode through the paved yard to the open, main door.

CHAPTER SIXTEEN

Pat looked at April in despair.

"I really liked living at the Wine Sellers with George," she whispered. "It wasn't perfect but we were warm and sheltered and always had food. And he cared about us, he truly did. I wish we didn't have to leave."

"I know," replied April. "But as George said, we wouldn't be safe there forever and then who knows what might happen to us? He's right; we've got to be on our way. Everything will be fine as soon as we reach my grandmother's. She may even know that we're not at Avondale House and that we're on our way. I wouldn't put it past her. She's a very clever woman and not a bit like a normal grandmother. She travels everywhere on her own and nobody questions her or bothers her. Imagine a life like that, Pat. Imagine being able to do whatever you want without anyone interfering. That's how it will be for us when we find her."

"But what about the wolves?" asked Pat.

"We'll worry about them if we come across them," answered April. "And we might not even see any. Everyone keeps talking about them but I don't know anyone who's actually come into contact with a real, live wolf, do you? It's not something we need to concern ourselves with right now. Our first priority is to get out of this town without being noticed. It's after curfew so if we're caught we'll be in such trouble. Come on, follow me. Luckily I fed Hope a little early so she may sleep for a few hours yet. How's that rucksack? Is it too heavy for you? Is there anything we can take out of it?"

"No thanks," replied Pat. "I'll manage and it'll get lighter as we go along. I only had time for a quick look inside and George seems to have filled it mostly with milk for Hope and some of the tobacco stash. I didn't get a proper look but we can sort it later."

April nodded at Pat and they set off. She felt a twinge of remorse having to leave George to fend for himself against the intruders but she was sure that he must have dealt with similar situations at other times in his life. And George was resourceful, to say the least. She needed to focus on safety; she needed to focus on looking after Pat and Hope.

It was a calm, clear night for their journey and when April looked up she was aware of a sky brimming with twinkling stars intent on lighting their pathway. They appeared warm and friendly. What was it that Tim had said? Always follow the brightest star. The brightest star was the Morning Star, the Star of Venus. If they followed it they would be heading in the right direction for the mountains. Tim had told her not to forget that and to use the star as their guide. And she could see it; she could see it shimmering at her most encouragingly. It was almost as if it deigned to shine this evening just for the three of them.

The street lamps seemed to be on their side too, shedding dim pools of spattered light here and there on the pavements below and gleaming just brightly enough for April to be able to see a short distance ahead. She could feel Pat close behind her and was aware of her breath coming in short, sharp rasps as she struggled beneath the weight of the rucksack. April moved to the inside of the footpath so that she and Pat were concealed within the shadows of the houses looming up on either side of the street and they scurried along like small, furtive creatures of the night having really no desire to be there. Conditions were perfect for flight and the streets were empty as everyone was indoors due to the curfew. April reminded herself how lucky they were. They always seemed to bump into kind people who looked out for them. Well, kind men actually and that came as a mix of shock and relief as April hadn't encountered many of those. She had heard so many awful things about men from Bertha and Pat and it was her own father who had made the decision to dispose of her and exclude her from family life forever. Had he known what was in store for her; had he cared? He had never shown any interest in her at home. He had paid great attention to her brothers but April and her mother had been treated as nothing more than unpaid servants, to be shouted at and given a good slap every now and then, not for any particular reason but just for good measure as her father liked to say. He enjoyed keeping them on their toes and he was almost fanatical in his demands. He liked the house to be kept in a permanent state of obsessive cleanliness; everything in its place and totally spotless. Whenever her mother went into labour at the end of a long, exhausting pregnancy April remained indoors to take care of the cooking and cleaning and household chores and then shortly after the birth her father would bully her mother back into action again. Her mother always gave birth at home; there was no comfortable, hospital bed for her to rest in and her father made sure that April was available with hands on help for the delivery. There wasn't much April didn't know about childbirth but there was a lot she didn't know about sex and even more that she didn't want to know. The very thought of it made her shudder with horror and disgust.

At home a curtain divided her parent's space from the rest of the sleeping quarters and April often heard her father grunting and groaning at night, sounds which brought forth images of pigs squirming and rolling about in dirt; but she heard very little noise from her mother. If April became aware of anything it was usually a sharp cry of pain and after that everything became muffled as if her father had placed his hand over her mother's mouth to keep her quiet and then suddenly there would be an intense burst of loud, rampant noise making April cringe and she would put her fingers in her ears thinking that the creaking, old mattress would either split or pop a spring at the very least with all the bouncing up and down that was systematically destroying it.

In Avondale House Pat was the one who seemed to know about sex and yet her only experience of it had been with Sister Charlotte and that had been quite innocent by all accounts. Pat had opened up to her an awful lot whilst she had been ill. Somehow she knew she had escaped terrible pain and trouble at Avondale Manor and that Sister Charlotte had been responsible for this. She was familiar with the trauma of childbirth and not only had she helped with the delivery of beautiful babies but she had also watched in despair and shock as many of the young mothers bled to death, afterwards helping to wrap their misshapen, yet fragile bodies in bloodied sheets and then tipping them directly from trolleys into the huge ovens that kept the rooms upstairs warm and cosy for the visiting male guests. She knew that the girls in those rooms weren't always treated well either. They never seemed to be allowed to leave. They remained confined, waiting for men to arrive, dressed in skimpy, revealing tunics, with their hair brushed until it shone and their makeup perfect. They looked so young and innocent, as indeed they were. On that first night of their coming of age the girls endured a traumatic shattering of their dreams. The handsome Princes that they were expecting simply didn't arrive. Instead, sleazy, leering men came into their rooms. Old, fat, dirty men who grinned in anticipation of what was to come and pulled down their trousers and forced the innocent girls to do unthinkable things with their mouths. These were men who wanted to squeeze and poke and pinch and grab and hurt, until finally they would force themselves upon the girls, thrusting over and over again until the poor, virginal creatures felt as if they would be torn apart with the endless, searing pain. None of these men wanted to marry the girls; they came to Avondale Manor purely for pleasure and it was after this first unspeakable encounter that many of the girls tried to escape and some even attempted suicide. They were horrified to find that their doors were locked and windows barred and that every night the same thing happened all over again. On that first night they were the property of only one man who paid highly for their virginity but after that they were considered soiled goods and men entered and left their rooms in quick succession.

Pat had relayed some of what happened at Avondale Manor whilst they were still at the House and it was this horrific information that had prompted April to plan her escape. She was glad she had rolled down the mountain as throughout their subsequent experiences neither she nor Pat had been disrespected or hurt in any way. In fact they had received nothing but help and kindness and this had been solely from men. So, in fact, there were good men out there. This didn't mean that April felt ready to trust any of them but she was able to relax a little and not jump to the immediate conclusion that men were out to harm her. Now as she walked along she hoped that there would be more help available if they needed it.

Although it was dark it wasn't cold and April found herself sweating under the weight of the thick, donkey jacket that George had given her. He must have worn it at some point as there was a familiar smell to it that was oddly comforting. As she walked her thoughts were constantly drawn back to him. She wondered what was happening at the Wine Sellers. She hoped George was safe and had managed to get rid of the long, loping men. He had risked everything for them. He had risked his livelihood and his home and perhaps now he was risking his life. April felt a twinge of panic. What if he hadn't been able to get rid of the two men? What if they were dragging him, even now, to the authorities and he was about to be thrown into some kind of hell-hole prison? She stopped suddenly and looked around her. Was there anywhere to hide? She frowned as she stared and found she could just distinguish the shadowy shape of a small shed in the front garden opposite her. She scurried across the road with Pat hurrying to keep up and thrust aside the tall privet hedge to get to it. She tried the door. It wasn't locked and after sliding a bolt across it opened.

"What's happening? Why have we stopped so soon? We're still in the town. We have to get out of here. What's going on?" asked Pat breathlessly.

"I want you to stay in the shed for a while until I get back," answered April. "I won't be long."

She pushed Pat inside the shed ahead of her and tugged off the heavy donkey jacket.

"Here, take Hope for me and cover yourself with this. She won't wake up for ages yet. I won't be long, honestly. I can't leave George without knowing that he's okay."

Pat eased the rucksack from her shoulders and sat down holding out her arms for Hope.

"You're right," she said. "I feel bad about him too. He's done so much for us and it's as though we just disappear as soon as the going gets tough. I'll be okay here with Hope but come back as soon as you can, won't you? I'm not so good on my own."

April nodded and turned to leave. She slipped the bolt across on the outside so that the door would remain closed and Pat and Hope would be safe until she returned. Then she began to run. A sense of urgency spurred her on adding wings to her flight so that it felt as if her feet barely touched the pavements. She had to get back to George as quickly as possible. She had left everything with Pat except the crowbar which she gripped so tightly that her knuckles turned white. She hoped she wouldn't need it and that all would be well but anxiety was churning sickly in the pit of her stomach. As she approached the Wine Sellers she could see that the door was still wide open and she could hear a lot of noise coming from inside. She was aware of the sudden appearance of lights illuminating the nearby houses and knew that at any moment people would be coming out into the street wondering what was going on. She hesitated in the doorway in order to get her breath back and to try and fathom what was happening. She could hear crashing and banging and great yells of pain, but also wild laughter amidst it all. April tiptoed down the hallway. The tumult was coming from the cellar. She opened the cellar door and crept down the stairs, the crowbar raised high as she went. As she got to the last few steps she knew that what she was hearing were the final sounds of some sort of struggle. She peered around the corner cautiously and immediately saw George. He was in trouble. The shorter of the two men was standing behind him holding his arms and laughing and the taller man was laying into him with his fists. There was no holding back. The taller man's punches were wild and frenzied, raining down thick and fast and he was enjoying every moment of the injury and pain he was inflicting. The wounded cries from George were becoming weaker and weaker and as April watched he slowly collapsed and fell to his knees. Soon he would be unconscious, if not dead. April gave a gasp of horror and then instantly she was consumed with a sense of outrage. Who were these men to think they could come in and attack her good friend George? How dare they? Who did they think they were? The shocking sight of George being viciously pummelled suddenly overwhelmed her and, without thinking, April positioned the crowbar for maximum effect and charged. Seconds later she brought the crowbar crashing down upon the taller man's shoulders. His legs buckled and he lurched forwards under the force of the unexpected blow and she struck him again. As he fell she continued to pound him with blow after blow upon his head and shoulders expelling pent up rage and fury, conscious of a hideous, screaming sound that ricocheted off the walls of the cellar and filled the entire space with its passion and anguish. She didn't stop until the taller man was no longer moving and then she looked up. The hideous, screaming sound continued and April put a hand to her throat to stem its flow aware that it had to be coming from her. Her face was aghast as she glanced down at what she had just done and noted the shorter of the two men staring at her with a look of incredulity and terror on his face. He was attempting to hold George up in front of him as a shield to protect himself from the frenzied madness of this wild, bloodied creature. George was in a state of collapse and ready to hit the floor. April approached the shorter man, curling her upper lip back in a bestial snarl.

"Let him go, let him go now!" she growled.

Immediately the shorter man lowered George carefully to one side, all the while keeping his eyes on April, and then raised his arms in submission.

"It wasn't my idea," he squeaked, glancing in horror at his inert friend and then back at April. April let out a great roar and rushed at him, swinging the crowbar wide. She struck him first across the side of his knees and then as his legs gave way she swiped him viciously across the chest. It was no more than the cowardly bully deserved. The man made no attempt to defend himself. April's blows were totally unexpected as he was obviously used to his friend taking the lead in every situation. He had no idea what to do or how to react now that he was under attack.

"Stop, please stop!" he cried, covering his head protectively with his hands as he fell to his knees.

But April had lost control. She was far too angry to stop now. She raised the crowbar as high as she could and brought it crashing down with as much force as she could muster. There was a gurgling sound as blood spurted from the side of the man's mouth and nose and then he collapsed in an unconscious heap on top of his friend. April stared at them, panting and breathless with the force of her exertions. Both men were decidedly out for the count. She dropped the crowbar and crouched down beside George. He was curled up in a ball of pain and misery. His eyes were so bruised and swollen that he could barely see through them. It looked as if his arm was broken too as it was swinging limply and at an odd angle from his shoulder. He tried to grin at April and in doing so he coughed and spat a bloody tooth from his mouth.

"Don't have to bother with the dentist now then, do I?" he grunted, attempting to make a joke of it. "Good to see you, April. Obviously you didn't get to your grandmother's?"

"Stop talking," said April. "We've got to get you upstairs and lock the door on these two monsters. We need to get someone to look at you. Can you walk?"

"I think so," answered George. "I may need assistance though."

April encouraged him to lean on her taking care not to touch his injured arm and after a few stumbles he managed to clamber to his feet. George nodded towards the crowbar and motioned for April to pick it up.

"Mustn't forget that, must we?" he said. "Didn't realise it'd come in so handy or that you'd make use of it quite so soon."

April grabbed the crowbar and began to half-haul, half-drag George up the stairs.

"I'm glad to see you've still got your sense of humour," she retorted.

Presently they were in the kitchen and George was seated, slumped forward at the table. People were starting to sidle in through the main door. Neighbours were arriving to offer their help.

"You okay, mate?" asked one of the men.

"I'll live," replied George. "There are two of them down there. They came in for the wine and then suddenly attacked me."

"Lucky your son was with you," remarked a well-rounded woman, staring hard at April. April lowered her eyes in embarrassment hoping that the woman wouldn't suddenly realise that she was a girl. There had been enough trouble at the Wine Sellers for one night and there was not much point in making things any worse. George nodded and April filled a bowl with hot water and then immersed a tea towel in it. She wrung it out and began to tenderly clean George's wounds. There was a lot of blood and swelling but most of the cuts appeared to be superficial. The main concern was George's arm and the well-rounded woman was taking care of that.

"I used to be a nurse in the old days" she said.

"Don't you do any nursing now then?" questioned April politely as she wrung out her tea towel for the fifth time.

"Not whilst The Twelve are in Government, dear. I'm at home with the husband keeping house and producing."

"Producing?" questioned April. "Producing what?"

The woman chose not to answer and turned to George. "Your arm's not broken but you do have a dislocated shoulder. If you hold still I'll pop it back in for you. It will hurt for a moment or two as I do it but that's all."

The woman sounded very casual about what she was going to do as if it was an everyday occurrence and not at all out of the ordinary. She nodded at one of the men who had come in with her and he reached out and clasped his arms around George's chest in order to keep him still. Then with great efficiency and determination she grabbed hold of George's shoulder and arm and with a single thrust she shoved the shoulder back into its socket. George let out a huge yell and then burst into nervous laughter. He clenched and unclenched his fist as he began to move his arm around, looking at the woman in awe and wonder.

"I'm surprised they don't make use of you at the hospital," he said. "Thank you. It feels much better now."

"It's all men at the hospital," replied the well-rounded woman. "No females are allowed to work there. You obviously haven't needed to visit one for some time or you'd know this?"

"No," replied George. "I try to stay clear of such places."

"Too right. The less experience you have of them the better. Most of the beds are taken up with women and young girls giving birth anyway. As soon as the doctors know a boy is on the way it's all hands on deck and action stations. Can't lose any boys, can we?"

April stared at the woman. She understood what the woman was saying but her tone of voice made her sound bitter and resentful. Did she hate boys? Was that it?

"What about the girls?" she asked.

The woman shrugged her shoulders.

"No one wants girls, dear," she replied tersely, "and it's best not to ask any questions if you know what's good for you."

She glared at April who flushed red and quickly turned her attention back to soaking the tea towel in the blood-stained, tepid water before cleaning George's face.

"I'll rinse this now," she said, picking up the bowl and carrying it carefully back to the sink. It would be much better when she was on her way again. That woman made her feel uncomfortable. The sooner she left the Wine Sellers the better. The more she thought about what she had just done the more horrified she felt. She couldn't believe she had lashed out so wildly with the crowbar. She had never hit anyone in her life. She was not in the least confrontational, always preferring to stay out of trouble and she had never been one to allow herself to be drawn into arguments at home. She felt pangs of dismay and disbelief run through her as she remembered the multitude of blows she had rained down on the two men. What had come over her? She had completely lost control. She flushed the water away and rinsed the bowl out quickly before taking a seat at the table opposite George. Her teeth had started to chatter uncontrollably and she was having difficulty preventing her body from shaking. She hunched over at the table wrapping her arms about her, trying to make herself as small as possible in the hope that no one would notice. A moment later the well-rounded woman placed a mug of hot, sweet tea in front of her.

"I think you need this, dear," she said. "The men have gone down into the cellar to see what the damage is."

April took a great gulp of tea. "I've got to go," she said.

"You're going into shock, love. You're not fit to go anywhere," responded the well-rounded woman. "Stay there and finish your tea."

April cradled the hot mug with both hands and forced her lips to curl upwards into what she hoped looked like a grateful smile.

"It's alright, dear," said the well-rounded woman. "Whatever your secret is, it's safe with me. There's no need to worry."

April looked at her and then across to George. She didn't know what to believe or who to trust. One minute the woman was grumpy and the next she was all kindliness and concern. It was most confusing.

"It's okay, April," George said. "Since The Twelve stepped into Government I've hardly seen my neighbours but they've always been good friends. You can confide in the nurse. She won't let you down. She had two daughters and they were both taken away. We've all been placed in uncomfortable situations and communication has been unnaturally awkward. It's dangerous for us to be seen talking to each other on the outside."

By this time the two men had returned from the cellar.

"It's bad down there," said one of them, shaking his head slowly as if he couldn't quite believe what he had just seen.

"What on earth happened?" asked the other, staring first at George and then at April.

Tears suddenly began to roll down April's cheeks and, without warning, she found she was making loud, gulping, wailing noises.

"I did it!" she cried. "It was me! I saw them using George like a punch bag and it made me crazy. They've been following him and watching him and then they came in and they were beating him and I had the crowbar and I had to stop them and once I started I couldn't stop."

"Hush now," said the nurse. "We know those men and someone was going to sort them out at some point. It was inevitable. They are amongst the worst of their kind. They simper and smile to your face rubbing their greedy hands together and all the time they're scheming and plotting behind your back and getting as many innocent people into trouble as they can."

"They'll not be getting anyone into trouble again, I shouldn't wonder," said one of the men. "That will be the last thing on their minds. It's about time someone had enough courage to tackle them."

He smiled at April and she felt the nurse's hands placed comfortingly on her shoulders.

"Yes and it's taken a child to do it. You put us to shame, love," she said.

George got up from the table, wincing as he gripped the edges of it, in pain and unsteady.

"Where are the others?" he asked April, unwilling to mention any names.

"They're in a shed," replied April. "I said I wouldn't be long. I shut them in for safety until I could get back to them. They're not far away."

"I'll go with you and we'll find them," suggested the nurse. "You should have a rest for an hour or so in the shed as you're in shock and then you'll have to leave and be on your way. We'll take care of the men in the cellar, no need to worry about that, but we don't want you getting into any bother. We'll tell the authorities that George had intruders and that his son caught them attacking him. We'll say we think his son took quite a beating and went to the hospital to have his injuries tended to. Of course we had no idea George had a son as we've never seen him and he must have been visiting. No one will come looking for you as they'll be checking the new arrivals at the hospital so you'll have a better chance of getting away. Don't worry, dear. Everything will be okay."

April nodded at her and looked at George, beginning to relax. She knew he was going to be alright now and was glad that he had rekindled his friendship with his neighbours. He wouldn't be on his own any more. He would be safe. She heaved a sigh of relief.

"I'll wait a while and then I'll come and find you," said George. "Don't doubt me on that. You're like family to me. You've all become so important in my life, even in such a short space of time."

April jumped up from the table, running round to hug him.

"Easy now tiger," said George. "I've just been attacked, remember?"

Even so he managed to place an arm about her as he gave her a peck on the cheek.

"The perfect protector," he said, smiling kindly at her. "And when I meet you at your grandmother's we'll be together again. That's as long as your grandmother doesn't mind, of course."

"She would never mind," responded April assertively. "Especially when she hears about everything you've done for us. I should think she'd be glad of a man about the house too. She's quite old you know and won't be able to do everything by herself forever."

George gave a chuckle of delight at her engaging innocence. Life was simple as far as April was concerned.

"We'd better get going then," interrupted the nurse. "We don't want to leave it too late and find there's no time for you to rest before the sun comes up and you're stuck in that shed. Get yourself cleaned up and we'll set off."

April pulled away from George and for the first time noticed that she too was covered in blood although, fortunately, none of it was her own. She refilled the bowl with fresh water and sloshed at her face and hands. Her clothes would have to wait. There wasn't much she could do about them right now. She turned towards the main door. The nurse was right. The sooner she, Pat and Hope were on their way the better. She raised an arm to wave goodbye to George and, clutching the crowbar for reassurance, exited the Wine Sellers, trying not to show how completely lacking in strength and courage she felt. Her savage and extraordinary behaviour had taken it out of her, in more ways than one. The nurse followed behind, neither of them speaking. Once they were outside April paused and took a few deep breaths before starting to walk quickly down the street towards the house with the shed in the front garden. Her mind was already on the next chapter of her life.

"Alright love?" queried the nurse as she stepped out beside her.

April turned to her. "I will be as soon as I know my friends are safe," she replied.

CHAPTER SEVENTEEN

Shortly afterwards they reached the shed and April pulled back the bolt on the door. The nurse squinted as she peered in, barely managing to make out the small figure crouching in the corner on top of a pile of hessian sacking. What on earth was she holding onto so tightly?

"You took your time," hissed Pat. "I thought you were never coming back."

"Of course you knew I was coming back, silly," responded April with a nervous giggle.

"Who's that with you?" demanded Pat suspiciously.

"She's one of George's neighbours. She's a nurse. There was a bit of an accident at the Wine Sellers and she arrived to help. We couldn't have sorted things out without her."

"Is George okay?" asked Pat.

"He is now," April responded. "His shoulder was dislocated and she shoved it back into its socket quick as a flash. She's amazing."

"What's that in your arms?" interrupted the nurse.

"That's Hope," replied April. "She's our baby sister."

And she smiled encouragingly at Pat. The nurse knelt down beside Pat.

"Can I hold her for a moment?" she asked. "I would really love to."

Pat cautiously handed Hope across to her and then rubbed at her arms. She had been holding Hope in the same position for so long that they felt stiff and aching.

"She's beautiful," said the nurse, gazing tenderly down at Hope. "You've been through so much together, haven't you? I wish I was coming with you to your grandmother's. I could do with starting again. Life has become increasingly intolerable over the past few years. Everything feels unsafe. We neighbours avoid each other in the streets, lowering our heads as we walk so that we don't have to speak or even acknowledge one another. But now the incident at the Wine Sellers has forced us to come together and that can only be a good thing. I couldn't ever leave my husband but I would like a new life. My husband's a good man and the loss of our daughters almost destroyed him. Maybe we'll come and find you later on, when things are more settled."

"I'd like that," said April. "It would be wonderful to think that we had friends."

"I'll wait with you until you feel ready to set off again," said the nurse. "It's a long time since I've held a baby in my arms. It's such a lovely feeling. There are medical supplies in my bag. I think you should have them. You never know when you might need something and I can always get more. The doctors at the hospital often throw out valuable stuff, especially on a Saturday night after a busy week. I hide in the shadows watching them and then I rummage through the bins to see if there's anything I can make use of. They never see me. I've picked up bandages and antiseptic cream and a plastic container with painkillers in it. You'd be surprised what they get rid of. As I said I can always get more and I really would like you to have them."

"That's very kind of you," responded April. "We'd be most grateful."

She slid down to the floor, putting her arms through the sleeves of George's old donkey jacket and pulling it around her body before resting her head between her knees. The familiar smell emanating from it was comforting. She didn't want to talk about what had happened at the Wine Sellers. She didn't even want to think about it. She wanted to gather her thoughts in preparation for the next stage of their journey. She had discovered exactly what she was capable of and she knew that she would have no qualms in defending Hope and Pat in the future if it became necessary. She had made new friends too so at least something positive had come out of the hideous episode. Those two awful men had been sorted and they would certainly never bother George again, if anyone for that matter. Not that the way in which she had handled the situation was something to be proud of but what was done was done and she couldn't change it so it was better to try not to think about it and to put it behind her. She heaved a deep sigh and closed her eyes.

CHAPTER EIGHTEEN

It seemed only moments later that the nurse was tapping April gently on the shoulder. She lifted her head and looked at her through bleary eyes.

"Time to go," said the nurse. "Time to be on your way. The sun will be up in a couple of hours and people will be leaving their homes to get to work. Curfew is almost over."

April shook her head as if to clear it and gave a huge yawn.

"You've been asleep," continued the nurse. "You've been asleep for two hours. I fed Hope and your friend dozed off too. Come on. No hanging around now. You can't leave it any later before you set off. You need to get moving."

April stood up hugging the thick donkey jacket closely to her. She reached out for Hope and secured her neatly around her middle and chest with the shawl and then buttoned up the jacket so that she would be hidden from prying eyes. Pat was ready and waiting. She had slept lightly and the nurse had packed the medical supplies for her. They added very little to the weight of the rucksack and now that Hope had been fed it was lighter anyway and Pat gave an audible sigh of relief as she slung it over her shoulders. The nurse stepped out of the shed and checked that the street was clear before beckoning the girls to follow her. There was a glimmering streak of gold on the horizon which meant that the sun was preparing to put in an appearance and Tim's morning star was defiantly making a last bid for freedom. April grinned as she glanced up at it.

Their new friend strode along beside the girls keeping to the road's edge helping to shelter them from sight as much as possible. The nurse knew April and Pat weren't boys although they were dressed as such and the subject had not been discussed. The less said the better, she thought, particularly under the ruling of The Twelve. She felt protective towards the girls as being with them stirred strong but painful memories of her own daughters. She hadn't been able to help them; she had been unable to do anything to stop them being taken away from her. At the time she had been too afraid to stand up to the authorities and had only half understood what was happening and had been even less aware of what the future held for her daughters. Now she knew. Now she was fully aware of what girls stood for in the society of today and how even their status as human beings had been diminished to such an extent that their only value was as playthings for the use and pleasure of men and ultimately for the production of male children. She shuddered violently. From now on she would try and help any girls that she came into contact with and she sent up a silent prayer that someone somewhere was looking out for her own girls, just as she was for Pat and April.

After walking for almost an hour they reached the borders of the town and a single road, not much wider or better than a dirt track, loomed up ahead of them surrounded on all sides by a stark and bleak landscape.

"I have to go," said the nurse. "I have to get back before people start noticing I'm not around for my everyday business. I don't want to arouse any suspicions. There are still people who don't like to take their troubles to the local hospital and who come to me for help. I need to be available for them. You must follow the road. Follow it as far as the mountain tunnels and then you'll see a narrow pathway going off to the left. Take that and it will lead you around the foot of the mountains. You'd be quicker going through the tunnels but there've been a lot of landslides in recent years and so they're quite dangerous and may even be blocked. Watch out for the wolves too. You don't want them prowling around you. Not that they'll stand much chance against you and that crowbar." The nurse chuckled as she directed this last comment at April. "I don't think you'll come into contact with anyone on the road. It's hardly ever used any more. There's no reason to."

The nurse turned away and began to walk off. She didn't trust herself to hug the girls or to reach out and offer any sort of physical contact. They were so young and vulnerable. Their anxious, little faces as they listened to her directions said it all. She felt almost as if she was betraying them in leaving them to face the unknown without any adults to help them but she had no option. The deserted town streets would soon be full of people scuttling about in the shadows trying to pretend they didn't exist as the less they were noticed the better and she didn't want to be observed either. Life was so different now. She sighed and shrugged her shoulders. It was really not much of a life at all!

April stared after the nurse's broad, comfortable back as she disappeared into the distance. They were on their own again and she couldn't help but feel scared. They had received assistance throughout every step of their journey so far but now, for the first time since they had climbed aboard the warship, they were completely on their own. The road stretched on and on in front of them for as far as the eye could see and in every direction she looked the land appeared barren and uninviting. Behind them the town was waking up and dim, twinkling lights were beginning to flicker before finally reaching a steady glow with the approach of daylight. April felt a yearning, a yearning to go back to the town they had just left. It looked positively welcoming in the cold light of the approaching dawn. The road ahead looked desolate and unwelcoming. She shrugged her shoulders just as the nurse had done, smiled at Pat and started walking. There was nothing else for it. The sooner they arrived at her grandmother's the better.

"Come on, let's keep moving," said April, gripping the crowbar tightly.

Hope stirred momentarily against her chest and April became aware of her warm, gentle breath tickling her shoulder. She could feel the delicate pulsing of Hope's tiny heartbeat and a wave of love swept through her giving her the confidence to carry on. She had two sisters to care for and to watch over and she had no intentions of letting them down.

"Stay close to me, little sister," she said to Pat and was rewarded with an eager, thankful grin as Pat quickened her pace to keep up with her.

"It will be wonderful when we get to my grandmother's house and even better when George arrives, won't it?" April suggested encouragingly.

"I'm looking forward to it," replied Pat. "We're so far away from Avondale House that no one will ever be able to find us. We must be over half way to your grandmother's by now, mustn't we? We've had such a lot of adventures. She'll be surprised to hear about them, won't she?"

Pat was almost fully recovered from her knock on the head and the fever that had come with it but still looked fragile. April knew that she would have to keep a constant eye on her if she didn't want her to fall ill again. She felt a rush of love for Pat too. She never uttered a word of complaint about anything. She just got on with things no matter how tired or unwell she felt. She was a stoic creature and had been through such a lot in her short life. She deserved better.

The sun was soon high in the sky, intent on tormenting them mercilessly, and it felt as if they had been walking for hours. The town lay far behind them and upon turning to glance back at it April saw that it was barely visible and appeared inexplicably as a hazy mirage hovering in the distance. April considered it time to take a break and looked around to see if there was anywhere they could sit and rest. There was a cumbersome looking rock on the left which might possibly provide shade and April pointed towards it and then stepped off the road. Pat followed. The girls had stopped talking some time ago, nodding towards each other in the acknowledgment that it was exhausting both walking and chatting at the same time. Hope had started to feel heavy against April's body and Pat was slowing down under the weight of the rucksack.

The rock lay on its back like a huge boulder that had been angrily hurled down at the side of the road by some enormous giant. There was a slight lip to it and this provided a shallow shelter for the girls to crawl into giving them protection from the harsh glare of the sun. The sun was beating down on the back of the rock and it wouldn't be long before it reached the front but for now the overhang offered a welcome respite. Hope was awake and grizzling. She was hungry. Pat opened the rucksack and rummaged around. George had somehow managed to procure and fill a baby's plastic bottle with milk and this was much easier than persuading Hope to suck through a straw especially when she had just awoken. She gurgled happily as April eased the teat of the bottle into her mouth and she felt the first mouthful of lukewarm milk squirt down the back of her throat.

"Sandwiches," commented Pat. "George packed sandwiches for us. I didn't know he'd done that. How did he know that we were going to be leaving?"

"He must have wanted to be prepared, just in case," answered April. "He may have felt the time was coming. What's in them?"

"Bacon," responded Pat in surprise and delight as she bit into one. She passed a sandwich over to April. A sandwich filled with crunchy bacon was more than welcome and gave great pleasure for the girls knew that George had been thinking about what they liked and not just about their needs. Chewing on the salty bacon reminded them of him and made it feel as if he wasn't so very far away after all.

"We can't go on in this heat," said April. "We'll have to wait until the sun has gone down a bit. It feels hot enough to be desert heat. It felt quite cool in the town, didn't it, but the further away we get the hotter it becomes? I'm sweltering under the weight of the donkey jacket and with Hope slung around my chest. She looks quite sweaty too. Even the milk is warm, isn't it? And you must be exhausted carrying that rucksack. Let's see what else is in it. Maybe there's something we can leave behind."

"We can leave the rubbish, that's for sure," suggested Pat.

"I don't think that's a good idea," said April. "If those wolves that the nurse was talking about find it they'll be able to track us. We don't want any wolves on our trail, do we?"

Pat shook her head as she tipped the contents of the rucksack onto the rocky earth below. George had included a couple of bars of chocolate as a treat and there were two enormous bottles of water! Now Pat knew why the rucksack was so heavy. It hadn't felt heavy to begin with but the longer they walked the more cumbersome it had become. The bottles must weigh more than Hope did. George had packed a corner of fleecy blanket which they could fold up and use as a pillow and then there were the medical supplies that the nurse had given them, just a few basics, but they would be ideal in an emergency. There was plenty of milk for Hope too, small packets of it, the contents of which could easily be squeezed into the bottle when it was empty and then there were some square pieces of cloth that could be used as nappies and a few plastic bags to contain the rubbish. Sealed in plastic bags the stench of the rubbish, primarily Hope's, would be considerably less pungent. There was even a discreet stash of tobacco which they could use to barter with if necessary. Somehow George had thought of everything.

"I think we should eat the chocolate before it melts," said Pat.

"Good idea," replied April. "Unwrap a bar for me please while I feed Hope."

Pat did so, breaking off a piece so that she could pop it into April's mouth. The girls smiled at each other happily.

"We're definitely on our way again," commented April. "How are you feeling?"

"I'm tired but I'm fine too," replied Pat. "I don't know if I can keep moving for long periods of time but I think I'll be okay if we have lots of short breaks."

"That's what we'll do then," said April. "I feel the same and there's no rush at the moment. We've got enough food and supplies to be going on with. And we have my trusty friend the crowbar with us in case we encounter any problems."

Pat finished her chocolate, took a gulp of water and lay down, placing her head upon the corner of the fleecy blanket. It seemed as if all they did was either travel or rest. April placed Hope next to her. She had no fear of wild animals here in this barren wilderness but the sun would be coming round very soon and then they would be without shelter. She needed to improvise. She picked up the donkey jacket and slipped its hood over the hook of the crowbar before wedging it at an angle between the lip of the rock and the earth below. That was a start. Then she picked up two large stones, securing the free ends of the jacket and spreading the sides out like the triangular sail of a yacht. The sun's rays definitely wouldn't be able to penetrate through such a heavy curtain and they would be able to rest in comfort. Shelter sorted!

CHAPTER NINETEEN

The whole day passed and the sun was beginning to set before any of them came round and they were surprised that they had fallen asleep so quickly and for so long. The air felt still and balmy, perfect for travelling. April had sat at the edge of the shelter keeping watch and staring out into nothingness until finally her head dropped to her chest and she had slumped against the rock where she drifted into the realms of oblivion. Her sleep had been filled with happy dreams; dreams of her grandmother waiting at the gate for their arrival because she knew they were coming. And there were hot scones and butter to tuck into as soon as they stepped inside the house. April remembered her grandmother's culinary skills from her visit all those years ago. On the very first day she entered the house she had rolled up her sleeves, taken over her mother's kitchen and baked scones for the entire family. It had been a simple matter of mixing a few basic ingredients together in a bowl, plopping them from a large spoon into small creamy heaps on greased trays and then loading them into a hot oven. April had stared in wonder as her grandmother did so. The dollops of mixture had risen quickly and the aroma that filled the room as she waited for the oven door to be opened left her eyes and mouth watering in anticipation. That first bite of hot scone came directly from heaven as the skim of spread throughout the middle of it melted and ran dripping down April's chin. Happiness was being able to use her forefinger to scoop it back into her mouth. That had been a peaceful and surprisingly pleasant evening. Even her father had enjoyed the scones and had asked for the recipe so that his wife could bake such morsels of delight in the future. Of course April's mother was never able to replicate that first heavenly scone experience no matter how hard she tried but they remained something of a treat to be looked forward to and then eagerly devoured whenever there was a little sugar and flour left over at the end of the week.

April smiled as she yawned and stretched. Perhaps her grandmother would bake a batch of scones to celebrate their arrival. That would be something. She was certain that everything would be wonderful as soon as they found her.

"We need to be on our way again," she said as she noticed Pat staring at her curiously.

"Can we have some water first? I don't want to carry so much in the rucksack. It's heavy."

April nodded and they took large gulps from one of the bottles before packing it away.

The donkey jacket and crowbar curtain needed to be dismantled and Hope had to be secured in the shawl once more. April rolled away the stones and shook out the jacket. As was often the case Hope was still deeply asleep and barely moved as she wrapped and tied her around her middle. Pat had everything packed in a couple of minutes and then they were ready to go.

"I didn't see you make that curtain with your jacket," said Pat.

"You were fast asleep, decidedly out for the count," replied April. "I had to do something. We'd have been burnt to cinders if the sun had been able to get in at us. Luckily dusk is falling now. We have to walk as far as possible before we end up in total darkness. Did George pack a torch?"

Pat nodded. "Yes, I spotted a couple of headlamp things in one of the rucksack pockets and some spare batteries. I think he's taken every precaution and made sure we have everything we need. I wish he was with us though. I'd feel a lot safer."

"Yes, me too," agreed April. "Come on, let's get back on the road and try not to think about it. We've got a long way to go before we get to the tunnels. George will join us as soon as he can, I'm sure of it."

She gazed up at the sky. It was going to be another clear night. The stars hadn't yet put in an appearance but were on the verge of doing so. She then scanned the area quickly for any other life forms but could see none. That was a relief. The thought of wolves roaming freely in the vicinity was neither a welcome nor an encouraging one. She gripped the crowbar tighter than ever, gave the shelter a last cursory glance to make sure that no trace of them would be left behind and stepped out. It was still warm but April knew that as soon as the sun disappeared it would become cold very quickly. She was glad she had the donkey jacket with her, no matter how cumbersome. Pat was wearing multiple layers of clothing and had taken off a couple of items and managed to stuff them into the rucksack to be worn later when the temperature plummeted.

It was quiet on the road, with no traffic whatsoever, which was as April expected. If the tunnels ahead were blocked by landslides then there was nowhere for people to go or to get to or even to come back from. Driving along the road would be pointless particularly as the scenery left much to be desired. She wondered briefly if anyone ever left the town. Perhaps they knew of a different route such as the one Tim had used on their way in? Or perhaps they remained where they were, being too afraid to travel far from their homes or to go against the authorities in any way? In any event a quiet road was a positive sign for their journey as it meant that no one was coming after them or attempting to track them. As April stared ahead into the distance she could see no sign of rocky hills or mountains with tunnels going through them which meant that there was still a huge amount of walking to be done. She sighed. Despite the fact that they were most likely to be the only travellers on the road she felt vulnerable. It was the sheer openness of everything and the fact that they could see clearly around them in every direction. On a positive note this gave them an advantage as they could see if anything or anyone was coming but it also meant that they were easy prey for watchful, lurking predators. She would be glad when the stars appeared and they could slip like shadows silently through the night.

It wasn't long before the last rays of the sun faded into insignificance and April agreed they should stop for a moment to allow Pat to rummage about for the headlamps. They were makeshift contraptions, obviously put together at the last minute by George, and they fitted around their heads with strips of elastic so that each lamp sat squarely in the middle of their foreheads. Nothing more than a dim glow emanated from these creations giving just enough light for the girls to see a few feet in front of them. April and Pat laughed at each other as they shook their heads up and down and from side to side making the beams dance and spin in zig-zagging spits and spats upon the road. The stars were now popping into sight and April raised her head to look at them, searching for the morning star. Of course it was there, shining bright and twinkling, twinkling, twinkling! It confirmed that once more they were heading in the right direction and the thought that the star was still guiding them was comforting indeed.

All too soon though, Pat insisted that she needed to rest. She had walked for as long as she could but was becoming breathless and was at the point where her knees and legs felt as if they were going to give way beneath her. April had been aware of Pat's laboured breathing for a while but could see nowhere for them to take shelter. There was nothing for it but to sit down in the middle of the road. It was time for Hope to be fed anyway.

"We'll rest here until you've got your breath back," said April, "but we can't stay here for long. We're sitting ducks if we do. We have to cover as much ground as possible at night and sleep during the day. We need to find somewhere where we're not quite so visible if possible. Drink some water and I'll sort out Hope."

Pat nodded but didn't speak. She didn't want to tell April that her chest was hurting. She gulped down some water and focused on her breathing, concentrating on slowing down her heart beat so that she felt ready for the next stint of walking. April was patting Hope on the back waiting for the inevitable belch that came after feeding. She was such an easy baby to deal with. They had been so lucky to find her on the warship. Her gurgling noises and contented smiles brought such pleasure. April never ceased to be amazed that they had actually been brave enough to rescue such a tiny, baby girl but it was obviously meant to be or they would never have found her amongst all those baby boys. She could feel Hope's tiny fists balling and her arms flailing as the belch rose up from the depths of her stomach and made its way out with a nose-pinching rumble of sound.

"She feels better now," said April, turning to Pat. "Look at her happy little face. She'll be asleep again soon."

Pat nodded again and rested her head lovingly against April's shoulder. April was the perfect sister. She knew everything and she knew what to do in every situation. The three of them made a strong family unit. It would have been better if George had been with them of course but Pat felt confident that he would find and join them as soon as he could. She closed her eyes, feeling calm and secure. April frowned, contemplating how far they might yet have to travel, and flicked off the headlamps. There was no point in wasting the batteries. They could barely be seen now that there was no longer any sunlight. Huddled together closely in the middle of the road they took on the semblance of a large rock that had somehow become displaced from its group and managed to tumble and bounce along before finally coming to a halt; an odd sight indeed but not unusual enough to merit investigation. April stared into the velvety darkness ahead of her and listened. Not a sound! The wolves wouldn't roam around an exposed area anyway, or so she hoped. They were far more likely to be prowling amongst the mountains harbouring the tunnels.

Time to get up once more! Pat's breath sounded soft and peaceful and April didn't want her to fall into a deep sleep. A short nap was enough. She shook her and Pat opened her eyes wide with a start.
"Where am I?" she asked.
April flicked the headlamps back on and helped her up.
"In the middle of the road," she reminded her.
Pat put her hands to her throat and stroked it with her fingers. Her throat hurt. She didn't feel too well but she wasn't prepared to admit that to April. After the long days of rest she had taken back at the Wine Sellers she ought to be fighting fit and raring to go. Her head ached too. She wasn't going to be the one to hold them back on their journey though. If April thought it was best for them to get moving again then that was what they must do. She stood up beside April and said nothing. At least it was cool at night time; much better than travelling in the heat of day. Pat could sense she was sweating and it wasn't a normal type of sweat, rather the feverish type. She hoped it wouldn't develop and that they wouldn't have to walk for too long before April found another shelter where they could rest and sleep for considerably longer. At least the rucksack was lighter now so that was a bonus. They had finished off one of the large bottles of water and Hope had drunk a whole packet of milk and as they travelled the rucksack would get lighter still. Pat gave a quiet sigh. Things were getting better despite the fact that she was feeling unwell.

The final hours of the day enveloped them as they walked, much like a comfortable, old blanket. Their footprints made very little impression upon the harshness of the pitted and stony road beneath them and they trudged on, on and on. April habitually gazed at the Morning Star to reassure herself that it was still there until eventually she looked for it and it was gone and there was the hint of a shimmering sun on the horizon. Somehow they had managed to walk all night and it was almost dawn. They had simply continued walking, without talking and without thinking. They had done it. April contemplated the surrounding landscape. She thought she could see a clump of trees not far away on the left and the distinct outline of rocky hills or mountains ahead of them. That was a surprise. Perhaps they were coming to the end of the road. They must have walked for miles. The light from the headlamps was almost non-existent and April knew that the batteries would soon be spent. They needed to get off the road before the sun came up and head towards the clump of trees. They needed to do that now. She glanced at Pat but it was difficult to see how she was faring. Her head and shoulders were bent forward under the weight of the rucksack but she was still walking, somehow managing to place one small, weary foot in front of the other in an effort to keep going. April stepped off the road. Pat followed her but made no acknowledgement of what she had done. April was tired, so tired that she just wanted to sit down right there and then on the side of the road as they had done earlier but she knew they couldn't. Sitting ducks, she recollected. But they would be even more obvious sitting ducks this time if they sat out in the open with the sun coming up. Exactly what they didn't want to be! She could feel the heat of the sun's eager, tendril-like rays creeping towards them. She could feel them on her face, the only part of her body along with her hands that was exposed to the approaching daylight. She took a deep breath. If she felt tired then Pat must be completely exhausted. They were almost at the trees. She thought the ground felt slightly damp beneath her feet, or maybe she was imagining it? That was strange. Not soggy, just a little damp. The damp was welcoming though as it meant that perhaps their next shelter would be cool and protective. There was grass here too and that meant water. But it also meant the probability of predators. April surmised that they wouldn't be the only ones drawn to the shelter and shade of the trees.

"We're here," she said at last, standing still and looking around.

She had stopped beside the trunk of a particularly leafy tree, one with branches that spread out like the spokes of an umbrella, in perfect symmetry.

"We'll stay cool here," she continued, "and it will also be a good place to rest."

She didn't add that others might have the same idea. Looking at Pat though, she could see her peering around suspiciously and thinking the same thing.

"There's water close by," said Pat. "I can't see it but I know it's there. I guess we'll have to take turns in keeping watch. You've still got your crowbar, haven't you?"

It was a rhetorical question but April raised her arm and held the crowbar high in the air in a gesture of defiance and triumph. Pat grinned and sat down, sliding the rucksack from her shoulders as she did so.

"Dibs on sleeping first," she said, retrieving the last bottle of water and unscrewing the cap. "So thirsty. Don't know how we made it this far in one go."

And it was a statement rather than a moan before she lifted the bottle to her lips and took a great gulp. She passed it to April along with a packet of milk and gently laid her head down upon the rucksack using it as a pillow. It still contained several packets of Hope's milk and two woollen tops that she hadn't yet worn and felt quite comfortable.

"It's warm here but it feels cool at the same time. I like it," she commented.

And so April took the first watch. Her body was exhausted but her mind was active. She had been thinking all night as they walked; thinking about the wolves and about their inevitability as they approached the tunnels. They had been lucky so far as there had been neither sight nor sound of them. But this wasn't going to last forever. She was worried but would never have admitted that to Pat. She rested her back against the trunk of the tree and watched as the sun began to rise in the sky. Pat had fallen asleep almost instantly and now Hope was waking. April squeezed the contents of a packet of milk into the bottle and popped it into Hope's mouth. She was aware of Hope's immediate satisfaction and gurgles of appreciation! The donkey jacket was still securely fastened around her body and so she unbuttoned it and allowed the fresh air to gently whisper and meander its way in. She took a few heartfelt, deep breaths and fixed her sight on the bleak and barren, surrounding landscape. They had found their own green, heavenly oasis in the midst of it all. She too was surprised that they had managed to walk throughout the night with only one brief, recovery break. They were obviously stronger than they realised. She decided that once more she would stay awake for as long as she could so that Pat would only have to keep watch for a short period of time. She stared and stared out into the distance but it became increasingly difficult to keep her eyes open. As before they insisted on closing and once she almost drifted off and then somehow managed to shake herself awake so that she could stare ahead for a little longer. Inevitably though her chin dropped and her eyelids became heavier and heavier until finally she could no longer resist the strong pull of slumber and she floated off into a world of dreams which were filled again with images of her grandmother and of baking and hot scones and happiness.

CHAPTER TWENTY

April awoke with a start feeling as if she had never been asleep. Something was wrong. She turned towards Pat. Pat was sitting bolt upright and had grabbed hold of her arm, gripping it tightly. It was this that had jolted April from her dreams. She could sense Pat's fear. She gave a sniff. There was something in the air; a strange smell. It was a smell of something vaguely familiar. What was it? Then she recognised it. It was the smell of fresh, raw meat - but that was impossible. Raw meat was just a distant memory. The only meat they had come into contact with recently had been bacon and that had always been well cooked. What on earth was it? Then she heard something. She heard growls; low, snickering sounds that came and went in sharp bursts intermingled with high-pitched yelps and squeals. Along with these fearful sounds she could hear ripping and tearing - but the ripping and tearing of what?

"The wolves are here," whispered Pat, gripping her arm even more tightly. "The wolves are eating. They've killed something and they're eating it."

"Let go of my arm," hissed April. "You're hurting me. At least if they're eating they're not going to be interested in us, are they? I should think we'll be the last thing on their minds."

They were responses that she didn't really expect Pat to answer. She was automatically delivering words to reassure them both. But even as she uttered them April felt terrified. The wolves were obviously devouring a meal of succulent, hot flesh. She had hoped that their appearance could have been avoided until they at least reached the tunnels but obviously not. She felt Pat relax the grip on her arm as she stared at her.

"So what shall we do?" she asked, trembling.

"Nothing," replied April. "They haven't noticed us, have they? Hold on to Hope so that I can be ready with the crowbar though, just in case."

She began to carefully and quietly unravel the shawl that secured Hope, unwilling to disturb the baby girl and not wanting to attract the attention of the wolves who were feeding voraciously. Hope gave a large yawn and an appreciative sigh of contentment. Pat couldn't help but smile as she cradled her. Hope was blissfully oblivious to everything that was going on around her. April reached across and picked up the crowbar.

"If we're lucky they'll finish feeding and wander away," she whispered.

"Or they might fall asleep," responded Pat. "What shall we do then?"

"Let's wait and see," said April. "There's no need to panic."

But of course there was a need to panic she thought, as she took a deep breath. She had only a crowbar with which to defend the three of them against a possible pack of slavering, predatory wolves. She had no idea how many wolves were out there, how many were eating or how many remained prowling and hungry. Although it was daylight and April knew the wolves were close by she couldn't see any of them. The girls had taken shelter under a particularly leafy tree and from the sounds reaching them the wolves were gorging on their prey a little further away somewhere. Maybe they were close to water? Maybe the heat of the day didn't bother the wolves? They obviously hadn't seen or scented the girls and she was sure that Hope's baby smell, if it wafted their way, would be particularly delicious and alluring. The wolves must have caught their prey and dragged it out of the heat of the sun and now, having torn into it, their senses were completely consumed by the pungent smell of the ripe, bloody flesh. The mild aroma that wafted gently towards them from two girls and a baby could never compare with the satisfaction of having caught and killed such a succulent treat, whatever it was. In fact if she and Pat could smell the fresh meat then maybe the wind was drifting in their direction and the wolves couldn't be aware of them at all. April tried to convince herself of this and to feel positive about the situation. They were concealed in the shadows under the tree and so any predatory wolves, unless they were searching for extra food, might not even see them. April relaxed her grip on the crowbar slightly. They were safe for the moment.

Suddenly, in front of her, a lone, prowling wolf appeared, as if from nowhere. April instantly stiffened and stared straight at it. The wolf returned her stare and curled its upper lip back into a quiet but menacing snarl. April didn't move, aware of Pat's body tense and rigid next to hers. She continued to stare fixedly at the wolf. A mixture of blood and saliva dripped and dribbled from its yellow fangs onto the damp earth below and its chest was stained red where it had zealously attacked its prey. The wolf flicked a long tongue slowly around its upper lip relishing the lingering taste of what it had recently swallowed and then purposely turned away as if deciding that the small group under the tree wasn't worth bothering with. It had let them know that it was aware of their presence but currently had no need for food. It was not going to attack purely for the sake of it. Its belly was full and that was enough. For some obscure reason it felt as if the wolf was giving April and Pat time to decide what they should do next and simultaneously showing that it was totally in control.

April could feel her heart pounding rapidly within her chest and her breathing had become shallow and raspy. She laid a hand against her collar bone and drew in a few deep breaths in an attempt to calm down.

"What shall we do?" whispered Pat, looking down at Hope who was still snoozing peacefully.

"We'll wait until we're sure they've finished eating and we can't hear anything and then we'll make a move. The tunnels can't be far away now and I've calculated that we should reach them in about an hour if we walk quickly. We've both had a rest so we should have enough energy to get there. You slept a long time and I dozed off too even though I was supposed to be on the lookout. If I'd managed to stay awake we might not be in this predicament."

"You can't blame yourself," responded Pat in hushed tones. "If we'd known about the wolves earlier and made our escape then some of them might have come after us instead of attacking whatever poor creature they've obviously mauled to death. It doesn't even bear thinking about. At least now they've eaten they might not be so much on their guard and we have more of a chance of getting away."

"You're right," agreed April. "But I'm not letting go of the crowbar, just in case."

And she forced herself to smile, a grim endeavour which didn't quite reach her eyes.

The girls sat huddled together feeling very uneasy. It sounded as if the wolves were now snacking on the final remains of their meal as their growls had become much less frequent, and once or twice there were yelps and barks as if scuffles and tussles were occurring amongst them. Gradually the sounds faded away though and there was silence. As the girls waited the short passage of time seemed interminable and despite April concentrating on her breathing she knew she was becoming more and more anxious as she tried to focus on the right moment for them to get up and leave. Eventually she inhaled deeply.

"Pass Hope to me so that I can get her sorted," she whispered. Pat did so and April took care not to awaken the baby girl as she secured her once more in the shawl. She stood up carefully and put her arms through the sleeves of the donkey jacket, making sure that at no point did she let go of the crowbar.

"It's not so hot now," she continued. "It must be late afternoon. We'll make our way quietly to the road and from there we'll walk as fast as we can to the tunnels. How does the rucksack feel? Let's have some water before we set off because once we start we're not going to stop until we're on the track taking us around the mountain. At least then we'll know that the wolves are behind us and we won't be taken by surprise unless of course there are more wolves out there. But we won't think about that. That's just another unnecessary worry. I want you to walk beside me and not behind me. I want you in my sight at all times. The wolves have become so quiet that they must be asleep."

Pat gulped down some water and wiped her mouth with the back of her hand before handing the bottle to April. Her eyes were wide with fright and her legs, as she clambered to her feet, felt as if they were about to give way beneath her. She hoped April wouldn't notice her trembling hands. The rucksack was thankfully very light indeed and she watched as April polished off the last drops of water. She packed the empty bottle away knowing that at some point they would need to refill it. Although the earth around the tree and the surrounding area had been damp beneath their feet they hadn't seen any evidence of water anywhere. This was possibly a good thing because that must be where the wolves had settled. They would have made their way straight towards water with their prey. Perhaps they had been there all along, had made their kill and then dragged it back with them? The two girls looked steadily at one another and without feeling the need to say anything further began to walk. Their main objective was to get back onto the road and to get as far away as possible from the wolves. Pat lowered her eyes staring down at the earth below. She didn't want to know if the wolves were coming after them. She didn't want to see any. That would be even worse than knowing where they were. The terrifying sight of one of them had been more than enough. She tried to pretend that everything was just as it had been earlier and that there were no wolves around. She focused all her energy into transferring one foot in front of the other and in keeping up with April.

April had a look of fierce determination on her face. That lone wolf had let them go for some reason and she hoped it wasn't part of a game. She hoped that it had perceived them as unworthy fodder and therefore not worth the bother of tracking or hunting. She didn't relish the thought that they could be the next edible prey and that the wolves might be after them as soon as they had rested and their bellies no longer felt so full. Well, she would make sure she was ready for them and she wouldn't go down without a fight. She knew what she was capable of after the recent episode at the Wine Sellers and although this was a side of her that she didn't feel particularly comfortable with she was prepared to protect Pat and Hope until death if necessary. It would obviously be better if it didn't come to that but she knew that she needed to keep her wits about her and to listen hard for the padding of any eager paws in pursuit.

Fortunately they heard no sounds at all other than the tenuous pit patter of their own hurrying feet and the girls reached the edge of the road safely. April let out a heartfelt sigh of relief. The stillness around them was absolute and they quickened their pace, scurrying hastily towards the dark tunnels looming eerily in front of them in the midst of the mountainous slopes. The sun was starting to go down and they needed to find the next part of the track before it became too dark to see anything. There were a couple of extra batteries for the headlamps but they wouldn't last long. Maybe they would be able to see by moon or starlight.

"Move as fast as you can," said April. "Keep up with me."

Pat gasped. She couldn't walk much faster. She felt more optimistic now that they had reached the road but their situation was still a precarious one. Their journey to the tunnels had become filled with a sense of urgency. They were out in the open on the road but somehow it felt safer. It would be easier for the wolves to spot them but hopefully they had achieved some distance between themselves and their predators and it would take a while for the wolves to catch up.

The yawning, black holes of the tunnels were growing larger and larger as they walked and suddenly, before they knew it, they were standing directly in front of one.

"We've made it!" said April, staring upwards, and with a degree of surprise in her voice. "Now let's head for the track!"

But neither of them moved. Pat was panting noisily as she tried to get her breath back and April could feel Hope beginning to squirm beneath the thick, donkey jacket.

"Can we just stop for a moment?" asked Pat. "I need to get my head around the fact that we're finally here and away from those wolves. I feel overwhelmed."

"I feel the same," responded April. "Can I pass Hope to you again while I hunt for a track that leads around the side of the tunnel here? I'm not quite sure what our next plan of action should be."

"What do you mean?" asked Pat. "I thought we'd already decided to follow the track?"

"Well, we might need to take a short break and stop for more than a moment while I think. The appearance of that wolf has quite unnerved me and I haven't thought everything through yet."

Pat settled herself on a rock at the side of the tunnel and cradled Hope.

"She's very beautiful, isn't she?" she murmured distractedly as Hope beamed at her making happy, gurgling noises. But April had gone. She was clambering over a pile of stubborn, craggy rocks and boulders. Pat sighed. She would let April get on with it. She always knew what she was doing and what was best for them. She stroked Hope's cheek with her little finger and was rewarded with a contented smile. Even if their journey ended here it would have been worth it. It would have been worth it for the adventures they had had and because they had found baby Hope. Right now everything felt beautiful and as it should be and she was filled with a sense of satisfaction knowing that they had finally arrived at the tunnels. Pat began to sing softly to Hope. There was nothing to worry about. They had come this far and once they were on the other side of the mountain they would be very close to April's grandmother's house. They would be there in no time. They were on the final lap of their journey and they had made good friends along the way and best of all they were still together.

Soon Pat could hear April making her way back. She was aware of her feet slipping and sliding amongst the rocks and the dislodging and tumbling of small stones as she approached. She could hear short, sharp cries of pain coming from April as she grazed her hands and once she heard an attempt to muffle a yell as she lost her balance and skinned her ankle.

"We've got to go now," she hissed as soon as she was close enough to Pat not to have to shout. "We can't go around the mountain. We've got to try and hide in the tunnels."

"Why? What's wrong?" Pat asked, with a tremor in her voice. Her moment of serenity had passed and she was ready to burst into tears.

"I found the track but there are wolves on it and they're heading this way. And these seem to be hungry wolves. They look very thin and they're constantly snickering and snapping at each other. We've got to hide. I think they're aggressive and I don't want them to pick up on our scent. They're very close. Come on. Pass Hope over and grab the rucksack. There's no time to lose. Get the headlamps out and put the spare batteries in. We need to be able to see where we're going in the tunnels."

Pat handed Hope across and fumbled around in the rucksack until she had located the headlamps. Her fingers were shaking so much that she couldn't insert the batteries. A small sob escaped her and she knew that her cheeks were wet with tears.

"Get a grip," hissed April. "This is no time to fall apart. In fact, you'd better take Hope as well as the rucksack in case I need to use the crowbar to defend us."

She grabbed the headlamps from her and inserted the batteries. Then she secured one of them around Pat's head before sorting out her own.

"I have an idea," she said. "The rucksack is almost empty. I'm going to put Hope in it with her head and shoulders out so that she can breathe. Then you'll have your hands completely free to help you as you climb and you won't fall on top of her if you slip, unless you fall backwards of course."

Pat simply nodded and watched as April tucked Hope securely into the rucksack. She looked like a tiny doll staring about her with a puzzled look on her face. This was a new position for travelling and she was intrigued enough not to make a fuss. She could see everything from the rucksack; it was a whole new world. Pat stood mutely with her arms outstretched whilst April fed the straps through and across her shoulders immediately becoming aware of the weight and warmth of Hope in the small of her back. Somehow April had managed to keep hold of the crowbar as she sorted everything. Pat knew that the situation was serious.

"You need to go ahead of me," whispered April. "You have brilliant eyesight and I need to take up the rear and keep an ear out for those wolves."

Pat stared at the yawning entrance of the tunnel rising up in front of her. She could see very little and could feel only a heavy gloominess from it. The thought of leading the way in or through or wherever it was they were going was daunting. And who was to say that the wolves wouldn't sniff them out and follow them? She took a deep breath, adjusted Hope across her back and walked forward. She walked without thinking; she walked almost without looking. And then she continued to walk - and walk.

The Inside of the tunnel was eerily silent and brimming with blackness. The dim glow from their headlamps made very little difference to what they could see as they were surrounded by high walls of craggy, grey rock on all sides. The walls stretched up and up and over their heads but even enclosed within the darkness of the tunnel they were aware that they were prime targets for the wolves for there was nowhere to hide. Pat began to walk as fast as she could into the voluminous folds of obscurity. The rucksack weighed very little even with baby Hope tucked inside it and Pat was filled with an adrenalin fuelled energy that she didn't know she possessed. She shook her head as if to clear it of doubt and started to take longer strides. The road beneath her feet was smooth and easy to manoeuvre. She could hear the comforting sound of April marching behind her but decided not to turn round. She didn't want to throw any flickering lights around the tunnel. She didn't want to do anything that would act as an open invitation to the approaching wolves. They had managed to escape unnoticed from one pack of wolves but now they were fleeing from another. When would it ever end? And where were they going? She didn't know how far ahead of them the landslide was but what would they do then? It didn't even bear thinking about. They couldn't walk through a landslide. That would be impossible. Her breathing was becoming more and more erratic and she was experiencing flickers of panic. She didn't know which was worse - the landslide ahead of them or the pack of wolves behind them. Perhaps there would be a small gap in the rock or a hole somewhere that they could climb through or hide in?

"I can hear them," whispered April urgently. "They've detected us and they're at the tunnel entrance. Run. Run now. We need to run."

And she pushed Pat from behind. Pat almost lost her balance before breaking into a faltering sprint as she sensed April catch up with her and run alongside her. Her heart felt as if it had moved from her chest up into her throat and it was beating wildly. She couldn't breathe properly. She couldn't catch her breath. Sensations of nausea were threatening to overwhelm her. The wolves were going to get them. This was crazy. They were running towards a landslide and what would they do then? Perhaps they should just stop and allow themselves to be caught? Perhaps that would be the simplest solution? But she kept going, her mind plagued with wild, tormented images. She kept running. Hope was making small noises of surprise and discontent. She was being jostled about in the rucksack and wasn't sure whether or not she liked it.

"This way," hissed April suddenly. She had seen a dim light over on the left. She grabbed Pat and pulled her along with her and then, quite suddenly, they were standing in front of a sheer wall of rock and there was nowhere to go. There was nowhere to hide and nowhere to run.

"Oh no!" April cried. "Oh no!"

Pat however was scanning the face of the rock in front of her. She could see the dim light that April had seen but it was high above them. She reached out with her hands and began to feel her way along the rock wall.

"We can climb here," she said. "It's quite steep but I think we can do it. The wall doesn't go straight up; it just looks as if it does. We'll go as high as we can and then we'll turn the headlamps off. The wolves won't be able to see us in the dark, will they, unless they have super x-ray eyes? They'll be able to smell us but they won't know where we are. I'm sure we'll be able to find somewhere to hide and if we're high enough and they try to follow us you can whack them with the crowbar, can't you? Come on, follow me."

For the first time in her life Pat knew exactly what to do. She was responsible for Hope and, at this moment, for April too. She began to climb, gripping hold of jagged edges of jutting rock with her hands and using her legs and feet to move onwards and upwards. She found she was able to scale the rocky incline with the surefooted adeptness of a mountain goat and the higher she climbed the more courageous she felt. April followed her, slowly and cautiously, not so confidently, and holding the crowbar tightly in her hand. Little by little they found they were ascending the rock face.

After the first few metres the incline became much easier to navigate as there were more obvious foot and handholds embedded in the rock surface and they were closer together so the rock face didn't appear quite so sheer. The wolves were practically upon them now. Pat could almost taste the hot stench of their putrid breath as it wafted upwards. The wolves were prowling and circling below, sniffing and growling, and a couple of them were even leaping into the air and then falling back against one another, snapping and biting with frustration and fury as they did so.

"We're almost at the light," said Pat, turning to look down at April. "I think it's a hole. I hope it's big enough for us to crawl through."

"Just climb," called April. "There's no time to talk. I feel as if the wolves are about to feed on my heels and it won't be long before they discover a way to get up here."

Pat did as she was told and very soon she had reached the shaft of light which April had noticed so far above them. It was the entrance to a hole just as she had predicted. She hoped it didn't simply drop into nothingness on the other side and that she wasn't going to climb through and then suddenly topple to her death. But there was light coming from the hole so it had to lead somewhere. It was a very small hole though. It would be impossible to negotiate it with Hope sticking up from her back. She carefully removed the rucksack, holding onto it with two hands and balancing precariously with the tips of her toes wedged into two small crevices. Staring into the hole she could see that it went back for quite a way. Perhaps it was some sort of hiding place and didn't lead anywhere? Perhaps they would be able to fend off the wolves from inside until they got fed up and went away? Or perhaps the wolves would never be able to reach them anyway? Whatever the hole was they had to explore it because at the moment that was the only option available to them. There was no other light to be seen anywhere inside the tunnel.

Pat pushed the rucksack ahead of her into the hole as far as she could, making sure that she was still holding onto one of the straps. Then she heaved herself up, supported by her arms, and began to crawl in after it. As she crawled she knocked her head against the roof and was forced to lie on her stomach and inch her way along. She dreaded to think how April would fare behind her as the space within the hole was only just big enough for a small body to squeeze through. She didn't want to look around in case she bumped herself again. She seemed to be continually suffering with head injuries lately. It was wet in the hole too. There was water trickling down from somewhere and it was most unpleasant. The cold drops splashed periodically onto her nose and into her eyes and she blinked rapidly trying to see where she was going. Moments later she heard a fizzing noise and a pop and the light from her headlamp expired. Water must have got into the battery compartment. Now she really had to concentrate on her surroundings. She could hear panting noises behind her and knew that April was following her. Every now and again there was a disgruntled squeal from Hope as water splashed onto her face. Pat continued to push the rucksack ahead of her. The space was becoming tighter and tighter. She didn't know how much further she would be able to go. She paused for a moment to get her breath and to allow her eyes to adjust to the remaining light.

Behind her April kicked out ferociously at the snapping jaws of the wolves. She had never thought that wolves could jump so high. But, strangely, that's all they were doing. They weren't attempting to climb the rock face but just hurling themselves as high and as far as they could into the air. She managed to dislodge a couple of stones with the crowbar, picking them up and throwing them down as hard as she could. She heard a few angry yelps but she had no time to focus on what was happening below. It was imperative that she keep moving upwards. Suddenly the air was filled with howls of pain and growls of frustration. The wolves had stopped jumping. Something had distracted them and their attention was diverted elsewhere. April cautiously turned her head and looked down. It appeared that other wolves had arrived and joined in the fray. April stared as hard as she could. It was difficult to see in the gloom but she could tell that they weren't friendly wolves and it looked as if they were from another pack. The new wolves were thickset and heavy-looking with a silvery edge to their fur. They appeared a lot stronger and healthier than the snarling, snickering wolves they were attacking. April was surprised. She hadn't heard of wolves attacking one another before. She had always assumed that they kept within the boundaries of their own territories, choosing not to interfere with other packs. She turned her head back to the rock face and as she did so she caught a glimpse of a solitary wolf waiting in the shadows. There was something familiar about that wolf. In fact, she knew that wolf. She recognised it almost instantly. It was the same wolf that had stood and snarled at them with slavering, bloody jaws earlier on and then had studiously turned and walked away. She stared at the wolf and as she did so she realised that its yellowy, amber eyes were staring right back at her. Their eyes locked for a moment and then the wolf drew its fangs back into a fearful grimace before it launched itself into the midst of the fray. April felt a surge of exhilaration rush through her as she continued to climb and climb and climb. Was the wolf protecting them because that was how it appeared? It obviously had no desire to seek them out as prey and she could only assume from its behaviour that it was the leader of its pack. She shouldered her way into the hole after Pat. A wave of relief washed over her. She knew they'd have no problem with the wolves now. She would have to tell Pat what she had seen as soon as she could.

Pat was wriggling along entirely on her stomach now with her elbows pulled in and her legs drawn tightly together, trying to make herself as long and as thin as possible. She pushed the rucksack a little further ahead and then, quite unexpectedly, something snapped and it was gone. But she was still holding onto it? Or at least she thought she was. But there was no weight to it? Where was it? Where was the rucksack? What had happened to Hope? There was no sound, nothing! It almost felt as if the strap she was holding onto had been tugged at or cut. She had heard a ripping noise and then the rucksack was gone. The light was brighter now though so she must be coming to the end of her journey through the hole. Hope couldn't be far away. Pat propelled herself along on her elbows as fast as she could, skinning them as she went. She knew she was still holding onto something. She could feel one of her hands gripping something tightly. It felt like a strap from the rucksack. She hadn't let go. Of course she hadn't. Something or someone had grabbed hold of the rucksack from the other side of the hole and wrenched at it, breaking it loose, and now Hope was gone. Where was she? What was going on? She began to feel nauseous. She had to find out what had happened to Hope.

A few seconds later, Pat found herself at the other end of the hole or tunnel or whatever it was she had been struggling to squeeze her way through and realised that her hands were flailing and flapping about aimlessly in mid air. She cautiously eased herself forward and peered outwards. She could see nothing. She looked down. There seemed to be lamps dotted here and there which shone dimly in the darkness. How on earth could there be lamps shining in the middle of the tunnel? Who could possibly have lit them? Perhaps she was not on her own? A shiver of fear ran through her. Maybe someone had been listening to her and watching her struggle as she inched her way forwards and had snatched the rucksack containing Hope at the first given opportunity. She hadn't seen or heard anyone though. She squinted as she continued to stare downwards. At least the descent on this side looked easier to manoeuvre than the ascent on the other side had been. The rocks below didn't look as if they formed part of the landslide but as if they had been dragged next to and on top of one another in order to assemble a series of uneven steps. Pat strained awkwardly as she wrenched the lower part of her body out of the hole and instantly lost her balance, tumbling headlong towards the first rocky step. Reaching out with her hands she stopped herself from falling any further, pulling herself upright into a seated position and striving, as she did so, to catch her breath. Crawling through the hole had taken more out of her than she realised. Attempting to scan the area she blinked, several times. She needed time to allow her eyes to adjust.

The scene below her was extraordinary and Pat shook her head in disbelief. She had never seen or could have imagined anything like it! It was incredible! She stared intently downwards and forced herself to slowly absorb the picture that she was being presented with. Her mind needed time to process it. She rubbed at her eyes in case she was hallucinating because she was tired. But no, there was no mistaking the ghostly vehicles lit up by the dim lamps overhead. They filled the entire tunnel.

There were empty cars and trucks and vans everywhere; stationary cars; trucks whose engines must have been turned off while queuing in the tunnel and then ceremoniously dumped whilst their owners fled, and vans that had been left with their back doors swinging wide. At some point whilst driving along the road and into the tunnel a landslide must have started. The drivers and their passengers would clearly have heard the rumblings of the rapid approach of falling rock and been forced to take action. They must have left their vehicles as fast as they could in order to escape. They would have had to run for their lives! Which way did they run? Was it forwards or backwards? Where was the first landslide? Had there been more than one? Pat could neither see nor hear any evidence of life, although there must be at least one person out there as the rucksack was nowhere to be seen and someone had obviously taken it. It couldn't have disappeared by itself. The vehicles had definitely been abandoned and had clearly been in the tunnel for some time. Pat knew very little about motor cars but even she could tell that these were old. She could tell by the shape and design of them.

Above her she was aware of April grunting and groaning as she heaved and strained to make her way through the hole that she had so recently negotiated.

"I'm down here," Pat called up to her. "I'm on the rock below you."

Within moments April was sitting next to her and had turned round to give a final, exasperated tug at the now filthy, donkey jacket. She had managed to remove it halfway through the hole as it hindered her passage and was sweating with the exertion of having dragged it along behind her. April was covered in cuts and scrapes as the hole had been a much tighter squeeze for her than it had been for Pat. She had knocked her knees, elbows and head so many times that she had lost count. She arrived on the rock next to Pat exhausted but elated and certain that she had been granted permission by the lone wolf to make her way safely through the hole. This thought had spurred her on when she felt too tired to continue and on the couple of occasions when she had become stuck for minutes at a time, being unable to wriggle either backwards or forwards and feeling so afraid. The removal of the donkey jacket had been time consuming and awkward but had eased her transition considerably. She might feel warm and clammy right now but there was no telling when it would come in useful as a blanket or for shelter or even just as protection in bad weather. And besides, George had given it to her so it was precious beyond measure.

"What a nightmare!" she grumbled, turning towards Pat. "I thought I'd never get through. Let's hope we don't have to return that way or you'll be on your own."

"Look down there," said Pat, ignoring April's grouchiness. "Look at what's down there!"

April followed the line of Pat's extended arm and finger, raised her eyebrows and then gasped aloud: "Wow! Unbelievable! This can't be real. I feel as if I'm seeing things. Just let me get my breath back and we'll go and explore. I'll take my turn with Hope now, shall I?"

Pat's face instantly crumpled and she dissolved into tears.

"Hope's gone!" she cried, throwing up her hands in a gesture of despair. "Hope's gone! I was nearly through the tunnel, pushing the rucksack ahead of me and it vanished, almost as if someone yanked it out of my hands. But I've still got the strap in my hand so that couldn't have happened. I never let go of her. I really didn't and you know I wouldn't. Someone must have cut through the strap or perhaps it tore on a jagged piece of rock? Either way, Hope's not here anymore. She's disappeared. I don't know where she is. I never heard a sound. I don't know who's taken her or what's happened to her. I really hope we can find her."

She began to sob loudly. With April next to her the trauma of losing Hope was suddenly a reality and the tears rolled down her cheeks. April frowned. She was deeply shocked by Pat's outburst. She couldn't register what she had just heard. She felt like crying too but she knew that wouldn't help either of them.

"We're going down the rest of these steps now," she declared loudly, hoping she sounded braver than she felt and making sure also that if there was anyone around they would be certain to hear her.

"We'll find Hope, don't you worry. We didn't rescue her and bring her safely all this way so that someone could snatch her from us. We might find her tucked up in the rucksack on one of the rocks below. Anyway, I've got my crowbar and am more than happy to use it if I have to. Come on Pat. You need to pull yourself together. Stop crying and follow me."

"But it's my fault. I was supposed to look after her."

"And you were looking after her. Wherever she is, she can't be far away, can she? What's happened is nobody's fault. So get up and follow me."

Pat gave a final snivel as she drew her arm across her face wiping away the remaining tears. It seemed as if everything was against them and they were going to spend the rest of their lives on the run. At this precise moment in time she doubted they would ever reach April's grandmother's house and even if they did who was to say that she would want an extra hanger on anyway, especially one who couldn't even take care of a tiny baby. April had talked about her grandmother so much and built her up into such an amazing and wonderful person but, in actual fact, she had only met her once and that was it. She didn't really know what she was like, did she? Pat sniffed. She generally considered herself a positive person so she didn't know where these negative thoughts had come from or why they had surfaced. She supposed she was feeling sorry for herself and April was right; she did need to pull herself together. It had been such a long journey though and full of stupid hazards along the way. She was so tired of travelling. Maybe they should have stayed with George but even he hadn't thought that was a good idea. He'd insisted that he would come after them and find them but she couldn't imagine him climbing through the hole to get to the other side of the landslide. He would be far too big. How on earth would he ever catch up with them? It was all a bit of a 'let's live happily ever after rainbow kind of dream' and Pat felt dispirited to say the least. She sat for a moment watching April as she clambered over the rocks carrying the crowbar and her awful donkey jacket. She shrugged her shoulders resignedly, heaved a huge, unhappy sigh and began to make her way down after her.

CHAPTER TWENTY-ONE

April dropped the donkey jacket at the foot of the rocky incline and set off to explore. She couldn't deal with Pat's emotions as well as her own at the moment as she wanted to appear as if she was on top of things the way she usually was. After the final jump to ground level she became aware of a strange, buzzing sound that filled her ears and turning her attention to the lamps above she decided they had to be the source of it. The lamps were roped together at intervals and strung randomly amongst the rocks and the glow that came from them seemed to fade in and out intermittently in sequence with the buzzing. April surmised that the energy for the lamps must be coming from a generator positioned somewhere close by. She knew about generators as she remembered her father going out one night to sort out an old generator in the neighbourhood. He'd been called out on an emergency when all the lights went out as he was the local engineer and it was his job to keep things going. She decided she would look for the generator later but what she wanted to do right now was to explore the stranded vehicles around her. She was totally fascinated by them. Maybe she would find Hope in one of them? Maybe someone had taken Hope to stop her from falling and had deposited her on a seat in one of the cars? She would have to systematically check through them, one by one, just in case.

It looked as if the motors were lined up, one behind another, as part of a desperate and helpless traffic jam and had been stuck there for a hideously long time, each one unable to move either forward or back. As April stared she could see that some of the motors were in better condition than others. She found her eyes drawn to an old jeep that was close to the front of the queue and headed towards it. Still clutching the crowbar she ran her free hand over the paintwork. It felt smooth to the touch and in the gloom appeared to be in pristine condition. She cupped the same hand around her face peering in through a side window and then tried one of the doors. It was locked or perhaps it was jammed shut because the thought of it being locked meant that someone had had the presence of mind to lock it before they abandoned it and anyone on the run from a landslide wouldn't think to do that – or would they? Perhaps they might if they assumed they would be coming back to it and they didn't want anyone else to have it because it was their most valued possession. April had heard of men who loved their cars above everything else but she had never come across anyone who owned anything like this before. She circled the jeep tugging at each door as she went but nothing budged. She reasoned that perhaps she might have more luck with the boot. She pulled at it but nothing happened. Time to use the crowbar, she thought? She rammed it under the lid of the boot door and tried to lever it upwards. No good, but wait, yes, there was a little movement. She gripped the crowbar tightly with both hands and, using the weight of her body, pushed down with all her strength. Suddenly the boot flew open with a loud crack and April lost her balance and staggered backwards still clutching the crowbar. She gasped aloud in surprise. That had been unexpected! It took a moment for her to regain her balance, standing as if frozen and waiting to see if anyone had been disturbed by the noise, and then, deciding that they hadn't, she scrutinised the inside of the jeep. Oh, it was beautiful! The seats were made of soft leather and there were sheepskin rugs laid out across them. No wonder the doors had been locked. No one would want those rugs to disappear. April tentatively reached out, to gently touch with her fingertips and then to stroke the sheepskin. Perfect bedding, she thought. This would be the ideal place to sleep and recharge their batteries and if she could find a way to open and close the doors then she and Pat would be safe. If there were any wolves around, and she sincerely hoped there weren't, they certainly wouldn't be able to get at them. The search for Hope could wait a little. It would have to. After all, she had to be close by as although they had made their way through one landslide in the tunnel the darkness around them meant that there was quite possibly another landslide to negotiate further ahead. There wasn't a pinpoint of daylight to be seen anywhere. Hope had to be somewhere in the tunnel and from the way that Pat had described the rucksack being tugged out of her hands, the strap having snapped or even possibly having been cut, it was clear that someone had taken her and certainly not the action of a wolf. If they remained here quietly and for long enough they would surely hear Hope cry. No one could keep her hushed forever.

"Pat, come over here," April called. "I need you."

Within moments Pat was standing next to her, gasping in awe at the jeep's interior.

"Wow!" she breathed. She had never seen anything like it either.

"I'm going to prop the boot open with the crowbar and I want you to make sure it doesn't drop," said April. "I need to check out how much space there is inside. Can you do that for me?"

Pat nodded. She held onto the crowbar with both hands as April wedged it securely in place. April smiled at her and then climbed in. The sheepskin felt luxurious beneath her hands and knees and such a relief after the sharp stones and rocks of the hole she had just, wonder of wonders, managed to squeeze through. She crawled to the front and eased herself into the driver's seat, putting her hands around the wheel. It was wrapped in soft leather and warm to the touch. What bliss! She closed her eyes and pretended for a moment that the jeep was moving. She imagined she was driving out through the other side of the tunnel and that Pat was sitting next to her cradling Hope and that they were arriving in style at her grandmother's house. As they approached the house her grandmother came out to greet them, standing expectantly at the gate. She had been waiting for them and was smiling and waving. It was such a reunion and filled with great happiness. April exhaled contentedly. Her grandmother's house couldn't be far away. They must have completed most of their journey by now. She removed her hands from the wheel and opened her eyes. Back to the real world! No point fantasising just yet. She had to try and sort out the doors. She pulled at the door handle beside her but it was definitely locked. There was no key in the ignition but there were plenty of buttons and knobs on the dashboard that she could play around with. She pressed and pulled and twiddled and soon she heard a clicking sound and a button at the bottom of the window in the door next to her popped up. April reached over and pushed down the handle. Yes, she could open the door. Wow! She had done it!

"Come in, come in," she called to Pat. "Bring the crowbar with you. It's okay! I know how to lock and unlock the doors. We'll be safe in here."

Pat climbed in, wrenching the crowbar out of its position and into the jeep behind her. The door of the boot fell shut with a huge, clanging sound that echoed around the tunnel and the two girls stiffened, waiting to see what would happen next. But there was nothing, nothing at all. It seemed that no one was coming after them and that they were the only two living beings inside the tunnel. Except of course they couldn't be because what about Hope? They mustn't forget that Hope had been taken. One moment Pat was pushing the rucksack ahead of her and in the next it was gone. Hope had to be somewhere. She just had to be. She couldn't have vanished into thin air. She wasn't an imaginary baby. She was real, made of warm flesh and blood, and they had taken care of her since they had rescued her from the warship, even though there had been no one to show them how. She was their baby sister and had to be in the tunnel somewhere! April grimaced and gritted her teeth. They would find her. She had no doubt about it. They had to. She was not prepared to continue the journey without her.

April stretched out on a thick piece of sheepskin and pulled another one on top of her. Pat lay down next to her and did the same.

"It's lovely and cosy in here," she murmured, "and so comfortable. I feel as if I could fall asleep in seconds. But I'm not really sure whether I should or not because I can't stop thinking about Hope. I can't stop worrying. What are we going to do about her?"

"Nothing," replied April pragmatically. "We'll do nothing right now. We need to get our strength back and then we can think about Hope. She'll cry at some point and we'll know where she is and what to do. So close your eyes and sleep. We're perfectly safe in here. I've made sure all the doors are locked so no one can get in unless we invite them and the windows are tinted so we can't be seen from the outside. Go to sleep. We both need to be able to think straight and to do that we need to rest. Pass me the crowbar, please."

Pat handed it over. Despite the obvious security of the jeep April wasn't going to take any chances. She was a light sleeper and would awaken if there were odd noises outside. She didn't think that anything would happen to them whilst they were inside the jeep but keeping the crowbar close by was a precautionary measure and she patted it to reassure herself. She really did need to get some rest. Her body ached and she felt bruised and battered after having dragged herself through the hole and due to the stress of having to ward off the wolves. She needed to feel strong and positive for the next stage of their journey. If they found Hope quickly perhaps they could stay in the jeep for a while before moving on. Perhaps they would be able to stay somewhere without worrying for once. She looked at Pat who was curled up under the sheepskin beside her. Today was the first time April had ever seen her really upset and she hadn't felt able to deal with it. Pat had been so brave throughout everything that had happened on their journey but the disappearance of Hope must have been the last straw. April reached out and tenderly pushed back a strand of hair that had fallen across Pat's face and into her eyes. Pat gave a small, appreciative smile at the gesture and April put her arm protectively over the sheepskin and across her body. Within minutes the girls were sound asleep.

CHAPTER TWENTY-TWO

April awoke thinking she could hear the sound of a bell accompanied by a murmur of voices and the restlessness of bodies moving around her. But as she strained to listen there was nothing. Perhaps it had been part of a dream. However, as she opened her eyes she was aware that she felt refreshed and relaxed. She yawned and stretched; feeling the heat of Pat's body pressed against her and then wondered where she was. It took a while before she realised that she was snuggled under a sheepskin and lying comfortably on a soft, leather car seat. Her first thoughts were that she was still at the Wine Sellers, cosy and warm in the windowless room that had so recently been their home. Then she thought that perhaps she was in the kennel on the warship. She felt quite disorientated and bewildered and it was only when she sat up and saw the steering wheel in front of her that she recollected what had happened and where she was. They were very close to the end of their journey. If they could get to the other side of the tunnel then they would be within reach of the foot of the mountain where her grandmother lived. She threw the sheepskin aside impatiently. There was no time to lose. The sooner they were on their way the better. Then she remembered. Hope had disappeared! Hope was gone! They had to find her before they could do anything else. Her recovery was a priority. They also needed to make sure they were completely rested before the last stretch of their journey. There was no point in rushing anything. Yes, she felt energised after a full night's sleep but they might benefit from a few of those before setting off again. She looked down at Pat who was snoring gently with her mouth open. Should she wake her or should she let her sleep? She decided to let her sleep. She would investigate the tunnel first and then come back for her. But what should she do about the doors? She didn't want to unlock them and then leave them unlocked. She would have to exit through the boot with the crowbar. She couldn't take too long exploring either as she didn't want Pat to wake up and worry when she discovered that she was on her own in a locked jeep. She levered the door of the boot up a foot or so with the crowbar and slid easily down to the road below. She then carefully lowered it behind her making sure it closed soundlessly and looked up and down the tunnel. The glow from the lamps gently illuminated everything around her. Perhaps the lamps were always on or perhaps she and Pat had slept so long that they had gone out and come back on again. She couldn't tell. That persistent buzzing was still there. Maybe she should search for the generator - but what was the point in that? It was probably better if she hunted for an exit at the other end of the tunnel. She would also keep an eye out for the rucksack that had miraculously vanished along with Hope as without the rucksack they had nothing. There was no food, no water, nothing. And worst of all, there was no Hope. Their only remaining possessions were the crowbar and the grubby, donkey jacket. She gripped the crowbar even more tightly as she reflected on their current situation.

April walked slowly alongside the queue of motors, trying to move as quietly as possible, peering to the right and left as she did so in case there were any holes anywhere that could be construed as exits. But there was nothing. The entire length and breadth of the tunnel was silent and everything seemed bathed in a veil of slumber. The only sounds she could hear were those made by the soft pit pat of her feet as she crept along and the helpless creaking of a car or van every now and again as it shifted and sighed in gloomy desperation. She walked to the very end of the queue and found that her first thoughts regarding the darkness in the tunnel were correct. There was another landslide but it was one that looked as if it would be impossible to manoeuvre. Nevertheless she felt compelled to try. The landslide consisted of small stones and earthy, black rubble that crumbled and slid and slipped away beneath her feet and hands as she attempted to negotiate her way upwards. She unexpectedly lost her balance after only a few feet of climbing, tumbling knee deep into sooty earth as there was nothing to grab hold of and no identifiable foot or handholds anywhere. Oh well, at least she knew. She would have to find another way out. She didn't relish squeezing her body through that awful hole again and neither did she cherish the thought of coming face to face with the wolves on the other side. In fact she didn't even know if she would be able to inch her way through. It had been difficult enough squirming along after Pat in the first place. The thought of the hole and what was on the other side of it made her shudder. It was obvious that they couldn't stay too long in the tunnel as they had no supplies - unless of course they managed to find something hidden in one of the motors. The very little they had managed to save on their journey had disappeared along with the rucksack. April suddenly felt trapped and, sitting alone in the dirt, she faced a moment of disillusion. Yes, it was warm and comfortable under the sheepskins in the jeep but they couldn't survive without food or water. She slid a little further into the rubble and reached out with her free hand to grab hold of something, anything! Eugh! Her hand was wet. It had landed in a sticky, damp patch. April kept very still. She didn't want to slip any further into the rubble and disappear. She had no idea how deep this patch was. She retrieved her hand slowly and, in doing so, became aware of a dripping sound close by. She cupped her hand around her ear, lifted her head slightly and listened. The more she listened the louder the sound became, although of course it wasn't louder at all it was just that everything else was so quiet. The sound was coming from somewhere above her head. Something was splashing rhythmically onto a stone close by. She stretched her free hand out cautiously and turned her palm up. She moved her hand around waiting a moment in each new position until finally she felt a tiny drop hit her thumb. She had found it; she had found the spot. She had found water. It had to be. She extended her palm until the drops were hitting the centre of it. Then she cupped her hand and brought it back just under her nose. There was no smell so it had to be water but she didn't want to lick her hand after it had been in the sticky mud and dirt just in case. And if it was water then it was coming in from somewhere so that meant that there had to be a way out! April suddenly felt exultant! There was always an answer. She had to go back and tell Pat. She must return to the jeep and let her know. She raised the crowbar and thrust it deep into the earth beside her and then used it to swing to the ground in one agile, deft movement. A pile of dirt and rubble came tumbling down after her and she hoped she wasn't about to start another landslide. She had no idea how either of them would manage to climb up to the water but if there was one exit then it was quite feasible that there could be another. It was something positive to tell Pat. She gripped hold of the crowbar with both hands and wrenched it out of the earth. Another pile of dirt started to shift and then to roll and slither downwards. April jumped nimbly out of the way but the downward movement of earth was over as quickly as it had begun. She ran on tiptoes back to the jeep keeping her eyes and ears open. She still didn't feel comfortable with the thought that there might be others around and she would rather be aware of them before they became aware of her.

She tugged at the door of the boot and found it lifted easily now that it had been loosened by that initial tussle with the crowbar. She clambered in.

"Pat, Pat!" she hissed. "There's another landslide at the other end of the tunnel but there's water too. What do you think of that?"

There was no reply. April pulled back the sheepskin rugs with a tut of exasperation and then gave a gasp of shock. Pat wasn't there. Where was she? She wasn't inside the jeep. She had gone. April pushed at the doors. The doors were open. Pat must have woken up and gone for a walk. Where could she have got to though? Perhaps she had climbed into another motor? April certainly hadn't seen her as she ran back after her futile attempt negotiating the landslide. Perhaps Pat had gone looking for her? April scrambled out of the jeep as fast as she could, running along the ghostly, desolate queue trying every door available to her and searching frantically for Pat. She didn't dare call out as a chilling thought had suddenly struck her. What if Pat had been taken too? Hope had simply disappeared; obviously someone or something had taken her, and now Pat was gone! The very thought was unbearable. A sense of loss and sweat inducing panic began to surface. It clutched at her intestines, squeezing them so tightly that she became overwhelmed with waves of nausea. Her knuckles turned white as she gripped the crowbar. If anything had happened to either Pat or Hope there would be hell to pay. April knew she was capable of murder where her friends were concerned and Hope and Pat were so much more than friends. They were family and April was supposed to be looking after them. As a surge of bile rose, threatening to fill her chest and throat with its acidic fury, she began to slam shut the rest of the open doors, gritting her teeth in frustration as she did so. No, she would not be quiet. She would make sure that whoever was hiding in the tunnel knew that she was a force to be reckoned with and a very angry one at that. And no, Pat was nowhere to be seen. Something terrible must have happened to her, April was sure of it. This was ridiculous, first Hope and now Pat. She stopped and put her head in her hands, shaking it with a gesture of despair. Then she slid down the side of a large, black van, sitting in the middle of the road, trying to stifle a scream of rage. For once, April had no idea what to do next.

CHAPTER TWENTY-THREE

Pat moaned softly in her sleep and stretched. She was having such a lovely dream! She was aware she was on the verge of waking and was trying desperately not to. In the dream she was sitting at a large table eating the most appetising of hot meals prepared by April's grandmother. Life seemed to focus very much on April's grandmother at the moment! The arrival at her house was the ultimate goal and so she was constantly in Pat's thoughts. George was in the dream and April, of course, and Bertha too, somehow. (That was odd; dreaming about Bertha!) Bertha had Hope on her lap and was feeding her with a spoon. Bertha was a different person. She was warm and loving and fitted in with everyone perfectly. George really liked her sense of humour and was telling her joke after silly joke, barely pausing for breath! Pat was tucking into a succulent piece of chicken breast, scooping the warm gravy back into her mouth with her finger as it trickled down her chin and licking her lips as she did so. She had once had chicken at Avondale Manor, prepared especially for her by Sister Charlotte when she was ill, and so she knew what it looked and tasted like. Her stomach gave a loud rumble in expectation. Pat sighed happily and reached out towards April. Her hand kneaded the sheepskin rug beside her like dough, opening and closing in pleasure as she savoured the final piece of chicken. What was she going to eat next? Would there be ice cream for dessert or would there be strawberries, or if she was really lucky perhaps she would be presented with a bowl filled with both?

"Come with me," she heard a voice say and she felt a warm, rough hand envelop hers. She was clearly needed in the kitchen and Pat opened her eyes to look at April's grandmother and say yes. But this couldn't be April's grandmother, could it? It was certainly a very old woman but she didn't fit the description that April had given of her grandmother at all. Pat shook her head in bewilderment and then suddenly remembered where she was. Someone was trying to pull her from the jeep. Someone had her hand in a vice-like grip and was trying to persuade her to go somewhere with her. Was it April's grandmother? If so, what was she doing here? Had she made her way into the tunnel to find them? Had she known all along that they were coming and set out to meet them? Pat was confused. She didn't know whether to feel relieved or afraid.

"Who are you?" she asked curiously and a little groggily. "Why do you want me to go with you? Where are you taking me?"

"Come and meet the others," replied the old woman encouragingly.

"Are you April's grandmother?" questioned Pat. "We've come a long way to find you. And we've lost Hope. Have you seen her? Was it you who took the rucksack away with Hope in it? Can you get her for me? I need to know that she's alright."

The old woman tightened her hold on Pat's hand without responding. She drew her woollen shawl protectively across her thin, twitching mouth with her free hand and pursed her lips. Pat stared at her as she climbed out of the jeep. She didn't feel scared but this old woman was absolutely nothing like April's description of her grandmother. This old woman was very wizened and scrawny looking and as she forced her features into an unbecoming grin Pat saw that she was toothless too. No, there was nothing glamorous about this old grandmother. Pat raised her eyebrows for a moment and then decided that there was no point in pulling away. She might as well go with the old woman and besides, perhaps she knew where Hope was, and that would be a relief. She attempted to draw her lips back into what she hoped resembled some sort of amenable smile, and not a grimace, and nodded at the old woman. She felt the grip on her hand relax a little as she shut the car door behind her and began to walk beside her.

"Where are we going?" asked Pat, but once again there was no response. The old woman shuffled along in the darkness next to the tunnel wall until they arrived in front of a rusty, old camper van. She opened a door and climbed the two steps leading up to it, dragging Pat along with her and then took a great step downwards. Pat fell after her.

"Ouch!" she cried as she caught her leg upon a large, circular grid that poked up in the middle of the van. "Ouch!"

A section of the floor of the van had been hacked out, leaving jagged edges around a rough hole and from there a manhole cover from the road below could be accessed. It had been opened up into the van revealing a yawning entrance into the depths of obscurity. No one would ever suspect it was there unless they knew about it. The old woman ignored Pat's complaints and pushed her towards the iron-runged ladder that led down into the manhole. Pat frowned and began to descend. She was sick of going up and down and hiding in dark places. When would it ever end? The old woman followed her pulling the manhole cover into place over their heads. It was all very secretive. They were soon facing a maze of tunnels at the bottom and there were lamps lighting their way here too. Curiouser and curiouser, thought Pat, feeling as if she was Alice on her way through the notorious rabbit hole. She remembered Sister Charlotte reading chapters of Alice in Wonderland to her and for a moment she wished she was back in Avondale Manor sitting next to her and listening. Sister Charlotte had always looked out for her and protected her. Pat smiled momentarily in fond recollection but then immediately felt guilty for having such thoughts for hadn't April always done the same and April hadn't even been aware that she was going to join her in that roll down the hill in their bid for freedom. April had planned a solo escape and yet as soon as she realised that Pat was with her she had taken care of her. There had been no moaning or complaining; she had just looked after her. And there was no ulterior motive either as there had been with Sister Charlotte. And now Pat was on her own. What had happened to April? Maybe she was somewhere down here; in whatever place this old woman was taking her to. The old woman pointed towards a tunnel on the left and Pat began to move quickly, smiling at the grunts and breathless pants coming from her companion as she tried to keep up. She reached the end where the tunnel forked and dusted her clothes down with her hands. Her hands felt sore from the rusty iron rungs and she rubbed them together. Which way would they go now? The old woman was soon standing next to her and pulling her along again. She was a lot tougher than she appeared.

"Where are we going?" asked Pat again.

"To meet the others," replied the old woman.

Pat sighed audibly. What others? What was the old bat talking about? They were now travelling along another gloomy passageway with random lamps gleaming here and there and seemingly without end. But all of a sudden the old woman stopped, bent over and lifted up her skirts. She retrieved what looked like a key from amidst the voluminous folds and stepped to one side, pushing it into a hole in the wall, although Pat couldn't see anything, and opening a door. Pat peered over her shoulder, squinting in surprise. Beyond the door was a well lit area which appeared to be a good-sized kitchen and it was filled with raggedly dressed women and girls slicing through vegetables, cutting up meat, hulling assorted berries and drinking mugs of something hot, which simply had to be tea. At least that was as much as Pat was able to take in at first glance. All the food was going into a huge pot on what looked like some sort of enormous stove. Pat sniffed. Whatever it was, it smelled delicious. Her mouth and eyes watered.

A tall woman put down a bunch of carrots and stood up, wiping her hands on her skirt.

"So you've found one of them then," she stated, addressing the old woman. She came over to Pat and looked her up and down. "What about the other girl? Where's she?"

"Who are you?" asked Pat bravely. She didn't feel afraid but she was taken aback at the sight of so many females together. She assumed the one standing in front of her was their leader, telling them all what to do and keeping them working.

"I'm Belinda," answered the woman. "And who are you?"

"My name's Pat. We escaped."

"So did we," responded Belinda.

Pat stared suspiciously at her. This place didn't look anything like Avondale House or Avondale Manor but it was full of women. She couldn't see any men anywhere but that didn't mean that there weren't any. This could be a terrible trick and Belinda could be one of Miss Abigail's spies sent out to hunt her down, find and catch her. Suddenly she heard the sound of a baby crying.

"Hope!" she gasped in astonishment. "Hope's here! That's my sister. I recognise her cry. Where is she? I'd know that cry anywhere. What have you done with her?"

She turned her head this way and that, straining against the fierce grasp of the old woman, who was once again clutching at her, scanning the area and growing distressed. Hope was crying piteously and she and April had never let her cry for more than a few seconds. They had always known how to comfort her or what she wanted or was in need of. In fact she barely ever cried when she was with them. Pat turned and twisted and pulled so much that she eventually managed to escape the old woman's clutches, running to where she thought she could hear Hope's cries, weaving her way in and out of the women and girls. No one stopped her. She found herself next to the stove beside a young girl who was sitting basking in its warmth and rocking Hope gently in her arms.

"Give her to me!" commanded Pat fiercely. "Give me my sister! You don't know how to look after her!"

The young girl stared up at Pat in bewilderment and then across to Belinda for guidance. Belinda nodded slightly and the young girl held out the crying baby. Pat reached down for Hope, snarling crossly at the young girl as she did so. She pulled her in close to her chest, holding her tightly whilst she soothed her. The young girl got up and gestured for Pat to take her place by the stove. Pat sat down, making a great show of not looking at anyone, paying attention only to Hope. The other women and girls, who had been watching the unfolding scenario with increasing curiosity whilst feigning great disinterest, turned back to what they were doing and Belinda walked over and settled herself opposite Pat. She waited as Pat comforted Hope, leaning her over her shoulder and patting her on the back so that she belched within moments and closed her eyes, ready for sleep.

"Where did you escape from?" asked Belinda finally. "What town was it?"

"It wasn't a town," explained Pat. "We ran away from Avondale House and we're on our way to live with April's grandmother. She'll be expecting us, I'm sure."

Pat sounded a lot more confident than she felt and kept her eyes lowered, murmuring gently to Hope and rocking her whilst she spoke.

"Whose baby is she?" continued Belinda. "She's not yours, is she? She doesn't look a bit like you. Does she belong to the other girl?"

Pat stared hard at Hope. It was almost as if she had never really seen her before but now that it had been brought to her attention she acknowledged that Hope had a completely different skin colouring from her own and that tufts of black, curly hair had begun to sprout from the top of her head. Pat had never taken much notice before or if she had she had never paid any attention to the differences between them. After all, Hope was just a baby and what did it matter where she had come from or who her parents were? If she and April hadn't taken her when they had there was a strong possibility that she might have been dumped somewhere for the wolves to devour or that she might have suffered some other hideous fate worse than death. After all, she had been the only baby girl left on the warship amongst all those baby boys and no one could say who or what kind of person would have discovered her there. Yes, it had clearly been an honest mistake on Tim's part but thank goodness she and April had found her.

"I already told you. She's our sister," Pat responded protectively. "We rescued her and we're responsible for her."

Belinda looked at Pat thoughtfully and then asked if she wanted anything to eat or drink.

"You must be very thirsty and hungry," she said and as she spoke one of the young girls immediately got up to bring over a mug of steaming, hot tea. Pat tucked Hope closer in towards the side of her chest and took the hot tea gratefully. It smelled of mint. A bowl of something that looked very much like vegetable soup was placed on a small wooden log beside her and Pat eyed it suspiciously. She wasn't sure whether or not she could trust these females or what they cooked but on watching some of the other young girls supping and one in particular who gave her a most encouraging smile she decided that the soup probably wasn't going to harm her. She gulped down her tea and picked up the bowl, raising it to her lips, whereupon she eagerly quaffed it, exuding a great sigh of contentment as soon as she finished.

Belinda laughed out loud and slapped at her knees in delight. She studied Pat. It didn't look as if she had eaten properly for some time. On the surface she appeared to be a fragile, thin child just like her own daughter but that was where the similarities ended. Pat had clearly experienced much already during the course of her short life and so Belinda waited until she felt that the soup and tea had helped relax her young guest before deciding to broach the subject of the journey and why she and her friend were making it. She placed a blanket around the young girl's shoulders and smiled amiably at her.

"We didn't mean to steal your baby sister," she began. "That wasn't our intention. The strap from the rucksack was about to break and she would have fallen and hurt herself; she might even have landed on her head? We simply took her before anything happened and then watched you for a while before deciding what to do. We're well hidden here and everyone is safe. The last thing we want are intruders. We didn't know how many others were coming after you when you crawled through the hole so we watched and waited. When we felt there was no danger one of us was sent to fetch you. There are only women and girls living here. When we arrived we made a group decision to remain hidden until things on the outside change and The Twelve no longer exist. There is no knowing how long that will take but until then we wish to remain here in peace and seclusion. You are the first person to have climbed through that hole in a long time. We considered it too small a space for any human to find or to bother with but you've proved us wrong. It may have to be blocked."

Pat looked up in panic. "No, don't do that. We have friends who may follow our tracks at some point and come to find us and stay with us at April's grandmother's house. They have to be able to find a way through or the wolves will get them. It's impossible to go around the side of the mountain."

Belinda considered Pat's words. "We won't do anything just yet. We need to find the other girl who came in with you. She's gone to explore, hasn't she? It's not safe for her. There are other holes that the wolves can squeeze through. Luckily they only come in at night, mostly seeking shelter when the lamps are out, and so far there haven't been any problems. Many of us sleep in the cars just as you did, making sure the doors are locked. There's no heat in here except for the stove and we have to be frugal with the wood. We have no control over the generator either. It's very old and so we've no idea how long it's going to last. Every day we wonder whether the lamps will come on or not and whether we can gather enough wood for the stove. So far we've been fortunate. But one day everything could change and so we've each chosen a motor as a night shelter and temporary home and what few belongings we have are stored inside. You and your friend broke into my jeep last night which is how we knew where you were. You're welcome to share it with me. The more bodies huddled together the warmer the nights are and the better we are able to sleep."

"We did sleep well, thank you," responded Pat, "and it would be great if you could find my sister April. She must be very hungry."

"There are girls searching for her already and it won't be long before she's here safely with you. Try not to worry. We mean you no harm"

Belinda could see that Pat was close to tears. She had been brave for long enough. She would question her about her journey later or maybe she would ask April when she arrived. There was plenty of time. Belinda got up and squeezed Pat's shoulder reassuringly before moving away, leaving her to gather her thoughts and reconnect with Hope. The pair of them were wrapped around each other so tightly and it was very important that Pat felt secure in her new surroundings and able to relax. The heat from the stove would help and time too; time always made everything better. Belinda and the other women had rescued many girls from the nearby towns over the last few years, meeting them as they were dumped from trucks and lorries at the side of the road but none had ever been resourceful and courageous enough to make their way along the road and through the tunnel on their own before. Trust was exactly what was required here and there was no need for Pat to feel rushed in any way.

CHAPTER TWENTY-FOUR

"Come with us," April heard a voice hiss beside her.

April frowned. Was she imagining things? She didn't dare move. It was necessary to feel composed before she transferred her gaze to the owner of the voice. It didn't sound like Pat's voice although it did sound as if it was a young voice. She removed her hands slowly from her face and opened her eyes. Two girls, roughly her own age, were crouching down in front of her. April held their curious stare whilst she slowly extended her arm in order to pick up the crowbar - just in case.

"Your friend is with us. She was famished. She feels much better now," offered one of the girls.

"She's my sister," responded April.

"We thought she might be. We're sisters too," said the other girl, smiling.

The two girls stood up. April unhurriedly did the same, dusting herself down as she did so and still regarding the pair with a degree of suspicion. She needed to collect her thoughts. The girls looked harmless enough and perhaps they did know where Pat was, besides which she was incredibly hungry. The mere hint of food was encouragement enough for April to accompany the girls wherever they were going.

"Let's go then," she said. After all, she had nothing to lose. It was pointless remaining where she was and she was at a distinct advantage with the crowbar in her hand even though there were two of them. April scowled and flared her nostrils just to let the girls know she wasn't a pushover and that she was quite capable of defending herself should the need arise.

The girls seemed satisfied with April's response and set off in front of her. They whispered a lot and April sniffed at their chuckles and titters as they walked. She felt irritated by their display of confidence and the sense of secrecy and intimacy that emanated from them. She hoped she wasn't being led into a trap. She had been in too many awkward situations already and didn't feel up to dealing with another at this precise moment in time. But no, the girls were very relaxed about meeting her and equally assured that April would follow them and soon they arrived at exactly the same van that Pat had been taken to by the old woman. Once inside they tackled the hole in the floor, climbing down the iron-runged ladder to the tunnels below and then finally speaking in normal tones.

"We're taking you to Belinda. She's in charge here."

April nodded but said nothing. She followed the girls along the dim passageway and then waited patiently whilst one of them retrieved a key from a chain around her neck and unlocked an unseen door beside her. April squinted and shaded her eyes as she passed through the doorway.

"The warmest place is by the stove and that's where you'll be able to get some food," said the girl who had unlocked the door. "I think your sister is there with the baby."

April gasped in surprise gripping the crowbar tightly. She stood rigid for a moment. She had to make sure she wasn't caught off guard. It all sounded too good to be true. The girls walked away and April watched as they disappeared from sight. She proceeded to look around her and take in her new surroundings, her body tense with anticipation. There was no knowing what was going to happen next. The same dim lamps that hung in the tunnel above lit up this place too. She blinked a few times whilst her eyes adjusted and discovered that she was in a large, spacious room that gave off an air of warmth and comfort, despite the rocky earth beneath her feet. She was in the very same kitchen area that Pat had been taken to. There were women and girls milling around everywhere but due to their dark, sombre clothes and subdued movements they gave an impression of near invisibility. April's eyes were drawn to a large stove and she moved cautiously towards it. This was where the heat originated. She found her nostrils quivering as they inhaled the savoury aroma which wafted towards her from the huge pot bubbling away on top of it. Her eyes and mouth watered and the hunger pangs that she had tried so hard to forget began to stab relentlessly at her stomach, almost overcoming her.

"April!" she heard an eager and familiar voice call. "April, I'm over here!"

April dragged her eyes away from the huge pot turning them to a most welcome sight. There, at the side of the stove and seated on an upturned log, was Pat cuddling her baby sister, Hope. April had never felt such relief or joy in her life. She flew across and knelt down, enfolding the pair of them in her arms and hugging them. Tears ran down her cheeks and she began to giggle uncontrollably, almost hysterically.

"Watch what you're doing!" Pat cried, laughing. "You've just whacked me with that crowbar of yours."

"Oh no, I'm so sorry," said April, pulling away. "I've been carrying it around for such a long time that it's almost like an extension of my arm. I'm thrilled to see you."

Pat leant forward and kissed her on the cheek.

"Here," she said. "You take Hope and cuddle her while I get you a bowl of soup. It's delicious; you'll love it."

April nodded, unsure as to whether she should be laughing or crying or continuing with both. She cradled Hope in her arms gazing at her beautiful, contented face. In Hope's world everything was peaceful and just as it should be.

"We must never lose her again," she said. "We must never let her out of our sight. Anything could have happened to her. My mind was filled with such terrible thoughts. I didn't want to frighten you but I thought she had been eaten by wolves and that if we found her, there would just be the scattered remains of her bones and some torn clothes. I tried to remain positive but inside I was churning with anxiety. I didn't know what had happened to you either. As soon as I got back to the jeep and you weren't there it was as if my worst nightmare had suddenly come true. I felt as if there was no point to my existence and no point in going on. Without the pair of you my life instantly became nothing. I just slumped to the ground in complete despair."

Aprils' concerns and fears, which she had been bottling up, poured out of her. Her words took her by surprise as she blurted everything out at once. Pat touched April's shoulder in sympathy. She knew exactly what April meant for she had experienced those very same feelings of despair and helplessness after Hope had disappeared along with the rucksack. As well as her misery though, she had been consumed with guilt. She ladled soup into a large bowl and placed it beside April. The last time they had eaten anything substantial had been at the Wine Sellers and that seemed aeons ago. She knew April would feel better very soon.

"So what is this place then?" asked April after she had gulped down so much soup that her stomach felt stretched to bursting. Not content with one bowl she had rapidly devoured three and it was only after her hunger was completely assuaged that she felt able to converse sensibly. With Hope wriggling contentedly on a blanket on the rocky earth below the two girls were able to catch up with their separate adventures.

"It's for women and girls," replied Pat. "They had to flee their homes and wherever they were living. They were helped to escape and now they live here in safety. No one knows they're here. There are holes everywhere above us that can be climbed through to get to the mountainside so that everyone can take turns in hunting or gathering food. They wash their clothes in the stream and that's how they keep clean too. They live a simple life and they're happy here."

"What about the wolves? Surely there are wolves on the mountainside?"

"Yes, that's a worry but they never go through the holes on their own. They always have at least one lookout and they've been taught how to make and use a bow and arrow. Nothing is wasted here. If they catch a wild animal not only do they cook and eat it but they skin it so that its coat can be used as a blanket or rug or to make clothes with."

"It sounds very primitive," whispered April, keeping her head down and making sure she wasn't heard by anyone except Pat.

"It is," responded Pat. "But it's how they survive and the greatest part of it is that they're free. They have sensible rules and no one is allowed to bully or abuse or hurt anyone in any way. I don't think anyone wants to anyway. They seem very content here."

"Sounds incredibly idealistic," continued April, still looking down. "I wonder how long it will last. It's not like that in the real world, is it? And they're very quiet, aren't they?"

"But that's the point," said Pat. "This is their real world and this is what they've made of it. They're waiting until The Twelve are no longer in government and things have changed and then they may decide to go back and find their homes and relatives. And they're quiet because they don't want to draw attention to themselves. Who knows what's roaming around on the mountainside out there?"

April shrugged. What Pat said sounded too good to be true. Here thrived the perfect community and if that was the case then why leave? Why not simply carry on living in the tunnels and continue with their survival plan? Just because there might come a day when The Twelve were no longer in government didn't mean that things would necessarily go back to the way they had once been. In fact that idea was almost incomprehensible as life was always about change and moving forward. Nothing ever stayed the same. And why would any of them want to go back to the very same families they had fled from in the first place? The whole family concept that they were clinging to was starry-eyed to say the least and April didn't feel optimistic about it. She, Pat and Hope had been through enough to know that a return to their old lives would be impractical and almost impossible and, although they had made friends on their journey, April wasn't convinced that she ought to automatically trust everyone she met. She liked the idea of a female commune where everyone helped one another and had useful and supportive work to do but she thought that sooner or later some of the girls and women would be drawn back to the world of men because they would continue to hold onto the perfect dream of getting married and being treated like princesses and finally having a family. She didn't feel she could discuss any of this with Pat though as although Pat was biologically the oldest she was naïve and innocent in so many ways. And due to her small height and petite frame it was always assumed that April was the elder of the two.

At that moment Belinda came over to join them. She had been watching keenly from a distance and whilst she knew the girls weren't related they did indeed make a lovely family unit. Belinda's heart felt as if it was tugged in so many directions. She had left her own home taking her daughter with her as soon as she discovered what was in store for the pair of them. She had been with her husband, a good man, faithful and true, for many years and it had been almost too late when, with sadness and despair in his heart, he informed her what had been going on at the meetings. He encouraged her to pack a few belongings and disappear as he didn't agree with the new plans for wives and daughters. And so Belinda had done exactly that, kissing her husband goodbye in the knowledge that she might never see him again and clutching her daughter's hand tightly as they left. She told her daughter nothing except that it was imperative they leave that very night. She said nothing of where they were going or why. In fact she had no real plans for the future thinking there would be plenty of time for discussion later.

CHAPTER TWENTY-FIVE

Belinda and her daughter walked for three, long, tiring hours to a rendezvous point where they flagged down a man driving a large truck filled with fresh vegetables. They climbed into the back of the truck and hid underneath a cumbersome piece of tarpaulin. Due to luck more than anything else they had managed to flag down the right truck or who knows what might have happened to them? There were several females already in situ beneath the tarpaulin, experiencing similar fears and worries, and also making their escape from the regime of The Twelve. They were fleeing from the terrifying prospect of having to become either baby mothers or sex slaves and, for their own safety, they remained as silent and as still as was logistically possible whilst the truck trundled from one town to the next with the earth-clad vegetables bouncing and rolling about enthusiastically on top of the tarpaulin. It was neither a pleasant nor a comfortable journey!

The women and girls were dumped early the next morning, aching, bleary-eyed and tousled, in the middle of nowhere, and it was from there that they set off along the road leading to the tunnels in the hope of beginning new lives. Belinda had previously been a teacher and so she was used to taking responsibility, making suggestions and guiding others. It wasn't long before the females she and her daughter were travelling with looked to her for advice. They walked, seeing nothing but a long, empty road stretching ahead of and behind them, Belinda leading the way with her daughter. They journeyed in an haphazard group to the tunnels, a sorry-looking, miserable bunch, wondering if what they were heading towards was going to be better or worse than what they had left behind. They met no one and nothing along the way which was extremely fortunate, as encountering wolves would have incited great panic and most likely have seen the end of the group as they scattered in every direction becoming easy prey.

Upon entering the tunnels they became aware of the earth and stones from both old and more recent landslides blocking the road ahead of them and they took this as an opportunity to rest and to contemplate their next move. Eventually one of the women spotted light coming from high above them and, taking the initiative, she clambered towards it to get a better look. It was a hole; the same one that April and Pat later discovered, although relatively larger at this point for there was another landslide yet to come, and so it was easy for the women and girls to negotiate their way through amidst the crumbling earth and stones. There were no strategically hacked out steps awaiting them on the other side, that would be a job for later, but the descent wasn't too difficult to manoeuvre. The lamps were on and the interior of the tunnel was filled with abandoned cars, vans, trucks, lorries, every conceivable type of stationary motor – exactly as April and Pat had found it!

On reaching level ground the women and girls gazed around them in wonder. The silence that filled the tunnel was disconcerting and coincided with an eerie draught that whipped and whistled around their feet like a cold, breathless breeze. No one knew what to do next. The view in front of them was totally unexpected. Most of the women and girls had never seen such motors before or so many of them all at once. Suddenly one of the girls ran forward, peering eagerly through the side windows of an old estate.
"Did you see that?" she cried. "There's something in there. I think it's a cat."

The silence was immediately broken and with excited exclamations the rest of the girls ran over to take a look. A door was quickly yanked open and a small, furry creature was pulled out, enclosed in a pair of thin arms.

"How do you think it got in there? How has it managed to stay alive?"

The girl who had first seen the cat turned to Belinda for answers.

"It must have been left there when its owners fled," Belinda replied.

"But how do you know its owners fled and how long ago would that have been?"

"I don't know," continued Belinda, "but neither do I believe there's anyone here right now except us. I think it's safe to go off and explore. In fact, I think we should. We'll split up into pairs and then regroup as soon as we can. As we have no idea of the time I'll call out when we need to meet up and we can discuss our findings. Hopefully we'll find some food. It's a pity we didn't take a handful of vegetables each from the truck while we had the chance. Make sure you stay together. I don't want any of you wandering off and playing heroics. Do I make myself clear?"

Almost before her words were out some of the younger girls had paired up and darted off. Now that they had been given permission to do so and Belinda thought they were free from danger this whole, new world they had discovered seemed full of adventure. Exploring the tunnels in the knowledge that there was a chance of finding cats and kittens would be a lot more rewarding and far less tedious than trudging down that long, weary road which thankfully now lay behind them. The day was suddenly heading in a new and more exciting direction.

It was Belinda who discovered the door hewn out of the rock in the tunnel wall and that was purely by chance. The women and girls had paired up and she had been left to wander about on her own. Even her daughter had deserted her. Belinda didn't mind though as being alone for even a short period of time was a welcome break from the endless doubts and concerns expressed by the other members of the group. Ignoring the abandoned motors Belinda made her way from one lamp to the next, down one side of the tunnel hunting for the elusive generator that had to be hiding somewhere. Eventually though, she was drawn to the camper van with the grid and iron ladder reaching down into the tunnel below. She could see the grid looming upwards through the partly open door and curiosity overcame her. Who would park in such a spot? Had it been done on purpose or had the owner just happened to park over a manhole leading into the bowels of the earth? Why was there a hole in the bottom of the camper van? Who would think to do such a thing? There must have been someone who remained in the tunnels and maybe they were still around – somewhere! Perhaps the cat belonged to them? It was most odd but definitely worth investigating. She remembered a similar van from her childhood. The engine had caught fire and it had been towed away and then dumped on a patch of disused land near her home and the local children used to meet up in it and play cards or share out and eat the apples and pears they had just scrumped. It was their very own special haven. Parents always knew where to find their sons and daughters if they didn't return home straight after school. Belinda smiled as she climbed into the van, memories flooding through her as she visually embraced the dusty but homely surroundings. She distractedly patted and plumped up a few cushions before deciding to find out exactly where the manhole led to. Taking a deep breath she stepped carefully onto the first iron rung.

Once at the bottom of the ladder and in the tunnel below she followed the wall until she suddenly hit a warm spot. It took her by surprise and she almost tripped over an uneven patch of earth beneath her feet. As she thrust her hands out to prevent herself from falling she grabbed hold of what felt exactly like a bunch of keys, one of which was jammed into some sort of hole in the tunnel wall. She held onto the keys until she regained her balance and then felt around with her fingers until she realised that she had located a huge door. It took all her strength to turn the key in the wall but eventually, after a great push, the door creaked and groaned open. She gasped as an intense wave of heat hit her. It felt like a blast from a furnace and was a welcome relief after the damp tarpaulin in the truck and the cold trek along the road. Belinda rubbed at her arms. She didn't want to move. This was bliss! Her muscles felt as if they were coming to life again. She stretched her arms and legs out and felt truly warm for the first time in weeks. Things had been so difficult at home that she had been forbidden to make up the small living room fire, even in the evenings when the pale, wintry sun had disappeared and her breath hung in the air around her head in dismal, wispy clouds.

Belinda looked around and found she was in a large, empty room. This area too was lit by lamps that appeared to flicker and fade before struggling to reach full strength for a few seconds and repeating the entire process all over again. Eventually Belinda gave a great yawn and headed in the direction of the heat. It came from a large stove which was hot as hot could be but upon inspection there was nothing cooking either on it or in it. This was confusing! There must be someone else around? There had to be. Someone had to have hacked out the hole in the floor of the camper van; that was certain. Someone had to be feeding the cat! But where were they? Belinda strained with her ears trying to catch any possible sounds but even as she listened the silence that ensued began to feel increasingly deafening. She stared about her but except for the heat blasting from the stove there was no evidence of life anywhere and the only logical explanation that she could think of was that the stove was set to come on with a timer. Perhaps that was the answer and anyone who had been here had gone a long time ago? Where on earth was that generator? Did someone switch it on and off? Did someone set the timer? She wondered if she was being watched but decided that no, she would have felt something, even if it was just the hairs prickling at the base of her neck. All was still and all was silent! Belinda decided to head back to the rendezvous point and call the group together. She had made her discovery, had news to impart, and it was positive. There were a couple of intriguing doors leading away from the stove area but they could be opened and explored later. She clutched the keys to her chest and retraced her steps to the huge door.

By the time she climbed out of the camper van most of the girls and women were already waiting. There had been no more furry, little creatures taking refuge anywhere and the one that had been found was a skinny thing, not much more than a bag of bones covered in fur, and had obviously been scavenging in the tunnel for some time. It purred madly now that it was being cuddled and seemed very friendly. The girls had decided to make it their mascot. They had no idea whether it was a boy or a girl but that didn't matter. The poor creature had been starved not only of food but also of human contact and was now lapping up the endless attention it was receiving.

The girls and women had discovered that many of the motor doors were unlocked and so anything that might be of any use was removed. Everyone was eager to please Belinda. There were lighters and coins and odd pieces of clothing and blankets and the boot of one car even contained a sack of potatoes. Unfortunately the potatoes had been left in the sack for so long that they were sprouting and after inspection Belinda thought it preferable that at some point in the near future they were dug back into the earth rather than eaten. But on second thoughts beggars couldn't be choosers and if they were cooked through and through they might be alright. At the moment she felt hungry enough to eat them raw. She called for the rest of the group and then showed them into the van and from there down the iron ladder, along the tunnel wall and finally to the heavy door.

"I would never have found this," said Belinda's daughter in admiration. She was a fragile child with great, luminous eyes which reflected her failing health. She had managed the long walk but was exceedingly tired now. She had spent what little remaining energy she had in exploring various motors with another young girl and was now in dire need of rest. Belinda took hold of her hand and squeezed it, acknowledging how small and cold it was. Her daughter would never have survived the trauma of being a baby mother. The decision to leave the family home had been the right one no matter what happened afterwards or where they ended up. She just hoped her husband was safe and that he hadn't been arrested after their disappearance. The Twelve were unscrupulous in their desire to publicly punish and persecute. She led her daughter to the stove and encouraged her to sit on a woollen cardigan that someone had found. Her daughter smiled happily at her before laying her head down and closing her eyes. Belinda knelt beside her and stroked her cheek gently. She instructed one of the women to put the sprouting potatoes into the hot stove, counting them out as she did so, thinking that if they were lucky there might even be enough for a couple each.

Their new circumstances prompted pause for consideration. What should they do next? The room with the stove in it was habitable but there was still the matter of their daily fare. In fact if they could solve the problem of how to feed themselves then maybe this place was the ideal solution – for now. Food, shelter and warmth were at the top of their survival list. And water of course! Who knew how long they would have to remain holed up in such a place? If they could sort out their basic needs then they could, in all probability, live here – until things changed and they were able to return home. And they had no way of knowing when that might be? Belinda sighed and watched as the girls ran about exploring whilst the women drew close to the stove warming themselves. Suddenly there was a loud scream and one of the girls slammed a previously unopened door and stood with her back pressed against it.

"There's someone in there!"

Belinda stood up slowly, dusting herself down as she did so.

"What do you mean, there's someone in there?" she asked calmly.

"See for yourself. Have a look yourself!" answered the young girl, quite brazenly, but still leaning with her back against the door. "I'm not going in there again. She looked like a right old witch."

"Move away," said Belinda, approaching the door.

The young girl scowled and then ran to join her friends. Belinda opened the door and stared into the gloom but could see nothing.

"Come out," she called. "Come out of there."

There was a slight scuffle and then silence. The sound could almost have been mistaken for the scampering paws of a mouse retreating into its hiding place. Belinda sighed irritably.

"Come out now or do I have to come in and get you?"

Still silence. Belinda waited patiently, hoping she wouldn't have to go in and tackle whoever or whatever was hiding, until finally she caught a flicker of movement. Someone was stepping out of the shadows. Belinda squinted, straining her eyes in order to see clearly. Shuffling towards her was an old woman, a wizened and very old woman. Her scarf had slipped down revealing a mass of wiry, grey hair sticking out at right angles to her head in tangled, corkscrew curls. She wore a full, woollen skirt which skimmed her ankles along with a grubby blouse and a patterned shawl that had clearly seen better days. She continued shuffling inch by inch towards Belinda.

"How long have you been here?" asked Belinda, warily.

"I've always been here," responded the old woman, sniffing disdainfully. Belinda nodded. She didn't think this was the truth.

"Come and meet everyone," she suggested.

The old woman shook her head. "I live here. I don't need to meet anybody. I'm fine as I am."

"It's warm by the stove. It gives out a lot of heat. There are no men with us," Belinda continued.

The old woman stared suspiciously at her, in two minds as to whether or not she should trust her. Eventually she seemed to come to a decision and took a step closer. Belinda gave a small smile. Curiosity was getting the better of the old woman and on some level she desired company. Belinda held the door open wide enough for her to step through. Everyone was watching and pretending not to. Everyone wanted to know whom it was that Belinda was talking to. All heads were half turned towards Belinda and the newcomer and the tension in the room felt palpable. Belinda placed a hand briefly on the old woman's shoulder.

"How shall I introduce you?" she asked.

"Gloria," replied the old woman after a pause, shrugging Belinda's hand away. "My name's Gloria. No one's used it in a long time."

She made her way directly to the stove and sat down on the rocky earth in front of it, folding her shawl into a cushion as she did so, as if this was something she was in the habit of doing. She then proceeded to turn her back on the group, assuming an air of disinterest and staring straight ahead, wrinkling her nose vigorously as she did so.

"We're baking potatoes," offered Belinda in response to her unasked question.

The old woman grunted and took out a handful of apples from her skirt pockets, laying them on the earth in front of her. Belinda's eyes widened.

"We'd be more than happy to share our potatoes with you. They smell good, don't they?" she said quickly.

The apples were pushed towards Belinda who instantly began to hand them out before the old woman changed her mind. There was a chorus of gratitude and general smiles and nods in Gloria's direction. No one felt the need to question her. She had given them red, crunchy apples and that was more than enough for her to be accepted into the group. Gloria feigned indifference. She had her eyes fixed on the stove and the mouth-watering smell that was coming from it. To Gloria it was the most appetising aroma she had experienced in months.

It wasn't long before the potatoes were ready to be eaten; hard on the outside but soft and creamy on the inside, and everyone indulged. The previously sprouting, white shoots had shrivelled so much during the cooking process that they were now strands of black, crispy threads rendering an almost normal appearance to the potatoes. Gloria clutched at her hot potatoes; one in each hand, taking a bite first from one and then the other and never letting go of either of them, no matter how much they scalded her palms. She found it difficult to bite through the charred skin as she had very few teeth remaining but she was determined. She glared suspiciously either side of her as she tackled her potatoes but no one was watching. They were too busy looking after their own stomachs. The only thing they needed to complete their meal was something to drink. And everyone looked to Belinda ……..

Belinda watched Gloria. She must know where to find food and water. If she had managed to survive in this place on her own and had gathered a handful of apples that she generously shared she must know where there were more. She couldn't have existed purely on apples either. Maybe she knew where there were berries and nuts and she must definitely know where there was access to water. She waited patiently until Gloria's hands were empty and then addressed her.

"We need to drink. We're dehydrated and in desperate need of water. Can you help us?"

Gloria chewed lengthily on her last mouthful of potato, turning it over and moving it around with her tongue until it was a mushy, liquid texture before finally swallowing. Then she raised an arm and pointed in the direction of another unopened door. Belinda crossed over to it and pulled at the handle. The door opened easily. Behind the door was a storage cupboard, lit by one of the now familiar lamps and filled with packets and packets of dried foodstuff and tins of fruit. And at the back there was a tap; a tap that dripped. Water had pooled onto the earth below suggesting that it had been very recently used. On a shelf above the tap were plastic beakers with names scrawled across them in black, marker pen. They were the names of men, men who had obviously worked or lived in the tunnels at some point and were no longer around. The rest of the cupboard was damp and dusty but as everything was in sealed packaging it didn't matter. Belinda took a beaker and wiped it on her skirt. Then she filled it with water. She stared at the water suspiciously for a moment before noting that Gloria was standing behind her, prodding her and encouraging her to drink. Belinda wasn't sure. Gloria tutted with impatience as she pushed past her, grabbing another beaker and filling it before throwing back her head and swallowing the entire contents in one great gulp. She shook her head patronisingly at Belinda with one eyebrow raised as she wiped her mouth with the back of a rough, grubby hand. Belinda couldn't help but stare at her nails which were long and claw-like and caked in dirt. It was clear that Gloria was a survivor and had been coping down here for some time. It would be better to have her as an ally than an enemy. Belinda gave a slight smile, raised her beaker to her lips and drank. She watched Gloria features visibly relax as she replaced her beaker on the shelf and waited for Belinda to do the same.

The rest of the group had finished eating by now and as Belinda came out of the cupboard they looked towards her to see what was going to happen next. She called them over and told them to drink, girls first and the women after. She noticed that her daughter was still sleeping.

"Where does the water come from?" she asked Gloria.
"Outside."
"Outside, where?" continued Belinda.
"The stream," replied Gloria.
"Show me," said Belinda. It seemed that Gloria had decided that she had said more than enough. Maybe this was because she hadn't conversed with anyone in a long time. Or

maybe she was just a rude, belligerent, old woman. Belinda decided to communicate in a similar manner and to keep her questions short and to the point. Gloria seemed to respond well to requests and so that was how she would communicate with her. She watched Gloria move to the door behind which she had been hiding and open it.

"Through there," she said, pointing towards the back of the dimly-lit room. "Wrong time now though."

"What do you mean?" queried Belinda. "Wrong time now?"

"Wolves. Can't go out, can't stay here. Sleep in cars. "

And that was more than enough for Gloria as she then pursed her lips in a tight, thin line and Belinda could get nothing else out of her. As far as Gloria was concerned she had said all she needed to say and the rest was up to everyone else. She took her place by the stove again, hugging her knees and staring into space. Belinda sighed and crouched down next to her sleeping daughter, stroking a few strands of loose hair from her face as she did so and making sure she was comfortable. She heard Gloria make a clicking noise with her tongue and then there was a slight sound of movement from her. Before she knew it Gloria was crouching beside her and had placed a protective hand on her daughter's shoulder. Belinda knew she had to see to the other members of the group and that she had to make a decision. Could she trust Gloria? If what she said was true and there were wolves close by then it was her duty to get everyone to safety. Could she leave Gloria alone with her daughter, even for just a few seconds? She barely knew her but nothing could happen in a few seconds, could it? She felt she had no choice in the matter. She would fill a beaker of water for her daughter and hand it to Gloria to give to her when she woke up. That would be a demonstration of trust.

Soon Belinda had rounded up the women and girls. She instructed them to return to the tunnels and sleep in pairs in the motors. According to Gloria they were in a place that could be penetrated by wolves and they would be much safer inside a motor with the doors slammed shut behind them. She didn't know how the wolves were able to get in but she would find out from Gloria in the morning. For now though they must find cars or vans or any motor that was unlocked and remain there for the night with a friend so that they could keep warm. The stove was cooling down rapidly which only confirmed Belinda's initial belief that it was set to come on and go off with a timer and the room would soon be very cold. She stopped for a moment to take a deep breath and as if in response a blood-curdling howl resounded from somewhere high above her.

"Go now," said Belinda. "Go and find somewhere to sleep. And don't wander about on your own."

She decided it was time to wake her daughter but Gloria had already gently shaken her from slumber and given her the beaker of water and a warm potato that she procured from the depths of her skirts. How had she managed to get hold of an extra potato without anyone noticing?

"Are you alright?" she asked and her daughter nodded. "We need to go too," she added.

Most of the women and girls had run on ahead after hearing the howl but a few remained, waiting to see which motor Belinda might choose. They wanted to be close to her in case there were any problems. She was their reassurance and security. Belinda followed Gloria. She had survived here the longest and would know the best vehicles in which to hide and sleep.

Fortunately the night passed smoothly and without event. The group slept too deeply to be aware of any outside or unusual noise. Belinda shared an old jeep type motor with her daughter and Gloria and tried to stay awake as long as possible. There were sheepskin rugs in the motor and covered with these they were snug and warm. Eventually, and due to great exhaustion, Belinda fell asleep and when next she awoke it was morning, or so Gloria indicated, as in the tunnels there seemed to be no way of knowing. When questioned as to how she knew this Gloria simply pointed to a small shaft of light streaming in from above and sniffed disdainfully. Belinda shrugged. She obviously had a lot to learn. The rest of the girls and women were up and about and had returned to the room with the stove in it and were trying to warm themselves. The stove was heating up and so was the room. They had slept huddled together but had not been fortunate enough to find any extra coverings and as it had been very cold during the night they needed to get their bodies moving again. They knew there was food available in the cupboard behind the door but they waited for Belinda's instructions as to how and when they should share it out. Gloria, of course, had no qualms whatsoever. She went straight to the cupboard, ripped open a packet of what looked like custard powder and tipped it into a beaker. Then she filled it with water, stirred it about rapidly with a dirty finger and gulped it down. The mixture couldn't have tasted very pleasant but Gloria devoured it eagerly, licking her lips with relish. The women and girls stared at her in vague disgust, stomachs rumbling but longing to do the same. Belinda searched through the cupboard looking for something she could use to cook with and eventually came across a large, heavy, old pot. She filled it with water, noting that last night's pool of water under the tap had miraculously disappeared so it had either dried up or drained away somewhere. She carried the pot to the stove and set it on top to heat the water. If they were going to use the pot then she wanted it to be as clean as possible so that none of them became ill due to avoidable, bacterial infection. She was surprised at Gloria's good health considering her grubby and dishevelled appearance and the manner in which she had obviously been living. Once the water boiled Belinda disposed of it and refilled the pot pouring in several packets of the custard powder as she did so. Now she just needed something to stir with? She went back to the cupboard and pulled open all the drawers available to her. Nothing! Each one was empty. This was frustrating. No wonder Gloria used her fingers. But there had to be something that she could use? She returned to the stove only to see Gloria stirring the pot with a long, wooden spoon. Belinda shook her head slightly but said nothing. Gloria had her back to her and her shoulders were moving up and down rapidly. It looked as if she was trying not to laugh.

"Mum," she heard her daughter call. "Mum, look at these."

Belinda looked down to where her daughter was sitting and there on a sheet of unrolled canvas next to her was a collection of cooking utensils.

"You just have to ask Gloria. Gloria knows where everything is."

Belinda stared at her daughter. Ask Gloria? That was a joke! The woman was a law unto herself. But her daughter looked well this morning. She had slept throughout the entire night for once and seemed to be embracing this new episode in her life. Something had changed. The cat purred contentedly on her lap. One of the girls had brought it over saying it was her turn to look after it. Gloria had asked where it had been found as it had been missing for a while. Her daughter's eyes sparkled as she responded and there was a hint of a rosy glow to her cheeks as she caressed the cat. Belinda hoped this wasn't the beginning of a fever and that she was about to take a turn for the worse; yet she couldn't help but smile at the picture in front of her.

"Thanks, Gloria," she said gruffly. Gloria nodded, still with her back to her, making no reply.

The custard soon thickened and was ladled into the beakers, Gloria carrying the first beaker over to Belinda's daughter. As Belinda watched her she knew that something had happened between Gloria and her daughter and that Gloria could be trusted, at least where her daughter was concerned. She gave a silent sigh of relief. Gloria might not say very much but it was apparent to anyone seeing the old woman and the fragile girl together that they had somehow formed a bond in a very short period of time. Belinda felt herself start to relax. There was someone else now to help her keep an eye on her daughter and offer support.

It was an unusual breakfast but a sweet and strangely satisfying one. There was a distinct feeling of camaraderie amongst the members of the group as they drank the hot custard from their beakers. There were contented smiles all round and the sounds of happy banter as their bellies were filled and their bodies warmed up. What was going to happen next, they wondered? What would they do today? A few of them thought they recognised certain labels on the tins of fruit in the cupboard and couldn't wait for Belinda to decide when they could fill a beaker with them. Maybe they would have fruit and juice for lunch? That was a welcome prospect! For the first time since they had left their homes and families there was a feeling of hopefulness as they acknowledged the present and anticipated a brighter future.

CHAPTER TWENTY-SIX

And so it began! The women and girls commenced their new lives in a new environment with new friends and new rules! And no men! Belinda set the pace for everything, taking responsibility for any decision making - and she was obeyed without question. Everyone learned to hunt and to forage and gather. Everyone learned to cook and to wash and clean. They looked out for each other and very soon a situation that had started as challenging and possibly of concern became something that was familiar and habit forming, and a productive way of life was established. The group was safe in the room with the stove during the day and safe sleeping in cars, vans and other motors when darkness descended. They discovered evidence of wolves prowling the perimeters at night and sometimes entering and marking their territory or leaving a pungent deposit but no harm came to anyone. Eventually Belinda decided it might be wise to leave the gift of a kill at one of the exit holes at night and this plan worked. The wolves were deterred from getting too close as fresh food was now always ready and waiting. They arrived, ate and left. Life was peaceful and pleasant and everyone felt safe. Belinda's authority was never questioned and even Gloria became a teacher, of sorts. She still refused to say much but if Belinda asked her to show the girls how to make and then use a bow and arrow she obliged. The group watched her and copied as best they could. If they didn't get it right Gloria would slap at their wrists impatiently and demonstrate again, tutting all the while in irritation. She taught them how to spear fish with sharply pointed sticks in the cool running water from the nearby stream and how to catch, skin, gut, dry and cure small animals so that no part was wasted. Everyone worked hard under her expert eye as hands and cheeks would often smart unexpectedly if attention wandered. The only person with whom Gloria was never cross was Belinda's daughter. In her presence she was always kind, gentle and protective. It was as if she had made up her mind that Belinda's daughter needed her and was determined not to let her down. Belinda watched as this intriguing relationship blossomed. It was clear that Gloria cared for her daughter and that she was prepared to do anything she could to make her life comfortable and happy. Belinda was relieved. She couldn't watch over her daughter's health and simultaneously pay attention to the behaviour and antics of the rest of the group. Her leadership role had begun to take up more and more of her day. She was glad that Gloria had stepped in and inadvertently eased some of her load.

In the evenings before the stove became cold and after they had eaten time was spent reading. There was not much else to do after everything had been cleared away. A lot of newspapers had been retrieved from within the motors and although the material was outdated and might sometimes be considered inflammatory the girls were encouraged to plough on with their reading skills and to learn as much as they could. The fact that they were living in tunnels with only each other for company didn't mean that they must remain ignorant or that they should lack any form of education! One of the older women had been an accountant before women's work became restricted, and in many places forbidden, and she was thrilled to work with the girls in a teaching capacity. There were photographs of eligible and sometimes handsome, young men in the newspapers and the girls would whisper and giggle as they pointed and read and thought about love and marriage and how their lives might be at some point in the future. In the tunnels they were segregated from the rest of the world, almost as if they were in quarantine, and so they had no idea what was really going on outside. They felt as if they were simply waiting; that they had patiently submitted themselves to a period of withdrawal in order to prepare for what was going to happen next. And yet nothing did happen next. It was always the same, day after day, week after week, month after month, that is, until the day April, Pat and baby Hope arrived.

It was on a day when Belinda felt despondent and as if she was losing faith; as if she was losing a little of her belief that they would ever be able to return to their homes again and engage in some sort of normal, family life. It was lovely to include extra members in the group and it was even lovelier to have a baby in their midst but the knowledge that things were still the same, if not worse, on the outside, left Belinda with heaviness in her heart. She was restless and she was disheartened. She had been restless for some time, confused as to why, and with this restlessness an urge to be on the move again reared its ugly head. She wanted to live in a house and to come and go as she pleased and to have as much fresh air as she liked. The group had established that they could survive on a daily basis and that they could survive without men. But their existence in the tunnels was making them pale and wan and as time passed Belinda could feel the women and girls around her becoming unsettled. She was first aware of minor irritations, never verbal but in a look or a glance and she recognised them as something that echoed her own restless feelings. Every day different women and girls left the tunnels and went outside, depending on whose turn it was to forage or hunt for food or to gather water for washing and cooking, but this short period of exposure to the elements was not enough. Looking at the group Belinda could see that they needed more sunshine on their faces and warm rain on their bodies and the breath of a mischievous breeze blowing away the cobwebs that had so recently and insidiously begun to penetrate their dimly lit lives in the tunnels. Belinda acknowledged that she missed her husband. She missed his arms around her at night and his light, dry peck on her cheek as he left in the mornings and she even missed the sound of his snoring. She missed the man she had married. She missed the man who was chatty and bright and full of laughter. She missed the man she knew before The Twelve had voted themselves into government. So much had changed then and she wished it hadn't and that life had remained the same as when she had first taken her marriage vows. The women sometimes sat and talked about the way their home lives had been and what loving men they had chosen as partners but as the conversations continued the gaps of silence between one woman finishing and the next starting grew longer and longer as they realised how different things had become and the grief at what they had lost and might never regain became almost tangible. It was not productive to reminisce on the past. It was much better to talk about how safe they were now and how amazing they had been in setting up their new lives and moving on. The past was behind them and only the present remained. They had to live in the moment and neither look backwards nor forward. They had always to focus on living for today.

But on that fateful day when April, Pat and Hope arrived Belinda forgot all this and became distracted and strong feelings of restlessness gripped at her heart and began to rage within her. She could not dismiss them and think about today. The girls were welcomed into the group and Belinda made it her mission to coax as much information out of them as she possibly could. She wanted news of the outside world; she wanted to know about April's grandmother. And yet the more she heard about April's grandmother and how she was waiting for the girls at the foot of the mountains in her lovely home the more she yearned to meet her and to have a home of her own. It sounded like a wonderful dream and something to hold onto and to work towards. April's grandmother sounded just the sort of person she would like to associate with. She sat and listened to April and as she did so a plan began to form. She would travel to the foot of the mountains too and somehow start a new life outside in the fresh air. She would take her daughter and Gloria, if she wanted to come, although of course it was inevitable that Gloria would come with them as she couldn't envisage her deciding to remain in the tunnels without her daughter. Belinda began to convince herself that the group didn't really need her any more as they were more than capable of looking after themselves and if a small group of females surreptitiously disappeared early one morning no one would be interested enough in going to the trouble of trying to find them. They would just shrug their shoulders and carry on with their chores. Already there were signs that one of the women was pushing to become a new and dominant leader and some of the females were gravitating towards her. This was a woman who had been meek and pliant throughout the journey to the tunnels but recently another side had begun to emerge. At some point confrontation would be inevitable and Belinda couldn't be bothered with any of it. Tensions were mounting and had been for some time. She and the other woman clashed on certain levels and the other woman had taken it upon herself to openly defy her on several occasions, in front of the whole group, thereby undermining her authority. Belinda was growing tired of being expected to know all the answers and it had crossed her mind more than once that she would be happy for this rebellious young woman to take her place as the new group leader if that was what she wanted. Belinda was rapidly losing interest in telling the others what to do. She had done enough for the group. It was time she had a break from such responsibility. She had encouraged the development of a strong and loyal unit and if a small part of it was starting to break away, so be it. Belinda would get out whilst she could and while she still occupied a well-favoured position. She had no desire to break down or destroy what she had worked so hard to build up. She knew that April wanted to get going again too. She was fond of April. She found her to be plucky and enterprising and the more she talked to her the more she liked her. She just had to get to know her a little better; that was all. There had to be trust between them just as there now was with

Gloria. She would talk to April about accompanying her to her grandmother's as soon as there was a suitable and appropriate opening in one of their conversations.

CHAPTER TWENTY-SEVEN

And that opening occurred sooner than expected. Belinda had been out foraging and had returned feeling very pleased with herself, carrying a huge armful of young dandelion greens and nettle leaves which could be used for making tea and adding to the pot. The moment she entered though she could feel the tension. The air was electric with it. She looked around but everything appeared perfectly normal. The only thing that was slightly unusual was the fact that April was stirring the pot with a pronounced vigour and force. Pat was crouched in a seated position behind her, tending to Hope. Belinda could tell from April's stiff stance and slightly hunched shoulders that something had happened and that she had been involved in it. She went straight over to her and dumped the greens. There was hardly anyone else around; most of the women and girls seemed to have disappeared.

"We can use some of these with tonight's meal," said Belinda calmly.

There was no response; April merely seemed to stir the pot even more vigorously. Pat didn't look up either. Instead she pulled Hope protectively towards her.

"Hope's teething," she said. "She wouldn't stop screaming and it's taken me ages to calm her down."

April gave a loud snort of disgust. "You would think she'd kept everyone awake all night the fuss people were making."

"What do you mean?" asked Belinda gently.

"Well, you can't just shut a baby up, can you? It doesn't work like that. Babies need to be looked after and sometimes they cry."

Belinda looked down at Pat who had begun to hum tunelessly to Hope and noted her tear-streaked face. Something had definitely happened and it was clearly something that would never have occurred if she had been there. April and Pat were both upset and obviously, although Hope was now sleeping, she had been the instigator of whatever upsetting situation had arisen.

"It's time we were on our way," continued April. "We can't stay here forever. We've been living here long enough. Besides, my grandmother will be waiting. She loves children and would never shout at a baby."

Having met her grandmother only once April didn't know this to be a fact but she felt adamant about it. Her grandmother was expecting them and had been for a long time and the sooner they got to her the better. Their arrival at her home would be the answer to all their problems. She was the reason they had made it this far and there was only a little further to travel and they needed to leave. What were they waiting for? Why had they stayed here so long, allowing themselves to be lulled into a false of security? They had been relatively happy until today and the tunnels had been a place of safety for them. But things had been changing recently. April could sense it. There was a constant feeling of unease in the air. It was definitely time to go. She couldn't use Pat as an excuse to stay any more as she was so much stronger and healthier and neither could they stay in a place where people shouted at babies. Babies couldn't look after themselves or take responsibility for their feelings. They were not guilty of anything and if Hope was teething then she was in pain and had every right to cry. And as well as all that, she belonged to the two of them and they loved her.

"Would you do me the honour of allowing me to travel with you for the remainder of your journey? I would like to bring Gloria and my daughter along too if that is acceptable?"

asked Belinda suddenly in a low voice, so that no one else could hear.

April froze. She frowned and her shoulders rose a little higher. This was an unexpected request. She did like Belinda though. Belinda was always reasonable and had shown her nothing but kindness. Her daughter was lovely too. She had often cuddled Hope and soothed her when she was upset. She wasn't sure about Gloria as she had been very grabby and clutching when she first met her but she generally followed Belinda's instructions without question and to the letter so perhaps she might be useful. She certainly wouldn't be a hindrance as she was a tough old bird and mostly kept to herself along with her strange mutterings. April stopped stirring for a moment and picked up a handful of greens to throw in the pot. Then she turned towards Pat.

"I'd like it," murmured Pat, lifting her head and looking directly at April and without even waiting to be asked.

"That's fine then," responded April, turning to look at Belinda whose face instantly lit up with a huge grin. April couldn't help but smile back at her. Things were getting better already.

"When are you thinking of leaving?" asked Belinda.

"After we've slept and before the sun begins to rise," answered April, surprising herself as it was something she had only just thought of.

"We'll be ready," said Belinda and April knew this to be true. No one would say anything to anyone. There would be no need. The decision to go had been confirmed in less than a few seconds and suddenly everything felt positive again. They would gather their belongings together and be on their way before the rest of the group was awake. If they were incredibly quiet and very lucky their departure might not even be noticed for a few hours. April felt her spirits begin to lift. She turned back to the pot and hummed as she stirred. This might work out even better than she had anticipated. They would have company on the journey and they would have the added protection of two knowledgeable and experienced adults with them.

The rest of the day passed quickly. No one mentioned baby Hope's teething problems and April and Pat chose not to discuss her or to engage in any conflict as they had better things to think about. Belinda noticed her adversary watching her surreptitiously as if waiting to pounce should there be a possible opening for confrontation and so she deliberately assumed an air of peacefulness and tranquillity, ignoring her and continuing with her daily chores along with the rest of the group. She could feel a sense of excitement welling up from deep within every time she thought about the journey ahead and was determined that this manipulative woman should not get the upper hand on this, her final day in the tunnels. There was still a small amount of tension in the air but it had mostly dissipated and as the day went on it disappeared completely and the atmosphere became much more relaxed. This was a good sign as without any suspicions being aroused their departure would be all the easier. No one would know that anything out of the ordinary was about to take place and when late evening was upon them and the women and girls retired to their motors to sleep it would be a relatively simple feat for the six of them to leave. Six of them! That was a lovely number! Belinda glanced at Gloria and wondered if she had overheard what she had said to April. She was certainly hovering constantly around her daughter and hadn't left her side all day. She managed to catch Gloria's eye and Gloria nodded slightly. Yes, she had heard and Belinda gave an inward sigh of relief. Gloria would gather her daughter's belongings together without any fuss and without anyone even noticing. She could depend on that. She decided to go to the jeep and collect a few things so that they could leave promptly once the time came. The sheepskin rugs would come in useful as the nights were still randomly chilly. She approached April, peering inside the pot as she did so. She noted the crowbar propped up next to her. For the last week or so it had been almost glued to her side. It was as if April had been waiting for something to happen. Well, something was going to happen but it would be a productive step forward as opposed to mutiny within the ranks.

"Must be more than ready by now," Belinda said loudly and then hissed the word 'provisions' in April's ear before walking away.

"Yes, it's time to eat," responded April without looking up. She had been stirring the pot and adding ingredients to it on and off all day and hadn't thought to do anything else. Her mind had been focused exclusively on her grandmother and on attempting to calculate how long the remainder of their journey might take.

"I'll get the bowls and start dishing up."

April moved away from the pot and went to the cupboard. She collected as many bowls as she needed whilst simultaneously scanning the shelves and taking note of what food items she could discreetly pack later. Pat had retrieved the rucksack and it would be best to take as little as possible. They were used to looking after themselves outside now and so could hunt and forage as they went along. The most important item would be water and there were a couple of empty plastic bottles available which could be filled from the stream as soon as they were out of the tunnels. Hope's milk had run out shortly after they had arrived as Hope had proven to be an incredibly hungry baby and had taken to consuming great quantities of anything she was given. It had been easy to get her used to drinking the thick, nutritious soup and in a very short space of time she had changed from a pallid, thin creature stupefied by drug-filled milk to a cheerful, chubby baby who enjoyed using her lungs. Each time April looked at her she was filled with a sense of pride and gratitude. It was still hard to believe that she and Pat had saved her when she was such a poor, helpless creature and had managed to feed and care for her, bringing her to optimum health. The love that April felt for Hope was overwhelming and she knew that rescuing her had been the right thing to do. She expected her grandmother would feel the same way.

The food was soon dished out and eaten and within minutes the bowls had been rinsed and cleared away. Stomachs were full and this meant the entire company would sleep well. April beckoned to Pat saying that they needed to get to sleep early as perhaps this would help with Hope's teething problems. They had no medicine to ease her pain but Belinda had steeped a little valerian and honey in hot water to soothe her and encourage slumber. Pat nodded and wrapped Hope in an old piece of sheepskin and a shawl which she slung around her shoulders and middle tying it securely so that she could carry her to Belinda's jeep without dropping her. The iron ladder that led up into the bottom of the camper van was always difficult to negotiate and two hands were required to grab hold of the rungs so that Pat could make her way upwards with Hope especially as she had become so much heavier of late. The rucksack, once it had been found and the strap repaired, had been hidden under sheepskins in the jeep and so could be packed quite easily with no one being any the wiser.

By the time April and Belinda arrived Pat and Hope were sound asleep. April thought she ought to stay awake during the night watching for the first slivers of light to appear through the holes in the tunnel roof above them as then it would be time to be on their way. It was difficult to know when morning arrived otherwise. Belinda managed to dissuade her saying that somehow she always woke up at least an hour earlier than anyone else no matter what time she went to sleep and if they packed now they could be gone in the space of about ten minutes if necessary. And actually there was hardly anything to pack. April had hidden a few pieces of meat under her tunic, not enough to be missed, and had taken the two empty water bottles which could be filled from the stream as soon as they were on their way. Several sheepskin pieces could be squashed into the rucksack and the rest tied around their bodies. April smiled to herself and closed her eyes for a few moments so that she could bring to mind the image of her grandmother's face.

Before she knew it Belinda was shaking her gently and telling her it was time to leave. April was pleasantly surprised. She had fallen asleep as soon as her head hit a corner of soft sheepskin and had slept deeply and well. She was more than ready to get moving. She woke Pat who took care not to disturb Hope and they grabbed hold of as many pieces of sheepskin as they could carry and climbed down from the jeep. After filling the rucksack April slid her arms through the straps and reached back to pick up the crowbar. Belinda smiled as she saw her. Gloria and Belinda's daughter were already waiting. Her daughter looked a little afraid.

"I don't know your name?" whispered April.

"It's Emily," said Belinda's daughter, with a small sigh of relief. No one had ever asked her name before and Belinda had never mentioned it. Perhaps she had thought she was protecting her daughter from harm in some way. But now that they were leaving it seemed right that they should know with whom they were travelling. Did Gloria know that Belinda's daughter was called Emily? Maybe the need to know had never arisen and she had simply been happy to take on the role of caring friend and protector without question.

"Come on, we've got to go," interrupted Belinda. "We can't hang about waiting for someone to wake up. We've only got a short amount of time before anyone stirs but you can never be sure that there won't be any early risers. We'll follow Gloria. She knows the tunnel best."

Although Gloria had shown the group various exit holes Belinda hoped that there were one or two she had kept quiet about as making use of an unknown exit would be perfect for just such an occasion as this. Gloria said nothing but began to walk quietly and quickly towards the front end of the tunnel. Everyone followed. Apart from April none of them had explored this area before. It had always looked gloomy and uninviting and no one had ever felt any need or desire to wander there alone. Gloria was leading them straight into darkness. They had to trust her. They had no choice. April reached for Pat's hand and she felt Pat squeeze hers firmly in return. It was very difficult to see even as they carefully placed one foot in front of the other and it was unnerving walking like this. April could feel her breath leaving her body in short, sharp rasps and she momentarily felt overwhelmed by a wave of dread at the thought of what might lie ahead of them. But suddenly they rounded a corner and a thin splinter of light stretched out in cheerful promise on the ground ahead. Gloria hurried them towards it.

"We need to follow this light!" she hissed. "It's only here for about half an hour while the sun rises and then it's gone. Hurry, hurry or we'll never find the way out! There's no time to lose."

Gloria hastened forward and the rest of the group scurried along behind her trying to keep up. It was a simple enough instruction: follow the light, but because the area surrounding the light was so dark it was disorientating. April felt dizzy as she tried to focus on the thin strip in front of them. Who was to say that she might not trip over something while she was scuttling along like an anxious, short-sighted insect? Who was to say that Pat might not crack her head against an overhanging piece of rock, unable to see it jutting out above her? She certainly had a good track record for blundering into things and injuring herself. April shuddered violently and gripped Pat's hand even more tightly. Fortunately her doubts and fears were unjustified. Within ten minutes the strip of light began to grow until it filled the space of a low doorway.

"Wow! I would never have found this!" exclaimed Belinda as she stooped down behind Gloria to pass through it.

"Wow!" exclaimed everyone else in turn as they too stepped through to stand beside her. Even Hope gave an expectant wiggle as she turned her head towards the other side of Pat's chest. Only Gloria said nothing, merely pursing her lips into a smirk of satisfaction.

Somehow and most unexpectedly they were outside the tunnel feasting their eyes on the welcoming daylight on the other side of the mountain and the view that swept across the horizon in front of them was an evocative sight indeed. The sun had risen and the sky above was laced with feisty blue and white, with continually evolving clouds scudding across it. Leafy trees lined the road ahead, beckoning them forward and grassy vales stretched nonchalantly into the far distance further encouraging them to continue their journey. Even the mischievous breeze that lifted strands of hair and flicked at their ankles was intoxicating and they drew in great gulps of it forcing the imaginary, sticky cobwebs of despondency and gloom that had been clinging to them to rise and evaporate. The entire landscape left them reeling and gasping in delight! After expecting a similar sight to the craggy, stark terrain they had made their way through and grown accustomed to on the other side of the mountain this was a breath of fresh air – literally! Hope opened her eyes and let out a surprised squeal before squeezing them tightly shut again! Her small outburst broke the ice and everyone relaxed; turning and grinning broadly at one another. Hope had reacted in exactly the same way everyone else wanted to but had been too much in awe to do so.

But there was something else out there and it was Emily who noticed it first. Far away, but not out of sight, soared a range of purple hued mountains and to one side of them something shimmered. Emily pointed and Belinda stared. Neither of them could say what it was. It was something they were unfamiliar with. Their eyes were fixed upon a never ending sweep of something that quivered and shook with sparkling, grey flickers of light as it rolled away gently into the distance. As the sun's rays reached down to strike against it the whole expanse flashed and glistened intermittently, creating instant and random rainbows of coruscating colour.

"What is it?" Belinda asked in hushed tones.

She had never seen anything so wondrous before. The shimmering expanse was simply breathtaking. Everyone turned and directed their gaze to where she and Emily were staring. Suddenly April's eyes widened in recognition.

"It's the sea!" she cried. "It has to be! I've seen pictures of it in books. It can't be anything else. I've never seen it for real though. I'm sure my grandmother mentioned it was close by on her last visit. Even so, I was never really sure it existed! Wow! This is so exciting! We're on our way to the sea!"

"What's the sea?" asked Pat. "I've never heard of it."

"It's made up of water!" explained April. "It's a massive amount of salty water, more than you could ever imagine and it goes further than the eye can see. It goes for miles and miles. Boats sail on it. You can travel from one place to another on it by boat. You must have heard of the sea. It's much bigger than any of the streams we've seen. And it's so deep we would drown in it."

"Yes, well, maybe I have heard of it, although not much," responded Pat, trying to sound as if she knew what April was talking about. "I heard that maybe fish swim in it, not the little tiddlers we caught in the stream, much bigger ones; only I don't understand how they can live in it if it's salty?"

"But they do; fish and other creatures live there, and plants too. I remember reading a story about a huge fish called a whale and a man in a boat on the sea. The man tried to catch the whale."

"Well, I hope we're not going to be doing anything like that?" queried Pat, raising her eyebrows.

April burst out laughing and so did Belinda. She too had a vague recollection of being told about the sea although she would never have recognised it if April hadn't suddenly announced that that was what it was in one of her flashes of inspired knowledge. April never ceased to amaze her. Somehow she managed to read and remember things although there was very little to read from any more. A few books had been found in the discarded motors in the tunnels along with yellowing newspapers and magazines and April had managed to systematically work her way through them. She had sat close to the stove with a book open on her lap on many an evening in the tunnels. The books and magazines were filled with knowledge and were a reminder of happier times and of what had once been.

"Let's go to the sea," called out Emily happily, flinging her arms out expansively. Belinda laughed even more. She had not seen such a display of joy from her daughter since they had fled their home.

"We'll fill the bottles with water first and then we can go," she said, turning to give Emily an impromptu hug.

Emily nodded and even Gloria gave an almost toothless smile in agreement. April pulled the two bottles from the rucksack.

"Where's the stream?" she asked. "I don't see it."

"But you can hear it, can't you, if you listen hard enough?" suggested Pat.

Everyone stopped what they were doing and listened. Sure enough the stream sounded as if it was close by. It sounded as if it was running beneath their feet. April turned back to look at the mountain noting a patch of dark green amongst the rocks. She climbed towards it and placed a hand on the earth below. It was damp. She began to pick up and toss small pebbles and rocks aside knowing that the stream had to be close by. But it was just the earth that was wet. There was no sign of the stream. Gloria came to stand next to her and watched her.

"You're in the right place," she said, "but you need to climb a little higher."

April stared at her in astonishment. It was the most she had heard Gloria say since that first meeting. She had become more and more monosyllabic in her conversation as time passed. She hadn't even been aware until now that Gloria was capable of stringing more than half a dozen words together, let alone a coherent sentence. She watched as Gloria sprang lightly up amongst the rocks, with the sure-footedness of a young goat. For such a wizened, old woman Gloria was incredibly nimble. And then she raised her eyebrows in astonishment as Gloria began to push at a large boulder above her. She put her back against it and pushed. It moved a little and then fell back into place. Gloria grunted and gave another shove but the same thing happened again. April sighed, knowing she had to help her, and then carefully picked her way through the rocks until she was standing beside her. She put her shoulder against the boulder, nodded at Gloria and together they pushed. It was much easier with two of them. The boulder suddenly rolled forward and proceeded to topple. It toppled down to the bottom of the mountain and onto the road ahead, crashing and bouncing noisily as it went as if it knew about their forthcoming journey and was prompting them to get on with it. In its wake came a gush of clear water. It sprang up from beneath the boulder like a frisky geyser before dashing irreverently onto the rocks below and finally meandering amongst smaller rocks and stones to pool in a dip at the side of the road.

"I'll fill the bottles," called out Emily, removing their tops and plunging them into the water as it raced frantically past her. She certainly seemed to have found her voice. She had always been so quiet in the tunnels. This was a new Emily. Perhaps it had something to do with the fact that she was now a girl with a name. Perhaps knowing that her friends were interested in her and wanted her company gave her confidence. April and Gloria headed back down the mountain. That was the water sorted then. They could get on with their journey now.

"So I guess we just follow the road," said Pat. "Will it lead us to the sea?"

"I don't know," replied April. "But it will definitely lead us to the mountains and that's where we need to be."

Pat nodded in agreement. April was usually right. The mountains looked as if they were a long way away but it was early in the morning and after all that time spent mainly in the tunnels their legs were more than ready for a good stretch.

"Let's go then," said Belinda. But Gloria slowly raised a hand. Everyone stared at her. What was she doing? What was the matter now? Who did she think she was?

"Wait!" she commanded. She turned to look back up the mountain and suddenly a blood-curdling howl reached their ears.

"We need to go right now!" repeated Belinda urgently.

"I said wait!"

Everyone looked at Belinda but she was frowning and appeared uncertain as to what they should do. Gloria obviously had the most survival experience but Belinda had always assumed the role of leadership no matter what happened. April turned her gaze back to the mountain and in doing so caught a glimpse of something large and grey which fleetingly appeared and then disappeared amongst the rocks and undergrowth. She moved to Gloria's side gripping her crowbar tightly with two hands, assuming a stiff, slightly hunched stance. Now she could see what it was! It was a wolf and it was hurtling down the mountainside in great leaps and bounds. Well, of course it was a wolf! What else could have made that awful howl? She gave an audible shudder of horror and everyone turned to see what was wrong. The wolf was near now and in full view. There were gasps of shock as the wolf flew ever closer towards them and then a terrified silence. Only Gloria remained unperturbed. Long strands of spittle could be seen swinging from the wolf's great jaws as it approached. Its hackles were up and it looked as if it was preparing to pounce. It would be upon them in seconds. No one dared move. No one dared breathe. They were transfixed with terror. What was going to happen next? What should they do? What could they do? April very slowly and carefully raised the crowbar, ready to defend the group if need be. Her heart was pounding but she had used the crowbar before and knew she would not hesitate to use it again. Gloria still had her hand raised in the air and as the wolf gave a giant yet final leap it abruptly attempted to pull back, tumbling and skidding its way to a halt just in front of her before crouching in submission. Gloria slowly brought her hand down to rest on top of the wolf's head and then knelt down before it. She stared directly into its eyes and began to talk gently to the fierce creature which let out a couple of small whimpers before promptly rolling over onto its back. Gloria began to rub its belly. No one said anything. What was going on? Did Gloria know the wolf or did she have some kind of magical powers when it came to animals? Why was this wild creature allowing her to touch it? April stared and stared and as she did so a feeling of familiarity struck her. And then she remembered. Indeed she recognised the wolf. It was none other than the pack leader; the same wolf that had seemed to protect them and had turned away rather than attack them on their journey.

"Give me some meat," said Gloria softly.

April nodded towards Pat who instantly began to rummage through the rucksack for the rabbit chunks that had been packed earlier. Her hands trembled so much that she almost dropped the fresh meat as she handed a piece across to April. She didn't dare get too close to the wolf. She was responsible for Hope and there was no telling how hungry the wolf was. If it caught a whiff of warm, sweet-smelling baby it might decide Hope was a better option than the rabbit. But there was no need to worry. The wolf snatched the meat from Gloria's fingers and devoured it quickly.

"More," said Gloria.

And April dutifully took the rucksack, digging deep for further pieces of prime rabbit. They were soon gulped down and the wolf sat up, ears pricked and waiting, responsive solely to Gloria.

Gloria addressed the group. "Before you arrived he was my only friend. We looked out for one another. Sometimes he would be away for days but he would always come back. I fed him whenever I could and he kept the other wolves away. I think he must have been someone's pet once but after the landslides he had to make his way in the wild. He has a lot of old war wounds so I guess he's had to stand up for himself. He's the pack leader now but he doesn't always run with the pack. I think sometimes he feels as if he's had enough of animals and seeks out human company. I believe he wants to come with us."

Belinda stared in horror at Gloria. The wolf had rolled back onto all fours and Gloria had a hand on its head once more and was stroking it absent-mindedly behind the ears. Belinda wasn't sure about this. The wolf might certainly be good protection and an assurance of safety if it came with them but who could say how friendly it was or that it wouldn't attack anyone.

"He won't hurt any of us," continued Gloria, almost as if she knew what Belinda was thinking. "He'll most likely stay away during the day and then sleep close by at night. What do you say?"

April stared down at the wolf and then nodded. The wolf would have attacked them before now if it had been inclined to. She believed Gloria. She had experienced the behaviour of this particular wolf already. She turned to Belinda.

"I know this wolf too," she said. "Pat and I encountered it on our journey. I think we'll be okay with it along. It will keep wolves from other packs away and its own pack will follow at a safe distance."

Belinda stared at her, then at Gloria and finally at the wolf.

"Let's go then," she said. "The sooner we're on our way the better. Not knowing what lies ahead, we need as much protection as we can get."

CHAPTER TWENTY-EIGHT

Bill was frustrated. During the last few deliveries at Avondale House he had barely seen Miss Abigail. He didn't think she was avoiding him but he couldn't be sure. He had caught fleeting and taunting glimpses of her as he unloaded the van but nothing more. He had been tormented with lustful thoughts of her every day since that first brief and unexpected encounter. He hadn't been able to get her out of his mind. At night when he closed his eyes he could hear her eager, panting breath and feel the moist secret of her inner thighs. He was consumed with desire for her and by the thought of their next intimate meeting. He felt as if he was floating in a heady sea of delirious intoxication. His wife didn't know what had come over him. He rolled on top of her every night and was ready within seconds to thrust away inside her. He said that they had to produce a boy or they would be in serious trouble but he hadn't been so active or impatient in years. It was all over within a few minutes, but he grunted and groaned and seemed to derive such pleasure even from the brevity of his endeavours that she felt stunned by the intensity of it. As soon as he was finished he let out a small sigh, pecked her on the cheek, rolled over and fell asleep. His wife raised her eyebrows, let out a breath of relief and did the same. She knew that something must be going on but she had no idea what it could be and she wasn't going to waste time and energy worrying about it. She could now enjoy a good night's sleep. The sex was done with until the next evening when she would close her eyes and complacently endure the same thrusting procedure all over again.

Yet every time Bill was with his wife he was thinking about Miss Abigail. He had to have her again and the less he saw her, the more determined he became. He found it very difficult to think of her as simply Abigail. The word Miss in front of her name made her appear more as an object of desire and less as a young, vulnerable woman. Perhaps Miss Abigail was playing hard to get? Perhaps she was teasing him and it was simply a game to her? The more he obsessed about her the more he knew he had to do something and he decided that today was going to be the day. He surmised that if he loitered around Avondale House for long enough it was inevitable that he should see her.

Having driven into the grounds of Avondale House he took his time parking, moving his van backwards and forwards until he felt he must surely have been noticed. Following this he slowly and meticulously unloaded everything, placing the packaged goods in neat, orderly piles on the slabs below. Then he solicitously took each package one at a time to the kitchen door. Cook was around but there was no sign of Miss Abigail. He hadn't seen his daughter either for a while and that distressed him, but the thought of tight buttocks and pert breasts took precedence. He couldn't wait to run his hands over Miss Abigail's body. She had previously taken him by surprise instigating the sex and now it was his turn. He had to have her and as he thought about her he felt a smouldering flame beginning to ignite below. He soon became so swollen with desire that walking was painful. He was surprised that Cook didn't notice. He carried the last package to the kitchen door and wondered what he should do next. Cook didn't invite him in. She seemed preoccupied. She had been preoccupied for weeks. The whole place seemed different lately as if something had happened and everyone was keeping quiet. The atmosphere at Avondale House had changed, but for the moment Bill wasn't interested. He just wanted Miss Abigail. He turned tardily away from the door and strolled nonchalantly towards his van attempting to adjust his engorged member so that it lay in a more comfortable position. And then as he reached the van there she was. A soft growl of desire erupted from the back of his throat. He could see the fullness of her breasts through the flimsy, white blouse she was wearing and her tight skirt skimmed her hips and thighs. She looked as if she had been crying. Immediately he felt concerned.

"What's the matter? Are you alright?" he asked.

"We've had a terrible few weeks," she answered and her face began to crumple. He took her in his arms and hugged her. He could feel the curves and warmth of her body as she pressed against him.

"Don't worry, I'll make you feel better," he said, opening wide the door at the back of the van. "I've missed you so much."

He felt her tremble and then, as she relaxed in his arms, he began to stroke her hair. Moments later she lifted her face to be kissed and instantly his mouth was hard against hers.

"Get in," he growled roughly, coming up for air and lifting her into the back of the van. She lost her balance and he caught her from falling, at the same time pulling open her blouse and reaching for one of her breasts. She moaned as he did so and reached down to caress him. His body was on fire. He couldn't think. He couldn't wait. His desire for her totally consumed him. He quickly flipped her over onto her hands and knees and unzipped his trousers. Tugging at her skirt and pulling aside her knickers he pushed her head and shoulders to the floor. Her bottom was high, her legs were apart and penetration would be much deeper. This was a position he had been dreaming of. It was something he would never have been able to persuade his wife to agree to. Those days were gone. As he began to fulfil his fantasy the fire in his body reached fever pitch and exploded. It was done. He turned her over so that she lay on her back. He kissed her gently and then put a hand down and stroked her, taking delight in her response to him. He watched his fingers moving back and forth for a while and then lowered his head. His penis was on the rise again.

Up above from a window on the first floor Bertha had seen everything. She had almost gone into shock as she watched Bill bundling Miss Abigail into the back of the van without even attempting to close the doors behind them. She had wanted to run down and scream at them but found that she was glued to the spot, frozen and unable to move. Now as she stared at Bill's hand moving over Miss Abigail's private parts she felt herself growing hot and bothered. She watched as Bill lowered his head and Miss Abigail contentedly adjusted herself. Bertha had never thought much about sex before. She had seen plenty of it through keyholes at Avondale Manor but had been merely curious as to what the men did to the girls and what the men liked the girls to do to them. The girls had mostly been coerced into performing sexual acts they were unaccustomed to and from which they obviously derived no pleasure. The men had been rough and forceful and the girls had tried hard not to cry and had done everything the men wanted no matter how much it hurt. None of it had ever bothered Bertha. As long as she wasn't involved she didn't really care about what was happening to the other girls. But watching Miss Abigail's evident enjoyment certainly had an impact on her. Suddenly she was forced to acknowledge something about herself and as the realisation hit her she clasped at her chest in disbelief. Now she knew why watching the men having sex with the girls did nothing for her. Now she knew why she had no interest in or respect for men. Bertha was instantly and mortifyingly aware that she liked women. And she didn't like just any women; she liked Miss Abigail. She too wanted to reach out and touch Miss Abigail and to kiss her. And as she acknowledged this she became flustered and reddened with shame. Then she felt angry. Then she felt jealous and confused. The conflict of emotions rapidly coming and going took her by surprise. She couldn't just stand there and watch. She had to do something about what was going on in that van. Who did this man think he was? That was her very own Miss Abigail that he was interfering with. He had no right to touch her. As Bertha continued to stare she saw that Bill was in the process of penetrating Miss Abigail once more and she turned furiously away from the window. She was going to stop them. She was going to go down and confront them. This was exactly the kind of opportunity she had been waiting for. At this very moment she had the upper hand and she knew precisely what she was going to do with it.

    Bill had just flopped down on top of Miss Abigail with a long, shuddering sigh when Bertha reached the back of the van. Miss Abigail's eyes were closed and her body language displayed absolute gratification. Bertha gritted her teeth and stood completely still with her fists balled at her sides. After a while Miss Abigail opened her eyes and as she did so she took in the comical picture of the outraged Bertha. She didn't move but a small smile played about her lips as she contemplated her. It was almost a smile of mockery. She tapped Bill on the shoulder so that he grunted and rolled away from her. He immediately caught sight of Bertha and sat up quickly, adjusting his trousers as he did so. Miss Abigail lay there, completely exposed. She could see Bertha staring and very slowly and deliberately she put a hand down and gently stroked herself before closing her legs. Bertha could barely tear her eyes away and it was only when Miss Abigail had rearranged her clothing so that there was no longer anything to see that she raised soulful eyes to her face.
    "Did you want something, Bertha?" Miss Abigail asked smugly, sitting up and letting out a contented sigh as she patted her hair into place. She was basking in the aftermath of unbridled passion and felt genial and mellow.
    "I'd like to work in the kitchen full time with Cook," replied Bertha boldly.
    "Why, yes dear. I've been thinking the very same thing for some time. Now run along and I'll let Cook know in due course."

Bertha stared at her suspiciously. Wow! That had been easy! Unexpected too! She wasn't quite sure what to do now or what to say. There had been no confrontation. There had been no scolding or telling off! She didn't know what to do or say because everything was over and Bill was climbing into the front of the van and turning the key in the ignition as if nothing had happened whilst he waited for Miss Abigail to close the van doors.

"Run along then," continued Miss Abigail. "Come and see me just before lights out."

Bertha blushed as she turned on her heels and strode off. Lights out! That must mean that Miss Abigail wanted to see her in her room. They would both be in their nightwear! Bertha rubbed anxiously at her forehead. She didn't know whether to feel excited or afraid. Miss Abigail's reaction, or lack of it, was most disconcerting.

Bertha needn't have worried though. When she knocked on the door later that evening Miss Abigail was waiting for her, resplendent in a pink, fluffy dressing gown and with two mugs of hot chocolate and a plate of biscuits on a small table beside her. They drank their chocolate together talking about Cook and the kitchen and what sort of responsibilities Bertha would have. Miss Abigail was more than happy that Bertha wanted to work in the kitchen as Cook was getting older and needed someone to help with the heavy work. She could teach Bertha an awful lot and Miss Abigail thought they would get on very well together. Of course the other girls would still take turns in sharing out the lighter duties in the kitchen but Bertha would soon be in a position to supervise them. They finished their chocolate and Miss Abigail stood up. Bertha stood up too and waited to be dismissed. But Miss Abigail had something else in mind.

"Would you mind kneeling for a moment, Bertha?" she asked.

Bertha raised her eyebrows slightly and then did as she was told. What on earth was going on? Had Miss Abigail simply been pretending to be friendly all along and now it was time for her punishment? Was she going to get out a cat o'nine tails like the one Sister Charlotte used and indulge in flagellation? Bertha remembered Sister Charlotte had once tried that on her and the instant she lashed out Bertha had grabbed hold of the dratted whip and wrenched it angrily from her hand. Bertha had been so indignant and full of fury that Sister Charlotte had never tried to whip her again but had chosen instead to make her miss her meals, or at the very least dessert, and that was a punishment indeed for the ever-hungry girl.

But Miss Abigail was smiling. Bertha watched as she slowly opened the pink, fluffy dressing gown and allowed it to slip from her shoulders. It fell to the ground in a soft, embracing heap around her feet and Bertha was left gasping in astonishment at the sight of Miss Abigail's naked body.
"Do you like what you see?" asked Miss Abigail.
Bertha was too stunned to reply but somehow managed to nod.
"You can touch me if you wish," continued Miss Abigail.
Bertha took a deep breath and didn't move. Was this a trick? Miss Abigail was still smiling though. Then, after a few moments she closed her eyes and tentatively reached out and stroked Miss Abigail's thigh with the tips of her fingers. She wasn't sure whether this was some sort of unkind game or not but she couldn't resist the invitation. Miss Abigail stood completely still and closed her eyes too. Bertha carried on stroking her, very gently. Then, when she could no longer bear it, she opened her eyes, leant forward and kissed Miss Abigail, right in the crease where her thighs met. She couldn't help herself. Miss Abigail caressed the top of Bertha's head. Now she was certain. She had had an inkling of Bertha's feelings for her for some time but hadn't been quite sure. She stepped out of the fluffy heap of pink around her ankles and moved towards the bed.

"Lock the door, Bertha," she said and Bertha got up to do so. When next Bertha turned round Miss Abigail was lying on the bed caressing her breasts in anticipation.

"Come here."

And Bertha obliged without hesitation. Having watched the behaviour of the men at Avondale Manor and, most recently, Miss Abigail's heated moments with Bill, Bertha had a more than shrewd idea of what was expected. But she wanted to take her time. She wanted to please Miss Abigail and to savour every moment in case it never happened again. Bertha was ready to put her heart and soul into giving Miss Abigail pleasure for she was completely infatuated with her. Miss Abigail closed her eyes in expectation and as she did so it struck her that perhaps she didn't love Bill at all and that she had been lonely and he had been little more than a welcome distraction. Perhaps she didn't need him in her life any longer and truth to tell, it would be very difficult explaining the circumstances surrounding the two missing, presumed dead, girls, especially with his daughter on the premises. She needed to make sure that her relationship with Bill was on a friendship footing only. There might come a time when she would need to call on him for help in some way? She would have to avoid him for a while but he would give up trying to seek her out in the end for he would be able to do nothing else and then everything would be as it used to be, except for Bertha. Bertha could come to her room in the evenings. She would invite her to spend an hour or so with her whenever she felt like it and her growing, sexual appetite would be well and truly sated. There would be no need for Miss Abigail to reciprocate in any way for she was aware that Bertha had such a huge crush on her that she would be delighted to be the one doing all the giving. Perhaps she would order some ice cream or a hot chocolate in her room as a treat for her. Bertha would be happy in the kitchen and happy in the bedroom. She would never have any trouble from Bertha again and she would be an invaluable ally. It seemed that everything was going to be sorted to her complete and utter satisfaction. Miss Abigail sighed with happiness and relaxed into the moment, awaiting the inevitable!

CHAPTER TWENTY-NINE

And so Belinda led the way and Gloria took up the rear with the wolf loping at her heels, head down and sniffing the ground. April and Pat took their places behind Belinda and Emily smiled uncertainly at her mother before standing next to Gloria and clasping her hand. If Gloria wasn't afraid of the wolf then she would try and conquer her own rising horror. She wanted to feel as if she belonged in the group and as if she was as brave as the others. She hadn't quite got rid of the cough that had plagued her since her arrival in the tunnels and which had made her feel self-conscious amongst the other women and girls. She had always felt different, especially with Belinda as her mother, but now all that was going to change. She needed her mother to be proud of her and being so close to a wolf was surely something that would make her mother realise how courageous she had become.

It was a quiet yet comfortable company that set off on their journey. Added to this it looked as if the breaking day was going to be lovely and so how could they not help but feel their spirits rising as they walked. They were putting their old lives behind them and there was nothing to stop them from looking forward to the future. The further away from the past they were the better. The sun's rays filtered through the thick army of leaves above and arrived dancing on the road beneath their feet in spattered spills of light. Belinda felt happy as she stepped out. She had picked up a long stick shortly before the wolf arrived and made use of it as she walked. After a fall a few weeks earlier she had twisted her ankle and it was still weak so the stick offered much needed support. Her mind was tired from the months of self-inflicted incarceration and the need to continually be in control. She hadn't realised until now the amount of stress she had endured in trying to keep order within the group, always having to be diplomatic and trying not to feel agitated whilst knowing that there was one amongst them who was watching her every move and just waiting for her to slip up. She knew Gloria looked out for her and would report back if anything was amiss but oh, how glad she was that she was away from the pettiness of it all. The sense of relief was overwhelming. She didn't even have to think about this small group; she didn't have to worry at all. She just knew they were with her, trekking along, each head filled with thoughts of reaching the mountains and that huge expanse of water that lay close to the end of their journey.

April too was pleasantly relaxed. The last few weeks in the tunnels had seemed more and more restrictive and she had been aware of the growing tensions around her. Even before she and Pat had been vociferously attacked over Hope's teething tears she had thought of nothing else but getting away. Somehow and most recently, she, Pat and Hope had become unwanted intruders. Nothing was said or intimated when Belinda was around but as soon as she was out of sight nasty comments and spiteful, unjustifiable remarks reached their ears. She glanced at Pat who was shifting Hope over to her right hip. Pat was a trouper. There could be no denying it. From the very first moment they had set out on their journey she had never complained. She had not moaned once, not even when she had cracked her head so badly and had subsequently fallen ill. April was glad that she had been given the opportunity to get to know her. At Avondale House she had never really been able to get close to anyone. None of the girls had ever bonded or sustained friendships. They had always had to look out for themselves, making sure they kept their heads down and that they didn't attract any unwanted attention. Miss Abigail had run a tight ship and nothing had been allowed to upset it. April was glad she was away from it all. Now they were on the last leg of their journey, literally, and there was nothing to stop them. She heaved a sigh of pleasure.

Pat heard her and grinned. She felt a lot more positive about life. Hope was snuffling in her sleep and although she had grown recently and was heavy on the hip Pat enjoyed her proximity. She was on the verge of crawling now and there was an undeniable satisfaction in watching her progress. She had come a long way from the fragile, drugged, tiny baby whom they had first rescued. She had put on weight, to the point where she was decidedly chubby, and she was so much stronger. She had always been a cheerful baby but now one could even add the word content to describe her nature. Pat adored her and she knew that April did too. They were the perfect family unit and the icing on the cake would be the warm welcome from April's grandmother when they finally arrived on her doorstep. As Pat pondered her heart gave an unexpected flutter and despite Hope's weight pressing down against her hip she could barely refrain from skipping in excitement. She quickened her pace to keep up with Belinda and smiled brightly at April.

The morning passed quickly and just as their legs were growing tired Belinda called a halt and suggested they have a short break. The only food they had with them was the raw rabbit meat April had packed and most of that had been gulped down by the wolf. There was still plenty of water though and they took turns in passing the bottles round. Belinda rested with her back against a tree trunk flicking her fingers through the cool, green grass beside her. When had she last felt unhurried enough to enjoy such a simple pleasure? When had she last seen such thick, luxuriant grass? She couldn't remember a time since she had taken flight with Emily when she hadn't felt worried or anxious. She had hidden her fears

concerning survival from the rest of the group but with the passing of time they had become all consuming. She had been fully aware of the impending mutiny amongst the ranks, remaining ever vigilant, looking over her shoulder and listening, listening, listening. If she hadn't left when she did who knows what might have happened. Whilst she was in charge in the tunnels she had managed to keep her emotions under control, dealing with the day to day problems with diplomacy and tact but it would have only been a matter of time before the inevitable flare up had occurred. And Belinda felt betrayed. She had tried hard not to feel that way, and yes, she had been glad that there was someone waiting to step into her shoes at a moment's notice, but the backstabbing and malice that had manifested recently had left her filled with a deep sense of treachery from those she had relied on and trusted.
Fortunately that problem was one she no longer had to deal with now that she had left the tunnels but there was still the issue of food to address. She looked around. Everyone was resting and sitting comfortably. Hope was happy with water for the moment but that wouldn't last long. It would have to be a short halt only before they moved on again. There was a distinct lack of suitable habitation around them wherein they could forage for food. Her attention turned towards Gloria and her daughter. Emily had just changed position and was lying with her head in Gloria's lap and Gloria was running her fingers gently through her hair. Emily had always loved such gestures, even as a small child. Belinda didn't know whether to feel pleased or jealous but decided against the latter as it was pointless and it was good to know that there was someone looking out for her daughter other than herself. But where was the wolf? Belinda scanned the area. It was nowhere to be seen. Had it returned to its pack? Was the pack even now moving in closer, circling at a distance and getting ready to attack? Perhaps she should have a word with Gloria? Even as such thoughts ran through her head the wolf suddenly appeared, as if from nowhere. It arrived at Gloria's feet and dropped something beside her. Gloria smiled and reached out

to stroke the wolf's head. Its fangs were bloodied as if it had already eaten and Belinda was curious to see what it had dropped. She got up slowly and moved towards Gloria. The wolf was now supine, waiting once more for its belly to be rubbed. It lifted its head as she approached, giving a small warning growl from the back of its throat, and then completely ignored her. In a flash Belinda realised that it was not the wolf that was the pack leader but Gloria. The wolf was protecting Gloria; it was acknowledging her superiority. What had it so nonchalantly dropped though? Belinda leant forward, knowing that it would be fine to look but that on no account should she touch. That would certainly be dangerous.

On the earth next to Gloria was a fully grown but headless rabbit. The wolf had eaten the head and left the body as a gift for Gloria. Well, well, well! There was a surprise! Perhaps it had often done this, even when they were living in the tunnels and Gloria had kept quiet about it. She had always brought in plenty of fresh meat and no one had ever thought to ask how she obtained it. They were just grateful it was there. There was no time to waste in contemplation though. They had to build a fire. There would be enough food to eat after all.

Belinda clapped her hands together lightly and issued instructions and shortly afterwards a bright fire was burning and the headless rabbit had been skinned and torn into several pieces before being placed in a light griddle pan along with the remaining morsels in the rucksack. Gloria had been forward thinking enough to bring one with her and had hidden it under her long skirts. She had chuckled with delight as she revealed it. There was no telling how long the pan had been there and Belinda didn't like to dwell on it. Gloria was full of surprises. Belinda joked about what else could possibly be squirreled away beneath her skirts but Gloria simply smiled and said nothing, handing Emily a stick with which to turn the meat every now and again so that it didn't char.

The unexpected meal of cooked rabbit was like manna from heaven and the fact that they were able to sit outside in the fresh air chatting happily together somehow made it even more delicious. Emily felt almost giddy with excitement as she handed the strips of meat round because she had done the cooking and she had never been given such responsibility in the tunnels. She felt accepted within this small group and it was a new experience for her. The confidence and camaraderie amongst them was growing stronger and stronger and it seemed that as long as they were together they could achieve anything. They were a team that nothing and no one could defeat. They even had a wolf for a friend and how awesome was that?

Baby Hope was miraculously managing solids. Pat had chosen to masticate small pieces of rabbit until they were soft enough to be passed from her mouth into Hope's. Hope blinked in surprise at the first mouthful but then made vague chewing motions before eventually swallowing.

"What a good girl you are!" Pat exclaimed in delight. "Look April, she's eating rabbit like the rest of us."

April came over and plonked a kiss on the top of Hope's head making her gurgle and ball her squidgy fists with pleasure.

"She's amazing!" she agreed.

Belinda, Emily and Gloria laughed. Life couldn't get much more perfect.

"We've got to keep moving," said Belinda eventually. "Those mountains still look far away. I don't know how long it will take to reach them."

Gloria rinsed the pan out with a splash of bottled water and then dried it on her skirt before tucking it away beneath the voluminous folds. Belinda discreetly looked away hiding a shiver of disgust. She had spent a great deal of time impressing the virtues of cleanliness on the group but there was nothing that could be done with Gloria. Gloria was a law unto herself. It was wiser to ignore her ingrained habits; nothing anyone could say or do would encourage her to change her ways and who could tell how long she had spent surviving on her own in the tunnels without human contact. Belinda stretched, then stood up and prodded the earth with her stick. Pat and April scrambled to their feet and dusted themselves down. April offered to carry Hope for a while but Pat refused, stating that it was her job to look after her and she would like to continue doing so. Emily and Gloria took up the rear once more. There was no sign of the wolf. It had disappeared whilst they had been eating.

The road loomed ahead of them for as far as the eye could see. It was easy to travel along as they were sheltered from the sun's rays and its ever increasing heat by the avenue of leafy trees on either side. The road was smooth and well made and it looked as if repairs had been carried out prior to the landslides so there were no potholes or uneven cracks. It spread out like a long, meandering ribbon of black, sometimes sticky, tarmac; a totally different cry to the rocky terrain on the other side of the tunnel. Where had all those abandoned cars and motors been going to, thought Belinda as she walked? There were no houses or villages anywhere to be seen. There was no sign of life at all, merely a vast expanse of empty, open road. And where had the motors come from? Somebody must have lived somewhere along the road? Or maybe everybody lived at the end of it? Or perhaps they had to reach April's grandmother's house first and then they would come into contact with people?

Time passed and the further the small company travelled the more they became aware of an eerie, yet sultry hush that had begun to hover thickly around them. The sun had dropped until it was hanging low and heavy in the sky and there was a distinct lack of breeze. Everything around them was now still and silent and as they walked it became more and more noticeable. The journey had felt peaceful at first but little by little the extreme quietness began to bear down upon them filling them with a sense of impending doom. The only sounds they could hear were the tramp, tramp, tramp of their feet as they walked determinedly on. There was something unnerving about the fact that they were possibly the only living creatures for miles around. There had still been neither sight nor sound of any bird or animal, except for random glimpses of the wolf, from the moment they stepped onto the road. It was odd to say the least and the confidence and high spirits that they had set out with began to be replaced with feelings of worry and doubt. April was the first to voice her apprehension.

"It's too quiet," she said, in a voice just above whisper level. "I don't like it. And we'll be on open ground soon without any trees for protection."

"And the sea doesn't look real. I feel as if we're imagining things and it's not really there," continued Pat. "The air feels so close I can hardly breathe."

"Same here," gasped Emily. "My chest is very tight. I don't think I can walk much further."

Belinda looked at her in concern and then back at the stretch of black road swimming hazily behind them. The tunnels were almost out of sight, they were so far away. They had travelled steadily over the course of the day, covering a lot of ground and perhaps it was time for another break.

"There's going to be a storm," said Gloria. "That's what the problem is. I can feel it in the air. We need to take shelter."

Belinda scanned the neighbouring terrain. The trees had been thinning out for some time but they had been so intent on their journey that they hadn't noticed. If they walked much further they would find themselves very much out in the open and crossing arid, dusty land. Already most of the flourishing growth beside the road was gone and in its place dry, yellowing shoots were sprouting feebly from a sandy soil. The sun beat relentlessly down and the remaining trees provided very little protection. They had been so eager to make good progress that none of them had thought to cover their heads and it was small wonder Emily felt unwell. Belinda was surprised that no one had complained of headaches whilst they were walking, never mind Emily and her chest pain. The stagnant air around them felt oppressive which was unexpected as they were approaching the sea. Gloria was obviously correct.

"There aren't many trees we can take cover under," she said. "I wasn't expecting a storm. Let's hope it passes quickly."

"We need to check the sides of the road. There used to be holes dug into the earth for people to shelter in during great storms. It would have been impossible for them to stay in their cars."

Everyone looked at Gloria. She was full of information. How did she know all this stuff, thought April? Exactly how long had she been surviving in the wild for? At the end of the day none of them knew anything about her. She was proving to be a veritable fountain of knowledge. And April smiled as she thought this; she must have read such a phrase in a book somewhere.

"Right," said Belinda decisively. "You, April and I will do that. Emily and Pat must rest for a moment or two. Pat must look after Hope and Emily needs to be able to breathe."

"I'm so sorry," interrupted Emily, looking as if she was about to burst into tears. "I'm so sorry."

"I need some help with Hope. I'd like to try and change her without waking her if possible," said Pat quickly. The last thing she wanted was for Emily to be upset. The group had been so content up until now. There was no need for anyone to feel unhappy. She frowned slightly as she walked back a little and sat down under the largest tree available, beckoning for Emily to join her. Emily sniffed and coughed, knowing that Belinda was right.

"There's nothing to be sorry for," said Belinda encouragingly. "It will be your turn to help out later and our turn to rest."

Emily coughed again, giving a final sniff before settling down beside Pat. She took Hope from her. Hope possessed the wonderful ability of being able to sleep through almost anything.

April scuffed at the earth lazily with her boots. She had no idea what she was looking for. It was obvious that they weren't going to suddenly come across big holes in the ground. If there had been any they would have noticed them by now. She was tired of walking and would willingly have taken a break with Pat and Emily. Why couldn't the adults just look for holes? Why did she have to? She felt irritable and cross, although she hadn't a clue why she felt like this. She had been walking along quite contentedly and then, for neither rhyme nor reason, she suddenly felt as grumpy as hell. Perhaps she was suffering from sun stroke; perhaps that was what was making her feel out of sorts? After all, it was incredibly hot. She turned towards the tunnels and looked back along the road. Everything appeared shimmery, like a rainbow mirage. Everything was calm and still and the tunnels were hazy, black dots in the distance, reminding her of how far they had walked that day. She couldn't quite believe it. What was that though? Something was moving. April stared. Maybe she was seeing things. Now it had stopped. She squinted and blinked and there it was again. Was it the wolf? No, it was far too tall. It looked like the washed out silhouette of a person bending over and moving about amongst the trees. Impossible! April rubbed at her eyes and when she next looked the person, or whatever it was, had gone. She was obviously more tired than she realised. She should mention it to Belinda though, just in case. Or perhaps not? After all, she didn't want to scare anyone and if there had been something then it was far away and there were five of them, six counting Hope, although she didn't really count as she was too little to do anything in an emergency. And she still had the crowbar. Yes, there was always the crowbar. April decided not to say anything and to keep her ears and eyes open, erring on the side of caution.

"Over here, over here!" she heard Gloria call suddenly. "I've found something. I never really thought I would but here it is. Come and see. Quickly, quickly!"

April turned towards Gloria, all thoughts of her sighting momentarily forgotten. Gloria and Belinda were kneeling a hundred yards or so from the edge of the road scrabbling at the earth with their bare hands. She ran across to them.

"I think it's an iron ring," explained Belinda, "and it's attached to some kind of manhole cover and if we can pull it up then we might have found our shelter."

April stared at the dry earth below. Gloria had the iron ring in her hands now and was tugging at it. But she wasn't physically strong enough to make any impact. Her hands kept slipping as she pulled. She couldn't get a firm grip at all.

"Out of the way," said April impatiently. She still felt irritable and as if everyone around her were complete and utter idiots. "Let me do it."

April knew exactly what to do. There had been a similar ring at the Wine Sellers. She hooked her crowbar underneath the ring and pulled. It moved a little but she wasn't strong enough either. She pulled again. Belinda grabbed hold of the crowbar with her and, on the count of three; they both gave it a good wrench. The manhole cover instantly flew up in a cloud of dust and dirt and April and Belinda landed in a heap beside it, coughing and spluttering.

"Get off me, get off me!" panted Belinda. "You're far too heavy."

But April couldn't move. She had dissolved into fits of hysterical laughter. Once she had stopped coughing she had seen the humour in the situation. The crowbar had gone flying and she had fallen back into Belinda's arms and was lying, straddled, on top of her. Soon Belinda was giggling too and Emily and Pat had come over to see what the commotion was. Only Gloria wasn't interested as she had her head inside the hole, trying to see if there was a way down.

"It's very dark and there's no ladder. We need a torch. Has anyone got anything we can use?"

Pat reached into the rucksack. There were still the head lamp contraptions that George had given them although the batteries were almost dead if she remembered rightly from the last time they used them. She passed one over to Gloria who switched it on. It flickered a little.

"This isn't much good," she muttered churlishly. "I suppose it's better than nothing though so it'll have to do. The hole isn't deep. We could possibly jump down there. We'd just have to be careful. I'll go first and then you can pass Hope to me."

"Wait," said April. She had finally managed to roll off Belinda and had retrieved the crowbar. "There's a rope attached to the manhole cover so that we can close it behind us. It looks quite long. Use that as you climb down."

She took hold of the thick rope and passed the end of it to Gloria.

"Go on, see if that helps."

Gloria nodded and threw the length of rope into the hole. April sat on the cover to add extra weight and then Gloria began to clamber downwards holding onto the rope with both hands and using her feet to swing herself into the darkness below. It was relatively easy and she was soon at the bottom of the manhole. Once there she reached up for Hope. Pat leant over and gently transferred her to Gloria's outstretched arms.

"Now it's your turn, Pat," said Belinda. "Lie on your belly and lower your legs into the hole. Gloria will help you if need be and I'll keep hold of your arms. Don't worry, you'll be perfectly safe."

Pat did as she was told and Emily followed suit. April was strong enough to climb down without any help. Her one concern was the crowbar which she passed to Emily before making her descent. There was only Belinda left now and she couldn't wait to get into the hole. She could almost smell the change in the air around them. The atmosphere felt electrically charged and as if they were in imminent danger – although of what she wasn't sure. She glanced around making sure they hadn't left anything behind and observed the heaving, black clouds that had suddenly appeared from nowhere. The sky had been a hazy blue a short while ago and now these menacing clouds were rapidly swirling closer and closer. Everything above her was about to be saturated in gloom and she knew that they had found safety just in time. Moments later she was with the rest of the group and April was pulling at the rope, manoeuvring the manhole cover into place over their heads. Suddenly a flying lump of fur and slavering jaws hurled itself down to join them. The wolf had arrived!

CHAPTER THIRTY

The storm flew in on wildly beating wings, exploding above them and then diving down like a whirling tornado. It descended from some abject space in the sky anxious to expel it. As the group heard the storm's approach they slid slowly from standing to seated positions and huddled close to one another as if in making themselves as small as possible they would be protected. It was almost pitch black in the hole but thank goodness they weren't outside. The storm sounded like a seething mass of wind, rain, thunder and lightning along with trees cracking, torn up and tossed aside, and earth moving and everything fearsome and destructive that could possibly be imagined. This was the first storm April and Pat had come across on their journey and April gripped the crowbar tightly whilst Pat held Hope close to her chest. Neither girl moved. Emily was squashed in between Gloria and Belinda and she wriggled around until she was able to link arms nervously with the pair of them. She needed to feel secure and comforted in the deafening darkness. The wolf had somehow managed to enfold the entire group within its long, lean flanks and tail, enclosing them on all sides, although of course this was logistically impossible but that was how it felt. They each considered that they had been generously allocated a furry, body part and they could feel its warmth penetrating the darkness and alleviating their fears as they waited and listened. No one spoke a word as the storm raged and howled above them until, hours later, and with a final, terrifying wail of devastation, it wore itself out. By this time everyone was exhausted from straining their ears in futile attempts to distinguish between the various crashing sounds and by the sheer intensity of the storm. No one wanted to speak. They were ready for sleep.

Everyone that is, except for April. She was beyond sleep. She was as rigid as a wound up clockwork toy and tense enough to burst. Along with the noise of the storm she had heard something else and this something seemed to come from within the hole. Although they assumed they were in nothing more than a cramped underground shelter, barely being able to see one another in the dark, April was convinced that it was much more. From where she was sitting she had seen a small, flickering light which encouraged her to believe that there could be a tunnel system leading away from the hole, something that no one else was yet aware of. The light came from somewhere behind Belinda and April was directly facing it. Pat might have seen it if she had looked up but she was engrossed in caring for Hope and in hiding her fear, so had kept her eyes lowered from the moment she dropped down into the hole.

At first the light had been barely visible, merely a pinprick, but as time went on it became something that danced and fluttered as it grew. April knew that the others were desperate for sleep and ready to drift off at any moment. They hadn't noticed the light so she determined to stay awake and find out what it was. Every now and again she heard vague, scuffling noises which she associated with the movement of the light and she surmised that whatever it was it couldn't be that far away. She listened and stared as her friends drifted off into the realms of gentle slumber and she waited. She felt no sense of impending danger; after all she had the crowbar, but she would like to know what was coming. For it was coming. It was coming nearer and nearer with every passing second!

April squinted into the darkness focusing on the growing beam of light. Her eyes were dry and itchy and her head began to ache with the fervency of her never-ending watchfulness. After a while she thought she saw a shape belonging to the light. It was a shadowy shape and much the same as the one she had earlier seen behind the trees. April tightened her grip on the crowbar. It soon became apparent that the shadowy shape belonged to a long, lean man and that he was making his way towards the area beneath the manhole where they were taking shelter. She felt the wolf's body stiffen by the side of her thigh and its hackles go up. April decided to surprise the unknown intruder so that she had the advantage.

"Who goes there?" she whispered as loudly as she could without waking the others.

"A Tracker," she heard in muted response. The long, lean man now stood perfectly still as if he was appraising the situation.

"What do you want?" continued April.

"Simply to rest now that I have arrived."

"What are you talking about? Arrived where? You could have rested anywhere back there. You don't have to rest here with us."

"It has been my job to find the group and then report back. I haven't found the whole group but I've found some of you and now I'm tired. Now that I've found you I can rest. I've been looking for you for a long time and my work is almost over. I guessed you were in the tunnels but the wolves kept me at bay so I could never get close enough to be certain. Sometimes I caught random glimpses of women and girls whilst they were out hunting for food but I could never discover any of the exit or entrance holes in the mountain. It was purely by chance that I saw you by the stream. I've been following you ever since. I mean you no harm and simply wish to rest. I will decide what action needs to be taken after I've slept."

"You mean us no harm?" questioned April suspiciously.

"My job was to find you and I've done that. Please let me sleep."

"Stay where you are then," said April. "I don't see that I can stop you from sleeping but I don't want you coming any nearer."

The man said nothing but bent his knees and slid down to the ground from where he was standing with his back against the wall. He looked as if he was no more than a few metres away.

"Where did you come from?" asked April. "We didn't see you following us. I thought I spotted someone once or twice but that was all."

"As soon as I knew the storm was coming I too found a manhole. They link up all the way from the mountains to the sea. I'm surprised you didn't come across them in the tunnels. They would have saved you a lot of bother above ground."

"We weren't looking for them," responded April. "We needed to be out in the fresh air. And we didn't know about them anyway."

She could feel the wolf twitching beside her and was aware that its quiet grumble was beginning to turn into a deep, suspicious growl. She tentatively put her hand out and found she was stroking its head. Somehow she didn't feel afraid. The wolf was instantly quiet almost as if it was taking heed and was aware that April didn't want the man to know it was there. April's eyes were very heavy but still she watched. Soon she could hear the man snoring. His head had dropped to his chest and his hands and arms hung loosely around his knees. April was finding it very difficult to keep her eyes open. Slowly but surely the desire for sleep overwhelmed her and her eyes began to close. With one hand resting on the wolf's head and the other around the crowbar April finally drifted off.

It felt only moments later that she was being roused by Pat. The rest of the group was already awake and standing. Belinda was reaching up and straining at the manhole cover. She pushed and shoved with all her might but it wouldn't budge. Sighing heavily she bent down to enable Gloria to climb onto her shoulders to see if she might fare any better from a higher position and maybe work with her fingers around the edges but after a while Gloria too gave up, complaining about her sore hands and broken nails.

"Let me try," said April, as soon as she realised what was going on. "I've got the crowbar. I may be able to do something with that."

Belinda crouched down again so that April could take Gloria's place. April was a lot lighter than Gloria. She skewered away as deeply as she could with the crowbar but she didn't have enough strength to make any impact either.

"This is ridiculous!" she said finally. "There has to be a way. We've got to be able to get out."

Everyone stared, perplexed, at the manhole cover. There was a minuscule sliver of light filtering through from above which meant that the cover wasn't quite in place and shouldn't be so difficult to move.

"Allow me," said a voice from the corner.

The wolf snarled, snapping noisily with its jaws, and everyone, with the exception of April, stiffened in shock. Even April gave a slight jump of surprise though. She had been unwillingly dragged out of sleep and away from a delicious dream by Pat's persistent nudging and had forgotten about her encounter with the Tracker. Now she remembered and obviously some sort of explanation was needed.

"He arrived while you were sleeping and wanted to rest. He's a Tracker and he's been looking for us. He's been following us since we left the tunnels and now he's found us. He came from somewhere at the back of this hole. Maybe he can help."

The long, lean Tracker rose to his feet and approached cautiously. He didn't want to startle or frighten any of them. He traced the manhole cover with his fingers and then straddled the space beneath it with his knees slightly bent. He lowered his head and pitted his shoulders against the corner of the manhole through which the sliver of light filtered. He pushed and pushed with every ounce of strength from his long, lean back but the cover wouldn't budge. He stopped for a moment, took a deep breath, and then tried again. No luck!

"Something must have fallen or rolled onto it in the storm," he suggested. "Were there any trees nearby? Did anyone hear any cracking noises?"

"There was a tree, not too far away," responded Pat timidly.

The Tracker turned to look at her. The fragment of light coming through shone directly down upon her beautiful face. April stepped protectively towards Pat and scowled at the Tracker. He was staring at Pat in wonder, almost transfixed, but there was something about the expression on his face that April didn't like. It was only there for an instant and then it was gone, almost as if it had never been there in the first place. April shook her head slightly. Perhaps she had imagined that sudden flash of intense desire?

"That must be the answer then," said the Tracker. "We can't do anything here. We'll have to continue to the sea through the tunnels."

Belinda looked at him in shock while Gloria gave a disdainful snort.

"What do you mean; we'll have to travel through the tunnels? Who do you think you are? You're nothing to do with us," said Belinda. "We don't know you and we don't travel with men."

The Tracker began to laugh. "Do you want me to travel ahead without you then? I can move very fast with these long legs. I'll be gone before you know it but rest assured, there will be others coming. I'm not the only Tracker this side of the mountains."

Belinda grimaced, curling her top lip back into a sneer as she did so, and made no response.

"I can offer a certain amount of protection, you know. No other Trackers will come near if they see I'm with you. We don't interfere in each other's business," the Tracker continued.

"And what business do you have concerning us then?" asked Belinda, folding her arms over her chest in a distinct display of hostility.

"Let's wait until we're out of here before deciding anything," responded the Tracker turning away, but not before April caught sight of him glancing salaciously at Pat and licking his lips as he did so. She cringed inwardly before speaking.

"Maybe you could walk in front and we'll follow. After all," she said, turning to Belinda, "there's safety in numbers and it will be better if he's ahead of us rather than behind, don't you think? Especially as he seems to know the way!"

Belinda looked down at the ground, frowning. April's suggestion was a sensible one. There would be time to get rid of the Tracker later. She had an uneasy feeling about him although she couldn't determine exactly what it was that worried her. Perhaps it was to do with the unseemly tales regarding Trackers that she had heard from others? They were stuck with him for now though so it might be wise to follow April's suggestion and try and make the best of the situation. At least if he was in front of them they could keep an eye on him and make sure he didn't get up to any mischief.

"Okay," she said. "Let's go."

Belinda picked up her stick as the Tracker moved forward, leading the way, and the rest of the group fell into place behind. April decided to stick close to Pat as she was decidedly the most appealing as far as the Tracker was concerned and she didn't want anything to happen to her. Gloria pushed the wolf behind her skirts, nudging it back with her hand so that it knew it must follow at a distance. Incredibly, the Tracker still hadn't spotted it and it seemed as if both Gloria and the wolf wanted to keep it that way. Gloria trudged along muttering obscenities beneath her breath and every now and again Emily would let out a loud chuckle, disguising it quickly with a cough, whenever she recognised one of them. There was something about Gloria that Emily simply loved, no matter what kind of mood she was in.

The pace the Tracker set was slow and steady as there was very little light around them and it seemed like hours before they stopped for their first break. By this time they were ravenous. They hadn't eaten since the day before and their insides were cramping. There was nothing left in the rucksack and only half a bottle of water which Belinda had decided to carry so that no one was tempted to gulp from it without the full consent of the group. Everyone sat and looked at each other in despair.

"How much further, do you think?" asked April. A question that was on everyone's lips!

"It's a good way yet," answered the Tracker. "You'll smell a change in the air soon and then you'll feel much better."

No one said anything. A change in the air? What on earth was he talking about? The last change in the air had been when the storm was on the verge of exploding and that hadn't been something to look forward to. They were so hungry. Their stomachs were grumbling loudly enough for each and every one of them to hear and they could focus on little else. The Tracker studiously set his bag down on the earth in front of them and opened it. Out of it he pulled a half eaten loaf of bread. The women and girls stared at it, eyes wide with longing. The Tracker began to tear the loaf into chunks and then to share it out. He presented the first portion to Pat making sure their fingers touched briefly as he did so. April frowned. He was up to something. She didn't trust him. The bread was dry but not quite stale and clearly the Tracker had been travelling with it in his bag for some time. Everyone tucked in, chewing at the bread greedily, desperate to assuage their pangs of hunger. The Tracker watched Pat as she took her first bite. He stared at her mouth as she devoured her chunk of bread. April shuffled a little closer. She didn't like the way he was looking at Pat.

"Thanks," she said, trying to distract him. The Tracker turned to April and gave her a lopsided grin. He appeared quite normal and perfectly affable and once again April wondered if she was imagining things. The wolf stayed out of sight and April felt more courageous because of this. The group had a secret weapon. She decided that she would remain extremely vigilant where Pat was concerned. There was something about the Tracker that unnerved her but perhaps it was simply that there was a man in the group and she had grown used to being around women. She gave the Tracker a falsely bright smile. It would be such a relief to finally meet up with her grandmother.

The rest of the journey that day passed without consequence. They trudged on and on behind the Tracker keeping their heads low and walking as close to the middle of the tunnel as possible. The walls at the sides of the tunnel were becoming damp and were streaked with a white residue. April stuck her finger out, wiped it on the wall and then licked it. Wow! It was salt! Yuk! The Tracker was right about the smell too. It was different. The air was fresh and cool with a saline tang to it and there was something about it that made the whole group droop and feel tired again. It was a yawning sort of tired, not a bodily tired, but one that couldn't be ignored. It had to be something to do with the change in the air.

"Can we sit for a moment?" Emily called from the back of the group.

She was lagging behind with Gloria. Gloria had her by the elbow for support but Emily was becoming more and more unsteady on her feet as exhaustion gradually seeped through her body.

"I can't go on much longer," Emily called again.

The Tracker stopped and turned round. The women and girls were slowing down. Their energy was low. He assessed the situation. The earth beneath their feet had been replaced by wooden boards some time ago and they would soon be so wet they would be slippery. They would need their wits about them to finish the journey without stumbling or falling. The Tracker wanted to hand each member of the group over without any broken bones and in perfect condition. He wanted his reward. Five absentees was enough for a very good reward especially as three of them were young, attractive girls, one of whom in fact was particularly beautiful and would fetch a high price if she hadn't been interfered with. Of course that bothersome baby would have to go. She had been grizzling on and off since they had last eaten and would be of no use to anyone. But that girl! She was exquisite. She would fetch a substantial amount no matter what. He would have to decide what he was going to do. If she had been tampered with he might be able to claim her for his own. That was an enticing thought! Perhaps he should keep her for himself. She could travel around with him and he would teach her how to be a Tracker. She would be available for him every night then. He would get a big enough reward simply by handing over four females. He would have to be careful though. He would be kind to the young girl and work hard at gaining her trust but ultimately his own needs were in a state of desperation. Every time he looked at Pat he ached. Images of his hands removing her clothes and then running them over her young, naked body constantly flashed through his mind. She was at that perfect stage where she was neither woman nor child. His desire for her made his loins throb. He would have to get that other girl out of the way, the one who clung like a limpet. She never seemed to leave her side and the way she carried that crowbar with her? It was as if she couldn't wait to use it. She might be more than just a bit of a nuisance. He gritted his teeth and addressed the woman in charge:

"A little further and we'll be outside. There is an exit point close by."

He could hear the sighs of relief around him as he turned away and began walking again. He smirked. They were in the palm of his hand. He definitely had the situation under control.

Ten minutes or so went by and then the Tracker stopped. He raised his arms and began to push at a square manhole cover above him. He knew these tunnels so well. There were short cuts through them that led everywhere. It was much quicker to travel by tunnel than to follow the road above, no matter how pleasant the weather. This cover was easy to dislodge and he pushed it aside, heaving himself up and through to the fresh air above. He took in a few deep breaths and gave a great stretch. He had felt hemmed in throughout the journey in the confined space of the tunnel. Then he lay on his stomach at the edge of the manhole reaching down so that he could haul each female upwards and into the daylight. He was in two minds as to whether or not he should leave the old woman where she was. She wouldn't fetch much of a reward. The only employment she would be suitable for would be permanent residency in an all male environment; one that required a tough, capable housekeeper to keep on top of all the dirty work.

Gloria dug her nails into the Tracker's palms as he pulled her upwards so that he almost dropped her. She could hear him cursing beneath his breath. He knew practically as many swear words as she did. She tried not to grin. There was something about him that repelled her and it was a stronger feeling than her general dislike of men. Like April she didn't trust him; but for different reasons. Why would a Tracker help a group of females in any way unless it was for self gain? She knew all about the reward system and was sure that his ultimate goal would be to hand them over in order to claim it. She would have to keep her ears and eyes open, but luckily she still had an ace up her sleeve. The Tracker knew nothing about the wolf. The wolf had quietly and stealthily padded along behind the group keeping well hidden amongst the shadows. Gloria had thrown half her portion of bread in its direction earlier on and had heard the wolf snaffle it down with a gulp a moment or so later. They were all hungry again as well as tired and needed to refill their stomachs.

Finally everyone was above ground and able to stand and absorb the beauty of the landscape around them. The group stared in disbelief and wonder. All evidence of the storm had disappeared as if it had never happened and the view was breathtaking! Lush green grass and foliage were in abundance and the sky was turning a deep but vivid blue, just on the cusp of dusk. They had come away from the road and were now very close to the volcanic mountain and the sea. The sea was much bigger than any of them could ever have imagined. The enormity of it was overwhelming. A sense of excitement arose within the group as they stared at it. They had almost reached their destination. They were nearly there! April felt tears pricking at the back of her eyelids as she yearned for her grandmother and she could see that Pat's eyelashes were wet and that she was working hard at holding back sobs of relief. The two girls glanced at each other keeping straight faces and without saying anything. They didn't want the Tracker to know what was going on. The Tracker pointed to a wooden hut sheltered beneath some trees and began to make his way towards it. Belinda turned to the group and discreetly put a finger to her lips so that they would remain quiet. They could discuss things later, in privacy hopefully. Emily squeezed Gloria's hand in delight as she grabbed at it and Gloria returned her gesture with a toothless grin.

"I'll replace the cover," she said, addressing the Tracker as he walked away and he lifted a hand in acknowledgement without even bothering to look back at her. He was certainly feeling confident. Gloria peered down into the darkness of the manhole, whistling quietly for the wolf and was instantly almost knocked over as it gave an almighty leap and flew, hurtling through the air, onto the grass beside her. It shook itself, licked her hand and then loped off, taking cover under some leafy shrubs nearby. Gloria knew it would be watching and waiting and would follow them when it could. The thought of the wolf travelling with them made Gloria feel safe. She had studied the Tracker's long, lean body and could feel the raw strength and energy that he exuded. She was sure that he would easily be able to deal with five females if he had to. One word from her though and the wolf would go straight for the Tracker's throat, clamping its jaws around it, worrying at it and not stopping until it had ripped it out and the Tracker had bled to death. She hoped she wouldn't be forced into making such a decision as a dead Tracker would encourage pursuit and the strong possibility of capture. And it would be difficult to dispose of the body here. Someone or something would find evidence of the Tracker and then there would be trouble. She didn't want that to happen.

April walked beside Pat. She had intimated in the tunnel that she would like to give her a break by taking care of Hope for a while but, as always, Pat had declined her thoughtful offer. It was a job she enjoyed doing. She loved the responsibility of looking after Hope. She had passed small masticated morsels of bread directly from her mouth to Hope's as the semi stale chunk which the Tracker had given her would have been far too hard for her soft gums and palate. Hope had a few teeth coming through now and was learning to use them. She had gazed at Pat quizzically at the first bland taste of stale bread but after an encouraging smile she chewed, swallowed and trustingly opened her mouth for more. Pat felt important and needed.

The two girls walked side by side amicably. Both could feel the significance of how far they had come as they approached the end of their journey. April was desperate to discuss how she felt about that first incredible glimpse of the sea and how it looked now they were so close to it and she knew that Pat would be feeling the same. They would have to wait until they were in the hut. Maybe the Tracker would go out for a while and then they could chat about what they had seen and their situation. It was difficult to say anything knowing that he was within earshot and could hear everything they said. They certainly didn't want him to know about April's grandmother.

Belinda walked directly behind the Tracker. She too was astounded at the enormity and proximity of the sea and the sight of the volcanic mountain. She thrust her stick into the earth as she walked and felt a renewed sense of vigour began to flow through her. She was positive that they would be able to get rid of the Tracker although at the moment she had no idea how. She wasn't going to expend energy worrying about it though. April and Gloria were strong allies and she could trust and depend on them for support no matter what happened.

The Tracker stood waiting for them at the door of the hut.

"You'll be safe here," he said, ushering them in. "I'm going to find food. Keep the door shut as wolves can often be found in this area."

Gloria stared at him. Did he know about the wolf? Had he seen it and known it was with them all along or was he simply making an innocuous remark? She followed the others into the hut, taking in the new surroundings as she did so. The hut was dry inside and slightly stuffy and there was a musty smell about it as if it had been unoccupied for a long time. There was a small, grimy window in the corner that let in a smidgeon of light.

"Can we open the window?" asked Belinda, fanning herself and almost reading Gloria's thoughts. "It's stifling in here and I don't think any wolves will be small enough to jump through."

The Tracker moved over to the window and wrenched at the latch. It was stiff but eventually, after a lot of tugging and pushing, the window opened. The latch snapped and came away in his hand. A waft of cool air blew in. That was better. The Tracker propped the window open using the broken latch so that they could see some of what was left of the daylight as well as enjoying the fresh air.

"I'll be back soon," he said. "Stay inside now."

He strode out of the door into the falling dusk. He knew where the padlock and keys were hidden but he didn't want to arouse suspicion. He wanted the group to feel comfortable with him for a little longer, just until he could make contact with his superiors, and locking them in certainly wouldn't help. He could do that later when everything had been sorted to his satisfaction.

As soon as the Tracker was out of hearing distance every face lit up. The women and girls turned to each other in wonder and excitement.

"We're nearly at my grandmother's house!" exclaimed April suddenly, unable to contain herself any longer. "We're nearly there!"

"And did you see all that water?" squealed Pat excitedly. "I could never in my wildest dreams have imagined anything like that."

"It looked awesome!" agreed Emily. "Do you think we'll be able to get really close to it?"

"I want to do more than get close to it. I want to be in it," added Belinda. "I want the experience of being in the sea. If a boat can float on top of it then I want to step into it and see what it's like. It has to be pretty much the same as soaking in a huge bathtub, although I don't suppose it'll be hot." And she chuckled even as she thought of it.

Gloria was standing by the window watching the Tracker as he strode away.

"We have to get rid of him," she said. "I don't reckon he's up to much good. We're almost at the end of our journey and we can't have him coming with us, can we?"

Vocal again and making a lot of sense, Belinda thought. She stared at Gloria, her brows furrowed. She had no idea how they might get rid of the Tracker.

"Perhaps we should tie him up and just leave him here?" suggested Emily.

"What with?" asked April.

"Rope of course."

"We don't have any."

There was silence after this as no one had any suggestions. They looked round at each other hoping for the hint of a sensible solution. Of course the Tracker would have to go. He couldn't possibly travel with them to April's grandmother's house. That was out of the question and they would definitely be heading for trouble if he came with them. He had helped them out when they needed it but he had more than likely done this with an ulterior motive in mind. No matter how kind or helpful he seemed he was not to be trusted.

"I wonder what he'll bring back with him?" Pat asked eventually, breaking the prolonged silence.

"Who knows?" responded April, shrugging her shoulders. "Let's rest. We can spread out the sheepskins. At least then we won't be lying on bare boards."

She proceeded to pull out the pieces of thick sheepskin from the rucksack and passed them round. Pat still had sheepskin secured around her shoulders, an emergency measure in case Hope became cold and also because there had been no extra space for it in the rucksack. Everyone grabbed a piece and settled down comfortably. Only Gloria considered the possibility that someone ought to remain awake and wait for the Tracker to return. Everyone else was ready to sleep. They were warm, they were dry and for the moment they were safe and it was time to rest.

Just as they were nodding off the door opened and the Tracker came in. A smell of something warm and doughy wafted in with him. April tried hard to open her eyes but only Gloria was wide awake, waiting behind the door, anticipating his arrival. She took the brown paper parcel that the Tracker offered and proceeded to unwrap it. The brown wrapping fell unnoticed to the floor as she held the contents up to her nose and sniffed long and hard. This was bread, freshly baked bread, bread that was perfect for eating, perfect for eating right now! There was nothing stale about this loaf! She turned her back on the Tracker and broke the loaf into soft chunks, respectfully keeping the largest chunk for their provider and sharing out the rest, placing a piece gently into the hands of each of her friends. The delicious smell was almost enough to encourage them to open their eyes but everyone was so tired that they simply lifted the soft, doughy bread to their mouths, murmuring in drowsy pleasure as they bit deeply into it and chewed. Each piece disappeared quickly, devoured in moments, and then everyone except Gloria fell into a deep sleep, the sleep that comes with full-bellied satisfaction and exhaustion.

Gloria was determined to stay awake for as long as possible so that she could keep an eye on the Tracker. The bread was definitely freshly baked and so this raised the question: where exactly had it come from? She hadn't noticed any other huts or dwellings as they made their way across the grass and through the trees but clearly the Tracker knew his way around. She watched him from beneath semi closed lids so that he would think she was asleep just like the others. What was he planning? Had he informed someone of their whereabouts? Was he even now waiting to collect his reward? Were others on their way? She watched as he sat with his back against the door, knees drawn up and shoulders drooping. He had no need to be on his guard – he was clearly at ease with his assumed role within the group. She watched until his head dropped and he began to snore. There was no longer any need for Gloria to remain awake and vigilant. It was time for her too to sleep.

CHAPTER THIRTY-ONE

April was dreaming. Her dream was filled with colourful visions of the sea and of George and her grandmother and even of baby Hope crawling. It was such a wonderful dream. They were having a picnic by the sea and Hope was crawling everywhere. But suddenly she was out of reach, crawling steadfastly towards the water and no one had noticed. In her dream April darted across the sand and reached down to scoop her up just as the first, salty waves dared to lap around her podgy fists, knees and toes. Hope giggled as April swung her round and carried her back to safety. Where was Pat? She always looked after Hope. Why hadn't she seen her crawling away? But Pat had finished eating and had fallen asleep amongst the dunes, tossing and turning restlessly, making distressed noises. She was obviously in the middle of a bad dream and April couldn't let her suffer. She had to wake her.

April half opened her eyes. Was she still asleep? She could hear muffled sounds around her. What was going on? And why was she suddenly filled with such a strong sense of dread? For a moment or two she felt disorientated and didn't know where she was. Was she dreaming or was she awake? She knew the sounds were coming from Pat but still couldn't figure out where she was or where Pat was either. All was darkness around her with only a minimal strip of light shining along a crack in the floorboards. Where was the light coming from? Was she back in the tunnels searching for a way out with the rest of the group? No, of course not, for they had left the tunnels some time ago. That thin strip of light could only be coming from the moon. April blinked a few times. What was going on? Where was she? And then she remembered. She was in the hut with her friends and the Tracker. Yes, they were with a Tracker and she didn't trust him. Without moving she opened her eyes wide and stared around her. It was difficult to see anything clearly but it was definitely Pat making the strange, stifled noises. A flicker of fear intermingled with the dread. What was that large shape by the door? Why wasn't Pat lying next to her? And why was she holding Hope and not Pat? Why was Hope sleeping soundly in the crook of her arm, her breath coming and going in short, contented pants, and not in Pat's arms? She was always with Pat. She didn't remember Hope being placed in the crook of her arm. How had she got there? Where was Pat?

Little by little her eyes adjusted to the lack of light and she found she could make out the large shape by the door. The shape seemed to be made up of two people. One of them was on top of the other and as she continued to stare she was able to make out Pat's face turned towards her and the whites of her eyes rolling back in what could only be described as terror. Someone was on top of Pat and had placed a hand over her mouth. Pat was kicking and trying to attract attention but the more noise she made the harder the hand pressed down. Who was on top of Pat and why? No, it couldn't be, but yes it was! It was the Tracker! What was he doing? Suddenly a large expanse of white flesh flashed into view. April could see everything now. The Tracker had his pants down and one hand was tearing frantically at Pat's clothes. A moment later and the Tracker began grunting with excitement. There was a ripping sound as he gave a final tug at Pat's clothing and pushed a knee between her legs to force them open. April couldn't believe her eyes. Was this really happening or was she still dreaming? Perhaps she was asleep and having what could only be described as a hideous nightmare? She had heard about the things men forced girls to do at Avondale Manor and once she had even seen her father in exactly the same position with her mother. And she hadn't seemed to be enjoying it! She had seen her father pushing his stiff penis in and out between her mother's legs and she had recoiled in horror behind the dividing curtain and stuffed her fingers in her ears so that she could pretend it wasn't happening and that her mother wasn't in pain. April rubbed at her eyes and sat bolt upright just in case she was still asleep and dreaming the awful scenario playing out in front of her. Pat's eyes were pleading for help and then suddenly her back was arching high as the Tracker attempted penetration. April could almost hear Pat's soundless screams whilst the Tracker's backside bobbed up and down like a hair strewn moon as he repeatedly jabbed between her legs. Was the Tracker trying to have sex with Pat? But Pat wasn't a woman; she was still a young girl! She was far too young for sex. Was that what was happening? Was he actually trying to have sex with her? April wasn't sexually experienced in any way but she had heard enough lurid tales in the past from both Bertha and Pat to know that men inflicted themselves brutally on the coming of age girls at Avondale Manor. She shuddered, horrified. Surely the Tracker couldn't be raping Pat? Surely he couldn't be stupid enough to force himself upon her in the middle of a small, wooden hut full of females? But what else could he be doing and why else would Pat look so terrified? Instantly April came to her senses and quietly and gently rolled Hope aside, unwilling to disturb her. Whatever the Tracker was doing it was against Pat's will and he was hurting her and that was unforgivable. He had to be stopped. April rose slowly to her feet picking up the crowbar as she did so. She had to do something before he hurt Pat anymore. She tiptoed to the door, raised the crowbar high above her head and then brought it down hard in the middle of the Tracker's back. He let out the most astonished and pained of yells. Everyone was waking now and beginning to take in what was going on. April brought the crowbar down again and this time it was upon the Tracker's head. The blow stunned him but not enough to discourage him from attempting to penetrate

Pat. He glared at April, growled angrily and resumed thrusting. April felt a surge of anger rush through her. Who did he think he was? She lifted the crowbar for the third time and directed it once more towards the Tracker's head. It caught him on the side of the neck and there was a loud crack. Instantly the Tracker slumped forward and stopped moving.

"Get him off me!" screamed Pat as soon as she could twist her face and mouth away from beneath his hot, sweaty palm. "Get him off me!"

April flung aside the crowbar and pushed at the Tracker. He was a mass of deadweight now that he wasn't moving and far too heavy for her. She took a deep breath and pushed again. He rolled a little but as soon as April let go he rolled back again. Pat cried out in pain. Belinda, who had woken up and had been watching April in horror, quickly grasped the situation and scrambled to her feet to help her. Between them they managed to roll the Tracker over onto his back. His eager penis instantly bounced upwards like a rocket prepared to launch and April gave a startled shriek. She had never seen the private parts of a man so closely before. Pat wriggled her way out from beneath the Tracker, struggling to compose herself and reorganise her torn clothing. Amidst all the noise and pandemonium Hope duly decided to make sure her presence was noted and began to screech at the top of her lungs. Emily was staring, wide-eyed and in shock, not understanding what had happened. She could see that everyone was awake and that the Tracker was half-undressed, lying with his head at a peculiar angle, and not moving. Gloria sniggered gleefully at the sight in front of her, shuffling across and putting two fingers to his throat to check his pulse.

"I think you've killed him," she said, grinning widely as she turned to April. "That pretty much solves our problem."

Emily gasped in horror and began to wail loudly. Pat frowned at her and picked up Hope, cradling her and hushing her back to sleep. She lowered her head so that she didn't have to make eye contact with anybody. She had her knees tightly pressed together and tried not to wince in pain as she attempted to settle into a comfortable position. It hurt where the Tracker had been trying to push his way in. April sat down next to her and placed an arm protectively around her shoulders, staring at everyone belligerently. She didn't care if the Tracker was dead. He deserved it for hurting Pat. She would sort out anyone who tried to hurt either Pat or Hope. Belinda put her arms around Emily to comfort her and turned her head away from the gruesome sight in front of her. Gloria put her finger to her lips to quieten them all and then moved over to the door, opening it slightly to see if there was anyone outside who had heard the commotion and was even now arriving to investigate. All remained quiet though. The moon shone gently, illuminating the hut and surrounding area with a haunting, silvery glow but all was stillness. Gloria peered into the distance looking for the wolf. Yes, there it was. She could see the outline of its powerful, muscular body at the edge of the trees. It was sitting on its haunches and waiting. Every now and then the light from the moon flashed down upon its fur, so that it shimmered with an ethereal sheen. It waited. Gloria nodded towards it. She had an idea!

"What happened?" whispered April in Pat's ear. "Why did you give Hope to me? I must have been sound asleep because I didn't even notice."

"The Tracker called me over," replied Pat. "He said he had some bread left and that I could have it for Hope. He told me to reach into his pocket and take it. I did but there wasn't any bread there. I could feel something else though, something squashy. Then he put his hand on top of mine and moved it around and the squashy thing became hard. I don't need to tell you what it was. You can easily guess." She shivered in disgust. "The next minute he was on top of me and my hand was trapped in his pocket squeezing his thing and his hand was over my mouth. Then he became really agitated and started trying to do things and I saw you were awake and you know the rest. If you hadn't hit him when you did there's no telling what would have happened ...."

"Well I did hit him and I'm glad I did. I didn't trust him and I was right. I'm glad he's dead too and I hope he stays that way. I don't want to have to use the crowbar again though. I'm getting to be a bit of a thug with it. When we get to my grandmother's I'm going to throw it away."

"We'll be there soon," said Pat.

"Yes, we will," confirmed April. She paused for a moment. "Did he hurt you?"

Pat nodded. "He really wanted to get inside me. You stopped him just in time but I am sore down there."

"Wish I'd bashed his bits off with the crowbar as well as breaking his neck."

And both girls stared with loathing at his naked, male parts. April began to snicker; making an uncontrollable, snorting sound. She was going into shock. Pat tried to nestle her head against her shoulder but was jostled up and down by the random spurts of laughter. She too began to giggle hysterically.

"I'd like to have seen you do that," she stuttered, when she was next able to draw breath.

"I still could," April responded. "Believe me I still could, but I won't. It would just make a mess."

"We need to get the Tracker outside," interrupted Gloria suddenly. "I think if we can do that we won't have to worry about disposing of him. Open the door for me."

She grabbed hold of his booted feet and began to pull. He was, of course, far too heavy for one woman alone. Belinda joined her and together they dragged him, painstakingly and inch by inch, across the wooden, hut floor.

"Can someone cover his thing, for goodness' sake? I don't want to have to keep looking at it," called out Belinda as she tugged. "It's not a pretty sight!"

April jumped to her feet, leaving Pat for a moment, and threw a piece of torn clothing across the Tracker's lower regions. It landed perfectly and stood aloft like a small pyramid celebrating his neglected manhood. She grimaced at the sight of it, running to the door to fling it wide and then doubling over and clutching at her sides to alleviate the stitch that had abruptly chosen to arrive with an impressive sting.

"We need to get him round to the back of the hut," said Gloria. "And then no one will see what happens to him. And hopefully, there will be no one to care."

Belinda grunted in reply. She had no idea what Gloria was talking about. After all, the dead Tracker wasn't going to simply disappear, was he? But at least he would be out of the way at the back of the hut. She continued tugging. One of his boots came off in her hand and she threw it aside, finding her hands now gripping at a bare ankle. Eventually the Tracker was out of the door and from somewhere in the distance she thought she heard an ululating howl. The wolf was still about then? She looked around for it. Yes, there it was. She could see its silvery grey outline silhouetted against the moon and its head thrown back as it let out another long and haunting cry.

"The wolves will be hungry," muttered Gloria in a low voice so that only Belinda could hear. "My friend is calling them. As soon as we are back inside he will be here, looking to see what we have left out for him."

Belinda understood now and her hands quivered as she continued to pull. Gloria was clearly intimating that the wolves would dispose of the Tracker. In that case they would have to hide his body some distance away from the back of the hut as it would hardly be appropriate for the younger girls to hear the Tracker being ripped apart and devoured by a pack of savage wolves. April had already shocked herself and some of the others by attacking the Tracker with the crowbar and that was more than enough for anyone to deal with. Belinda knew that she had previously used the crowbar under extreme provocation but as far as she was aware she had never killed anyone before. She had extricated the group from a worrying and troublesome predicament and that was wonderful but she had been through enough for the moment. She was still not much more than a child, after all.

The two women dragged, pulled, tugged and pushed until finally they were able to shove the Tracker under some bushes out of sight away from the back of the hut. They rolled him over as far as they could and then Belinda retrieved his boot and hid it. She pulled his pants up as far as she could in order to cover his naked parts. Why she bothered she had no idea but it seemed as if giving him a little dignity in death was the right thing to do. Now they needed to return to the hut and reassure everyone that everything was going to be alright. There was nothing more they could do tonight except rest. Gloria let out a long, low whistle and was rewarded by a series of sharp, short barks in return. Belinda raised her eyebrows. That woman was an enigma. There was always something new to learn about her.

Once inside the hut Gloria picked up April's crowbar and wedged the door shut with it. She didn't want anyone or anything disturbing them for the rest of the night. April, Pat, Emily and Hope were cuddled closely together under a couple of sheepskins and were drifting off. The late evening's events had taken on a surreal quality, almost as if the whole episode had been nothing more than a bad dream and as they snuggled up next to each other they found the warmth of their bodies conducive to deep and restful sleep. Gloria took a seated position close to the door whilst Belinda settled down next to Emily.

"I'll keep watch for the next few hours," said Gloria. "I'll wake you when I can no longer keep my eyes open."

"Thanks," said Belinda. She was exhausted, not just on a physical level but also on an emotional one. The Tracker had been very heavy and her arms ached. The thought of what he had been trying to do to Pat was appalling. She noted that April had an arm extended towards the crowbar with her fingertips outstretched even as she slept. Gloria must have watched her as she used it but had said and done nothing. Belinda smiled to herself. April was another one who was full of surprises. She shook her head slightly and closed her eyes, allowing fatigue to carry her away.

CHAPTER THIRTY-TWO

The remainder of the night passed without further disturbance. In the morning everyone was bright and cheerful and except for the missing Tracker it was almost as if nothing had happened and that perhaps they had merely dreamt his existence. He had been of no consequence anyway; just someone who had helped them out for a brief period of time, given them some bread, both stale and fresh, and then disappeared.

Gloria had waited until she heard the wolves dragging the dead body away and then she had shaken Belinda out of her sleep so that she could get some rest. She was used to thinking only of herself and this newfound consideration for others was becoming tediously relentless. She didn't know how long she could keep it up for or even if she really wanted to. Once they arrived at their destination she would say goodbye and get on with her own life once more. She had grown attached to everyone, particularly Emily, but Emily would be starting a new chapter in her life, one with her mother, and would probably no longer need her. Gloria shrugged. She was used to being on her own and so she would just return to previous, familiar patterns. Even as she acknowledged this she felt a strange ache inside. This was unexpected. She gave a disdainful sniff. She was turning into a sentimental, old fool. Somehow she had allowed herself to get used to female company and had even begun to enjoy it. There was no need to worry though. She would easily be able to switch off. She had done it before and she would do it again. She gritted her teeth and turned to Belinda.

"I'll check outside," she said.

Belinda nodded. She knew exactly what Gloria meant. If, as she anticipated, the Tracker had been devoured by the wolves then Gloria would want to make sure there was no trace of him. It would be awful if any of the girls happened upon a pile of mangled and bloody body parts as they set off. And it would be even worse if somehow they were unfortunate enough to be able to identify them. It was time to put things behind them and move forward towards a brighter future. Belinda scoured the hut making sure that all their belongings were gathered and that there would be nothing left behind. There must be no evidence of any of them having been there. Apart from the broken latch on the window and the fact that the air inside the hut was fresher than when they had first arrived, everything looked much as it had done. The latch could have been broken at any time and that would also account for the ventilation. Belinda still felt anxious regarding the Tracker as he must have conversed with someone in the area in order to obtain the freshly baked bread but hopefully no one would be concerned enough with his whereabouts to make inquiries after him and perhaps his arrival in the area was nothing more than an occasional and random visit.

Gloria was back in the hut almost before Belinda had finished her musings.

"We're safe to go," she said and was rewarded with a cheerful smile from Belinda and beams of optimism from the girls. Their guileless enthusiasm struck at Gloria's heart and she felt that strange ache again and knew she would be sad to leave them, subsequently depriving herself of their friendship.

"We're very close to the sea. It's not the quickest route to the mountain but it will do us good to fill our lungs with all that salty air."

Belinda agreed with her. There could be no harm in walking along the water's edge. How did Gloria know anything about the sea though? That was another thing. She had kept quiet for so long, joining in as and when she pleased, and now she was revealing herself as prolifically knowledgeable. Now there was nothing they could say that would stop her from talking. She was a totally different person from the surly, old woman they had first encountered hiding behind the door in the tunnels. And thank goodness she was! Belinda ushered the girls out of the hut and into the sunlight. It was going to be a beautiful day and with the incredible experience of the sea to look forward to it ought to be a memorable one too.

The girls could hardly contain their excitement as they feasted their eyes on the sea. Emily let out an instant squeal of delight. With the sun coming up the water sparkled and shone with flecks of rainbow colours flickering across its surface. It had rained at some point during the night and the grassy patch of green leading down to the sand caressed their feet with dewy coolness as they stepped onto it. Life was good. They were near the end of their journey and soon to meet April's grandmother. As they reached the sand Emily began to run. She couldn't help herself. She didn't know what she was going to do when she actually arrived at the water's edge but she knew she had to get there. April began to run too, wincing as she did so. Belinda looked at the disappointment on Pat's face and quickly reached out for Hope.

"Go on," she said, "run along with the others. I'll take care of Hope for a while. You don't need to miss out on the fun."

Pat hesitated and then grinned.

"Thanks," she said and darted happily after April and Emily. By the time she reached the water April had removed her boots and Emily had discarded her socks and trainers.

"Your feet!" cried Pat. "Your poor, poor feet!"

Emily stared down at her feet. There was nothing wrong with them. What was Pat talking about? They were pale and squashy-looking as they hadn't seen the light of day for some time but that was all. She wiggled her toes; yes, they were still working, just a bit grubby and that was on the verge of being resolved too. She grinned at Pat.

"My feet are fine," April responded with a grimace. She knew to whom Pat was referring.

But clearly they weren't. By now both Emily and Pat were staring at her discoloured, lumpen feet in horror. April let out an exasperated sigh, ignored them and hobbled quickly into the water. She didn't want anyone to make a fuss. Her feet had been painful since leaving the Wine Sellers and she hadn't ever felt brave enough to take off her boots and examine them. She knew that once she managed to peel them off she probably wouldn't be able to get them back on again. As it was it had taken some time to ease the cracked, split boots over her stiff, chapped ankles and heels and a great deal of holding of breath and she had been shocked by the sight of her poor feet when finally they were sticking out in front of her. At first glance they looked dark and swollen and rather like lumps of raw meat. They didn't look like her feet at all and right now she didn't want to talk about it. She wanted to step into the sea and enjoy the feeling of cold water lapping against her legs. And so off she hobbled. It was soothing standing up to her knees in the water and although the water was chilly the longer she stood in it the more she thought she felt life begin to return to her feet and ankles. Hopping from one foot to another she found she was able to wiggle her toes. In all honesty she had been wondering how much further she would be able to walk anyway. She had only held out because she knew that they were close to her grandmother's house. With every step lately it had felt as though red hot knives were being stabbed viciously into the soles of her feet. She hoped her feet were not infected in any way and that they just needed a good clean. She wiggled her toes even more. Her feet didn't look too bad. She frowned down at them through the salty water noting that the coldness seemed to alleviate some of the intense throbbing. She remembered reading somewhere that salt water was a great healer. She would stand and walk in the sea for as long as she could. The water would soothe her feet and help wash away the pain. How she had managed to run that short distance with Emily through the sand and down to the sea she had no idea but she had done it and now she was in the water. She had made it! Her feet felt less troublesome than they had done for a long time. April squeezed her eyes tightly shut so that no one could see the tears that were threatening to fall.

By now Gloria and Belinda had arrived. Belinda undressed Hope and watched as she attempted to crawl after the girls. Her chubby hands squelched open and shut up in the damp sand and she crowed with delight. She sat and slapped at the water as a shallow wave rolled in and then out again. She dug into the sand with her fists and crammed them into her mouth, spluttering and coughing as she consumed a mix of gritty sand and salt water. Belinda grabbed her, laughing, swinging her up into the air, slipping off her own loose ankle boots with ease and then striding into the sea to catch up with the girls. Gloria had quickly stripped down to her underwear and by now was far away in the distance, swimming, and all that could be seen of her was her head bobbing up and down amongst the waves. When had she learnt to swim? Who had taught her? Belinda decided then and there that she was going to have to find out more about this enigmatic, old woman they were travelling with. She knew so little about her. None of them did. Even April and Pat had opened up about their lives, revealing snippets of disturbing information about Avondale House and Manor and their former family situations. But Gloria never said anything. Everyone assumed that she had always lived in the tunnels and surrounding mountains. She had been the one to teach the group the basics of survival and so of course she must always have been there. The truth was that no one had really been interested enough in Gloria to ask her anything. Gloria was just a grouchy, old woman that no one liked to cross. But with the passing of time Belinda had seen something else. It had started as she watched her behaviour with Emily and her fierce protectiveness of her. She had later been taken by surprise at the sight of Gloria's complete ease and comradeship with the wolf and finally it was the surprising amount of knowledge she possessed and her obvious enjoyment and familiarity with the sea.

Belinda walked through the waves towards the girls. She was soon waist deep in the water and loving every moment of it. Pat and Emily were jumping up and down splashing one another. When was the last time they had played, as youngsters and children were supposed to? Belinda contemplated the happy scene in front of her with a smile tinged with sadness. She hoisted Hope a little further onto her hip and Hope clapped her hands together and reached out for Pat. Pat laughed as she saw her, wading through the water towards her and grabbing hold of her. Emily and Pat each took an arm and swung Hope back and forth through the waves. Hope loved it. April stood and watched, deep enough in the water now for the rolling swell to almost cover her thighs and the bottom half of her rolled up trousers to be wet through. She trickled her fingers dreamily and distractedly through the water as she gazed at her friends. Belinda pushed her way towards her.

"It's beautiful, isn't it? It's not even as cold as I imagined it would be. In fact the further out you get the warmer it is."

April nodded. She wasn't sure whether or not she trusted herself to speak.

"Are you alright?" asked Belinda. "You've been very quiet today. Seeing the Tracker on top of Pat must have been very traumatic for you. But you dealt with it and if I'd been awake I would have done exactly the same thing."

April turned to her. "My feet are sore," she replied with a taut smile. Why she had chosen to mention her feet she had no idea. Perhaps it was Belinda's kindly concern for her? The words had trickled out without any thought behind them. She had never had any intention of telling anyone about her feet. After all, they didn't have far to go now and maybe she could walk bare-footed for the rest of the journey? She dreaded the thought of putting her boots back on. She could barely contemplate the agony such an action would bring; if indeed she were able to manage it.

"We'll have a look at them before setting off again, shall we?" said Belinda gently and April turned her head away so that Belinda couldn't see the misery on her face or the hot, stinging tears that she was trying to prevent from rolling down her cheeks. She hated feeling vulnerable. She had tried to be so strong throughout the entire journey and now that they were close to the end of it she could feel a knot of buried emotions clawing their way up from her chest, threatening to drown her in an ocean of grief-stricken sobs. Suddenly she felt a strong, warm arm placed around her shoulders.

"Don't worry. I'm here for you," said Belinda and instantly the tears ran. April's chest crumpled and her shoulders began to heave in ragged, spasmodic jerks as she allowed herself to relax into Belinda's comforting embrace and for a minute or two the floodgates were open. Belinda waited, allowing the tears to freely fall. Eventually they subsided and April gave a few snuffly, embarrassed hiccoughs.

"Better now?" asked Belinda giving her a final hug. "You're not on your own, you know."

"Thank you," whispered April, bending down and washing the telltale tears away with a splash of salty, sea water.

CHAPTER THIRTY-THREE

The entire morning was spent in the sea, playing, splashing, swimming and cementing friendships, but most of all enjoying a newfound sense of freedom and the exhilarating giddiness of expectations about to be fulfilled. All too soon however Belinda announced that it was time to move on. Standing at the water's edge, wringing out wet clothes and grinning at one another, they turned, one by one, to look at the mountain. It was so close now and so huge, looming up in front of them; and it appeared well within a few hours walking distance. Everyone was eager to get there. Belinda had examined April's feet, cringing inwardly but outwardly making light of their discoloured, swollen appearance and reassuring April that they would heal very quickly in the fresh air. There was no need for her to put her boots on again. In fact why didn't April throw them into the sea and allow the waves to dispose of them? The boots were misshapen, cracked and split and no longer fit to wear anyway. She didn't know how April had managed to walk in them for so long. They were an offence to leather and to footwear. Gloria announced that she had a small pot of homemade, herbal salve in one of her skirt pockets and that as soon as they reached dry land she would rub some into April's feet. She would also tear one of the sheepskin pieces into long strips and bind April's feet with them. They would be most comfortable as a pair of temporary, makeshift shoes. Belinda nodded in agreement.

It was decided that for the moment the group would follow the coastline and so they could either paddle at the water's edge or indulge in squelching their feet in the damp sand, whichever appealed most. When they arrived at the rocky perimeter of the mountain they would stop and tend to April's feet before journeying on. April gave a thankful smile of relief. She no longer felt tearful. She was with her family and friends and they cared about her. There was no need for her to keep quiet about her needs or her painful feet. As long as she was able to dip her feet into the sea whenever they began to throb or hurt too much she knew she would be able to cope.

Everyone was content. The sun was shining and the salty, sea air was fresh and invigorating. The gentle lapping of the waves added to their enjoyment as did the knowledge that they were practically at their journey's end. Gloria glanced behind her every now and again hoping to see the wolf but there was no sign of the wary creature. She knew the wolf was around though; she knew it would be tracking them, maintaining a safe distance and keeping out of sight. There was just one thing that slightly marred the perfection of the day and that was the fact that none of them had eaten since the night before and now their stomachs were rumbling, rumbling, rumbling with hunger. They had gulped down the last drops of water instantly upon rising without considering whether or not there were any streams or rivulets in the vicinity of the hut with which to refill their bottles. Not to worry though as April's grandmother's house and other dwellings would soon be in sight.

They walked on and on and before they knew it they were on dry land, gazing up at the rocky terrain that rose more and more steeply ahead and above them. They sat for a while as April had her feet ministered to. Gloria's hands were rough and gnarled but she could be surprisingly gentle when she chose. Belinda watched her as she worked. From dubious beginnings Gloria had turned out to be an unexpectedly positive asset to the group. Once again Belinda surmised that Gloria was well worth getting to know. She turned away and clambered across a few rocks to get a better perspective of the surrounding area. They were only moments away from the perimeter of the mountain and yet she couldn't see any houses. Maybe they were hidden in recesses or behind rocks and she just hadn't spotted them? Maybe they blended in so well with the landscape that she had to be standing outside a door before she actually saw anything? Or maybe, quite simply, they had arrived at the wrong mountain? No, that wasn't possible as there were no other mountains anywhere to be seen. Belinda shrugged, feeling puzzled. She wouldn't be surprised if the houses were well hidden. After all with The Twelve in Government it was best to be as inconspicuous as possible and preferably not even to exist. That was obviously the answer. She climbed back down to April to check on Gloria's handiwork.

"Wow! That looks much better. I'm sure you won't have any problems walking now."

Gloria had torn and wrapped strips of sheepskin around and around each foot finally securing the ends with lengths of string pulled out from the waistband of her skirt. She had cleverly managed to make comfortable and protective pieces of footwear for April with the soft sheepskin.

"Get up and see how they feel," said Gloria.

April stood up and tentatively began to walk about. Her feet felt much better. There was still a degree of tenderness as she transferred weight from one foot to the other but it was nothing like the pain she had been quietly enduring since their departure from the Wine Sellers. This pain was manageable. The salve that Gloria had rubbed in had provided almost instant relief. April had no idea how her feet had managed to get so sore in the first place. The removal of the boots had been hideously painful and the initial contact of her feet with the air agonising. It had felt as if trapped and stagnant blood had suddenly been able to flow freely from her swollen feet up into her legs. It had been an excruciating experience; one that she didn't wish to go through again. Maybe she should have pulled her boots off at an earlier stage of their journey but she hadn't wanted anyone from the tunnels to steal them. Why on earth she had been so worried about her awful boots she had no idea! She let out a heavy sigh and forced herself to step across a few rocks finding that she could grip much better with the sheepskin than she had ever been able to with her crummy boots. She didn't need to worry so much about slipping now. Gloria got up and followed her. Impulsively April turned and hugged her. Gloria stepped back in surprise, her arms flailing as if she didn't know quite how to react and then slowly and cautiously she wrapped them around April, returning the hug and patting her clumsily on the back. April grinned at her. A new level of understanding had been reached.

"We need to find the houses," said Belinda. "They have to be here somewhere. Perhaps we should split into two groups and check out the area?"

There were nods and murmurs of agreement. April, Pat, Hope and Gloria would form one group and Belinda and her daughter Emily the other.

"You take the left and we'll take the right," said Belinda and each group set off.

They moved up and around the steep incline slowly and yet no matter how much climbing they did they found they barely covered any ground. It was challenging work pulling their bodies upwards and then lifting their legs high enough to heave their way onto the next narrow sliver of bare rock. There were neither footholds nor handholds to aid them and the higher they went the more they realised the imminent danger they were in of falling back onto the sharp rocks below. As Emily reached her Belinda put out a hand to stop her going any further. Belinda had arrived at a flat sheet of rock and from here the mountain sheered abruptly down towards the sea. One step further and they would tumble onto the rocks below. Pat and April had also come to a halt. Pat could climb no further with Hope in her arms and it was too dangerous to leave her shuffling around on her own. Only Gloria clambered on. Belinda turned to watch her, goat-like and foot sure as she negotiated her way upwards and onwards. She made the ascent look effortless. But eventually even Gloria reached a point wherein she could go no further and so she called back to say that there was nothing to be seen. There were no houses hidden anywhere. There was simply nothing but a never-ending expanse of exposed and slippery-looking, slate grey rock! There was nothing to see and nowhere to go!

"This is all wrong," said April when finally they regrouped. "My grandmother said that she lived at the foot of the mountain and that I could visit her any time I wanted. Why would she say that if she wasn't going to be here? I don't understand it."

She felt so confused. She had been talking about her grandmother for weeks now and had been looking forward to reconnecting with her. The entire journey that she, Pat and Hope had undertaken had been based on meeting her grandmother at the end of it. Her grandmother's house had been the carrot she had dangled in front of Pat every step of the way. Pat stared at her. She too felt confused and disappointed. She didn't relish the thought of going back to live in the tunnels or even of returning to Avondale House but what other options were there? Perhaps they could go and live with George but that was probably impossible too. The situation appeared hopeless. Where could they go from here? The two girls sat down and Hope began to cry. She was hungry, as indeed they all were. Pat rocked her back and forth trying to comfort her. Were they going to have to turn back? Had they come all this way for nothing? Emily joined them. She said nothing; simply staring discreetly into the distance. April looked at her. She had colour in her cheeks and appeared so much healthier than she had ever done in the tunnels. The short time they had spent out in the open together had done her the world of good. Belinda and Gloria stood a little apart from the girls deep in conversation.

"Let's leave it to the adults," sighed April. "I'm tired of trying to sort things. I've had enough."

Pat lowered her gaze focusing her attention on Hope. Although she was the eldest she had left everything to April. She had been happy for her to absorb the role of trusted guide, big sister and friend throughout but now even April had had enough. It was a devastating thought. Without April Pat didn't know what she would do. April had come to mean everything to her. She buried her face in Hope's shoulder bestowing gentle, butterfly kisses so that April couldn't see the fear and uncertainty she felt. Everything had to work out. They couldn't possibly have travelled all this way for nothing.

Suddenly they heard a shout!
"April! Pat! You made it!"
Both Pat and April looked around in surprise. There was someone else on the mountain, someone who obviously knew them. But that was absurd! They didn't know anyone here and they had looked everywhere and there had been no sign of anyone else around. It couldn't be April's grandmother because she hadn't seen April since she was a little girl and would hardly recognise her and besides, the voice sounded male.
"You've still got the crowbar then?" continued the voice, with a hint of banter. April stared at her hand which was gripping the crowbar tightly. Who knew about the crowbar? Was the Tracker still alive somehow and had he found them? No, she didn't believe it for a second; she knew what she'd done to him. She knew that Gloria and Belinda had dragged him from the hut and hidden his body and that the wolves had probably torn him to pieces and devoured him, disposing of his remains during the night. There would be no trace of the Tracker. He was done and dusted. She shuddered. So who and where was the voice coming from? At that moment someone leapt lightly down from the rock above them, landing next to Pat. April raised her arm protectively, prepared once more to use the crowbar if she had to, but a strong, sinewy hand instantly reached out from nowhere and grabbed it.
"Stop! It's me. Don't you recognise me?"

A slight but wiry man with long, wavy hair and with the lower part of his face hidden beneath dark stubble stood in front of her. April stared at him in confusion. He looked vaguely familiar. She thought she knew him but couldn't be sure. Pat got up and stepped towards the man, hitching Hope closer to her left hip.

"It can't be!" she said breathlessly. "You don't even look like him anymore. But it has to be because you smell like him. I would remember that smell anywhere!"

And she flung her free arm around the man in excitement.

"It's George, April! It's George!" she called. "How did you get here? And how did you get here before us? This is incredible! I can hardly believe it!"

George let go of the crowbar and hugged Pat, taking care not to squash Hope who was wriggling around disconcertedly. April stared at the two of them in astonishment. Of course it was George. Who else could it be? It was just so unexpected, that was all. He was supposed to arrive after they were settled with April's grandmother. He wasn't supposed to get to the mountain before them. How had he managed it? Where had he appeared from? How had he avoided the wolves and got here safely on his own? George looked over Pat's shoulder at April.

"I'm glad one of you knows who I am," he said, with a cheerful grin. "Your grandmother's waiting. We thought you were never coming. It's taken you so long that we feared the worst."

Belinda stepped forward. "We've heard a lot about you," she said.

George turned to nod happily at her, extricating himself from Pat so that he could extend a hand in friendship. Belinda shook it eagerly. Gloria was scowling. She didn't want any men joining them, no matter who they were. In her experience men meant only one thing and that was trouble. She dug her hands deep into her skirt pockets and glared at George. Despite her feelings of mistrust she couldn't help but be curious as to where he had come from though. She sniffed loudly, intentionally drawing attention to herself.

"So how did you get here?" she asked stiffly.

George contemplated Gloria. How had April and Pat managed to pick her up? She looked a veritable eyesore, to say the least.

"Her bark is worse than her bite," said Belinda quietly, and then more loudly. "This is Gloria. She taught us how to survive."

George reached out to shake Gloria's hand but she spat on the ground in front of his feet and thrust her hands even further into her pockets. She saw no reason for physical contact. She wasn't having any of it. She had no reason to trust this man. She just wanted him to answer her question. George turned his head away and spotted Emily. He smiled encouragingly at her.

"That's my daughter Emily," said Belinda. "We spent time together in the tunnels."

And that was enough explanation for the time being. Belinda's words revealed immediately why Pat and April had taken so long to arrive at the base of the volcanic mountain, why George had never found any trace of them and why they had arrived as a group. It was more than enough information for now. No more questions or answers were needed. Their adventures could be relayed and regaled over later. George's job was to get them to April's grandmother. She would be so surprised and thoroughly delighted.

"You'd best follow me," he said. "I've been coming here every day for weeks hoping against hope that you would be here and today, finally, you are. I was almost in despair thinking you were never going to arrive. Another day or so and I might have given up."

He turned towards Gloria. "You were nearly there," he admitted in grudging admiration. "You just needed to climb a step or two higher and then you would have seen it."

Gloria grunted. It was a compliment, she knew. She had no idea what he was talking about but he was openly acknowledging her skill and ability. No one else in the group was capable of climbing as effortlessly or as high as she could without help. But she still wasn't ready to trust him. He couldn't get round her with his smooth patter and flattery. George gave a brief chuckle and then began to scramble up amongst the rocks. The first part of the ascent would be straightforward but getting high enough to go down again would be a challenge for the women and girls. Well, maybe not for Gloria. Fortunately George had thought ahead and hidden a length of rope under one of the rocks some weeks ago. He just had to reach it and throw it down. He might need Gloria's help though.

George was soon out of sight and the group began the laborious task of climbing after him. Gloria, still suspicious, proceeded quickly. She didn't want George to disappear. Who knew what thoughts were really going on in his head or where he was leading them? She had no intention of letting him get away with anything. Suddenly she found herself kneeling on a narrow ledge beside him and saw that he was staring upwards in horror. Gloria lifted her head to see what the problem was. Then she laughed. She couldn't help herself. Above him was the wolf. Its body was rigid, fur bristling, and it was getting ready to spring. Snarls and growls were erupting from the back of its throat; its yellow fangs were exposed and slavering in anticipation. Gloria clapped her hands so that the wolf transferred its attention to her. Slowly and in response to her command it settled back on its haunches, giving a disgruntled snap at the air and then finally a conciliatory thud of its tail. Gloria gingerly stood up and snipped her fingers. The wolf immediately sprang down to settle beside her. She rested a gnarled hand upon its head and began to knead her fingers through the thick, coarse fur. George looked on in shock and astonishment, flinching as the wolf acknowledged him with a warning grumble and a curl of the lip. But the wolf was barely interested. It only had eyes for Gloria. Gloria was the pack leader and it would always respond to her commands. George didn't dare move. He wasn't certain of Gloria and he was even more uncertain of the wolf.

"What now?" asked Gloria, rather smugly. George glanced sideways at the wolf. He wasn't sure whether or not he trusted himself to speak.

"Well?" continued Gloria.

George cleared his throat. "I have a rope," he rasped. "We can use it to help the rest of the group up here."

"You don't need to whisper," responded Gloria with a cackle. "The wolf is perfectly safe unless you try to attack me."

She couldn't resist that last jibe. George looked at her in alarm and saw that she was having difficulty keeping a straight face. She was teasing him. He instantly smiled and began to relax. The wolf was just an overgrown dog and with Gloria as its pack leader nothing was likely to happen unless she ordered it. He crouched down and began to tug at something under the rock next to him. It was the rope. One end of it was already securely fastened around a stump of root leaving the other free for use. George pulled and tugged until the length of rope was lying in a heap on the ledge. Then he gently eased the end of it over the side. He didn't want to throw it down in case it landed on top of someone or knocked someone off balance.

"Who needs help getting up here?" he called. "Grab hold of the rope and I'll pull you."

Emily was the first to make use of it. Belinda tied it around her waist and she held on tightly with both hands, pressing her feet eagerly into the rock as she searched for footholds. She was on the ledge in no time. Then it was Hope's turn. Pat secured her in a piece of sheepskin before tying the rope around it so she too was quickly and carefully lifted onto the ledge. Gloria grunted in approval as she watched George and then grudgingly offered to assist with April, Pat and Belinda. It wasn't that she didn't want to help; she simply enjoyed watching George at work. The girls were easily hauled up but Belinda wasn't the lightest of women. Tall and sturdy she held back until the end expressing her doubts regarding George's ability to help her.

"Get on with it," shouted Gloria scornfully. "Stop wasting time. We haven't got all day. Everyone else is here and we need to be moving on. What's the matter with you?"

Belinda raised her eyebrows and pursed her lips, grasping the rope firmly between both hands. She was being forced to rely on George, someone she didn't know, and it made her feel very uncomfortable. Suddenly she heard April's voice.

"Don't worry, Belinda. We're all going to pull. You'll be with us quick as a flash."

Space was limited on the ledge and movement was difficult. A large, sharp and craggy rock jutted out above their heads. It was so low that only Pat and Emily were able to stand upright without knocking against it. Belinda and George stood with their heads thrust forward, shoulders hunched and knees bent in order to avoid it. Now that they were on the ledge the whole group felt as if they were practically standing one on top of another. Where could they go from here? The wolf had disappeared and only Gloria had seen it go. Somehow it had made its way down from the ledge. Gloria wriggled around carefully until she was crouching on all fours and from there she stared at the spot where she had last seen the wolf.

"There's a hole here!" she cried.

"Yes," agreed George. "We're going to go through it. We're almost there. I'm surprised you found it though as it's well hidden."

"My wolf went through," said Gloria. "I watched him. Let's hope he's waiting for us on the other side."

George nodded. The others looked curiously at Gloria. None of them had seen the wolf so they were surprised to hear her words.

"Would you like to go first?" asked George. He felt apprehensive as to how the wolf might react without Gloria within sight and assuming the role of alpha male. "I'll hold onto your hands and lower you down. It's just a small drop. You can catch the others then. I'll come down last."

Gloria sniffed in agreement and began to lower her legs through the hole. George let go of her wrists for the final part of the drop and she landed safely below on another ledge. The wolf was nowhere to be seen.

Before long everyone was through the hole and waiting on the ledge with Gloria. There were no problems with height here and being able to stand upright was easy. Pat had tucked Hope closely into her hip once more. Glancing down they could see that there was a staggering drop to the sea but unexpectedly the ledge on this side was part of a narrow pathway that led around the side of the mountain.
"Nearly there," said George, reassuringly.
They stood with their backs to the mountain and began to edge their way along. No one looked down for fear of becoming lightheaded and losing balance. Even Gloria, sure footed as she was, stared fixedly ahead. Although she had a good head for heights, the drop to the sea was terrifying in its abruptness and made worse by the waves resounding in a thunderous and all consuming cacophony of noise as they crashed against the rocks. Some of the waves leapt so high that the spray splashed against their feet and legs forming instant puddles which just as quickly drained away as they continued to inch their way along. Pat held Hope tightly placing her free hand against the rocky wall behind her to maintain balance. April gripped the crowbar; that familiar feeling of reassurance surging through her as she did so. There was no need to worry. George had arrived and had taken control. Everything was going to be fine.

It felt as if they would creep along the narrow ledge forever. Luckily there was neither wind nor rain or the consequences might have been disastrous. Everyone was eager for this part of the journey to be over. Shuffling their way along in single file was an infinitely slow and laborious process as they could do little more than move sideways one tiny step at a time. It felt as if they were undertaking an endurance test. They looked neither to the right nor the left but stared straight ahead to a vista where sea and sky blended into a spangled and frothy foam of grey, white and blue.

"I can't do this much longer. My body is so tense it aches," called out Emily. "And if I relax I'm going to fall and then I'm done for. And I feel as if I'm going to fall anyway. I'm just going to have to stop. I can't carry on."

"Only a little further," encouraged George. "The first time is always the worst."

"The first time?" muttered Gloria under her breath as she reached back for one of Emily's hands to offer extra support. How many times did he expect them to make this journey? And how many times had he done it? Once it was over she hoped never to have to do it again. This whole experience was incredibly nerve wracking, not that she would ever have admitted this to anyone. Her friend the wolf seemed to have disappeared and each one of them was vulnerable on this narrow ledge. They needed to arrive somewhere in one piece and then sit down and take a few, deep, calming breaths. April's grandmother had to be close by or Gloria was going to stop believing. She had always doubted April's story anyway as it had never sounded much more than a glorified fairy tale. It had simply been something for the group to hold onto whilst they journeyed and something to inspire them to keep going. Gloria gave an extra loud sniff and then spat over the side of the ledge in disgust. George chuckled. He felt he would get on well with this tough, wiry, old woman, if she would allow herself to trust him of course. She appeared as hard as nails on the surface but watching her take hold of Emily's hand he knew there was more to her.

"We're here," he called, moments later, stepping through an unexpected arch. "Come."

The group followed him through to the other side where the ledge broadened out considerably. Great sighs of relief were heard as everyone slumped into seated positions. Thank goodness they were away from that terrifying plunge to the sea!

But where were they? That was the question. After that long journey where exactly were they? Where was April's grandmother if indeed she existed? Where were the houses? Exactly where had George led them? Had they arrived at a place of safety? And where was the wolf? Where had Gloria's friend, the wolf, disappeared to? For the moment each of them decided not to care. Just for the moment they needed to get their breath back.

CHAPTER THIRTY-FOUR

Looking down from the ledge they could see a set of steps hewn roughly out of the rock, much the same as those that April and Pat had navigated on their way into the tunnels - but a lot more foot worn and hopefully easier to manage. The steps led across and down to what could only be described as a village – a hidden village! They were witnessing a village that was hidden deep inside the heart of the mountain and yet somehow it was still out in the open! No one would ever be able to find such a place unless they knew where to look. And gazing at the village it felt almost as though they had stepped back in time! It was extraordinary!

"I don't believe it!" exclaimed April. "I can see a donkey! Look! It's carrying baskets and has a rope around its neck. It's tied to a tree. Can you see it?"

Everyone turned to stare. Sure enough, there was a donkey tethered to a tree. Almost as if it knew April was passing comment the donkey lifted its head and began to bray. Slowly, silently, one at a time, men and women began to materialise from behind rocks and trees and from within dark spaces. George waved and called out an eager greeting and then proceeded to leap down the steps, taking them two at a time. He charged past the men and women who had gathered around the donkey, clapping a few of them on the shoulders in camaraderie as he did so, before disappearing into a dark hole in the side of the mountain. Moments later he reappeared.

"April," he called. "April, there's someone here to see you!"

An old woman dressed in a bulky, black skirt and an off white blouse had followed him out and was standing directly behind him. April stared at the old woman in some confusion and then turned to Belinda.

"I don't know who she is," she said. "Why would I know who she is? She's more likely to be a friend of Gloria's than anyone I would know. Look at her. She's even dressed like Gloria. What shall I do?"

Belinda stood up slowly, dusting herself down, and squeezing April's hand in reassurance.

"We'll go together, shall we? We've taken this journey as a group and we'll finish it that way. Come on. I'll go first."

She waited until everyone was on their feet and then cautiously led the way. It was all very well for George to leap down the steps with eager familiarity but they would proceed with deliberation and care. Their journey had taught them that much at least.

They reached the bottom of the steps and approached the crowd that had gathered around the donkey. There was a feeling of expectation in the air. People were smiling and nodding and generally looking on hopefully. The old woman had moved to stand next to George and there was a huge beam on her face.

"April!" she cried. "April! I'd know you anywhere!"

She reached out to envelop April in a warm and loving embrace. April recoiled in horror as she did so, standing stiffly with her arms at her sides and gripping the crowbar so fiercely that the knuckles of her hand turned white.

"Who are you?" she asked when the old woman had finished hugging her. "I've never seen you before. I don't know you."

"I'm your grandmother of course," responded the old woman. "I'm Amelia. You look so like your mother it's incredible. It's wonderful to see you."

April grimaced and took a step back.

"You don't look like my grandmother," she said. "You don't look like her at all. I don't believe you. My grandmother wore pearls and beautiful suits and heels. She told me to come and stay with her whenever I liked and we've travelled a long way to see her. What have you done with her? Why would you pretend to be her? Or maybe there's another village and we're in the wrong one. You can easily fool George because he's never met you but you certainly can't fool me!"

The feeling of expectation began to change to nervous tension as April's angry words of disappointment erupted but the old woman laughed and it dissipated quickly.

"You are certainly your mother's child, April. Come with me and I'll show you where I live and then perhaps you'll understand. Bring your friends with you. You must be very hungry especially the baby. That's Hope, isn't it?"

By this time Hope was screaming and arching her upper body back and forth with tiredness, hunger and boredom and Pat was jiggling her frantically upon her hip in a futile attempt to soothe her.

"Let's go April. Let's have a look at least and maybe someone could get some milk for the baby instead of just standing around and staring. That is, if there is any milk here of course?"

Pat felt upset and her voice grew louder and louder as she spoke. Hope was wriggling about in such agitation that she didn't know how much longer she would be able to keep hold of her. She hoped they hadn't come this far for nothing. They needed somewhere to stay and they needed to eat and rest but most of all they needed a home. Pat had had enough of travelling. She was at the end of her tether and didn't want to go any further. She sincerely hoped this woman, Amelia, as she said her name was, was April's grandmother, although she wasn't convinced as she looked much more like Gloria than she did April, except for the fact that she clearly washed and took care of herself and wasn't grubby with dirty fingernails and bird's nest hair.

Belinda squeezed April's hand again.

"Pat's right. Let's go and see where she lives."

The old woman, Amelia, turned and walked back towards the dark hole from which she had emerged. Someone tapped Pat on the shoulder and handed her a clay pot filled with a frothy, white drink for Hope. Pat peered at the contents suspiciously, sniffing at them and then raising the pot to her lips. She took a large gulp before deciding to give any to Hope just to make sure she was drinking milk and nothing else and also because her throat felt parched and she couldn't resist. It tasted like milk; there was no bitterness to it and why would anyone poison a baby anyway? What would be the point? She shrugged. These curious, old people didn't look as if they even knew the meaning of the word poison. They stood nodding and grinning at her, willing her to drink more. She took another mouthful. It was delicious, creamy and fresh.

"Great," she grunted, unable to hold back a grateful smile. This huge, clay pot brimming with milk would certainly satisfy Hope.

The dark hole turned out to be not so much of a dark hole as a cave entrance with a large wooden door across the front of it. Amelia pushed the door inwards and suddenly they were entering a bright and welcoming room; a room that twinkled and shone, a room which reminded April of a book she had read a long time ago about a hero called Aladdin and a cave full of gold and jewels. This particular room was lit up by the flickering flames of fragrant candles which were strategically placed in every corner, nook and cranny. Shadows danced on the walls, long and short, wide and thin. Everyone blinked and shaded their eyes. Amelia and George chuckled with enjoyment at their surprised reactions.

In the centre of the room a shabby sofa and a smattering of easy chairs faced inwards to embrace the last embers of an open fire. The wooden sitting furniture had been made to look inviting and comfortable with the strategic positioning of cushions and colourful, hand-woven throws. There was a long table at the far end of the room and a passageway leading into darkness beyond it. Amelia marched forwards and the rest of the group followed, trying not to knock into or trip over anything as they went. She led them down the passageway to a bedroom. This room was also suffused with candlelight, gently quivering in every recess, and in the room there were two single beds and a couple of large chests. April frowned. Who did this old woman live with? Was it George? She couldn't possibly be staying in the same room as George, could she? That would certainly be a predicament. Amelia turned to smile confidently at her as she threw back the lid of one of the chests.

"Come and take a look," she invited April happily. "I think you'll find everything you need in here. What you see should certainly put your mind at rest."

April frowned as she knelt down in front of the chest. She reached inside and carefully retrieved an item of clothing, holding it out in front of her. She found herself staring at a flimsy white blouse with seeded pearls at the collar and cuffs. It was soft and delicate and had been lovingly folded between layers of old, crackling tissue paper. She shook the blouse from the paper pressing it against her cheek and cradling it against her skin. Her hands began to shake. Next she pulled out a tweed jacket and skirt to match. Putting these to one side she withdrew pairs of expensive shoes, three heeled pairs in different colours and tucked inside each shoe was a silk stocking. It was not enough though. Although there was a degree of familiarity about the shoes and a certain smell that emanated from each garment April was still not convinced. Amelia put a hand into the chest and rustled around. April had missed something, and it was something important. Right at the bottom of the chest was a small, red, jewellery box. Amelia grasped hold of it and handed it to April with trembling fingers, smiling gently, and in the candlelight there was something about her smile that tugged at April's heart. April's hands trembled too as she took the box and she suddenly felt consumed by a strong and poignant ache. She longed to shout out, saying yes, yes, this woman is my grandmother. Who else could she be and why would she lie anyway? How would that help the situation? April turned her head away from Amelia's smile and looked at the box. She didn't want to be duped by her. She wanted to be sure. She had waited so long for this moment and needed to be quite certain. She prised back the catch of the box and opened it. A double row of creamy, lustrous pearls gleamed up at her.

"Do you remember these?" asked Amelia.

April threaded the delicate pearls through her fingers and lifted them up to the candlelight.

"Put them on," she said. "Maybe I do."

"You put them on for me. You don't need to undo the clasp; you can just slip them over my head," said Amelia.

April reached forward and lifted the necklace over the old woman's hair and as she did so the fluttering began. She caught her breath and clasped her hands across her chest as a tight yearning began to spread. Now she remembered. She had done this before. She had done this many years ago for her grandmother after she had been allowed to try the pearl necklace on. As she lowered the necklace gently around Amelia's neck the old lady tenderly took hold of her hands.

"Do you recognise me? Would you like to try them on, April?"

April burst into tears. She couldn't help herself. It was her grandmother. It could be no one else. It could never have been anyone else. She was close enough to inhale and absorb the soft fragrance that lingered on her grandmother's skin and instinctively a previously guarded part of her acknowledged the tone and vibration of her voice. Everything was finally so obvious. It was such a relief. April felt the stress, strain and worry of the past few months begin to drain away. The ache that had caused such pain moved from her heart to her throat producing an outpouring of grief. It was the grief and shock April had carried with her from the day that her mother had left her at the surgery, the day when she was informed that her family no longer wanted her. Amelia put her arms around April once again and cradled her while she sobbed. And as for April, there was no holding back. There was no reason to. Her barriers and defences completely dissolved. She flung her arms around her grandmother's neck claiming her for her own. Someone cared about her; someone had been waiting for her and was ready to love her. The long and arduous journey with Pat and Hope had not been in vain. It was a precious, private moment meant only for the two of them and for the eyes and ears of no one else. Belinda wiped away a tear of her own and then discreetly chivvied the remaining group members out of the bedroom and back into the living space.

As they relaxed on chairs and cushions in front of the dying fire George left the cave-like dwelling. He returned soon after with his arms laden with food. He began to chop and prepare vegetables at the long table and as he did so villagers appeared in the doorway, slowly filing through, in twos and threes, bearing welcome gifts. George had told everyone so much about April, Pat and Hope during his time in the village that they were eager to meet them. Their arrival had been anticipated with great curiosity and turned out to be even better than expected as more than just two girls and a baby had turned up and the general feeling was that it would be good to have newcomers in the village. Warm, woollen blankets were placed respectfully in front of Pat. Some of these were so small that they were obviously for Hope and had been knitted with great care by an elderly woman with stiff, swollen fingers. She gave a gummy smile and cautiously extended a crooked finger to stroke Hope's cheek. Pat tried not to pull a face and thanked her for the blankets. Hope gurgled in delight. Her belly was full to stretching and she was extremely content after her pot of creamy milk.

A large, earthenware pot was held out to Belinda and she blushed with pleasure as she accepted it. Thick skirts and woven tops were passed across to Gloria. She sniffed somewhat disdainfully as she clutched at them, attempting to hide the thrill of excitement she felt at the thought of being able to sort through fresh, clean clothing. She could hand items out to whoever she thought they would fit and she might even keep one or two pieces for herself. Emily was given a canvas bag of coloured beads and although she thought the beads were pretty she had no idea what she was supposed to do with them. She smiled politely as she opened the bag and then suddenly caught sight of a bracelet on the wrist of her gift bearer. It was made with the very same beads.

"Oh!" she gasped. "How lovely! I can make jewellery!"

Gloria nudged her. "I'll help you," she cackled.

A beam of pure delight lit up Emily's face as, one by one, she inspected each and every bead under the flame of a flickering candle. She was ready to start creating.

A meal was soon ready and April and her grandmother came out of the bedroom to join the group. People were sitting wherever they could, around the table, on rugs, on wooden boards; anywhere they felt comfortable enough to eat. The cave dwelling was spilling over with villagers and the air was filled with the warmth of camaraderie. A sense of contentment resounded in the light hearted chatter that bounced back and forth. Before April could say anything Amelia announced that Pat and Hope would be more than welcome to live with her and her granddaughter. In fact she made it quite clear to April that nothing would please her more. April couldn't remember when she had last experienced such happiness. She had no idea where any of them would sleep as she had only seen two beds but was sure that something would be sorted out. Her family was complete and the reunion with her grandmother was all and more than she had dreamt of or could ever wish for. Perhaps there would even be an opportunity to learn how to make scones at some point. A flicker of sadness ran through her as she thought about her mother and siblings but she quickly dismissed such wistfulness. Now was neither the time nor the place. She might talk to her grandmother about them at a later date.

George agreed to take responsibility for Belinda, Emily and Gloria and said that they could stay with him for as long as they liked as there was plenty of room in his cave dwelling. There was something about Belinda that intrigued George. He couldn't put his finger on it but he wondered if she felt the same way. He noticed her giving him a couple of surreptitious glances and blushed with pleasure, turning his head away so that she couldn't see the bright red flush that stole, rapidly and unbidden, across his cheeks and neck. His awareness of her made him want to wash his hair and have a shave and put on clean clothes. He hadn't felt like that since the girls had stayed with him at the Wine Sellers. It sent a thrill through him and he decided that he would tidy himself up later on and make himself presentable. Perhaps it was something about certain females that made him react like this. For the moment however he concentrated on dishing out food so that Belinda was unable to discern his confusion. He realised he felt quite nervous in her presence.

Every group member, with the exception of Gloria, was satisfied. They had come to the end of a long and often difficult journey and had somewhere to stay where they would be safe. They felt that their days of wandering and scavenging were over and that it was time to settle. They were on the verge of a new life. The sea was close by and there was plenty of fresh air. Food was freely available and the villagers had welcomed them with open arms. Gloria was restless and distracted, needing to know where her friend, the wolf, was and after eating she stepped outside to look around. Suddenly she heard a long, keening howl and looking up she spied the wolf on a rocky peak by the archway through which they had entered the village. Her friend was fine. Gloria heaved a sigh of relief. They were protected. The wolf had no intention of leaving and would always be with them. She gave a grunt of pleasure and rejoined the group so that she could finish her food.

Once they had eaten George offered to take the newcomers on a tour around the village. He pointed out the various hidden dwellings, the livestock, the herb and vegetable plots, the fruit trees and bushes and the different communal areas. The best bit of the tour though was a hot water spring which tumbled into a secluded, steaming pool for washing and bathing. Everyone stripped off and jumped in. George stood guard at the edge of the pool with his back to the group as they splashed about, warding off any unannounced visitors. Bathing with the villagers could come later when a sense of trust had been established. By the time everyone was willing to leave the pool dusk was falling and they were ready to retire. Amelia had pushed her two single beds together and encouraged April, Pat and Hope to make use of them whilst she unrolled a large, thick rug in front of the fire and covered herself in woollen blankets. George allowed Belinda, Emily and Gloria to make use of his room whilst he curled up in his old donkey jacket near the front door; a most welcome return from April, along with the crowbar. He had encouraged his guests to explore his home whilst he made use of the pool and on his return he noticed Belinda staring at him appreciatively. The warmth of her gaze fuelled his desire to make the most of himself. Gloria informed him that the wolf would protect them so he didn't have to worry but George felt the need to impress. His home would be the first to be discovered should anyone enter the village from the other side of the volcanic mountain and although he had been told that there had been no strangers around for a very long time George decided it was his duty to assume the responsibility of village guardian and keep the crowbar close by at all times. It was inevitable that at some point outsiders would arrive and being prepared could only be an advantage. Tonight he would rest by the door, alert for as long as possible, just in case his friends had been followed.

CHAPTER THIRTY-FIVE

And so the group settled into the village and their new lives unfolded. Life was calm and easy and each group member carried out daily chores according to their age and ability. Everything ran smoothly and comfortably without any trouble. There were no arguments; there was no conflict; the villagers simply accepted one another and got on with what they had to do. The group began to forget that they had ever lived in the tunnels and memories of their early lives faded until they had all but disappeared. They felt safe. They felt useful. They felt looked-after, needed and cared for. And best of all, they were treated with trust and respect.

The majority of the villagers were elderly and had fled their homes as soon as The Twelve had stepped into government. They knew that the method of rule soon to be inflicted upon the ignorant and easily influenced masses did not bode well. It reminded them too much of a bygone era that they had moved on from, determining never to return to, one that was not conducive to progress. There had always been a number of people who chose to live close to the foot of the volcanic mountain but recently the numbers had doubled or possibly even tripled and now with the addition of April, Pat, Emily and Hope there were youngsters around. The villagers kept away from the outside world, making sure that they had no need of external assistance and continually working towards the sustainability of the village for present and future generations.

There was always the possibility of volcanic eruption but that would be dealt with if and when it happened.

The houses were not at all as April had imagined they would be but instead were long, low cave dwellings distinguished one from another by handmade, wooden, door-like structures strategically hidden behind shrubs or at the back of narrow crevices and there was a certain amount of squeezing in and out which had to be done which made many of them difficult to access. April's grandmother had hidden her jewellery, hanging on to it covetously throughout the years. She had travelled with it secreted under her clothes on her final train journey to the volcanic mountain, smiling and nodding complacently at the inspectors as they passed through the carriages, looking altogether the epitome of innocuous and genteel senility. Once settled in her home she had concealed the jewellery amongst her beautiful clothes and these remained folded neatly in one of the chests, rarely to be disturbed as there was no use for them in village life. She had taken pride in wearing such clothes in her earlier, travelling years but knew she would never need them again. They probably wouldn't even fit her. She had made the journey by train to visit her daughter when April was young but trains were no longer in use and many of the tracks had become overgrown, rusty and unsafe. There was a track leading out from the back of one of the cave dwellings which had originally been part of a small train station and perhaps there would be a time, one day, when the disused, single carriage resting there would be overhauled and brought back to life but very few people were aware of it and for the moment the less who knew about it the better.

George had travelled around the mountain instead of through it and had set off much sooner than originally intended. He had quickly concluded that there would be no point in remaining at the Wine Sellers after his beating and the thought of being dragged in for questioning and then incarcerated whilst he waited for the inevitable, harsh punishment had played on his mind considerably. Invariably someone in his neighbourhood would have spotted the two lowlifes loitering outside his home and the reward for reporting suspicious behaviour was often too much to resist. He considered his neighbours to be trustworthy up to a point but even an accidental slip of the tongue could put him in danger. Besides, his life had been so much better and he had felt much more optimistic whilst the girls had been around. He felt actively encouraged by their bravery to set out on the journey to the mountains himself. If they could do it so could he. It was a big decision but indisputable, and one that he felt pleased with. Luckily he hadn't encountered any wolves as he circled the perimeter of the mountain and his journey had been decidedly uneventful. He had come across evidence of wolves here and there but no actual sightings. They clearly had bigger and better prey to concern themselves with. He had chuckled cheerfully to himself as he strode along gripping a long, sturdy stick - just in case. He had taken a leaf out of April's book there. Better to be safe than sorry!

It was quite by chance that he arrived at the village and then only after persistent questioning combined with multiple and repeated explanations was he finally introduced to April's grandmother, Amelia. The villagers needed to be sure he could be trusted as the majority among them were elderly and vulnerable.

Close to the end of his journey George had reached a stage whereby he felt he could go no further and so had squatted on a small plateau to rest. Presently the sounds of several voices wafted up into the air towards him and although he knew he couldn't be seen he instinctively shrank as far back into the rock on the plateau as he could, barely daring to take a breath. He waited until the sounds had almost faded away and then began to climb after them. He was so eager to investigate that he completely missed the hole, toppling into it and hurtling through the air along with randomly dislodged stones bouncing gregariously against the rocks around him before splashing into the sea below. It was purely by chance that his body wrapped itself around a protruding boulder, painfully halting his rapid descent towards certain death. Winded and unsure as to whether anything was broken or not he waited patiently until he felt there was no longer any movement around him and that he was able to regain his balance. Unravelling his body from around the boulder and standing up slowly on the ledge he tested his limbs. Everything seemed fine. He felt bruised and battered but able to go on. He could still hear people talking and he needed to locate them. He sidled along the ledge with his back to the rock face, looking straight ahead, until he finally arrived at the arch. From here he stepped into another world, into a village frozen in time.

Dazed and bewildered, George had slumped to his knees and stared downwards. The scene below was extraordinary, reminiscent of a bygone era, an era that he had only previously heard of or read about in books, a long time ago. It looked like a scene from a perfect village life. His eyesight left much to be desired but as he stared he surmised that the people milling about were elderly. He could tell by their body shapes and garments and manner of movement. There were no youngsters anywhere to be seen. He watched for a while; watched as water was drawn from a well; watched as goats and donkeys were led away – somewhere. It seemed as though they were led to a certain point and then suddenly they melted into nothingness. For a short while George was looking at them and then seconds later they were gone. He blinked and rubbed at his eyes. One by one the elderly inhabitants walked off and simply disappeared until the village below looked deserted. George scrambled to his feet wincing at the pain in his ribs. He began to make his way down the steps. He had to discover the secret of this amazing, vanishing act.

And that was the last George knew of anything until he came round in a wooden hut tied to a post next to a braying donkey. He had been ambushed from behind at the bottom of the steps and then dragged into the hut to be questioned. Three men crouched in front of him and a bowl of thick soup was held up to his lips. Someone had bandaged his head with a strip of grubby cloth and it ached considerably. He had clearly been knocked senseless with something hard. George waited until he had drained the last drops of soup and then nodded his thanks. The men stared at him saying nothing. After what seemed to be an inordinate amount of time George felt he ought to speak and informed them he was looking for April's grandmother. One of the men got up and withdrew from the hut. Shortly afterwards he returned with Amelia who asked George to explain himself. George told his story, trying not to leave anything out, and at the end of it, after another period of unnerving silence, Amelia and the three men left. With the falling of darkness George found himself drifting in and out of a restless slumber.

Amelia arrived the next morning with a few other women and George was obliged to repeat his story before a plate of food was deposited in front of him and he was left alone for the rest of the day. This went on for three days and nights until finally Amelia entered the hut with a large, hunting knife, cutting through his bindings and instructing him to follow her and not to try anything stupid. As if he would, George thought. Amelia was the one holding the knife, although he doubted she would use it, especially if everything April had told him about her was true and as long as Amelia was April's grandmother, of course, as she had insisted earlier. He shrugged his shoulders concluding that the inhabitants of the village wished him no harm and such being the case he would find out as much as possible.

Once George entered Amelia's home she became friendly and decidedly garrulous. She made sure he was comfortably settled before she asked him to tell his story again, right from the beginning. George sighed and gave a great yawn. How many more times could he repeat himself?

"Tea?" Amelia suggested encouragingly. "Tea?"

George nodded wearily. He was bored with his story now and it really felt as if there was nothing more to tell. But Amelia asked questions. She had so many questions for him. She wanted to know what April looked like and was she well and how was she coping and had she been ill treated at Avondale House? She asked no questions about her daughter. It was almost as if she knew the answers or perhaps she felt afraid to ask. She was only interested in April. She barely drew breath as she fired her questions at him. George was momentarily taken aback wondering how she knew so much and who or what was the source of her information? She revealed nothing however, merely asking more and more questions until eventually she appeared satisfied and a gratified silence ensued.

George remained a guest in Amelia's home until she was certain that he could tell her no more about April and that he wasn't a threat but an ally. Eventually she took him to an empty dwelling which she told him he was welcome to inhabit and consider as his own. Delighted and surprised George shook her hand vigorously and proceeded to settle into village life, making himself as useful as possible, helping out whenever he could and going beyond the archway and climbing through the hole every day in order to wait for April, Pat and Hope. He was almost on the point of giving up when they finally arrived and when George spotted them he was intrigued to see that they were not on their own. There were other females with them. Curious, George had spied on them for a while, unseen from his vantage point, as they clambered over the rocks in different directions, searching for houses, before returning to regroup, disappointed. It was at this point that he had called out to April and Pat, leaping down from the rock above, taking them by surprise, and then leading them to the village and Amelia – so that they could put down roots thus changing their lives for the better.

CHAPTER THIRTY-SIX
EPILOGUE

Miss Abigail felt uneasy. Things were changing at Avondale House and none of it was to her liking. Cook felt perturbed too. A core group of men had lost interest in Avondale Manor and were starting to call directly at the House. They were coveting younger and younger girls to relieve them and to satisfy their needs. No longer captivated by the coming of age girls and acutely desirous of Miss Abigail's innocent charges, some of whom were now as young as ten years old, they had taken to driving up in their expensive cars and parking outside Avondale House on a daily basis. It was a most uncomfortable situation and Miss Abigail was now locking and double bolting all doors and instructing the girls to keep away from the windows and preferably to stay out of sight as much as possible. Previously the girls in her care had been at least fourteen years of age before their arrival at the House and she had helped to collect them but recently there had been an influx of prepubescent girls, none of whom had undergone the compulsory physical examination and none of whom had any idea what was going on or what was about to happen to them. They often arrived most unexpectedly, dumped outside her door in twos and threes, and sometimes Miss Abigail wondered where she was going to put them all. Miss Abigail was not only concerned for the safety of the girls but also for herself. Men had taken to getting out of their cars and slouching idly against the bonnets whilst smoking. There was a sense of sulky rebellion and aggression about them especially as they were blatantly ignoring the tobacco ban. Who knew what they would do next? Cook had even caught one of them sneaking around the back of Avondale House and had knocked him on the head with a frying pan as he approached the kitchen door. The blow had momentarily stunned him but how long would it be before he tried again or before other men began to pluck up the courage to come forward and pushed their way in? Miss Abigail had no idea how she would handle such situations and dreaded the very thought of them. And then of course there was Bill!

Bill had arrived one day with a group of tearful, frightened girls who had been taken from their homes and bundled roughly into the back of his van. Bill was in the driver's seat as this happened and had kept his mouth clamped tightly shut, longing to get out and throw a few timely punches. Shame, anger and frustration overwhelmed him as he drove to Avondale House listening to the girls sobbing in the back and he knew he had to say something. He didn't know what to do about the situation just yet but he certainly had to say something. His job description had changed recently; he had been handed a new contract and instructed to deliver whoever and whatever was given to him - no questions asked. His deliveries were no longer restricted to food, products and medical supplies. This new turn of events was both confusing and distressing and he determined to let Miss Abigail know in no uncertain terms. He needed to know how her girls were and what was going to happen to them. He made his way to the kitchen, cap in hand, and informed Cook that he wouldn't leave until Miss Abigail came down to talk to him.

"I don't like it, you know," he blurted out. "It's wrong. They are too young to be away from their families. Who knows what will happen next? I've heard some bad stories. There's not enough room for them all here, is there? And what becomes of the older girls, like my daughter? Where do they go? I need to see my girl to make sure she's safe."

And Bill planted himself firmly on a chair at the kitchen table refusing to budge. He had only a week ago heard terrible rumours about the coming of age girls and about what transpired after they left Avondale House, many of whom were never seen or heard of again. And he wanted his daughter out of it. He wanted her away from it all. In fact, truth to tell, he wanted all the girls out of it but that was something else. There had been deep discussions held at the basement pub and many of the men were in agreement. They had to watch what they said in front of one another as it was sometimes not altogether clear who could be trusted but the general consensus of opinion was that the delivery of very young girls to Avondale House was a shocking turn of events and could anyone think of anything that could be done about it? It was clear that things would have to change as the situation was becoming more and more untenable. Feathers were ruffled and although no one had any firm ideas as yet there was a growing feeling of mutiny amongst the men, particularly those who had young daughters. Miss Abigail privately agreed with Bill about the younger girls and in fact more recently about all her girls but was not currently in a position to say or do anything. She could however alleviate his worries regarding his daughter and let him know that she was safe and on the premises, but who could say when she would be required to go to Avondale Manor as one of the men lurking around outside might catch a glimpse of her and speak to Sister Charlotte. It was a source of constant worry and the girls required were looking more and more childlike.

"Thank you, Bill," she responded, her face pale and drawn. "I understand and appreciate your concern. If you stay here a moment I will get Bertha to take the crockery through to the dining area with your daughter and you will see her. Wait behind the doorway please."

She knew that Bill still hungered for her and didn't wish to upset him. She was aware that she needed to stay on the right side of him as she might require him as an ally in the near future and was glad that his opinion was similar to hers. It made her feel confident that she would be able to rely on him if things became too difficult.

She watched as Bill grudgingly rose from his chair, twirling his cap nervously in his hands, and moved to stand out of sight behind the door where they had first had sex. He was a ruggedly handsome man and she couldn't help but feel a stirring of emotions whenever she looked at him. She inadvertently clenched her pelvic floor muscles and then forced them to relax. No more of that. It was too dangerous and much safer and easier to explore her options with Bertha who always delighted in giving pleasure. She beckoned Cook over and whispered her requirements and shortly after she was able to smile at Bill knowing his mind was temporarily at rest. Waving him on his way she experienced a huge sense of relief. Now she could turn her attention to the hand delivered note that she had received that morning from Sister Charlotte.

The note expressed a barely concealed distress at the changes taking place at Avondale Manor. There were fewer and fewer visits to the Manor and if Sister Charlotte couldn't do anything to encourage the men to return there was the distinct possibility that she would be out of a job and that the Manor would close. What would happen to her girls then? And what sort of impact would such a predicament have on the much younger girls at Avondale House? She was deeply disturbed by the recent turn of events and didn't know what to do. The note asked openly about her beloved Pat and hoped she was well. It also intimated that there had been a sighting, not too long ago, of two girls heading towards the mountains and did Miss Abigail know anything about this? Of course Miss Abigail, in her return correspondence, denied all knowledge of anything; she had no idea who the two girls were, she had heard nothing, but the apparent sighting left her thinking. It played on her mind, especially with the current situation as it was. If things got too bad there might be an option. It would require careful planning but life did not always have to be entirely black and white. Her own situation at Avondale House was becoming increasingly unstable and she didn't know how long she would be able to stay there or what was going to happen next. She felt as if she were somewhat precariously balanced on the tip of an iceberg and that it was ready to melt at any moment, dissolving with her into stormy waters below. But if April and Pat had survived as Sister Charlotte had given her reason to believe then there was hope. There was hope for all of them and that was what she must hold on to; that was what she must think ahead to and perhaps start planning towards ....

Printed in Great Britain
by Amazon